THE PENGUIN CONTEMPORARY AMERICAN
FICTION SERIES

NORMA JEAN THE TERMITE QUEEN

Sheila Ballantyne's fiction has appeared in *The New Yorker*, *American Review*, *Ms.*, and other magazines. She won an O. Henry Award for her story "Perpetual Care," which was published in the O. Henry *Prize Stories* collection of 1977. Her most recent novel, *Imaginary Crimes*, is also published by Penguin Books.

D0851307

Norma Jean
the Termite Queen

Sheila Ballantyne

PENGUIN BOOKS

Penguin Books Ltd, Harmondsworth,
Middlesex, England
Penguin Books, 625 Madison Avenue,
New York, New York 10022, U.S.A.
Penguin Books Australia Ltd, Ringwood,
Victoria, Australia
Penguin Books Canada Limited, 2801 John Street,
Markham, Ontario, Canada L3R 1B4
Penguin Books (N.Z.) Ltd, 182–190 Wairau Road,
Auckland 10, New Zealand

First published in the United States of America by
Doubleday & Company, Inc., 1975
Published in Penguin Books 1983

LIBRARY OF CONGRESS CATALOGING IN PUBLICATION DATA
Ballantyne, Sheila.
Norma Jean the termite queen.
(The Penguin contemporary American fiction series)
I. Title.   II. Series.
PS3552.A464N67   1983   813'.54   82-22254
ISBN 0 14 00.6551 2

Printed in the United States of America by
R. R. Donnelley & Sons Company, Harrisonburg, Virginia
Set in Electra

ACKNOWLEDGMENTS

"I See It Now" from the film *Open the Door and See All the People*. Lyrics by
William Engvick. Music by Alec Wilder. Publisher: TRO. Copyright © Hollis
Music, Inc., 1964. Used by permission.
Osiris and the Egyptian Resurrection, Vol. 1, by E. A. Wallis Budge. London:
P. L. Warner, 1911. Retitled *Osiris, the Egyptian Religion of Resurrection*. Copy-
right © University Books, 1961. Reprinted by permission of Lyle Stuart, Inc.
The Horizon Book of Lost Worlds by Leonard Cottrell. Copyright © American
Heritage Publishing Company, Inc., 1962. Reprinted by permission.

For *Philip, Anya,* AND *Stefan*

When you think on the human condition, remember the need for illusion, and its role in sustaining life.

—Norma Jean Harris

My mother reads the newspaper. She sits by the window and reads the newspaper while she waits for me to come home from school.

—Ruth Ann Harris, 7

The years go racing by;
I live as best I can.
—Mabel Mercer*

* "I See It Now." From the film "Open The Door and See All The People." Lyric by William Engvick. Music by Alec Wilder. TRO—© Copyright 1964 Hollis Music Inc., New York, N.Y. Used by permission.

1

"Mrs. Harris, a woman is not required to testify against her husband and children. It is never done."

"Not even to save her life?"

"Your honor, the witness has continually ignored counsel's advice; if it please the court, I request permission to remove myself from the case."

"You don't understand!"

Fuck the pay; there's no fee in the world worth the aggravation of representing a crazy woman. "Listen you dumb broad, are you aware that he's the most important judge in the country? You'd better not push this thing any further. That's my parting advice to you."

"If he's so important, what's he doing sitting small-claims court? This *is* a small claim; you said so yourself." These WASP pricks are all alike; even while I'm talking to him he's shoving his papers into his briefcase and zipping up. The judge is nodding; it's not an affirmation, he's just dozing. See, his jaw has grown slack, his delicate fingers probe the gavel in soft spasmodic strokes.

"Listen!" I scream. What else can I do? They're all here because of me, the least they can do is hear the charge: "It's the subtle way they continually create crises and demands which draw me away from my work; the unwarranted claims they make on my mind and body. Surely that deserves a hearing!" Even the jury has grown restless. They're not my peers; they couldn't get the peers. They were all excused for cause. In some cases that meant they had professional commitments; but for the most part it meant both hands were in the toilet shaking out diapers. In any case, I know the plumber over there, third from the left—Mr.

1

Beemer—has his mind made up already. His picture was in the paper just last week, in the "Question Man" column, where they interview people on the street. The question was: "Is Your Wife Liberated?"

> Yes. My wife has always been liberated. I've always been very liberal with her and the children. Sure, she does all the housework, but only because she wants to. I avoid all work by preference. Never been even tempted to do the housework! I've always told my wife if she felt moved to express herself in other areas she had my total consent.

Someone just tripped over a chair on the way to the bathroom. The noise brings the judge to his feet. As he fumbles for the gavel his robes part, exposing bare flesh. Since the death of his wife he has never dressed himself—so the rumor goes. "Case dismissed!" he squeaks, collapsing to the floor.

Pleasant Valley lies within commuting distance from San Francisco. The newspapers refer to it, along with its satellite suburbs, as a "bedroom community." The implication is clear: San Francisco has the culture; Pleasant Valley has the beds.

The drive between the city and Pleasant Valley arouses no pain if undertaken by freeway, except during those times when traffic is stalled. The drive between the two communities arouses pain in some, indifference in others, if the route chosen is Coronado Avenue. Coronado Avenue is a linear garden, generating the types of vegetation required to support post-industrial life: gas stations, laundromats, body shops, used-car lots, television repair shops, bars, beauty salons, and three major discount supermarkets. On Coronado, you can eat your way through twelve miles of Taco Bells, McDonald's', Jack-in-the-Boxes, Denny's', Foster's Freezes, A&W's, Doggie Diners, and Big Boy Burgers without hesitating for a block.

The streets in Pleasant Valley bear such names as Riviera, Flamingo, Capri, Ranch Road, and Palm Court. The homes are late California split-level, except where an occasional architect from the city has made his statement in redwood and glass. One must be on guard against drawing conclusions and being deceived by appearances: the residents of Pleasant Valley bear little resemblance to one another in background, political orientation, or

2

moral standards. On the other hand, neither is it a "melting pot." It is a place in time marked by a high rate of social mobility and a resistance to definition.

The families of Pleasant Valley have a special kind of twentieth-century heroism. Being pioneers in a time without geographic frontiers, their attempts to contain their sense of personal and collective confusion center around such devices as block parties (once a year, on the Fourth of July); sporadic "grass-roots" political gestures which center on threats to their immediate environment; hastily organized vigilante maneuvers, designed to curb what is loosely referred to as "the growing threat of crime in the suburbs"; and repeated attempts on the part of the fathers to organize "growth-promoting" activities for their children, usually the boys, and mostly involving balls of one sort or another (base; basket; volley; foot; and occasionally stick and hand—the latter an attempt on the part of transplanted New Yorkers to relive their childhoods through their sons, and usually doomed to failure). California-born fathers have a somewhat better edge, encouraging tennis as the outlet of choice among their sons; and its popularity is slowly spreading in a way that cuts across sexual, age, class, and —in two isolated cases—racial lines. The mothers bear their daughters, floating in undulant suspension on the eight-cyclinder, dual-control tail-gated wings of their Country Squires, to pre-ballet and mixed-media art, and participate one day a week in their children's classrooms at the recently integrated school. Some play tennis, some don't.

Palm Court has three palms in addition to native California live oak, loquat, eucalyptus, sycamore, pine, and redwood—an arrangement which intensifies the sense of confusion and ambiguous environment. Number 29 is the home of Norma Jean Harris and her family. On applications, Norma Jean has referred to herself variously as: Housewife; Homemaker (mentally adding "Creative"); and Mother. Of course, those terms do not belong under the heading Occupation; they never did, because they do not adequately describe what you do. Doctor, teacher—these terms are descriptive; they carry an imprint that fixes readily in the mind and graphically illustrates the nature of the work done. Housewife? We all know how sloppy that one is, the tendency it has to evoke a kind of back-room imagery, where all the trivia is stored. With Housewife the image usually centers on some vague woman going after dust balls with her Electrolux, slipping an endless array of pies and cakes into her oven, swatting the kids, matching fabric samples, running up curtains on her Singer, having orgasms in the laundry room while inhaling the whiteness of her wash. It varies. Some don't swat the kids; they offer them plates of hot cookies, or pour them glasses of Tang from bottomless pitchers. Taken in its most literal sense, the term arouses the image of a woman dancing with her house, which has just slipped a half-carat diamond ring on her finger. She is embracing her house, out of gratitude. Then she straightens its tie, brushes the leaves off its roof, gives it backrubs, and finally copulates with it.

So you see, while something always has to go on the dotted line under Occupation, it's obvious that the term that's been assigned to me doesn't say much. Even if I attached a separate sheet (which is sometimes allowed), how would that change anything? What could they possibly make of the one consistent thing I do (besides swatting the kids and petting the wash)? If I put down: Reads newspaper, what would that explain?

The kitchen is where Norma Jean sits by the window and reads the San Francisco *Chronicle* each weekday morning, after the children have been delivered to school. It required three months of planning to coordinate a schedule by which they would all three be in school or nursery school during the same two and a half hours, so she could read the paper without interruption. I have always taken the newspaper seriously. It is an absolutely accurate mirror of the period it describes. It's hard for me to understand Martin's attitude on this point. At times, when I subject him to my reactions, he accuses me of "taking things too seriously" (as in Warning: The Associate Professor of Education and Dean of Students Has Determined That Taking Things Too Seriously Is Dangerous to Your Health); at other times, when he would walk by just as I was spreading the paper across the breakfast table, concentrating deeply and taking it all in, he'd say something like, "Reading the *paper?*" in that tone which, when translated, meant: Aren't there some beds to be made? dishes to be washed? buttons to be sewn on? It really made him nervous, my "lethargy" and "preoccupation"; that's why I had to change my M.O., rearrange my schedule. His value judgments were interfering with business.

4

It took some experimenting to settle on just the right method of incorporating my news. As my "window" to the outside world, it not only informs and alerts, it reactivates feelings connected with that world, from which I have become detached over the years—such feelings as: rage (universal, as opposed to the kind produced by family life); horror; empathy; excitement (the excitement of ideas, as opposed to sexual excitement or the excitement that arises from seeing your daughter make a piece of conceptual art instead of an ashtray, or your son score [base; basket; volley; foot; and occasionally stick and hand]). Having sustained me in all these ways, it was absolutely crucial that I find the appropriate atmosphere in which to continue the perversion, uninterrupted. Being uninterrupted, for at least some portion of your waking hours, as every mother knows, is a condition rating nine points on a scale of ten. Before Martin put his foot down, I also subscribed to the San Francisco *Examiner*, the Berkeley *Barb*, The Oakland *Tribune*, and Freedom *News*. "You're pissing all my money away on newspapers!" is what he said. So now we just take the *Chronicle*, but I pick the others up on the stands from time to time, whenever the need to know what's going on becomes intense. A dime here, a dime there; there's no way he can control that, without appearing ridiculous. Some husbands make you account for every cent; not mine.

At first I took it into the bath after everyone was asleep. I can't say that didn't have its advantages, while it lasted; at least two basic requirements were met: quiet, and an uninterrupted stretch of time for the mind to dwell on, and bend to its own variations, any event, catastrophe or idea presented it. What finally got me in the end was the lack of natural light and the sense of overwhelming enclosure. How can you envision the images of the outside world—how can you let your mind play on them, preparatory to some imagined reunion in the future—from the confines of a steaming, locked bathroom, with all its symbols of self-absorption spread from floor to ceiling? (Soap, razors, Tampax, mirrors, make-up, devices to promote "healthy" teeth—brushes, paste, floss, Stim-U-Dents—toilet paper . . .) What made you think it was the rubber ducks? ("Oh, Rubber Duckie you're the one!/You make bath time/Lots of fun . . ." —Sesame Street.)*

* "Rubber Duckie," words and music by Jeffrey Moss © 1970 Festival Attraction, Inc.

5

Rimming the edge of the tub, spilling freezing water down your neck out their squeakers. If it's never happened to you, under the circumstances I'm describing, I won't belabor it. But for those who assumed that that kind of thing might have had something to do with the decision to give up doing it in the bathroom, it's only fair to acknowledge that the ducks were definitely a factor, along with the boats (tug; steam; row; sail; outboard; paddlewheel), though not the major one. It was the *confinement*, the growing feeling of being sealed in, as in the inner chamber of a pharaoh's tomb, that precipitated the move to the window (kitchen; eastern exposure; view of live oak and the freeway beyond), where I sit now.

DOUBLE SLAYING

Mother and Daughter

Chicago

A 29-year-old Bible peddler and ex-convict yesterday admitted beating to death a young woman and her infant daughter whose bodies were found in a suburban church parking lot, police said.

Lee Charles Jennings confessed to killing Barbara Flanagan, 27, and her 18-month-old daughter, Renée, in his apartment and taking their bodies to the Mt. Prospect Presbyterian Church, police said.

Church

Police quoted Jennings as saying he took the bodies to the church lot because "I wanted to take them to a church of their own denomination."

Cook county Coroner Andrew Toman said Mrs. Flanagan died of head injuries apparently inflicted when her assailant held his hands around her neck and slammed her head on a hard surface.

The child died of asphyxiation and had been sexually assaulted, he said.

Prison

Police said Jennings was arrested October 14, 1964, on charges of rape and armed robbery. He was convicted on both charges and served six years at the Illinois State Prison at Menard, investigators said.

Mrs. Flanagan's husband, Dennis, told police his wife posted a card in a supermarket offering to baby-sit. A man phoned the home September 9 and offered Mrs. Flanagan a job.

She took a bus to meet the man, police said. They said a bus driver identified Jennings as the man he saw picking her up.

UNITED PRESS

SNOWY OWL

Washington
The snowy owl lives in the barren tundras of the American, Asiatic and European Arctic.

ASSOCIATED PRESS

Norma Jean folds the paper neatly, all the sections in order, one under the other. Her eggs grow cold in their bowl. It was seven years ago this month that I brought Ruth Ann home from the hospital, wrapped tight as a bee in her blanket. I was feeling weak but I tried to smile for Martin's camera, attempted to imitate the women in the Bringing The New Baby Home pictures, who always exhibited a glowing radiance and inner confidence. My only thought, walking up the path, was how would I survive the next two weeks alone in the house with this new creature. We were new in the neighborhood and didn't know anyone; our respective families were either dead or scattered throughout the far corners of America, unable to assist. Martin had suggested hiring help, but I believed that a mother's reputation rested on being able to care for her baby, and her home, herself. Some of my friends with babies had help, but still conveyed the attitude that, even when it went well by objective standards, it represented some kind of failure on their parts. Others went it alone, like me. We never compared notes with any degree of honesty, because none of us wanted to appear weak or incompetent. As a result, we all suffered alone. It was 1964. We had the following aids at our disposal: pacifiers (Nuk-Sauger; Binkey; Playtex; Carters); our breasts, in the cases of those who nursed; Similac and Enfamil, in the cases of those who did not; our pediatricians; books on infant and child care and the psychology of the child, most of which were written in the forties and fifties. Foremost among these was, of course, Spock's *Baby and Child Care*. We loved him; he bent over backwards to avoid promoting guilt in

7

the new mother, offering dozens of possible solutions to every crisis, none of which worked.

Having broken with tradition and lost the guidance and support of a previous generation, women have been exposed to a wide variety of pamphlets, books, and magazine articles which often are confusing and conflicting, expressing sometimes irreconcilable professional advice . . .

—Lawrence K. Frank, *On The Importance of Infancy*, Copyright 1966, Random House, Inc., New York, p. 155.

We also read *The Womanly Art of Breast Feeding*, and imagined that, eventually, when we had mastered the art sufficiently, we would take our babies to the Chinese restaurant and nurse them over sweet-and-sour, until that crushing little item in the paper in May 1964 whose headline read NURSING MOTHER EVICTED FROM S. F. RESTAURANT. So we stayed propped against our pillows ("A pillow, placed under the elbow when nursing, often alleviates the strain." —*Handbook of Infant Care*, Chapter IV); we worked overtime to be womanly, alone in our quiet homes.

He came to the door on my first day home from the hospital. I had just lifted Ruth Ann's legs on the changing table to slide a fresh diaper under her when she shit halfway across the room.

When the pressures within the bladder and rectum build up through accumulation of their contents, the sphincters automatically release and allow the contents to be discharged.

Ibid., p. 144.

I had read that newborns who are breast fed tend toward runny stools (*Handbook of Infant Care*, Chapter II), but nothing prepared me for this terrible yellow mess which was slowly seeping into the rug, my nightgown, the walls. I was still in my nightgown, although it was eleven o'clock in the morning. That was how it was four days after birth, when you were home alone with a newborn infant. A mental image of Martin, in class with his students, flashed through my mind: his white shirt, not a trace of yellow shit anywhere, his mind probing, soaring, cross-fertilizing. It was my first experience hating the father and the child simultaneously.

I decided to wash her first, then lay her down while I changed. The very last order of business would be to call the cleaners to find out what I should use to take out the stains. I prided myself on the fact that my mind was still capable of functioning in an orderly manner, especially in my first emergency. She was lying there, wet and screaming on the bathroom rug, and I was throwing a dress over my head, when the doorbell rang. I hadn't learned yet that you didn't have to answer it. It had cost fifty dollars to have the electrician rewire it so a new mother could hear it.

I threw her over my shoulder; it really unnerved me how she screamed. I knew they cried, but no one mentioned that they were capable of screaming for hours, without interruption, after you had done everything humanly possible for them. The stitches hurt as I ran to open the door. He was about six feet tall, with a dirty blond crew-cut and black horn-rimmed glasses. Although he wore a sport jacket and slacks, they bore stains. I looked up at him in the way that new mothers and housewives look at strangers who come to their doors: expectantly, with a trace of suspicion. *Please don't kill me; I have a new baby.* I smiled weakly, to indicate an apology for Ruth Ann's screams. I still felt I had to apologize then. He bent toward me and spoke softly—barely above a whisper.

"I have discovered a method for making fire without matches," he whispered. "Would that be of interest to you?"

"What? Oh, I'm sorry; I can't hear you too well," juggling Ruth Ann on my shoulder, realizing too late I should have left her on the bathroom floor—who says you have to have them over your shoulder when weirdos come to your door? "I'm afraid I don't understand."

"I have developed a method for making fire without the use of matches," he repeats, slowly withdrawing a pamphlet from his pocket. "For one dollar you may have a copy of the book I have written on the subject. Then you would understand." He stares at me intently. He has in no way acknowledged that I smell of shit and have a screaming baby over my shoulder. I am beginning to feel chills and don't know just what to do. I know I should say no, and close the door on him, but he looks so strange, I don't want to make him angry. On the other hand, if I put the baby down and go looking for a dollar, I would have to trust that he would not come in and (do what to us? Make a fire right here in my living room?).

"One dollar?" I couldn't ask him to hold the baby. With some you could—the milkman, for instance. I stepped back slightly and my eyes raced around the living room. My purse was on the floor. I was only four days post-partum, but I could do the Deep-Knee-Bend-With-Screaming-Child-Over-The-Shoulder with some skill already, in spite of the stitches.

Withdrawing a dollar bill with my free hand, I accepted his pamphlet. My shoulder ached. The pamphlet felt strange in my hand; it had an aura of transient rooms and sidetracked minds. After he had gone, I remember having hysterics in the bathroom while Ruth Ann screamed from her bassinet. I stared at the dried yellow stains, fixed now in rivulets on the wall, and wanted to die.

> Only three things are required for my method of starting fire without matches: a piece of wood, or stone, with the center hollowed out, forming a bowl, which we will call the "Female" part; a wooden stick, or rod, with a pointed, but slightly rounded bulge at the end, which we will refer to as the "Male" part; and a small pile of dried grass or leaves.

Ruth Ann screamed and screamed as I sat on the side of the bathtub, crying and studying how to make fire without matches. Nowhere in the pamphlet did he say where one got the "Female" and "Male" parts, so essential to the task; you were left to figure that out yourself. Presumably you could whittle them from the slats in your new baby's crib, then add a little mattress stuffing, and you'd be on your way. I threw the pamphlet in the tub, where it withered in its deranged juices, and gathered up Ruth Ann and began to feed her, in spite of the doctor's warning: no oftener than every two hours. She became quiet, and we both slept.

The dishes simmer in the sink. The house is without sound. The only indications of life in the neighborhood are the bark of an occasional dog and the distant hum of commuter traffic from the freeway. Norma Jean picks at the congealed egg yolk on the plates, her hands listlessly scraping back and forth under the steaming water. She dreams of snowy owls in the far tundras of the world.

NAME	Norma Jean Harris
DATE OF BIRTH	8/12/38
ADDRESS	29 Palm Ct., Pleasant Valley, Calif.
OCCUPATION	Housewife
SOCIAL SECURITY NUMBER	563-52-5143
PERSON RESPONSIBLE FOR PAYMENT	Martin Harris
RELATIONSHIP TO PATIENT	Husband
CHILDREN	Ruth Ann, 7; Scott, 5; Damon, 3
PRESENTING SYMPTOMS	Fatigue. Depression. Anxiety.

The appointment is for 10 A.M. Norma Jean sits in the air-conditioned chill of Dr. Rudolph Arndt's waiting room. She thinks she has listed the symptoms accurately, the way Martin explained them when he convinced her of her need to "get a little professional help." She thinks her social security number is correct, but she's not sure; it's been over ten years since she has worked.

She looks at her watch. Five after ten. Maybe Dr. Arndt has forgotten. Maybe she is in the wrong building. She wonders if his split-leaf philodendron is getting enough water; it looks pale. It has seemed a long wait and has increased her anxiety. She attempted the magazines on the table, but couldn't understand *Scientific American,* and felt *The New Yorker* didn't speak to her needs. *Life* magazine was too overwhelming, especially the color pictures of the war. Wasn't it just last month that she had whispered to *Life:* "Please, no more color pictures of the war?" It was the evening Martin had said, "Jeanie, you're talking to yourself again; I think it's time you considered getting some outside help." He hadn't meant a cleaning woman.

Martin only sees the tip of the iceberg. It didn't start with the talking, it was further back than that. It's hard to pin down. . . . Suddenly the door to Dr. Arndt's inner chamber opens. "Hi," he says, motioning for her to come in. It wasn't what she had expected, neither the relaxed and friendly "Hi" nor Dr. Arndt's appearance. Impossible to tell his age—fifty? sixty? No cigar, not even a pipe. No piercing eyes, just a human being, standing now at the door, waiting for her to go through.

"My husband felt I should talk to someone about my . . . problems. He thinks I'm showing signs of not coping, the way I always used to. One of my neighbors is in treatment; she says it has helped her, made her better able to understand her children, tolerate her life. . . ." Norma Jean wipes the perspiration on her hands onto her skirt, in a gesture she hopes Dr. Arndt won't interpret as incipient hysteria. She attempts to do it casually, but how do you keep rubbing your skirt without its taking on sexual overtones? *What am I doing here? Was this what I wanted?*

"What signs of not coping?"

"Well, he would come home from work and the kids would be hanging on my skirt, crying, fighting, wiping their snot all over my skirt. And I'd think: who needs all this snot? Not me." Norma Jean stares at the floor. After a long pause, Dr. Arndt says, "Well, what were you doing?"

"I was leaning over the washing machine, crying into a pile of dirty laundry. I was also drunk. I never planned it that way, but somehow that's the way it always ended up: Martin coming in the door just as I was beating one of the kids. . . ." She waits for him to say, *"Beating your kids?!!"* but he remains silent. She goes on, "Or having hysterics over a pile of dirty laundry."

"It must have been quite upsetting to you."

"How would *you* know how upsetting it was? How many times has your wife come home and found *you* drunk over the laundry, kicking the kids?" (Patient exhibits initial hostility and guilt.) "My neighbor was doing it too, though not as often and she doesn't drink. She screamed a lot. Martin just couldn't stand it; I don't blame him. It's gotten awful in the past few months. I never dreamed this would be how I'd end up; it was how others ended up."

"Well, you've told me how your husband feels, and your neighbor. How do you feel?"

"Me?" Norma Jean stares across the beige carpet. How is it possible to say how you feel, after so many years of others, others?

"Well, it's almost impossible to say any more; I'm too far away from it. Martin says I overreact to things. I guess what he says is true, though frankly, with the pressures, I sometimes feel people have two choices: to do what I do, and fall apart; or to anesthetize themselves and carry on as best they can. Am I making any sense? You could add confusion to the record. I am confused. I'm very definite about my confusion! Ha ha." She starts wiping the sweat on her skirt again. Dr. Arndt is silent. *Why does the mind wander when under scrutiny? Where do you begin?*

"I see you have three children." The comment startles her. *Why did he say three?*

"There were supposed to be four," she hears herself answering, "but I lost the last one." Lost, little, last one; little lost last one. I'm sorry, Norma Jean; I'm afraid we've lost it. Under no circumstances are you to blame yourself; we did everything we could. It was an accident. No! How can you think of it as an accident? I wanted it. Four was the perfect number. Everyone had four. You didn't question it, you just tried your best to achieve it. "The armaments race," as one of Martin's friends had called it then. Those of us just getting our start in the early sixties had a tradition to maintain, inherited from the families of the fifties: two of each sex, if you were lucky. We did think togetherness lowbrow, and unsuited to our tastes, so we substituted creative homemaking in its place. Other than that, our goals were to keep up our end of what we thought to be the deal. The deal clarified itself at the social events: the dinners, cocktail parties, business socials and faculty parties which centered around the work of our husbands. No woman could escape learning about the deal. It was hovering behind the folds in the curtains, written in invisible ink on the undersides of coffee tables, lurking in the canapé trays, wherever women huddled together in groups, serving time. Having acknowledged that the party, as a whole, was the husband's terri-

13

tory, they set out to establish their own, on the fringes: digging, scratching, clawing, planting seeds, erecting fences.

"Hi. I'm Vern's wife."

"Hi. I'm Martin's wife."

"How many children do *you* have?"

Those who could say "four" had clear territorial rights, moved like queens among the hors d'oeuvres. There was nothing to be gained by comparing the status of husbands; they were all more or less on equal ground. The only way for a woman to jockey for position, establish her own status, was with reference to the number of young she had borne.

Norma Jean is fending off images. She realizes it is probably the wrong thing to do, here, in this situation; in fact knows that the reverse should obtain. The more she attempts to crystallize them in her mind, the more deeply she resists saying anything about them to Dr. Arndt. The old anger centers on the image of the doctor, she knows. Instead, she says:

"Yes. I guess I could start with the children; it's as good a place as any. Nothing in my single years prepared me for them, for the life they bring. Before they came, dreaming of them, I imagined they would be still as dolls, and never require more of me than I could give. Or I could begin with the house. They all fit together. The house, the family, the way they numb. I no longer have serious thoughts; everything is leveled, diluted. The days wrap around me; I suffocate." Is this really how I see myself? It bears no resemblance to myself as I remember me, as I once was. How many selves is a person awarded in a lifetime? Can you shed one for another, like skins?

Tears come to her eyes; she wipes them on her sleeve. New images appear. Unfocused at first, then shimmering, and in color. It is a film. It is the El Rey Theater and she and Martin are sitting together in the dark. It is the night they saw *The Hellstrom Chronicle*. The scene is taking shape; she doesn't want it, but it continues to bloom there in her mind, like a rich nightflower. *Surely the fifty minutes must be up. When this is over I will go to Pay and Save and pick up the groceries.* She begins to form the list in her mind; it is an involuntary reflex. But this time all she gets is: eggs, peanut butter, coffee, eggs, chicken, toilet paper, eggs,

eggs, eggs. . . . It is the scene in the termite colony. There on the screen are two enormous termite queens, throbbing side by side. She feels herself sinking lower in her seat, hoping the darkness of the theater will hide her from everyone. She is four months pregnant with the little lost last one, halfway down in her seat, hoping people won't notice they have a termite queen of their very own in the fifth row. It is herself she sees up there, magnified a thousand times.

The camera invades the colony, softly, with no obvious intrusion. It shows the various roles of each termite: the workers, whose entire life-spans are spent building and maintaining the fortress; the day-care workers, whose function is to care for the young until they reach maturity (then presumably to grasp—in a flash of primordial insight—their own respective roles); the feeders, whose only function is to stuff the queens; and lastly, the queens themselves: inflated and rolling, like silken parachutes. Their sole purpose is to produce young. All their lives, masses of rippling eggs pour from their bodies, increasing the species. Day after day, they accept the food that is brought and stuffed into them. Does the termite queen question her role? She does not. Billowing, corpulent, pulsating, she knows what she knows. It is elementary, inescapable. It has been written absolutely and for centuries in the history of her cells.

My head was spinning. I was relieved when the killer insects invaded the colony and all the workers died in their attempt to defend it. I knew the queens were doomed. The feeders tried their best to push them back under the rocks, where they would be hidden. But you see (and it would take another queen to know this, even before the camera picked it up), you can't *move* a body like that. It simply isn't possible. They tried, though: frantic, obedient to instinct, straining to protect the ancient home, the ancestral mothers. Let them die, I was thinking. Let them be eaten alive by invaders. They will forgive it.

I couldn't stop the tears. I tried to explain it to Martin later, in the car. He patted me on the shoulder and murmured something about my being too hard on myself. I had three glasses of wine when we got home and slept deeply. It's been a year since then. And every month I feel my body getting ready to have new babies.

15

It is a sly animal, can't be trusted. Shifts its gears and moves in mysterious ways. Sometimes I stand in front of the color TV and whisper, "Sterilize me!" This always upsets Martin, especially if he's watching a ball game at the time.

"Yes. Well, our time is up, Mrs. Harris. I will be available at the same time next week, if you would like to continue."

Is it permitted to speak of longing while buying apples? That's often where it strikes, right in the middle of the store. There I am, with my longings, surrounded by pyramids of apples, oranges, and—in winter—persimmons. All that abundance, and in my hand, the list:

mayonnaise	cat food	lettuce
peanut butter	coffee	cereal
toilet paper	floor wax	fish
bread	toothpaste	chicken
tomato sauce	fruit	cheese
eggs	vegetables	potatoes
orange juice	bacon	lunch bags

I need something else, very badly, but I can't think what it is. This often happens when I get to the store; the list is all right, as far as it goes. But then I get overwhelmed by the feeling that something is missing, that I have forgotten to list something and can't leave the store until I discover what it is. Many days I do not leave the store. I cruise up and down the aisles, pretending interest in the spice section, for instance, so that others won't be able to read my confusion. It's easy to pretend you're not confused in the supermarket—just act as though you're looking for something. Most people are.

Norma Jean pulls up in front of Fairyland Nursery School. She is ten minutes late. All the other mothers have arrived on time, fetched their children, and gone. She opens the door, anticipating the unspoken message in the eyes of the teacher: you're late. Again. Damon is anxious. Damon wonders if you have died. Damon is wondering if he has been abandoned by his mother.

"I'm sorry I'm late, Miss Rogers. The lines at Pay and Save were terrible." It's a weak excuse, and she knows it. Why do I have to feel apologetic all the time, about everything?

"You're late, Mommy," Damon says, from behind the book table. How terrible and alone he looks in the empty room. "Damon, you know Mommy always comes for you . . . eventually."

"Mrs. Harris," *Oh here it comes, just as I always knew it would . . . eventually.* "I've been meaning to speak to you about Damon. Now that you're here, and the others have gone, this might be a good time, if it suits you."

"Well, I do have another hour and a half before the car pool delivers Scott from his nursery school, Miss Rogers." And another hour and a half before Ruth Ann comes home from school. *A life measured out in hour and a half portions, five days out of seven, week after week, month, year.* Miss Rogers is looking at her in a peculiar way. Not unusual for Miss Rogers, but under these circumstances Norma Jean is clearly on the defensive, in the wrong, the weaker of the two, and recognizes these facts.

"Yes, this is a good time," she says.

They sit down; Damon is given permission to play with the fire truck. All to himself, no rivals, he accepts the bribe, to Norma Jean's great relief. There is nothing worse than trying to discuss your child's problems with an expert while the child is pulling on your skirt (loaded with snot, sweat, tears), or otherwise clearly indicating that you do not give him the attention he needs.

"Well, Miss Rogers. What is it about Damon?"

"I trust you are aware, Mrs. Harris, of his imaginary playmate?"

"Yes," she begins, cautiously. "All kids have them, don't they? Yes, I'm aware he sometimes has imaginary conversations." *Don't we all?*

"Yes, Mrs. Harris. But are you aware of his . . . this figure's *name?*"

"Oh. Yeah. Well, I guess you couldn't be referring to anyone else but Fokey. Sure, Fokey I think he calls him."

"I mean his full name, Mrs. Harris. This is rather difficult for me, but I can't believe you haven't heard Damon refer to him by his full name, and that is what concerns me."

The jig is up. She means Fokey Fuckerhead. "Yes, Miss Rogers, I'm aware he has an imaginary companion named Fokey Fuckerhead." Miss Rogers is getting red. It's hard to tell whether it is menopause or Fokey. Norma Jean knows. It's Fokey. Good old

Fokey Fuckerhead; if the real kid doesn't get you, the fake one will . . . eventually.

Leaning over the stove, Norma Jean reads the recipe on the back of a package of slivered almonds. She is going to make the family dessert tonight, although they rarely have desserts. (Martin's cholesterol level; her difficulty losing the weight gained through years of pregnancies; the pediatrician's warnings concerning early childhood eating habits and their influence on such things as hypertension, heart disease, and general social unacceptability.) Today, though, she feels they need a dessert. She feels they need it because somewhere, in the inner recesses where mothers look from time to time to see how they are doing, something tells her she has been negligent in some way. And dessert is an easy way of making this up: a tangible, basic statement of her love.

Raspberry Almond Gems
Cut (margarine into flour, sugar, etc.).
Blend (in yolks, etc.).
Chill (2 hours).
Divide (Dough).
Roll (on well-floured board).
Cut (with floured, 2½-inch doughnut cutter).
Place (on ungreased baking sheet).
Brush (with egg whites).
Sprinkle (with almonds).
Bake (at 350 degrees; 8–10 minutes).
Spread (raspberry preserves over each circle).

Her stomach hurts. Roll-Cut-Chill-Divide; Place-Brush-Sprinkle-Spread. She throws the slivered almonds back into the cupboard and pours herself a vermouth instead. Place (ice in glass); Pour (over ice); Drink. She begins to think. It's a risk, especially around the dinner hour. She thinks of what she might have been. She recalls the sense of purpose during the years spent in the college library, in the basement stacks, studying the major figures in ancient Egyptian history, even then suspecting that her major in art had less to do with art and more to do with that ancient civilization. Why it had fascinated her then, and why she felt it coming more to mind in the past year, she didn't know. There wasn't much you could do with a passion for Egyptian history then. She did what most of her friends did: worked a few years, married, and had children. Some author she had read recently had called this pattern "the natural route taken by women in the fifties who wanted to achieve and preserve the identity required of them by their culture." Of course you didn't know that then. They didn't write things like that about women. They wrote things like:

The Feminine Mother

How does the proper mother bring up her children? That is a question easily answered. In the first place, she does none of the things that are done by the other types. She does not reject, over-protect, dominate or overfondle her child.

More positively, she accepts herself fully as a woman, which means that she fully accepts her sexuality and enjoys it without parading it. She does not understand when she hears other women speak bitterly of the privileges of men. She does not see things that way. Men, to her, are useful objects and if, being useful, they extract enjoyment from various of the strange things they are up to it is quite all right with her. She knows, at any rate, that she is dependent on a man. There is no fantasy in her mind about being an "independent woman," a contradiction in terms. She knows she is dependent on the phallus for sexual enjoyment, which, as she is genitalized, she is in need of. Having children is to her the most natural thing possible, and it would never occur to her to have any doubts about it. When she hears someone question the advisability of having children she is bewildered unless she is told of some trenchant medical reason. Then she feels sorry for the woman deprived. If a woman does not have children, she asks ingenuously, what is everything all about for her?

* * *

Women with one or no children, excluding from consideration those with adverse organic conditions (present in few instances), are, with occasional exceptions, emotionally disoriented. That is to say, they are unhappy women, whatever may be their conscious testimony to the contrary.

—Ferdinand Lundberg and Marynia F. Farnham, M.D., *Modern Woman, The Lost Sex,* p. 319. Copyright 1947, Harper & Row.

Would have been, could have been, might have been, should have been . . . and saddest of all, was to have been. The oven is

hot, getting hotter. Oh, the variety of ways to describe lost possibilities. She chronicles them all.

Ruth Ann and Damon are screaming. They are coming her
way. Quickly, shut off the thinking; attend to the children. Do
not stand anywhere near the knife rack.

"I hate him. I'm going to kill him. I have a right to beat him
up," screams Ruth Ann.

"No, you don't," Norma Jean hears herself saying.

"Oh, yes I do. He's my brother."

"You don't have to like him, but you can't kill him. He's here
to stay."

"Well you always say 'take care of it yourself,' and I am. I am
going to kick his ass."

Scott flies in. "Nobody will play with me," he screams. My poor
neglected middle child. "They can't play with you right now,
Scott. They're tearing each other apart. Wait awhile, see what
materializes." She has another swallow of vermouth and lights a
cigarette. Martin will be home in ten minutes. Something has to
be done about dinner.

"Mommy's going to make dinner now," she begins, referring to
herself in the third person, something she detests, but finds herself doing more and more often. "I want you all to play quietly
for ten minutes. Here are some carrot sticks."

"Daddy! Daddy! Here he comes! Daddy's home!" screams Scott,
running to the door.

"Oh, there you are, Daddy!" cries Ruth Ann. "You handsome
man!"

"Hi, kids." Martin's deep voice drifts kitchen ward. "How are
my children today? What have you been up to while Daddy was
away?" It is understood that it is the kind of question which requires no answer, because Daddy doesn't want to know. Daddy
likes to preserve his myths.

"Mom's cooking dinner and she was going to make a dessert,
but now she won't," pouts Ruth Ann.

"Why don't we ever have desserts, Mom?"

"Because we're all too fat, Scott, that's why."

"We never have desserts in this house. You deprive us." (Ruth
Ann)

"Where did she learn 'deprive'?" says Martin.

"At school, where else? It's their explanation for when she gets her lunch money stolen."

"Something bothering you tonight?"

"No, Martin. Nothing out of the ordinary."

"Oh, by the way, how did things go with Arndt today?" *Did you see that? The way his mind works? The sickening logic of it? All I have to say is "nothing out of the ordinary," and he suddenly connects: Oh, yeah, just the usual. I almost forgot. She's crazy.*

"I'll tell you about it later, after the children are in bed."

Ruth Ann leans over the dinner table and puts her hand on Martin's arm. "Did you have a hard day, Daddy?" she whispers lovingly. Norma Jean glances up quickly from her plate. Where was I when she was growing into such a lovely creature? When did it happen? While I was asleep? ("Enjoy them now; they grow so fast!"—stranger in grocery store, Ruth Ann eighteen months. "They drink your blood." —cynic at cocktail party, 1964, when informed of Ruth Ann's birth. "They take years off your life." —Mrs. Hatch, neighbor, on seeing Ruth Ann in carriage for the first time, age three weeks.)

"You look just like a king, Daddy," Ruth Ann presses on. Norma Jean's eyes narrow, fighting off her deep love for Ruth Ann. He's *mine*. I think.

"What did you learn in school today, sweetheart?" asks Martin, leaning toward Ruth Ann. Norma Jean studies him: his thick hair, with traces of grey, like her own; the same profile that once stood on the other side of the wedding cake, now bearing signs of things having been endured. It surprises her to find herself thinking he looks better now than he did then.

"We learned about Malcolm X and how he was shot dead. And we learned about President Kennedy, and how he was shot dead, in the head. And then we learned about Martin Luther King. He was shot dead too. He tried to help his people."

Martin looks over at me, the way he does when something takes him by surprise. He thinks I have all the explanations. I stay at home, spreading my apron wide, gathering answers. Even when I don't actually have them, I make them up; I've got a big mouth. I try hard to accommodate all my family's needs.

"She's learning about our leaders and how they all get shot in the head when they try to help their people," I say. "I think the teacher was attempting to stress the importance of standing up for values one believes in, even in the face of powerful opposition. But they don't grasp that; they're too young. All they remember is how many times someone was shot in the head."

There is a sudden sound of dishware hitting the table. Damon speaks: "Mommy, I peed in my pants and I spilled my milk."

"Yes, I can see that, Damon. Ruth Ann, you and Scotty clear while I tend to Damon. Did you feed the cats?"

"Oh, do I *have* to? I *always* have to feed those damned cats. Scott and Damon *never* have to do it, always me. I'm going to find another home. I'm going to trade homes with Jennifer; *her* mother feeds *their* cats." Whine, whine, whine. You can see the way it is designed to wear you down, little by little, until you end up doing everything yourself. That is, it wears most of us down. Not me, though. Taking everything too seriously, overreacting as I do, hard as I am on myself, I never give in. I am relentless. I fight them right down to the last unit of energy, the last faint breath, the last morsel of Kitty Queen Chopped Liver: "If you don't feed those fucking cats in five minutes, I'm taking them all back to the pet store and you'll never see them again."

("Meow, meow, meow." —*Three Little Kittens*, p. 1.) They sit there on the kitchen floor, expectantly, never doubting the bounty which comes their way, without fail, twice a day, one enormous overfed cat for each child: Fletcher, Percy, and Snow White. It's always a strain, when taking them to the vet to be wormed or spayed or given booster shots, to have to spell their names for the receptionist. Yes, Snow White is the girl's cat (How did you guess?); the other two belong to the boys. They were named by my husband in a fit of hostility before they achieved the age of consent. He did this because he had wanted a dog. I said: No dogs. That's why we have two black cats named Fletcher and Percy. Why do I feel I have to explain things like this to the vet? Only someone on the brink would feel under such an obligation.

Norma Jean slips between the sheets; it is her favorite time, eleven o'clock: all children sleeping, Martin downstairs lapping up the eleven o'clock news. Getting to the bed first, while the room is still absolutely quiet and dark, has become another secret perversion—something which, like the newspaper, if explained, would be likely to arouse speculation concerning some mental slippage. Martin would make a sincere attempt to understand: "Well, what is it about the quiet and dark that's so special?" That's just it. If you haven't put in eight to twelve hours wiping snotty noses, quieting piercing screams, wiping blood off heads, fingers, knocked-out teeth, you can't grasp it.

The most exciting thing is what occurs in that space just before sleep: the drifting, letting your thoughts out on parole. It is nothing less than amazing to Norma Jean what happens just before sleep; the process reaffirms for her that her brain cells were not destroyed by the years of being jolted awake by babies screaming in the night; by the endless repetition of menial tasks during the days; and by the omnipresent sense of enclosure that is a by-product of mothers with young children, and other shut-ins, especially in winter.

Before getting into it, Norma Jean meets the conditions of her conscience: tiptoes into both bedrooms, lightly kissing all three children, replacing covers where needed, sometimes lingering against her will, being torn between the impulse to adore, and the thought that, sometimes, looking at their faces in sleep, I think: I would really like to get that bastard who first said, "Be fruitful and multiply."

Tonight there are stars, the winter constellations: Orion, the Pleiades, and Sirius, struggling for its place in the order of things on the eastern horizon. At first they are just stars and I am just Norma Jean, and I acknowledge the distinction. Then gradually the distance shrinks, and it is as though I had been expected; they wait: order, stability, my link with all selves past and future, with the beginning of all things, with the origins of mystery. I always terminate the stars when I arrive at that point where I realize I am seeing what the Egyptians saw. The knowledge becomes unbearable; I am overwhelmed.

Norma Jean closes her eyes. There are some who can afford to do stars pretty much at their leisure—drop-outs, campers, outdoor suicides. There is nothing to be lost by getting carried away; nothing intrudes. Norma Jean feels she cannot afford it too often, or for too long a stretch. She brings herself back to reality because to become lost in stars is to leave four dependents in an even greater state of dependency than they currently enjoy. "Where's Mom?" "She's in the stars." "Well tell her to come back, I wet my pants."

Why has it become so hard to cope? Is it because I am beginning to want something for myself? Whenever that happens, there are bound to be shifts in the degree of tension governing the ties that bind each member of the family to the unit as a whole. Currents begin to vary in intensity, upsetting the balance on some other line. You have slack here, corresponding pressure there. She views the family as a network, with herself at the center. She wants to move away from the center, but doesn't know how. Arndt probably thinks I'm still mourning for the lost one, but the truth is, I was relieved. It forced me to decide what to do with *myself*. I only pretended to go along with all the babies; after the first two, I had already begun to see myself as a termite queen, even before I knew the name for it. I thought of myself as Toueris, one of the ancient Egyptian animal gods, the pregnant hippopotamus. That was a year ago, right after I lost the baby, when I began to read again. Strange, thinking of it, that I chose a book called *Lost Worlds*. Could there have been a connection? That's what Arndt is sure to say. Martin probably thinks so too; I can read it in his manner, especially when he gives me that look when he catches me reading the Book of the Dead. The hell with them both. It was sheer coincidence; the book just happened to be near the bed when I was recovering. The only connection I allow is that I was trying to get back a part of some original self which lay buried, deep as any pharaoh, all those years. Of that I stand accused. Why did the following passage thrill me?

Anubis, the god of the necropolis, appears . . . as a jackal, the beast that prowls at night in Egyptian cemeteries. Other animal gods . . . were Bastet, the cat goddess of joy, and Toueris, the pregnant hippopotamus, a symbol of fecundity, who watched over childbirth. Both goddesses had other roles as well. Toueris was a patroness of vengeance. . . .

—Leonard Cottrell, *The Horizon Book of Lost Worlds*, p. 42. Copyright 1962, American Heritage Publishing Co., Inc.

It seemed absolutely logical that the goddess who symbolized fecundity, who was forever pregnant, should have been awarded the title Patroness of Vengeance. Toueris, the termite queen of the ancient world. And as I began to fight my designated role of primeval archetype, I studied again the ancient cast of characters; then I began to know them well. Martin began to show concern when I started becoming them (I am Queen Hatshepsut. I am Queen Nefertiti).

> In Egypt women enjoyed a high status rarely equaled elsewhere in the ancient world. They had complete legal right to inherit property and dispose of it without reference to the wishes of their husbands. Monogamy was generally practiced (although the rich supported harems), and men often traced their ancestry through the maternal rather than the paternal line.
>
> —Ibid., p. 85

How do you describe the exhilaration of discovering a civilization that supported and encouraged matrilineal values? They can be forgiven their harems. First things first. What counted was that there were queens, important in their own right, not mere decoration for their kings. And Toueris, goddess, patroness, rescued from the functional, her dignity assured by means of such a simple, yet ingenious, assignation: vengeance. It meant anything was possible, even for me.

3

It is morning. Norma Jean stirs. Martin has already left the house; it is his early day. He will have breakfast en route. She knows it will elevate his cholesterol level, but can't get as aroused about it as she used to. The children are still sleeping, but it is only minutes before they will be waking, with such comments as: "Mommy! I peed in the bed. The bed is *soaking!*" She looks out the window, over the trees, the yard, with its rusting swing set and overgrown camellias. *What am I doing here?* I am renting my life; haven't finished payments, and never will.

"Mommy!" Ruth Ann, the nubile maiden, has arisen. "I hate to tell you this, first thing in the morning, but you'll never guess what Damon did. . . ." There is a disturbing amount of pleasure in her voice.

There is only one thing that Damon could do while still asleep. Damon. Demon. My Aries child, who leaps tall buildings with a single bound, takes whole corners off the walls with one touch of his head. Are you the one destined to drink my blood?

de-mon (dē/mən), n. 1. an evil spirit; devil. 2. an evil passion or influence. 3. a person considered extremely wicked, evil, or cruel. 4. a person with great energy, drive, etc.: *He's a demon for work.* 5. daemon. -adj. 6. of, pertaining to, characteristic of, or noting a demon. 7. possessed or controlled by a demon. [defs. 1–4: ME, for L *daemōn(ium)* < GK *daimónion,* thing of divine nature (in Jewish and Christian writers, evil spirit)

26

neut. of *daimónios*, deriv. of *daímōn*; def. 5: < L; see
DAEMON]

—*Random House Dictionary of the
English Language*, p. 384. Copyright ©
Random House, Inc., 1966, 1967.

Did I err in choosing your name, too, along with everything else?
Did its unconscious meanings seep into your amniotic fluids? Did
you undergo the metamorphosis there? Or was the metamorphosis mine, beginning with the lost one's homeless spirit, and
my attempts to lay it to rest? Was there a transformation at all?
Were you divine from the start?

Slowly Norma Jean gets out of bed and makes her way to the
bathroom sink, where she stands staring at the face in the mirror.
It has begun to show subtle signs; she reads them in the way
that Indians once read signs of an early winter. There is some kind
of betrayal going on, under the guise of natural processes. It's not
surprising that it should show itself first in the face.

"Mom! Mom!"

"What is it, Scott?"

"I can't find my green pants!"

"Well, wear some other pants." Why can't he figure those
things out for himself? Norma Jean throws on her Levis and
sweater, decides it is too late to give them individual breakfast
choices. They'll all get granola. She has made their lunches the
night before; they are all lined up in a compelling little row on
the third shelf of the G.E. two-door refrigerator.

"I want the *green* ones."

"Well I don't know where they are, Scott. If you can't find
them, wear something else and we'll try to find them tomorrow."

"Oh Mom! I *can't* find them. *You* find them. I don't want any
pants except the green pants!"

"God damn it, Scott, it's *late!* I am going down to get your
breakfast and I am not looking for your green pants. If you don't
hurry you'll be late for nursery school." No matter how many
times she vows not to begin the day screaming, one way or
another there she is at 8 A.M. at the top of her lungs. She strips
Damon's bed quickly, piling the wet sheets, blankets, bedspread,
and bear on the floor, at the same time scanning the room for the

27

green pants. Scott has fixed himself in the tantrum position: stiff as a corpse on the floor, thumb already in position in case he doesn't win, snot running out his nose in giant rivulets. Stoic little Scott, waiting until 8 A.M. to have his fit, the one time when she can't forgive it. A bad mother, acting individually and on her own, can occasionally pick up a child late at nursery school; but it is unthinkable to hold up a car pool in the morning. It is never done.

"You will miss your car pool, Scott, if you don't get something on your ass this minute." She ties Damon's shoe laces and gathers up the urine-soaked bedding. Scott has panicked, as she knew he would, at the thought of being left behind by his pool. He is frantically throwing on his brown pants. "That's a clever boy, Scott. Mommy promises she will find your green ones today and put them where they will be ready for you tomorrow." *Stop referring to yourself in the third person.* I can't help it. *Well it's disgusting and it confuses the children; when YOU refer to MOMMY, they wonder how many of you there are.* That's not confusing; I am at least two people: her, and me.

As the last child disappears into the communal mass that twists and writhes in the interior of the late model Country Squire, Norma Jean throws the wet bedding into the washing machine and spreads the morning paper across the table. She knows how it will affect her, even before she begins. She also knows she could abstain from the paper for, say, one to two weeks, and see how things turned out. But she's not motivated to seek a cure; she prefers to continue mainlining the morning news, as she's been doing for years. Her coffee grows cold as she injects the headlines on page 1.

NAPALM SAVES BASE	PENTAGON PLANS LASER
U.S. Airpower Does Its Job	'DEATH RAY'
BOY SHOTGUNNED IN FACE	WOMAN, 60, RAPED AT KNIFEPOINT
MORE BOMBS FOR VICTORY, SAYS GENERAL	MOTHER LOCKS IN KIDS, BURNS HOME

BOTANIST SAYS MAN
MAY VANISH SOON

Why are some people fascinated by what they fear, while others screen it out? What accounts for the difference? She finds it hard to eat, and turns to page 4 so she can finish her breakfast. She knows, of course, that she could eat first and then do the paper; but we don't always act on what we know. Norma Jean is no exception to this rule.

KIDS VICTIMS OF	HE BEGS FOR LIFE,
DRUNKEN ARGUMENT	GETS SHOT 5 TIMES
They were shoved from a car	

Norma Jean wipes her tears with a napkin. I mustn't start my day overreacting. The news is a reflection of the time and place in which we live. If you repeat that idea often enough it should permit enough distance so that you can come to some terms with it, absorb the reality, without always (coming apart; breaking down; overreacting; getting overinvolved, overstimulated, overidentified).

QUIET MOTHER MURDERS HER FAMILY

Corpus Christi, Tex.

The quiet mother of a Pennsylvania military family killed her husband and children in their beds yesterday and fired a .38 caliber bullet through her own brain.

Police could not establish a motive. Three notes left by the 32-year-old woman, Mary Jean Whalen, gave no clue. The messages told only who should be notified and what should be done with some personal property.

Officers said the woman first shot her husband, Robert Wayne Whalen, 33, a Navy chief petty officer. Then, police said, she shot her children—Deborah, 12; Kelly Ann, 10; Robert Wayne Jr., 8; and Mary Kathryn, 3.

Police said they heard a child calling for its mother when they broke in the front door. By the time officers got to the bedrooms, all the children were dead.

Police Commander Ted Bullard said his investigators found nothing in talking with neighbors that could give a reason for the shootings.

"We were unable to come up with anything," he said. "The people out there said they seemed like they were such fine people.

"They said she never raised her voice and that there wasn't a lot of screaming and carrying on."

A police officer of 25 years said the crime was "the most bi-
zarre and the worst I have ever seen."

—UNITED PRESS

Norma Jean thinks of Martin and the children. It will never happen to them, because she's not quiet. All the complaining they
do because I scream, and they owe their very lives to it. She is
haunted by Mary Jean Whalen. Would it have made a difference
if she could have screamed? Imagine not being able to speak of
it, even in a note. To be so mute, so immobilized, that the only
creative act possible becomes an act of violence. Still, the logic
of her action is as searing, as authentic, as the logic of Toueris'
double role of procreator and vengeance-wreaker. It's the kind of
significance that is always missed by local preachers, chiefs of
police, and husbands. "Now why would she want to do such a
terrible thing; she must have been crazy." Not necessarily.
Not in every case. Sometimes being without what you perceive as
alternatives is enough to justify any act. It's interesting how many
times "craziness" is applied as an explanation for a woman's
behavior. It's always soothing to have a term which captures the
unfathomable.

DISHWASHER DEATH

Burleson, Tex.
A housewife was fatally stabbed Monday when she slipped
and fell on two butcher knives jutting from her front-loading
dishwasher.

—ASSOCIATED PRESS

Norma Jean pushes herself away from the table, alerted to the
fact that it is now ten o'clock and all her dishes are still settling
into their slime at various locales around the kitchen. With great
care she loads her Kitchen Aid front-loading dishwasher; with
great respect places the knives pointing down. She pours herself
another cup of coffee, and settles in at the table to finish the job.

COUPLE SLAIN IN BED

Police are investigating the slaying of a man and wife who were
shot to death while they slept early yesterday morning.
Arthur Oakes, of 135 45th Avenue, was found in his bed, lying

30

in a pool of blood. Neighbors, aroused by the sound of gunshots, reported the shooting to police at 5:45 A.M.

Officers responding to the call reported that, although shot once in the right temple, and once in the mouth, Mrs. Oakes still managed to stagger to the door to admit police. She died before an ambulance could arrive.

Actually, I prefer the fillers, especially the ones from England. I often wonder if they are put there by some wistful editor longing for another era, who wishes to add to our future shock by means of contrast. Two examples should suffice:

SEX-CRAZED ORGANIST JAILED

Cambridge
A church organist was arrested today on the complaint of female parishioners for making improper advances.

COURTROOM KILLING

Manchester
Court officials adjourned a case Tuesday at Manchester county magistrate's court while police inspector Harry Glover chased and killed a mouse with a rolled-up newspaper.

—UNITED PRESS

Here we are at the dregs. The dregs are similar to fillers only in that they are not "main news." They reflect our particular part of the world, in a manner which could be described as "pop." Dregs are low culture.

Your Horoscope

Leo. There are pressures on you now that are puzzling to you, but this is because you have been thinking negatively. Don't blame others. A cheerful attitude brings best results.

Your Health
by Dr. R. G. Anthony

CONVULSION WORRIES HER

Dear Dr. Anthony:
A few days after I had my first baby I had a convulsion. Does this mean that I should not have any more children, or that this will occur again if I do? —Mrs. R.M.

Dear Mrs. M.,
. . . Examination by a neurologist, with a brain-wave test, can

help establish the exact diagnosis. I would do this soon so that you can be relieved of the anxiety you apparently are feeling.

Ah yes, examination. When in doubt, seek examination. Especially if you are female.

"I just can't understand it, Martin. We've been trying for three months."

"It's not really such a long time, honey. On the other hand, it doesn't hurt to have an examination. Just to make sure everything's functioning all right. Why don't you call Dr. Ward, go in, get yourself a complete check-up. It can't hurt. Go ahead, it's O.K. We can afford it." When you begin to want that first baby you want it immediately; it becomes an obsession. Wasn't it the greatest shame a woman could know, to be found barren? A field that yields no crop, a tundra that supports no life; a glacier, a stone, a vacuum. When your calling is to fill the space, you dream always of rivers, or seeds, endlessly.

Martin, so generous, solicitous; there should be nothing but the best for me, even if he didn't think three months cause for concern; even if he was in the middle of a thesis, up nights on Dexedrine; even if we were barely making it in the small three-room apartment, tenaciously clinging, engaged in the early struggle. And I knew I would be the one to fail him, knew from this moment on that because there was something so desired, so absolutely necessary to complete the picture we held of the future, that it would be withheld; knew then that this was the end of a period in our lives. The specifics were still unclear, but things were shifting; and the shift was bound to be irreversible.

Dr. Ward's waiting room: the rug and walls a dull off-white, the couch and chairs putrescent aqua; and against the wall an enormous tank where exotic fish were driven mad by the sight of their own extravagance, and consumed themselves each week, and were replaced. And on the walls, seascapes: waves rolling, tumbling, cresting, breaking; shores spread smooth as glass. The whole room a gigantic womb, filled with the imagery of reproduction. And his office: the paneling, the journals, the wife and five little Wards, their six sets of perfect teeth flashing from the ebony frame. "Well now, Norma Jean," (they never call you "Mrs.") "you say you've been trying for three months? It's a bit early to become concerned. On the other hand, it's probably good in the

32

sense that if we find something wrong, we're on to it that much earlier." He takes the history. "Cramps?" It's the only bad sign he can come up with. Once so commonplace, the word now has a malignant and ominous sound.

We started out simply enough, flat on the table, doing the pelvic. Everything feels O.K. I am scheduled for a tubal insufflation next week. "No, no, it doesn't hurt. Meet me at the hospital at ten o'clock in X-ray. In the meantime, here is a chart. Get yourself a basal thermometer and take your temperature every morning *the first thing on waking*, before you even *move*. It will establish for us whether or not you ovulate." "But I know I ovulate; I can feel it." "Ho ho ho," he chuckles. "Really. Every month, fourteen days before my period, on the left side or the right, depending." "Ho ho ho." He musses my hair, in the manner reserved for children and dogs. "In addition, put a pillow under your pelvis right after intercourse. It will elevate the body and keep the semen in place for a longer time. Every little bit counts. Ho ho ho."

The following week, as I am strapped to the table in X-ray, he assumes what is to become his intensely familiar position, down at the end of the table, between the legs. A dye is being injected into Norma Jean's tubes. She has been instructed to hold her breath until the technician has taken the picture; the dye will show whether or not the tubes are clear. Her whole abdomen is filled with searing acid. She can't hold her breath. The picture is ruined. Now we'll have to do it again. She hears herself screaming. "If it feels like this, I don't want children!" "Just do it right this time; we can't afford to mess this one up." Oh agony beyond imagining. If the tubes weren't clear before, they're sure to be shot now. How is it possible for frail tissue to hold up under such pain?

"Don't you think the pillow is a bit too much?"

"Dr. Ward says it might help." It's a lousy way to fall asleep, like being hung in a tree by your legs. The thermometer and chart crackle on the bedside table in the moonlight.

"This is a disgusting way to make love."

"Well, it was your idea."

"*Whose* idea?"

"Yours. You're the one with the drawers full of baby clothes. I'm not worried. Hell, it's only been four months."

"*You're* the one who said 'get an examination!'" Tears, tears, burning the nights away. "It'll be all right. Don't cry. A year from now you'll be complaining about having to get up in the night, feeding little Peter."

"Scott!"

"Ruth!" Embracing each other, there among the graphs, charts, pillows under the ass. True love can endure anything. All the books say so.

"Norma, your tubes are clear. What is this now, the fourth month? Fifth? I'm going to give you some diethylstilbestrol. It's a mild hormone, will thin out your vaginal secretions, make it easier for the sperm to penetrate. Often in these cases it turns out to be a very minor thing, a matter of the female secretions being too thick to admit even the most vigorous sperm." He described it as the female secretions being *hostile* to the male. I knew that psychological hostility, and the attendant implication of vaginal hostility, was right around the corner. He didn't fail to mention it as a possibility, giving me a look which said: Now what would a nice girl like you want to tighten up at a crucial time like this for? "Sometimes when we worry about these things we become anxious, tighten up. That of course just makes things more difficult. Try to relax. I'll want to see you in two months. Bring your charts with you when you come. We should be able to establish a pattern by then."

She remembers the trip home on the bus, staring out the steaming window, thinking: No chemicals. Years before someone at the office had lent her a book called *Poisons in Your Food*; it described what stilbestrol did to cattle, when they put it in their feed, or slipped it under their skin. The author noted the artificial and sudden weight gain, and spoke of cancer. The consumer is always the last to know, was the argument. Walking home from the bus stop, the sidewalks shining like steel in the rain, thinking: Where was it decided that these procedures should be done on me?

That night, dreaming of feed lots, herself one of the herd. Knowing that in refusing to take the pills she would be her own person, but at whose expense? Martin's? The possible baby's? A doctor wouldn't prescribe something dangerous. She took the stilbestrol, and waited for change. ("Don't be difficult." "Be a good

34

girl." "You want a baby, don't you? Well, you'll have to co-operate." —Mixed chorus for anonymous voices from the past.)

Month after month, the pilgrimages to Dr. Ward's office continued: tubes clear, eggs rolling, secretions thinned, and still no baby. *Is there anything left for him to do to me?* Occasionally it crossed Norma Jean's mind that the trouble could lie with Martin. The idea was crazy, absolutely insane; but it was possible, wasn't it? she asked Dr. Ward timidly. *It's clear neither one of them wants to consider the possibility. I've let them do all they're going to do to me. Now it's their turn to answer the questions.*

"Well, Norma," he begins slowly, reluctantly, "yes, it is a possibility we sometimes have to consider, eventually. I think we've explored just about everything as far as you're concerned, so it wouldn't hurt at this point to have your husband go in for a check-up." Wouldn't hurt? Why didn't he suggest it earlier? If there's a mystery, always look to the woman first. Woman, with her deep interiors, full of hidden treasures and malignant secrets.

"Yes, Norma. We've ruled out just about all the possibilities in your case—except of course psychological factors. But I think before we get into that it might be a good idea to have Martin examined, just so we will have as complete a picture as possible of the problem." You see, Dr. Arndt, that's where the fury started; it had its origins right here, in this room, with its obscene fish biting each other to death in the filtered waters of their tank. Right here, among the seascapes. But I appreciate that you won't understand. You're brothers in the same order. You stick together.

"Dr. Ward says he's done just about everything to me he can think of. He says it wouldn't hurt if you were to go in for an examination, just to rule out all possibilities."

"God." She remembers Martin scratching his head. She was prepared to really give it to him, but now feels sympathy instead. He says, "It's something I've thought of, of course, but you never really want to acknowledge the possibility." No, you sure don't.

And Martin's going. And Martin's disbelief, and Martin's deep despair, as he reported the outcome: low sperm count. And Norma Jean's rage, and Norma Jean's triumph, and Norma Jean's fear. True love can endure anything. All the books say so. Norma Jean clings to what she's read of true love, and endurance. It is her turn to hold Martin in the night and whisper, "It's low, that's all, it's not absent. There will be some way. The baby isn't that important. We have each other, that's what really matters." And Martin's inability to be consoled, Martin's turning away, Martin's deep wound.

Well, Ward. What do you say now? Got any other ideas on what we could do about a baby? Norma Jean has entered her sarcastic phase; it protects her from "the nameless terror." —(See Edward Albee, A *Delicate Balance*).

"Well, Norma, I'm sure Dr. Silver had gone into it with your husband, but men are often reluctant to speak about these things. So I'm going to ask *you*: what state of health would you say Martin is in, in general?"

"He seems all right to me. He's overworked, but what man isn't?"

"Well, you see, that could just be it," says Ward. "When the semen analysis reveals a deficiency, physical exhaustion, overwork, nervous strain, are all important factors to consider. I'm sure Dr. Silver will get a complete history of the more serious causes, but we must do what we can on our end." I felt I had done all I could on "my end," so to speak. "Are you feeding him nutritious meals?" "You've got to be kidding," I say. Three hours a day spent selecting, washing, preparing fresh vegetables, irresistible salads; adapting Julia Child recipes to high protein, low cholesterol meals.

"He's been up half the night for months now, on Dexedrine, trying to finish his thesis. No, he doesn't get any exercise. Of course he's under strain." *What more do you want from me?*

"Well, Norma, I don't have to tell you, one of the most important functions of a wife—in addition to emotional sustenance, comfort, and love—is to feed her husband well and see that he gets enough rest, exercise, and relief from the pressures and strains that men are subjected to." I couldn't help thinking that it seemed as though he were describing the things a mother is supposed to do for her baby.

And Martin, jogging around the block, then quitting after two nights. "I can't keep this up, Jeanie. I feel like an idiot. I've got work to do." Martin, refusing to walk to classes. "I'm on a tight schedule." Martin, going on one weekend hike. "I've got a *thesis* to finish! God damn it, leave me alone!" Norma Jean, nagging: "What about the *baby?* Don't you give a shit about the baby?

Get more sleep! Get more exercise! Stop worrying about your goddamned thesis! Give me a baby! Give me a baby, you son of a bitch!" Norma Jean, staring out the window in the middle of the night, seeing not the stars that lovers see, but the stars of sterility and death, the chill of eternity. Norma Jean, cuddling the babies of her friends, folding and refolding the little vests, caps, sweaters that spilled from every drawer. And all that time, no one with whom to speak of it. Those things weren't mentioned then. And every night locked in the deadly infertile embraces, growing further and further apart, but still adhering. I can't explain it, to this day. It didn't seem anything like true love, but then it's possible love means different things than we've been told.

Martin, finishing his thesis. Martin's career assured. "Oh, God, do I need a vacation!" "It's wonderful, Martin." *Now maybe we can have a baby.*

And the trip to Mexico. The long days lying stretched on idle sands, the languorous nights under low stars. The hot afternoons, biting into ripe fruits; the eroticism of cold melon sliding down the throat. The rediscovery of textures, the electric smoothness of skin on skin. The two of us encapsulated in a timeless womb of sea and sand and basic desires. There was never a time like it before, or since. And of course there was a new level of love achieved, and of course there was a new life borne of it. Things always come out right in the end.

4

How can it be Thursday again so soon? Where do the days go? Norma Jean prepares for her second appointment with Dr. Arndt. What shall I wear? I know it doesn't really matter, but it might help if I didn't *look* crazy too. She selects a red sweater. Red: positive, attractive. She has time only for a quick cup of coffee and the briefest consideration of the paper.

WOMEN SLASHED BY KNIFE-WIELDING ASSAILANT IN SKYSCRAPER RESTROOMS

CO-ED STABBED	HITCH-HIKER HACKED
SIXTEEN TIMES	TO DEATH

MISTAKE BOMBING OF CIVILIANS

I don't know what's wrong with me lately. I can't seem to make out the grocery list. I start it, the way I always do, but can't seem to keep up my interest. Lettuce. Peanut butter. Bread. Then it trails off. I find I've been staring into space a lot and can't seem to concentrate. It doesn't seem to matter if there's any food in the house. I know it should matter, but it doesn't. Our meals have been gradually getting smaller and smaller. No one has complained yet, but I know they've noticed. I wonder if I'm unconsciously starving my family, trying to make us all disappear. Dr. Arndt is silent. I no longer feel liquid and alive. I feel brittle, about to break, and completely without desire.

"Do you *know* what it is you want?"

"No. I only know what I don't want. And even that is imprecise. I sometimes stop suddenly and realize I'm screaming all the time, or angry in a way I've never been angry before. It's an insidious thing, creeps over you and has you in its throes before you even realize what brought it on. I am speaking of a rage so inarticulate that to even attempt to describe it is to court accusations of insanity."

"Are you afraid I will think you crazy?"

"Yes. But I don't really believe I'm crazy. I think things are making me this way, but I can't pin it down, and that leads to confusion; and then I realize I appear and feel crazy."

"You spoke last week of the child you lost. Would you say these feelings began around that time?"

There he goes. They always think it's natural for women to go crazy over losing a child, can't imagine her going bananas because of the ones she didn't lose. But I was expecting this, I came prepared.

"Listen. I don't think there's too much purpose in trying to explain all this to you. You're from another world, another generation, another sex, another attitude . . ." He cuts in, "How do you know I won't understand what you say? I can only go by what you tell me." Well, I just know. Or do I? Norma Jean is torn between a desire to come to terms, and the feeling that she's lucky these days if she can make it home from the store by herself. Maybe it can help, giving this a try, sorting it out. She decides to trust Arndt, give him a chance, until she has proof to the contrary. *What have I got to lose?* "I have no part of my life that I can call my own. It's all for other people, centered entirely on their needs. You know the little sign the Red Cross used to stick on your window? The one that read: I GAVE? Well that's how I feel. And then I feel guilty for feeling it. And that's where it ends. I can't seem to go on from there."

"What were your goals for yourself before the children?" A memory so forbidden, she can scarcely bring herself to speak of it.

"Well, before I married I did a lot of ceramic sculpting. And I'm interested in ancient Egyptian history." Should I tell him about Osiris?

There are at least two passages in the Theban Recension of the Book of the Dead which show that the Egyptians believed in

39

the possibility of a "second birth." . . . Osiris is addressed as "he who giveth birth to men and women a second time."

—E. A. Wallis Budge, *Osiris and the Egyptian Resurrection*, Vol. 1, P. L. Warner, London, 1911, p. 141. Copyright 1961, University Books.

Osiris, the eldest son of the Earth-god Geb and the Sky-goddess Nut, ruled as a just and benevolent king over the whole earth, instructing mankind in the various arts and crafts and converting them from barbarism to a state of civilization.

—I. E. S. Edwards, *The Pyramids of Egypt*, Copyright 1947, © 1961, 1972 by I. E. S. Edwards, The Viking Press, New York, p. 19.

The briefest sketch of the origins of the Osiris myth is as follows:

Osiris succeeded to the throne of his father and governed the world wisely and justly, aided by his sister Isis, whom he married. Seth, jealous of his brother's power, plotted to destroy him and eventually succeeded, afterward cutting the body of Osiris into pieces which he buried in several parts of Egypt. . . . The faithful Isis recovered the scattered fragments of her husband's corpse and with the aid of the jackal-god Anubis, who subsequently became the god of embalment, re-animated it. Though unable to return to his life on earth, Osiris passed to the underworld, where he became the god of the dead and later the judge of souls. . . .

* * *

. . . It was during the Middle Kingdom that the conception of Osiris as a *judge of souls* became predominant, and for the first time the idea of accountability . . . began to take hold in the human mind.

—Leonard Cottrell, *The Lost Pharaohs*, Copyright © 1961 by Leonard Cottrell, Universal Library, New York, p. 25.

The brief sketch leaves out details such as the fact that when Isis was recovering Osiris' dismembered parts, she retrieved everything but "the virile member," which had been thrown into the Nile and devoured by the fish; that Osiris, although reborn, became god of the underworld—because there is no way you can generate life without a virile member. But he did very well there, judging souls and so forth; no one's life is just a matter of procreation, not even a man's. The brief sketch also fails to adequately chart the length of time it took Isis to find all the pieces; she really worked to put those pieces together. It also neglects to mention that she was, at the same time, busy giving birth to their son, Horus. E. A. Wallis Budge, in *Osiris and the Egyptian Resurrection*, Vol. 1, has a description of that which will strike a chord in the heart of any mother:

> From the fact that Amen-Ra and Thoth are present, these gods representing the husband and witch-doctor of modern days, we may assume that Isis suffered greatly, and that her labour was "difficult." This assumption is supported by the description of the birth of Horus, given by Isis in her narrative on the Metternich Stele, in which her agony is insisted upon, as well as her loneliness.

I know this must seem tedious to you, but if you want to know what I mean when I speak of Osiris, you have to have the background. Sometimes, in the night, I find myself calling his name.

> The ever-waning and reviving life of the earth, sometimes associated with the life-giving waters, sometimes with the fertile soil, or again discerned in vegetation itself—that was Osiris. The fact that the Nile, like the vegetation which its rising waters nourished and supported, waxed and waned every year, made it more easy to see him in the Nile, the most important feature of the Egyptian's landscape. . . . As a matter of fact the Nile was but the source and visible symbol of that fertility of which Osiris was the personification.
>
> —James H. Breasted, *Development of Religion and Thought in Ancient Egypt* 1972, University of Pennsylvania Press, Philadelphia, p. 23. Copyright 1912, Charles Scribner's Sons; renewal copyright 1940, Charles Breasted.

Last month, I cleared out the garage and made myself a studio. I got some clay and found myself making peculiar little jars. I started going out there every night, making the jars. Martin was shocked. (Why do you want to be out here at night? What are those weird little jars for? What could you possibly keep in them?)

First the embalmers made an incision and removed the viscera: heart, liver, lungs, intestines—all the most decomposable parts. These were installed separately in a set of stone vessels, later called canopic jars. . . .

—Leonard Cottrell, *Lost Worlds*, p. 48.

Do you really want to know about the funerary practices? How the canopic jars were buried in the tombs, along with the bodies, whose viscera they contained? How all the parts were guarded by special gods and protected from decay? Some of the jars were fashioned out of alabaster; you can see them in museums. They have a translucence that is indescribable. Now, of course, you understand why I'm here. If the neighbors knew that Norma Jean Harris sits in her garage at night, making canopic jars, it would upset the balance of things. It's not the kind of thing good wives and mothers spend their time doing. Only one conclusion could be drawn: (one guess; begins with the letter "c").

It doesn't have to do with the jars themselves. They were a beginning—in the way the Egyptians regarded death as a beginning. Poor crazy woman, trying to resurrect her dead child; knows her child-bearing years are over, spends her nights fashioning symbolic children out of clay.

"I knew it would be hopeless to try to explain."

"You're the one who has pronounced the verdict of hopelessness, not I. My role is not to judge, but to help you hear yourself, to understand."

"I know what you think."

"You're the one who is thinking it."

True, true. But you can't be too careful. If you're not on your toes, can't anticipate the judgment, down it comes just when you're at your most confused. I must fight to preserve that which is mine. My vision, even my confusion. Something may come of it and, when it does, it must be mine.

"That's just why I intervene as little as possible. So it will be clear that it is yours, and not mine." He has a point there. But it's hard to shake the image of the doctor as judge.

In the beginning, I was happier than I'd ever been; there was never a baby more wanted than Ruth Ann. The pregnancy was perfect, no complications, not a day of nausea. I was strong, radiant. I even stopped smoking. I wanted natural childbirth, but

Ward laughed, said, "You Amazons, can't you accept that medical science is here to help in case you find you can't tolerate the discomfort?" I began to realize that he wanted to control as much of it as possible, as though my role in it had to be made minimal. It wasn't until much later (Scott? Damon? The Lost One?) that I realized his obsession. He had to be there, giving orders, medication; guiding, directing, manipulating the whole thing. I wasn't having a baby, *he* was. That was Ward's secret.

The feelings of fury had their genesis somewhere around here; how can I say just which event marked the turning point? There never are actual turning points in these matters. All the events simply accumulate, and it is often years before you are aware of the feelings they generated. Was it the brief infertility or the Rh factor? ("They're working on a new drug now which they think will make worry over Rh a thing of the past; but it won't be on the market in time to do you any good, ho ho ho." —Michael Ward, M.D.) Was it Damon's prematurity, his having to stay in the hospital a week before I could bring him home? Where do you begin? At first you are so proud; your space has been *filled*: I am whole. I am loved. If I am especially blessed, I will bear a son! Well, I'm describing the way it was then. Martin gave me a book for Christmas that year called *The Great Mother*; nothing pleased me more.

Every month, lying on the table, enjoying the probings, the solicitation. You are important, because of this thing inside you. You are the focus of attention. Is it any wonder that so many women were tempted to bear baby after baby in order to recapture that languorous, child-like state? At first I enjoyed the infantilization and Ward's concern. In the end, it was his theatrics which gave him away. The relish with which he would flourish his instruments, all his brow-wiping and carrying on. They were his ways of participating, playing a vital role, and robbing me of my claim on the event. It took me three and a half babies to realize how much I hated Ward.

And it wasn't just Ward. It was Anderson, the pediatrician, too. And it wasn't that they didn't try. They probably did their best. It's just that their best wasn't enough. They withheld information. And perpetuated misinformation. Sitting on Ward's aqua couch, six months pregnant with Scott, flipping through the magazines on the table, and coming across one of his old Ameri-

43

can Medical Association journals; turning to the article "Maternal and Other Factors in the Etiology of Infantile Colic," scanning its conclusions.

The occurrence of colic showed no relationship to maternal emotional factors, whether estimated clinically or measured by a standardized psychological test. Most mothers of infants with colic were stable, cheerful, and feminine. This evidence, and other evidence when critically reviewed, does not support the frequently stated view that colic results from an unfavorable emotional climate created by an inexperienced, anxious, hostile, or unmotherly mother. By so advising parents, physicians may relieve them of unwarranted self-blame and anxiety.

—Jack L. Paradise, M.D., Journal of the American Medical Association, Vol. 197, No. 3, July 1966.

Feeling the fury rise as I remembered the voices:

"Well, Norma, if she's screaming as much as you say, she must have colic. You can have Dr. Anderson prescribe some medication for her, which will calm her down. But Norma, I would suggest you try relaxing more. You know (you're a bright girl) the relationship between anxious mothers and nervous babies." —Michael Ward, M.D.

"If you've fed her, changed her, cuddled her, and she still won't settle down, let her scream. It's good exercise." —Erik Anderson, M.D.

"She needs her mother. Hold her." —Martin Harris

A longstanding conflict exists between obstetricians and pediatricians and other professionals concerned with infants and children, so that an individual mother may be subjected to sometimes radically conflicting advice on the care of her newly born infant.

—Lawrence K. Frank, op. cit., p. 156.

I think this is where the feelings of disorientation first began. I never experienced them before this. At first I assumed it was simply lack of sleep, or, more accurately, the continual interruption of the sleep pattern which is sufficient to produce disorientation even in male subjects during experiments. Looking back, I realize it was also the screaming, the drained resources, the conflicting advice, the ensuing guilt. Or was it earlier still, in the hospital: waking to the strangeness, the dream of parents, grand-parents, family all gone; realizing: I have just started a new one. Screaming, "Where has everyone gone?" A *new generation is here; who will bear witness?*

On the way home Norma Jean stops at the drugstore to pick up the snapshots she left to be developed the week before. They are of the children on Halloween. It is now February. She experiences a transient feeling of incompetence, but it evaporates as she realizes that in twenty years, when she comes across the pictures in the children's baby books, she will remember only that Halloween, not her incompetence. (VANDALS RAID PUMPKIN FIELDS. RAZORS FOUND IN HALLOWEEN CANDY. POISON VICTIM, AGE 5, SUCCUMBS.) She pays the clerk and opens the folder. There is Damon looking cross-eyed at the camera, from beneath his Arab head-band; Ruth Ann glimmering as (Snow White; Cinderella; Sleeping Beauty; Angel; Fairy; Queen; Bride) with aluminum foil wings; and a giant cardboard garbage can that must be Scott. "Why do you want to go as a garbage can, Scott?" "I just do. That's what I want to be." Why did I have to feel I had to question it? Why did I invest so much energy worrying about the implications? "Martin, I'm concerned about Scott. He wants to be a garbage can this Halloween. I think he sees himself as a cast-off." "You're reading too much into it, Jeanie. The kid wants to be a garbage can, let him be a garbage can. What difference will it make twenty years from now?" And Ruth Ann, insisting on the white gown with silver trim. Why was I so concerned that she was sex-role stereotyped at seven? Would I have felt better if she had gone as the garbage can? And Damon, weeks before Halloween, whining, pulling on my skirt, badgering, "Can I be a monster for Halloween? Can I? Can I? Can I be a monster?" And Norma Jean screaming, "You won't even have to dress up; you can go as you are!"

Now home, with an hour before she has to pick up Damon, she lovingly inserts the pictures in the baby books: those absurd little histories that she has kept over the years because good mothers keep records of their babies. She resisted them for a while, but was always haunted by the idea that in twenty years there the children would be, demanding their baby books, and what could she say to them? "I'm sorry, kids. But I thought baby books were a lot of bourgeois crap, so you don't have any history"? So she had bought ones which she felt were creative. She had rules concerning their use. They would definitely *not* contain: (1) the first tooth; (2) the first lock of hair; (3) the foreskin. They would be as authentic and unsentimental a record as possible. They would contain only photographs; drawings which the children had done themselves; and her own record of things they had said which she considered either devastating or very funny.

Turning the pages now she comes across the record of sayings for 7/29/69. Ruth Ann: "I hate you! I am hating you!! I hate you forever, 'til you die off." Scott: "I go wee-wee on you. I put you in the toilet and flush you all the way down and you will never be a mommy again." *If I thought it would have worked, I'd have flushed it myself.* On the same page is a picture of the children with Grace, the live-in baby-sitter they had for six months after the lost one. Ah, Grace. The university student who used to assume the lotus position in the little downstairs room off the kitchen, after the children were in bed, smoking dope and reading the Berkeley *Barb*, learning about sin at our house. "They all go through that phase, Jeanie, their first time away from home. It's nothing to worry about. Just so long as she's not stoned when she's with the kids, and just so long as she does her fucking at *his* place."

It was hard adjusting to a stranger in the house. But Grace was good with children. "Nothing fazes her!" Martin would marvel, as I grappled with my first youth envy at the age of twenty-nine. "Of course it doesn't faze her," I would shout, "she knows she's getting out in six months!" The envy grew intense, exposed as I was each day to the spectacle of Grace and her friends—shining, long-haired creatures: flashing, flaunting, tasting their freedom with absolute abandon. The comparison with Norma Jean's youth in the fifties tormented her.

In college, there had been two choices: study and social life. Working her way through, she studied: buried deep in the basement stacks, making it with Osiris, a fifties freak, sealed in her silent tomb, while the others pursued the ritual of the time: getting a man. Pursued it in the backs of Chevy convertibles ("Stars Fell on Alabama" —Frank Sinatra), on fraternity staircases, in dim little cellars with sawdust on the floor, drinking beer. Beer beer beer, we couldn't get enough of it; at the beach, at cookouts, after the prom, at swim parties. It filled us, swelled us, coursed through our veins like carbonated lead until it was up to our throats, weighing us down. We drowned in beer. It made us so heavy we could bear to endure the clammy hand-clasps, the layers of smeared lipstick, the crew-cut, can-crushing embraces. Grace. You blink, you shimmy, you don't stand still long enough to grasp how it was with us. Why should I care that you bear witness, show respect? If it were possible for them to be taught, I could instruct you in those lost arts: our awkward tenderness, our fear. We knew nothing of cool; we were hot, hot. With nowhere for the hot to go. We rubbed against each other, we danced slowly, we groped, we knew desperation. What would it take to make you realize we feared the state? We were skilled in the art of ducking around corners. Would you find it too ridiculous that the worst thing we did, as a group, was to burn someone in effigy because he had failed to fix the Coke machine? And were relieved when the punishment came, that the reprimand seemed appropriate to our guilt, that justice had been done? It restored our order. The silent generation, we spoke in whispers.

By graduation, those of us who had failed to get our man went to work. We worked in department-store basements selling scarves, and we worked in offices typing letters. The orders, too, were silent, but we never doubted that they came from above and were explicit: now that you've had your fling and "improved your mind," you are as fit for a man as any woman could ever hope to be. Go out and work until you find him. And when you've found him, use the tools you've been given to accomplish two things: help him in his rise to the top. And hang onto him.

I held out longer than most. I had done time with Osiris long enough to know I could bear loneliness. I looked around and saw the alternatives. ("My wife has had a nervous breakdown; they're not sure when she'll recover, if ever. You know, you've got great legs." —Ralph, on the 8:41 bus. "I've got a red convertible, a thermos of gin, I've been accepted to law school, and have two tickets for next Saturday's game. Why won't you sleep with me?" —Nelson's eyes, in the lobby of the Alta Mira Hotel.) I said: I can wait. Grace, stop thrusting your pelvis just long enough to imagine it, as it was. Please. As a favor to me. Because it's important. Do you know how we waited then?

There was waiting and there was getting, and they both had as their sole focus the same objective. When you weren't getting, you were waiting to get. Everything else was peripheral to that aim, although some of us managed to hide that fact better than others. Well, I won't bore you with narrative, Grace; I know you like your information short and fast, so I'll just describe some of the things we did while waiting, and you can let your imagination fill in the rest. It might come in handy one of those times when all the good rock bands are out of town, or the dope supply is low, and you find yourself, you know, like alone, and there's nothing on the tube but talk shows. You never know when a little history will make a difference in your life.

We cleaned our apartments a lot. We spent a lot of time on that, just in case a man should come by and want a cup of coffee. When it got to be about seven o'clock, and it was clear that no one was coming, we went to the foreign films. We walked, because we couldn't afford cars. (Can you understand why I resent the patches on your Levis? Why weren't they flaunting poverty when I was poor?) And there, for ninety cents, you could sit in the dark of a tiny theater, in the third row, with your feet on the seat in front, and be swept inside two light-spotted black and white films which always (they never failed) took your mind off getting.

There was no candy or popcorn; when we went to films in those days we went to lose ourselves. We didn't go to eat. During intermissions, we smoked a lot and turned around in our seats, letting our eyes move nonchalantly around the audience. It's what people often did, casually, to see if there might be anyone there they knew. No one suspected we were looking for men (eyes running down each row, starting in the back and working our way down front, left to right, just the way you do when reading). We read the entire theater for men.

When the lights dimmed, there would be Giulietta Masina, in Fellini's *Nights of Cabiria*, strolling along a river bank with her man. We admired her. She wasn't sitting around in some dark theater, waiting; she was getting. There would be her man, grabbing her purse and pushing her into the river. Then there would be Cabiria being given artificial respiration, vomiting, choking, shaking her fist, going back home, putting on dry clothes, starting all over again.

There was Cabiria out on the street, hustling. She had a mangy little fur coat, and a cheap whitewashed house on the outskirts of Rome. She was poor. We were poor. We loved her. She twirled her purse around and around with one hand, with the other on her hip; she pointed one foot toward the street and turned her head in the other direction, whistling a little tune. She was waiting to get, but she wasn't letting on. That's how we saw ourselves.

Here is Cabiria standing on the curb, watching Amedeo Nazzari, playing a famous actor, having a fight with his girl friend outside a nightclub. The girl friend gets into her convertible and roars off. Amedeo Nazzari throws his cigarette into the gutter; his tie is loose. Cabiria's eyes are round as moons. She is thinking: what is that lucky woman doing, throwing away this rich, generous, handsome man? Amedeo Nazzari sees Cabiria staring at him. She assumes the waiting to get position: foot toward street, face toward blank wall, hand on hip, purse going around and around, whistling. "Hey you," says Amedeo Nazzari. "Me?" says Cabiria, dumbstruck, full of the rarest innocence, pointing at the mangy fur. "Yeah, you. Come here."

There are Giulietta Masina and Amedeo Nazzari going into the nightclub together. Anything is possible! They hang around in there for a while; he gets drunk. Cabiria gets lost in the curtains. Rich women stare at her from great heights, blowing smoke out their nostrils. She could care less. She has Amedeo. And there is Amedeo driving Cabiria home to his mansion in his convertible. There is Cabiria, sitting next to him, inhaling the night air. Here they are in Amedeo's bedroom! The butler wheels in a post-midnight snack on a silver cart to the strains of Beethoven's Fifth Symphony. Cabiria picks up a lobster and rolls her eyes. Amedeo Nazzari leans back on the satin pillows and laughs.

Here is Amedeo about to open a bottle of wine. He stares at the label and repeats the year, over and over. This is to indicate that he knows he, too, has aged. He sighs. Cabiria is about to comfort him when the butler rings that the girl friend is at the door. She won't go away. Amedeo says "Damn!" Cabiria freezes. The girl friend is coming up the stairs! "Quick, in here," says Amedeo to Cabiria, as he gently shoves her into his bathroom and locks the door. Here is Cabiria sitting on Amedeo's bathroom floor. There are the sounds of love-making in the other room. Here is a little puppy which Fellini has placed in Amedeo's bathroom for this scene, in order to emphasize the poignancy of Cabiria's plight.

Here is the puppy whining. Here is Cabiria comforting the puppy; she has it to give. She's been waiting all night to give it. If Amedeo doesn't need it, she won't take it out on the dog. It has to go somewhere. She's not stingy with her tenderness. They fall asleep together on the bathroom floor.

Here is Cabiria the next morning, looking out Amedeo's bathroom window, listening to the church bells. Here is Amedeo, tiptoeing into the bathroom, finger to his lips, showing her the way out. She casts a glance at the girl friend, asleep there in Amedeo's bed, between satin sheets; it goes straight to your heart. Here is Amedeo patting her on the head, offering her money. Here is Cabiria refusing. Is this boring you? You want some *Clockwork Orange*? Some Peckinpah tomato juice? Wait. Wait. There are tortures far more exquisite than beating the shit out of people. I can prove it. I was there.

Here is Cabiria, going on a pilgrimage with her friends. Bells are tolling; it is a long climb up the hill to the church. Everyone is sweating and crowding in for the miracles. Cabiria's mouth is turned down at the corners; she, like us, is cynical. Why then are her feet moving along with the others, shuffling up the stone steps, inching through the doors, straining toward the altar? She is given a lighted candle. A draught blows it out. Quickly she relights it. She faces the altar; her eyes are filled with tears. Everyone is sighing, whispering, imploring the Blessed Mother for this or that. A man drops his crutches and falls. There is a lot of wailing. Some faint. In the middle of all this, here is Cabiria, on her knees, whispering, "Help me change my life!" We know how she feels.

Afterward, they all sit around on the grass eating chicken. Cabiria gets up and starts staggering around. She is shouting, "It's all lies! Nothing has changed! We're all the same!" or something like that. "What's wrong with her?" "She's had too much wine," say her friends. They never expected anything in the first place.

So here is Cabiria wandering around alone on the outskirts of the city. She is not waiting to get. We all did that at one time or another. Papers blow on the wind; night is coming on. It is at such times that things which are decisive can happen, and often do. Cabiria enters a seamy little theater. A magic show is in progress. The audience is made up mostly of men in undershirts. She slips into a seat, as the smoke rises through the spotlights toward the ceiling. She is inconspicuous, as she is wearing loafers, a trench coat, and a shoulder bag. That's how we dressed when we were not waiting to get.

You will notice that I refer to: waiting to get; not waiting to get; and getting. Those were our three basic states. Even when we were not waiting to get we thought of it only in terms of not waiting to get; it had no other name. Occasionally there were deviations, and I was stubbornly deviant, for a while. For instance, instead of thinking of the middle state as not waiting to get, I would sometimes find myself conceiving of it as doing something for myself, without reference to the projected "one" for whom we always waited to do it with or for. But these occasions were transient and short-lived, even in the strongest of us. This is one of those occasions. Here is Cabiria sitting in the smoke-filled theater as the lights dim. On the stage an elderly magician goes through his routine. The crowd spits and guffaws. Their mouths are turned up, in derisive smiles. There is more than one kind of cynicism. This kind laughs and laughs; they've paid their admission, they claim full rights.

Here is the magician, bending over the footlights. He needs a subject for his next demonstration of hypnosis; would the little lady in the third row be so kind as to oblige? His eyes water slightly. His smile is sweet, defeated. He has done this many times, has nothing to lose. She's refusing? Ah, *bella signorina*, can you refuse all these men who are waiting to be convinced? There are cheers, there is clapping. They urge her on. She accepts, reluctantly. Her mouth is turned down and up, at the same time. It is her basic facial expression. This is known as cynicism with hope. Or: the wish to believe, accompanied by absolute disbelief.

She is helped onto the stage, and stands there daring him to make her make a fool of herself in front of all these men. "It's all tricks," she tells him. The magician responds, "Oh? You don't believe? Well, we'll see," or something like that. Then he goes into his routine, and the next thing you know, she's in a trance. He places a crown of flowers on her head, and begins to whisper to her. He suggests she is a young girl again. Here is Cabiria, closing her eyes. She smiles. She begins to pick imaginary flowers. The orchestra plays sweet music to match the delicacy of the mood. She is lost in her innocence. She makes confessions. The magician's face loosens for a fraction of a second. His worn eyes betray the fact that she has touched him. She offers him a flower, in a gesture of radiant and delicate love. He plays along, acting the part of her first lover, until the pretense becomes unbearable, even for an old pro like him. In desperation, he signals the orchestra. Cymbals crash, the lights go up, the audience roars. Here is Cabiria, startled out of the trance, looking wildly around, remembering nothing, snatching the crown of flowers from her head, running from the theater in agony and shame.

Here she is back on the street, in the night wind, among the blowing papers. Out of the shadows steps a gentleman. He removes his hat; he bows. His eyes are deep, gentle, penetrating; they have known sorrow. "Excuse me," he says. "I saw what happened in there, and I wanted you to know I was touched." He goes on and on about her basic purity, her innocence, her incorruptibility. Here is Cabiria, mouth down, eying him cynically. "You sound as though you swallowed a book," she says. And here they are in the following scenes, doing the dance: he courting, she playing not waiting to get. She reluctantly promises to meet him again.

But here little touches begin to creep into the film to make us suspect his sincerity. He speaks of life and love, and she is impressed, she is beginning to warm; but all the same, notice his overcoat, how wrinkled it is, how sloppy he is about his basic appearance. In the fifties that was always a bad sign. In addition, when he throws his cigarette away, he does it with his eyes squinted. We are on guard, just as she is beginning to lose hers. He buys her a box of candy; she takes it back to the street corner with her, to show the girls that someone cares. Her friend Wanda eats it all. "If he's so wonderful, how come we never see him?" she wants to know, licking the chocolate off her fingers. Cabiria says something to the effect that that is how she wants it; he shouldn't see how she has had to make her living; he is too good for her. He is too good to be true.

Here is Cabiria packing her belongings, selling her little home. Marriage. He has proposed marriage. Blessed Mary, she does not deserve such a man. Here is Wanda, crying. "Don't cry. I'll write. It will work out, you'll see." Here is Cabiria, boarding the bus with just her life savings in her purse. "*Ciao*, Wanda!" "*Ciao*, Cabiria." Here is the bus disappearing down the road, bringing up clouds of dust. Here is Wanda waving good-bye.

Grace, don't fall asleep now. Don't get stoned on me just when you're about to hear how we found ways of facing life then. Films like these were our basic instruction. Waiting to get was made bearable in just this way. I know you can fuck anyone you want any day of the week; I know that for you none of this applies. But if you're going to live in my house, if I have to witness how it is with you, the least you can do is show some respect for how it was with me. That is the ground rule. Is it my fault that times change so fast?

So here is our final scene: Cabiria and her man, sipping wine at a little table. It is on a balcony somewhere, overlooking the sea. She is completely transported by the wine, the sun, the man. It is a dream she never thought could come true. In a gesture of gratitude, she withdraws her bank roll and extends it across the table to him. For you, my love, for us! Her man looks around furtively. "Put it away," he whispers, his cigarette dangling from his lips. He has put on his sunglasses. We know what's coming next, but we don't want to believe it. The tension builds. The conflict is unbearable, we fight it almost to the end. She's come so far, she's *got*. He looks around again and suggests they take a walk through the woods.

The sun is beginning to go down. No. No. No. Hand in hand they go, through the fallen leaves, down toward the cliff overlooking the sea. Cabiria runs ahead, he lags behind, puffing away on his fag, looking around nervously. She goes right up to the edge of the cliff and drinks in the sun, shimmering its last over the water. "What a strange light!" she whispers. You son of a bitch, if you push her over, I swear, I swear, I will never come to another movie again as long as I live. We light up our fifteenth cigarette. We do not breathe. Cabiria turns. She is just beginning to sense something wrong. It happens this way every time with ambivalent believers.

They are facing each other now, she has her back to the sea. She reaches out her hands to embrace his face: "What is wrong?" He backs off a little and throws the cigarette away. She starts to back away from him, her arms still outstretched. She is inches from the edge of the cliff. They stand utterly silent that way, as her purse sways gently over one arm. The shadows lengthen. Ah, Grace, you're waking up. I think he says, "I don't want to hurt you." She makes a little whimper; it sounds like an animal in distress. "The money," she whispers, though it's more of a choke. Beads of perspiration appear on his forehead. In the next frame his eyes appear in close-up. There is a struggle going on there, between what might have been decency, at one time, and desperation. She reads it too. Her eyes are liquid. She holds out her purse to him. There is a brief scuffle in the leaves and then there he is, grabbing the purse and running through the woods. And there she is, lying in the leaves, pounding the ground, sobbing, choking, rolling over and over, covered with debris. Then the sun goes down. And she is absolutely still. Then slowly she pulls herself up. Her face is streaked with tears, mud, I think there may have been a leaf or two still adhering to her hair. She walks slowly down the road. In the distance you hear the faint buzzing of a motorbike, then music. A group of young people comes by; one of them is playing an accordion. Their gaiety is in terrible contrast to her despair. As they pass her, a girl on the back of the bike calls out, "*Buona sera.*" She has a radiant smile.

Here is Cabiria smiling back at them through her tears. She nods. She smiles again. Her mouth is turning up and down, at the same time. A little more up than down. She turns full face to the camera and smiles at us. She had lost her money and her man, but she still had herself. That was something I could never forget. It seemed important, even then. It went against the times. Some of us forgot and some of us never knew. I am thinking of Roberta.

After graduation Roberta found a job in a law office, typing. Together we rode to work on the 8:41 bus. On weekends we went to films while we were waiting to get. Roberta couldn't wait to get. The films didn't sustain her; Roberta would take anything that came along. I told her she always had herself, but all she said was, "Big deal." That's how we talked in the fifties. She thought Cabiria made too many critical mistakes, the worst being that she allowed herself to believe in love. You never did that; it crippled your ability to get. Her losses were proof of her stupidity. Roberta admired Marlene Dietrich's style in *The Blue Angel*. There was a woman who knew how to get and hold, and eventually crush. While you were getting, holding, and crushing, you not only proved your superiority, you freed yourself to "fall in love" later, with someone else.

Here is Marlene, tickling the professor under the chin. Here is the professor blushing, casting shy, tender glances. He's hers. Here is Marlene in the cabaret, singing: "Falling in love again/Never wanted to/What am I to do?/I can't help it." Here is the professor watching from the balcony, overcome, thinking she is singing for him. Here is the professor proposing marriage! Here is Marlene laughing. Here is the professor pressing on. Here is Marlene marrying the professor. Here is the professor, resigning his teaching post to take part in her nightclub act as a clown. Here is Marlene, kissing a young man on the stairs as the professor goes onstage and says, "Cock-a-doodle-doo!" Here is the professor collapsed across his old desk at night in the empty classroom. We are unable to tell if he is dead, or simply crying. Here is Marlene, back in the cabaret, singing, "Falling in love again/Never wanted to/What am I to do?/I can't help it."

By September, Roberta and I had been working for over three months, and still hadn't got a man. You couldn't help playing "September Song" in your mind as the leaves turned brown and started falling. There was a message in all that wrinkling and drying up. Roberta read the leaves on the way to the liquor store with the grocery money; what they had to say brought tears to her eyes: her birthday at the end of the month, twenty-two years old and still single! There wasn't enough cheap wine in the entire city of San Francisco to erase that fact, lodged like a knife under the heart, where it moved each time she breathed.

Here is Roberta, playing Marlene Dietrich, tickling her boss under the chin. Here is Roberta's boss blushing, rising to the occasion. Here is Roberta, discovering she is pregnant. Here is Roberta's boss, into his third martini, explaining why marriage is out of the question, but offering to pay for the abortion. Here is Roberta, calling her friends for the abortion list. In those days the abortion list was guarded like a crown jewel; anything happen to it, anyone abuse the rules and regulations governing its use, and it would ruin the whole setup for everyone. Here is Roberta making the long-distance phone call, using the code name. Here is Roberta receiving her instructions (read, memorize, swallow). Here is Roberta checking into the small Mexican clinic for the abortion. Here is Roberta coming back, changing clothes, starting all over again. "An affair either ends in marriage, or it ends," she is telling Jason, the young lawyer whose child she now carries. Here is Roberta, biting her nails, weeping, listening to Miles Davis, waiting for Jason to make up his mind. Here is Jason, offering to pay for the abortion. Here is Roberta, holding out for marriage. This was known as playing all your cards; it was the most desperate form of getting. Here is Jason panicking, doing the honorable thing. Here they are setting up house, with revolving charge accounts.

With Roberta having gotten, it was a little lonely for the rest of us, back at the bar each Friday night, dipping our fingers into the peanuts while our eyes roamed around the dimly lit room. Getting a man became more of an obsession whenever one of us actually managed to do it; it threw the others off balance, set methods of operation into motion which hadn't been considered necessary before. Every Friday after work now we gathered in the business district bars, jockeying for the well-lit tables, visible from the door, ordering our whiskey sours, playing with the cherries, feigning nonchalance. We all wore black: black dresses, with long sleeves, usually wool; black cardigans over the black dresses; black shoes from Leeds. We were secretaries and everyone knew secretaries wore black. We even wore black gloves, don't ask me why. We spent one fourth of our salaries on stockings. No one questioned the necessity. Ladies wore gloves and stockings; whores did not.

Norma Jean replaces the baby books in the drawer. It is time to pick up Damon. She gets into the car and heads for the freeway; it will be faster that way. She's late again. She sees the accident up ahead, brakes quickly. The freeway is backed up for miles. She forces from her mind the image of Damon sighing alone at the book table, and Miss Rogers' eyes, waiting to devour her with recriminations; she switches on the radio. There are two things you can do when trapped on the freeway: you can hyperventilate the gas fumes and go out of your mind; or you can flip on the radio, settle back, let your thoughts wander, and remain intact. It helps to keep a book in the car, she thinks, remembering the time she put in an hour on some off-ramp reading Simone de Beauvoir. Today she doesn't have a book. She leans against the headrest and reaches for the switch, listening to Albinoni and thinking of Grace.

Who, after graduation, went for a walk in the woods and discovered the Spirit of Christ commune. Grace, coming back the following spring to visit the children and save Norma Jean. ("I was saved. Things got so bad, nothing worked any more. Dope didn't do it for me, sex didn't do it for me, I thought I was going to have a nervous breakdown, and then I met Fran and Larry, who run the commune, and they said, 'Grace, if you really want to be saved, it is possible. Get on your knees and say to the Lord, "Lord, I, Grace Grovener, humbly ask to come into your heart." ' And I did that, Mrs. Harris, and the Lord took me into His heart. I have seen the Truth. If I die tomorrow I will be happy, I am fulfilled.")

Albinoni fills the car. If you have to be trapped on the freeway, your day isn't a total loss if you can manage a little Albinoni on the radio. This is the Sonata in F, for trumpet and organ. She has it at home, plays it sometimes, lying on the floor, after the newspaper has overwhelmed. There are two kinds of being overwhelmed: current events and those things which are timeless. How is it that this trumpet can move inside the blood with indescribable delicacy, saying things for which there is no language?

The traffic begins to move again, and by the time she pulls into the driveway of the nursery school she hears the screams. As she runs up the steps, she becomes alarmed. They are Damon's. There he sits in Miss Rogers' lap, screaming away and holding his ear.

"Damon has been screaming for three quarters of an hour, Mrs. Harris. He seems to have a terrible earache." His face is flushed and his eyes are streaming. "He often gets ear infections, Miss Rogers. I'm terribly sorry to be late; there was an accident on the freeway." For once Miss Rogers does not offer advice. Norma Jean carries the hysterical child to the car, and heads for the doctor's office. There she phones Scott's nursery school and explains, asking the teacher to ask the mother driving the car pool to keep him at her house until she can pick him up. Damon gets his perfunctory ear exam and penicillin prescription, which Norma Jean now heads toward the pharmacy to fill. If the wait isn't long, she should make it home before Ruth Ann gets back from school.

Pulling into the parking lot, she sees three police cars nosed in together, and a crowd just breaking up. She rolls the window down and asks a bystander what happened. "There was a robbery, a Brinks car; they executed the guard in those bushes next to the drugstore. He was on his knees, looked like he was praying. They shot him anyway."

"Mommy, lookit all the police cars! I want to get out and see them, can I?" "No, Damon, you stay right where you are." Norma

57

Jean rolls up the window. She is horrified that Damon missed witnessing the execution by ten minutes. The crime lab men are sifting the earth around the bushes, and hosing the blood off the asphalt. My God, where can we go? She has asked the question before: when the woman three blocks away was murdered in her sleep. They never found her killer, or a motive. She asks the question every time there is a killing that strikes anywhere in the vicinity which she considers "close to home." She always ends up feeling that there are few, if any, alternatives. One's basic commitment is to the life one leads, in the place where one lives. You do not leave a community, a country, when there is trouble. You stay and fight, and vote, and lock your doors. She drives to another drugstore and secures Damon's prescription, then picks up Scott. She gets home just as Ruth Ann is wetting her pants on the porch. "I can't help it, Mommy! I can't *go* in the bathroom at school; they beat you up in there!"

"It's all right, Ruthie. Let's go in and get you some dry clothes." She lets the children watch cartoons on TV. She refused for nearly six years, then decided to allow it, selectively. There are absolutely times when you have to forget that they're poisoning their minds if you want to hang on to yours. She takes a Librium and goes out to the garage.

The little jars are sitting on a shelf, waiting to be fired in a friend's kiln, on the other side of town. They have been sitting there for a month. She isn't even sure she wants to fire them yet. The urge is to shape them. She sits down and kneads. The clay is cold and solid under her palms. She closes her eyes. She gives herself over to the rhythm she has imposed on the elastic mass in her hands. In her mind an image forms: dark birds perched on ruins, and the words "All things pass."

5

"O.K., Johnella. Do you have a story for me today?"

"Yeah."

"What shall we call it?" Johnella rolls her eyes a few times across the ceiling. "Call it 'The Blues Monster,'" she says, languidly. The Blues Monster, I think to myself; that's pure. This will be a story from the heart, not another serial. It's hard to extract original material from these children; black, white, oriental, they all have one thing in common: their "made-up" stories are almost all likely to be variations on a Warner Brothers theme, adapted by sadists especially for children's television. I lick my pencil lovingly in anticipation of Johnella's pure gift. It comes like an easy birth, sliding in on the liquid tones of her even, measured voice.

The Blues Monster
by Johnella Franklin

Tall Harry went in the house. And he saw a big big monster. And he looked all around and he didn't know what to do. And he couldn't get out. He was in a trap so he went in a car and left his family.

That's what I'll be doing soon: getting in a car and leaving my family. When Martin told me about the conference in Palm Springs, I thought: this is it. Here's my chance to erase all the events of February from my mind, an opportunity to just lie around a pool and let certain irritants evaporate on the lean desert air. We'll get a sitter for the children and, while he confers, I will feign indifference to the world; and, if we stay long enough, and if the sun is hot enough, and the water seductive enough, perhaps even achieve the most sought-after condition said to obtain in places like Palm Springs: complete indifference. It wasn't easy keeping my mind on my duties as a participating second grade mother, but Johnella's story kept cutting through.

And he didn't never come back and they called the police and the police didn't know what to do and the children started to cry. Then they ran away. They called home and they speaked to their mother and their mother hanged up in their face. And then they called back to 675-7277. They said "Hello Mother" and she didn't say nothin. She hanged up again.

Then they called 675-7277 again. And they said "Hello Mother; what are you doin?" "I'm doin nothin. Pack up your clothes and leave. I don't want you never, never again." And they started to cry and pack up their clothes and ran out of the house. And they never came back to their mother.

A lady tried to stop them and the lady killed the monster. Then I got killed. A man came and killed me with a knife. I got stabbed in the stomach. Then I said: "I'm callin my mother and I don't care if she don't speak to me; I'm goin home. I still be callin 675-7277."

THE END

"That's quite a story, Johnella. You could be a writer someday. Would you like that?" Johnella rolls her eyes across the ceiling a couple more times; it's her way of dealing with people like me who lay far-out things on her.

"Naw," she says finally. "I'm gonna have lotsa babies like my momma." She pushes herself away from the story table. I gather up the pages of her story, lining up the left-hand sides evenly for the stapler. I weigh whether or not to let her take the story home. ("You told 'em *that?* What you tell 'em that for, girl? Pack up your clothes and leave.") My eyes roll around the ceiling for a while. They come to rest on the blackboard, where the teacher has written:

Tuesday, February 29

1. Today one baby rat was stepped on and he died.
2. His body was stiff.
3. We now have 9 baby rats.

4. They have to be cared for carefully, until they are old enough to take care of themselves.
5. We will handle them gently.

The newly opened section of Interstate 5 stretches over two hundred miles between Tracy and Bakersfield. We accelerate through the night at eighty-five miles an hour, surrounded by swirling air-conditioned chill. The freeway is just one month old; every so often a sign looms in front of the headlights: WARNING: NO GAS FOR NEXT 80 MILES. The state built the road, but there are no gas stations. The first week it was open, over three hundred cars ran out of gas, and were abandoned. The sense of isolation is terrifying, if you allow yourself to dwell on it. If anything should go wrong with the car, you would sit in the middle of the state of California in complete darkness, absolutely alone. Occasional tumbleweeds spring up in front of the car, making endless revolutions through the night. There is nothing else but cold stars and the hum of hundreds of cars burning up the night at eighty-five miles an hour; their passengers look neither right nor left. You go as fast as you can on Interstate 5 because your goal is to get to the end of it as soon as possible. We turn on the radio and receive a Mozart bassoon concerto. It fills up the miles and eases the dread.

The motel room in Bakersfield contains one hard bed with Magic Fingers which do not work; one twenty-three-inch color television which broadcasts people with Day-Glo orange skin; and one Bible, on top of which rests a card reading "Chaplain-on-Call."

A clergyman is available at any time to our guests
who have a spiritual need.
Our Chaplain-On-Call is
THE REV. BILLY RAY GIBBONS
857-2138

I imagine a man with fading skin, vomiting in the bathroom and rasping to the girl in the bed with the broken Magic Fingers, "Call the chaplain for me, will you baby? I have a spiritual need."

Tubes, wires, and grounders pour out of the wall into the color TV, feeding it intravenously, juicing it up to survive another night in Bakersfield. I finger the edges of the Chaplain-on-Call card and wonder what kind of advice Billy Ray Gibbons would give if I dialed his number. Martin is stalking around the room nude, doing his Motel number. It's something that comes over him whenever we manage to get away from the children for the night. The minute the key is turned in the door, the minute we step over the threshhold, a leer pulls at the corners of his mouth and a narrow light appears in his eyes. What is it about motel rooms that permits an abandon unlike anything since before the wedding? Is it the ghosts of all the other couples who have stepped through that door, thrown themselves on this bed, and fucked themselves blind? The room shimmers with their exhausted forms, played out and spread in every conceivable position. We throw back the covers, and switch off the light. We are breathing fast, and haven't yet touched. As Martin closes in on me I hear a voice calling out, "My bed is soaking!" It comes from two hundred and fifty miles away. I'll have to take this up with Arndt.

In the morning we go to the motel dining room for breakfast. It is situated so that you can look out the window and watch the custodian sucking the paper cups out of the swimming pool with a six-foot-long suction tube. The hostess who seats us has been flawlessly cast in styrofoam, in the Holiday Inn Dining Room Hostess mold. No sooner are the orders given than two giant plates come floating down, and before us swim two polyethylene eggs and two side orders of shredded plastic hash browns. You'd almost swear they were real.

Heading down the road you can barely make out the Tehachapi Mountains; the valley is encased in smog from one end to the other. Still, incredible fruits continue to bloom, with a peculiar native defiance, as though knowing they have the last word, since they were the first to arrive. Every mile or so enormous signs tell us what to do: EAT.

We stop for gas, and I take over the driving. The car surges ahead, doing just what I tell it to. At what point in evolution did we become equipped to deal with such power? As the miles slip by, I try to concentrate on lush pools and sweet desert air. They are there, somewhere, over the mountains. They will make everything come out all right. Wasn't it written somewhere that such things restore? On the left we pass a little bar, with a sign twice its size, reading

THE SAND BOX
Paul's Nude Girls   Topless, Bottomless   7-Up

It brings on images of droves of nude girls, all belonging to Paul, owned and operated by Paul, bearing his brand on their thighs: "Paul's."

"What do you think of Southern California?" Martin asks. It is my first trip. "Beautiful, isn't it?"

ACE EXTERMINATORS
Our Motto: *"We Kill to Live."*

"I think I'm going to be sick," I say. He is admiring orange groves, patches of wildflowers, date palms—things like that. We travel the same road but somehow manage to see different things.

"Look, we're on *vacation*; can't you enjoy it? Why do you always have to be so critical? Relax, let it happen to you."

Yes, I tell myself, I'll have to work on that, I really will.

Entering Palm Springs we are forced to slow; the traffic is almost bumper-to-bumper. I look in vain for a glimpse of landscape which will in some way correspond to the mental image I have erected of this area. You know that you are surrounded by mountains, because the map tells you they are there. The smog is so pervasive they can't be seen; but the imagination is a clever animal, it fills in what it wants to see, superimposes tall brown mountains on the pale yellow screen presented it.

As we pull into the hotel grounds, the air is static with the sounds of small birds clustered in the tops of tall palms. There is a sense of arrival. I head for the pool; they have not one, but three: large, medium, and heated Jacuzzi. Everyone is in the heated Jacuzzi. It seems incongruous to be sitting in a hot pool under an intense desert sun, but I get in anyway. By six o'clock the pools are filled with behavioral scientists, floating in varying degrees of embryonic trance. The sun flecks in small patches on their sunglasses and their drinks rest on their stomachs in clear plastic cups. The liquid in the cups moves in rhythm with the water in the pools.

The woman next to me is speaking of the "Negroes," and the

habit they have of invading the swimming pools "back home." Her pale flesh billows and floats on the swirling streams of bubbling water. "Mmmmm, this feels so good," she says, pursing red lips. She shows me the little label sewn to her swimsuit. It reads "O.K." That means she is allowed in the community pool back home.

"Do they have guards at your pools back home?" I ask her. Does the heat I feel owe itself only to the Jacuzzi?

"Guards?" she raises her eyebrows at me. "Did you say guards, my dear?"

"Yes. How do they distinguish you from the Negroes?" Don't insult her; you'll embarrass Martin and he won't take you to any more conferences. Her face turns the color of opals in the reflection of the water.

"Well it's quite obvious isn't it?" she asks, her voice rising. "They check the label on your suit."

The next day I make a solemn vow: I will relax and enjoy the desert sun and radiant pools, even if they are overheated. I force myself to go to the pool for a swim. A wind has come up and the palms are making paper noises and nervous birds begin to fill the skies. Sand is blowing in from the desert, covering the perfectly irrigated lawns with a fine layer of silt and dust. Within an hour, all the pools are filled with sand; they no longer look lush and inviting. The sand begins to clog the Jacuzzi filter system.

"When our children were small," muses the mother in the restaurant, filling her hours.

"Just put it all on Dr. Davidson's bill," says the wife buying dresses in the gift shop, biding her time.

"First they want your pool, then they want your daughter," says O.K., serving her sentence inside herself.

Back in the room I take some chilled wine from the tiny refrigerator while the air conditioner hums and the Mexican maids sweetly spread fresh sheets in ⚡23, ⚡22, ⚡21, ⚡20, all the way down the line. *What am I doing here?* In two more hours the conference will be over and we can go home. I will pack up my clothes and leave. I don't want it never, never again.

Scenario for Three Voices, Walnut Panels,
and Air-Conditioned Room
FIRST VOICE: Not only are the emotional needs of these children being neglected; their spirits are corrupted by ambivalent values

and the rampant consumerism which surrounds them. To what end do we presume to speak of integrated ego functions and well-defined controls, when a child is forced to cope with uprooted family ties and ever-increasing environmental dangers? And this is just the tip of the iceberg; I am speaking of the experience of the middle-class child. What of the children of poverty, who deal with unimaginable chaos, who are abandoned, bitten by rats, and who witness personal violence on a daily basis?

He was in a trap so he went in a car and left his family.

Our society creates greater stress and makes greater demands on its members now than at any other time in history. With greater stress, we have to expect higher levels of anxiety and dysfunction. As social scientists, we are obligated to examine root causes which obtain from the culture, and work for change; to speak of treatment in any other context is to continue treating symptoms. We must work to eradicate their causes.

SECOND VOICE: It is not our role to deal with socio-political issues. To do so is to weaken our focus and ultimately abandon our commitment to examine and illuminate the patient's inner life. As clinicians, we are obligated to honor the inner world which, by its very nature, is individual.

5. We will handle them gently.

THIRD VOICE: Well, they are utterly devoid of respect for personal property. There are too many of them, swarms; hordes. No, I don't have any objection personally if the polite ones, the educated ones, want to swim in our community pool; it's just that it is not permitted. If they had the patience, the inner controls, to wait—in twenty-five years it could change. But my dear, I'm speaking of *hordes*, you see; who has the answer to that?

1. Today one baby rat was stepped on and he died.

The members of the conference are departing; they carry their suitcases to their cars through the dust storm, and find their windshields pitted with sand. There is something about the wind that makes me feel confused and wild inside, without my usual well-defined controls. I seem to be suffering from a case of revenge, although I can't put my finger on its exact origins. My mouth is filled with sand; there is sand in my eyes and all through my hair. There is something taking shape in me that wishes to see the storm lay waste to everyone and everything here. The air is charged, electric, as though a lesson were forming: a lesson on the dangers of insulating oneself, of erecting fragile barriers. But where nature is impartial, I am particular: the one in the white shirt, kill. The one with the briefcase, spare. The trouble with mass murder or natural catastrophes is that individual judgments cannot be rendered. How are you to tell which are genuinely concerned and lovingly informed, and which are governed by certain resistant strains of myths? Here in the desert, they all seem peculiarly equal—as vulnerable to the forces bearing down on them as the mannered landscape through which they walk. As we drove away from Palm Springs, it pleased me in some enormous, elemental way to see that presumptuous oasis being eaten away on all sides. It seemed only a matter of time before the center would fall.

6

Being a Parent
by Dr. Haim Ginott
HOW TO REACT TO A CRISIS
Crises are turning points in a child's life. Winning his heart, in moments of distress, is a victory. . . .

For Women Only
by L. R. Curtis, M.D.
MOTHER SEEKS STERILIZATION;
CLAIMS THREE CHILDREN ENOUGH
. . . "Yes, that's true, Ramona," I said, "and sterilization is becoming a very popular method of birth control. Nevertheless, I still maintain . . ."

Dottie's Helpful Hints
WHEN IN DOUBT, THROW IT OUT

Norma Jean is interrupted in the middle of her dregs by the doorbell. "Oh, hi Rachel, come on in." It is Rachel Swartz, who lives on Ranch Road. She is wearing faded Levi's and sandals. Her hair is loose, in contrast to Norma Jean's, whose dark hair is now piled back in a twist, so that it won't drag in the clay. Rachel, the friend who has come to replace other friends who moved away; who herself has come to Pleasant Valley after six moves in the past ten years. She has lived here longer than anywhere previously: three years. Rachel, who has overcome endless broken friendships and who has settled into the community as though it might be for good; but who still refuses to "do" her house, fix it up, make it "hers," because after a while you refuse to invest in something which you perceive as being temporary.

We are the two most deviant wives in Pleasant Valley, where women tend to act and dress in a way which attempts to deny their social isolation. (If you dress for tennis, you're sure to find a partner. If you have enough fantasies, you're ready, in the event that something happens.) This phenomenon is an example of positive thinking in its final stage of decay. It is an exercise in futility, but the others haven't caught on. You have to seek out the event first; any fool can see it isn't going to come to you— not here. But here is where so many of them are, buying clothes and waiting around for the cards to fall. A frequent comment is: "Something better happen soon, or I'm going to go out of my mind."

"Are you in the middle of something?"

"Dregs. Just dregs. Want some coffee?"

"Better make a lot."

"Ah, you have gossip!" Norma Jean senses it immediately; it's a reflex. And she thinks of the ancient malice that once thrived in women ghettos. If we're no longer "gossip-mongers," then what are we now? Gossip connoisseurs? Are our ghettos simply more fluid, more resistant to definition?

She pours, and Rachel lights a cigarette; they prepare for the ritual. How we have refined this ancient art, in our spotless kitchens (our husbands absorbing it kinetically as they walk through the door, hours later: "Rachel's been here; you've been gossiping again. What did you tell her about last night?" And in their minds, the image of witches, burning). But the process is already beginning to mutate. Even now, as I set Rachel's coffee before her, I am a dividing cell: I want to hear; I do not want to hear. It would be oversimplified to assume that this is because I fear I will be next. It would be equally oversimplified to think it owes itself exclusively to any new-found sense of closeness with my neighbors, mobile though they may be. I do admit to receiving the phrase "No man is an island" rather frequently of late. I accept it as appropriate to the times and applicable to me. I also fight it. I cherish my privacy with a jealousy borne of the early, intense, nuclear beginnings common to most of us. I value isolation as a restorative state. I am aware that this attitude is counter-revolutionary. I know it is being eaten away on all fronts. And I have not resolved my ambivalence concerning the two kinds of isolation: that which is self-imposed and helps define inner resources; and that which is a by-product of my time and place and results in alienation and panic. I sometimes have dreams of communal life, and awaken with intense longing.

Norma Jean finds that the gossip reflex hasn't disappeared entirely. It surfaces at appropriate moments, like a vestigial condition that suffers from time-lag, hasn't gotten the message, has developed a resistance to change. "Who is it? Let me guess! Evelyn Tucker is pregnant again?"

"Nope."

"Hm. Pat's sleeping with that guy who services her car?"

"That's three months old. Besides, they never made it to bed."

"*Really?*"

"Yeah. She met someone new, at school. They've been together for a month. Don't you talk to anyone any more? Where have you been?" (Egypt; out in the garage; you know, the usual. . . .)

"The Epsteins have split?"

"You're getting close." Rachel pauses for effect. "The Folletts."

"No!"

"*She* left *him.*" This phenomenon has become more and more common, but Norma Jean still experiences a mild jolt when she hears it. It always used to be the other way around. How is it that one minute you're changing a diaper, and by the time the dry one is on and the wet one in the pail, the earth has already made a complete revolution around the sun, effecting in its wake a century's worth of changes?

"They seemed as happy as anyone we know."

"They put on a good show: the parties, tennis, happy hours, and running to gallery openings. It was all a front; they couldn't communicate. Marilyn has a lover, an artist she met at one of the openings. Ted's moved out, found a little apartment over on the other side of Coronado. The kids spend weekends with him." Rachel swallows the last of her coffee, pushes her cup toward Norma Jean, who is slow to respond. As if awakening from a trance, she gets the pot, pours.

"Thanks."

"That makes the tenth couple we know who've split in the past year and a half." ("It's a goddamned epidemic! People are going crazy." —Martin Harris.) Norma Jean recalls Martin, listing causes, after the sixth divorce: married too early; delinquent culture; envy of the young; mid-life crisis; longer life spans; more options; crazy, immature women, not knowing their place. He stopped listing after number eight, because they didn't fit any pattern, defied all available explanations. It threw him. He was silent after that, as was Norma Jean. They just ran out of things to say. It is also true that the sheer weight of numbers begins to have a subtle effect: you find yourself scrutinizing things about each other which formerly were taken for granted as having been adjusted to, and which wouldn't have been thought worthy of consideration in the old days (say, five years ago). It was as though all the previous advantages and disadvantages connected to the marital state had reversed themselves. It was another of the growing number of areas where old attitudes no longer applied.

"Everything seemed too perfect with them," Norma Jean is saying. "For one thing, they never fought. Marilyn told me once, 'Tom can't tolerate discord; whenever we disagree, he just withdraws. We wait it out; sometimes it takes a day, sometimes two weeks.' I used to think they were more mature than we were; I even tried 'waiting it out' the next fight we had. It lasted twenty minutes. Then I went at Martin with a kitchen knife."

Rachel smiles. "What did he do?" she asks.

"He threw a chair at me. I was so surprised, I put the knife down. I told him, 'You stupid bastard, don't you know better than to provoke a woman with a knife? If I weren't so mature, so *intact*, I would have killed you.'"

"I once emptied a dresser drawer on Paul—while he was sitting on the toilet. There wasn't a thing he could do. I went to a motel for the night, so he couldn't kill me."

"I've never done that. Gone to a motel."

"It's lonely, except for the feeling of revenge; you know: letting him sit there and stew, wondering if I've cracked up on the freeway; letting *him* change the diapers and get the kids off in the morning. That aspect was exhilarating."

Norma Jean muses. "The best fight we ever had was the Christmas of '63. I can't even remember what it was about." (Why do we forget the absolutely critical, life-and-death *issues*, yet retain those graphic details of battle that manage to rescue it from the banal and elevate it to high theater?) Looking back, I see that we defined ourselves that way, each time we extended our perimeters. It established the absolute outer boundaries of both personalities, within which each was free to inquire. It was an early form of learning, through play. Never mind that the game loses some of its appeal with time, that the infinite pressures associated with maturity can bring about sometimes deadly alterations in content and style. This was one fight that stood alone in its dramatic purity and over-all absurdity.

We were standing on opposite sides of the living room. It was eight or nine at night. I had a bottle of wine in my hand, which I was waving around in a menacing manner. Martin was holding a chair up in front of him, the way lion tamers do (he must have a thing about chairs; I never thought of it before now). I hiss. He snarls.

"Nagging bitch!"

"Mama's boy!"

"Cunt!"

"Prick!"

Well, you get the picture. I can't remember the dialogue because I've forgotten the issues. What I recall most clearly is the advance toward the middle of the room, where we're both doing the dance with the feet, like boxers, neither wanting to lose ground to the other. Everything comes down to territory, in the end. Just as the wine bottle and the chair were about to connect, and we were hurling our most vulgar epithets at each other in long, twisting, utterly disconnected strings ("assholewhoremotherfuckerpigslutpansycocksucker"), there came a knock at the door. We paused in frozen silence: through the window we could see the little group of Salvation Army carolers, singing "Silent Night"; and they could see us: arms raised high and streams of saliva parting our bared fangs. (". . . All is calm, all is bright . . .") Our minds were racing: Who is going to answer the door? Should we go on fighting and ignore them? Buy them off? "God bless you for the work you're doing for the underprivileged. Merry Christmas to you, too."

As Martin paid off the Salvation Army, I carried my bottle

out under the oak tree, fell to the ground, and leaned heavily against the trunk. We made a very striking combination there, the bottle and I, had there happened to be a painter around. Of course it was raining. The wind was blowing hard, too. The only things lacking were a little lightning and Beethoven's Eroica. A stray cat happened by, circled me twice, then crawled into my lap to get out of the storm. We made an even more striking combination, now that a touch of pathos had been added to the scene. I began to drink from the bottle, waiting for Martin to find me and carry me upstairs, the way they used to in the movies. He didn't come. I could see him through the window, rearranging the furniture and pouring himself a drink. It was getting very cold, even the cat took off. What do you do in a situation like that? That is, if pride is an essential part of your make-up? I stuck with it for another twenty minutes or so, killing the bottle, lying on the ground, addressing the storm: ("Take me! Take me!"). Martin finally came out, well after the "right" moment had passed, and said something like "Get up and come in the house; you're getting wet." "Fuck off, futhermucker." I always give it all I've got, even when a fool can see it's over. Then Martin said, "Come to bed, we're both exhausted." So that's what we did, just went to bed and fell asleep, exhausted. Who knows what might have happened if the Salvation Army hadn't interfered?

Norma Jean lights a cigarette to bring herself back. That was a time when there was the freedom to challenge boundaries, when they both had what seemed like unlimited elasticity of personality; it not only bore up, it bounded back, assumed new forms. It was a time of intense discovery. After the children came, their disagreements took on a different means of expression. You just couldn't do the bottle-and-chair routine in front of them. Now that we had responsibilities to others, we began putting the lid on. And once the old margins are gone, it's amazing how your life changes. The changes can affect you in unexpected ways. And sometimes years pass before you know this.

"Should I make more coffee?"

"Might as well; I still have a half hour before I have to pick up Peter. There's nothing you can do in a half hour, by the time you've found a parking space. How about you?"

"I have to get Damon about the same time." Norma Jean pushes herself away from the kitchen table, reheats the water for the coffee. "How are things going with you? How's Paul?"

"Oh, you know. Being back in school and working part-time have required some terrific adjustments. I almost don't want to get into it, it's had me so upset this month."

"You don't have to talk about it."

"I know, I know. I'm just so mad at the son of a bitch right now. I know he's trying; we've been through the whole equality thing and he accepts it intellectually. But when the chips are down, guess who still does the dishes, the laundry, picks up the house, bathes the children, hauls them to the doctor when they're sick, gives them their medicine, calls the sitter, takes out the garbage, takes the animals to the vet, makes the grocery lists, buys the food, cooks it, cleans up after it, takes his crap to the cleaners, picks up his crap at the cleaners, oh *you* know, I don't have to tell *you!* Sometimes I feel I'm going out of my mind. You'll see what I mean, Norma, when you get something going just for yourself, or start working again." *Should I tell her about the jars? No. Why? I don't know. I don't know why.* "You hardly have time to breathe, and there he is, always claiming he's coming home tired from work. It's a syndrome; all men have it. They've been claiming it as an excuse to get out of just about everything for so long they're not even aware they're doing it. The Coming Home Tired from Work syndrome always begins *after* he's closed the front door behind him, and *you're* there to witness it. Its major symptom is repeating over and over, 'I work *hard* all day!' It usually surfaces right after you've asked him to help with some simple task, you know, like the garbage or screwing another safety lock on the door. 'I work *hard* all day!' he says. As though you didn't.

"And he badgers me about sex: 'Your nightgown looks like a rag,' he says. 'I can't get turned on any more, looking at you in that thing.' 'Well, it keeps me warm,' I tell him. 'It's *winter!*' 'You don't look sexy any more,' he says. 'All the romance has gone out of our lives. Can't you do something to get the romance back?' 'Well I'm *tired*, you goddamned son of a bitch!' Then I let him have it. I say, 'I work *hard* all day!' And you know what he does? He gives me a withering glance. No work can compare with the hard work *he* does. You know why? Because he *earns the money!*" Rachel has whipped herself into a frenzy of confession. "I think of grocery lists while we're making love. Lettuce, barbecue sauce, Oh yeah, that's good; mayonnaise, tomatoes, cornstarch, cleanser, Ah! Pickles! Zucchini! Cucumbers!" They bend over the table in hysterics, knowing it's a pathetic way to achieve revenge. They laugh anyway because that is one of the functions of ghetto humor, to hurt without hurting, kill without having to go to jail for it. Ghetto humor is the social twin of fantasy; together they sustain the powerless, who accomplish miracles through illusion.

"Damon, we've got an hour and a half before Ruth Ann and Scotty get home. Want to go to the park for a while?" Norma Jean drives to the park, looking at the sky. It will rain, it's just a matter of when. Damon runs off to slide, while she settles on the bench, pulling her Ancient Egypt paperback from her purse. The park is almost deserted, except for a pack of stray dogs and one other mother and child. Norma Jean has deliberately chosen the bench that does not have the other mother on it. Sit down there, and it will be another half-hour discussion of the school system. How many times do they think a person can discuss the school system? Every time she does it she feels as though she's been on amphetamines. It isn't enough that you have to feed, clothe, comfort, nurse, and raise them; you've got to educate them too. Fuck that. I absolutely refuse to get involved any further. We pay taxes; why can't they educate our children? *Because they know that mothers can be coerced, manipulated, and played on like rare instruments; so finely tuned is their guilt, they can be counted on in almost every instance to hold up the pillars of any crumbling institution on an hour's notice. What else do they have to do with their time?*

"Mommy! Watch me go down!"

"I see you, Damon. That's very good."

"I didn't do it right that time. Watch again." She watches again. "That's enough watching now, Damon. You're doing fine. Mommy's going to read a little now." Everything they do has to be witnessed with an intensity and focus unequaled anywhere outside a theater. I love him, he's adorable. I'm proud of them all. They're exceptional, as all children are. But am I up to the task of being their sole audience for another fifteen years? That's an unbearably long time to sit and watch. Norma Jean opens her book and although she stares at the page in front of her, she is thinking of the scene in the kitchen the night before. The stove had broken down and she was standing there, reading an advertisement in the paper for microwave ovens, and wondering how to convert the original ingredients that were to have been (should have been, could have been, might have been) dinner into cold sandwiches, while the children fought, tripped over Tonka trucks, walked into walls, and otherwise vied with each other for her immediate attention.

Our microwave ovens have been checked and meet federal radiation standards, and leak no more than 5 milliwatts of radiation per square centimeter.

And then Martin came home, right on cue. He sensed immediately that things were rotten, as they usually are, especially between 5 and 6 P.M. His guilt began its usual dance over hot coals:

"What's the matter with you, Norma?" He always calls me Norma when there is distance to be observed. "Do you want a new microwave oven? Do you want a new kitchen floor? How about redecorating the bathroom?" Anything, anything, to get this woman running again and dinner on the table.

"I want to die, Martin."

"Don't talk that way. How about another weekend away? Just the two of us. You like that, Norma?" *Jesus, what do they want?* "Here, here's twenty dollars. Forget the budget. Go out to lunch. Get your hair done."

In the earliest versions of the Book of the Dead . . . the deceased says of himself: "I am Osiris, I have come forth as thou (that is 'being thou'), I have entered as thou . . . the gods live as I, I live as the gods, I live as 'Grain,' I grow as 'Grain.' . . . I am barley."

It is evident from these earliest sources that Osiris was identified with the *waters*, especially the inundation, with the *soil*, and with *vegetation*. This is a result of the Egyptian tendency always to think in graphic and concrete forms. The god was doubtless in Egyptian thought the imperishable principle of life wherever found, and this conception not infrequently appears in representations of him, showing him even in death as still possessed of generative power.

—James H. Breasted, op. cit., p. 23.

Back home, Norma Jean gathers up the sections of the newspaper which are lying all over the kitchen table, along with the debris left over from her talk with Rachel. She notices that her plants seem lifeless; it is suddenly clear that they are not flourishing. *It's been a long time since I've watered them. I also forgot their fish oil this month.* They hang and squat there, clustered around the window of the breakfast room: fifteen additional dependents, in varying degrees of atrophy, because of my neglect. *Had you supposed all this time that the only life form capable of reproach was man? All organic things engage in it, when the balance between their needs and your ability to sustain is disrupted. Even inanimate objects do it* ("Dust me!" —Coffee table. "Remove my stains!" —Hall carpet.)

Scott appears on the threshold, emitting Country Squire smell as he peels off his jacket and throws it on the floor. "Scott, you know the jackets go on the hooks, not on the floor. Pick it up."

"I can't! I have a sore throat!" *Should I take him in for a strep culture? Everyone else's kid has it.*

"Come on, boys, I'll read you a story until Ruth Ann gets home; then Mommy is going to go out in the garage while you watch cartoons." *The urge for solitude is becoming overwhelming.*

"What do you do out there, Mommy? Are you making toys for us to play with?"

"No Scott, I'm making . . . some jars for myself."

"What are you going to keep in them? Cookies?" *Grain, barley, my vital organs.* ("I grow as 'Grain' . . . I am barley.")

Once upon a time there lived a little old woman and a little old man. They lived in a little white house at the edge of the woods. The little old man was busy hoeing his garden. The little old woman was busy baking cookies for her grandchildren. They were very busy. They were very happy in their little house at the edge of the woods.

What is this shit? Things aren't that way any more. Grandparents do not live at the edge of the woods. There are no more edges. They live in rest homes. They do not hoe and bake; they swallow twenty-five milligrams of Thorazine with meals and play cards and lose control of their bowels and lose control of their minds and wipe the blear from their eyes and forget they have grandchildren. We do not know if they also mourn lost desires. They are unable to tell us.

> After baking the cookies, the little old woman discovered she had just enough dough left over to make one gingerbread man. "I will make a gingerbread man!" she said. "He will have raisins for eyes and white frosting for a mouth." She popped him into the oven and when he was done, she put him on the table to cool.

"Those kids are lucky; their grandma bakes them lots of cookies."

"I bake gingerbread cookies for you, too, Scott."

"You don't do it very often." True. Once a year, at Christmas. I am not a grandmother. I am not happy. I do not like to bake. Shouldn't these books be rewritten?

"Why don't we have a grandpa?"

"Because both your grandpas are dead, Scott."

"How did they die?" You expect questions about death at five. Answer them directly and honestly, lest the child get the impression that death is too frightening a subject to be discussed.

"Well, your Grandpa Harris died of a heart attack. That means" *his cholesterol level was too high? He was hypertensive? Suffered from inactivity and stress?* "that he became very sick."

"What about our other grandpa? Jimmy has two of them. Does everyone have two of them before they die?"

"Yes, honey; everyone has two."

"Well what happened to my other one? How did he die?"

> A healthy, honest, and open approach concerning loved ones, about whose death the child has a natural curiosity, can help him in his own eventual struggle to come to terms with his mortality.

—*How to Talk to Your Child About Death,* p. 13.

"Your other grandpa" *walked into his garage one morning and blew his brains out with a small gun. In the kitchen, just before it happened, he turned to your grandmother and said,* "I can't compete with the big interests; I'm just a little man." *She kept on frying the eggs because he had said things like that before, which she didn't fully understand. But she knew they would manage; they always had* "got sick and died too. It happens to everyone, but usually people just get old and then they die. But your other grandma" *who was frying the eggs when it happened* "is still alive! Remember when we visited her in Minnesota last summer? She lives with Auntie Alice and Uncle Hal" *and takes lots and lots of Thorazine* "and on Sundays they take her for drives in the country."

"Was she the one with the funny eyes?"

"Yes, she does stare into space a lot, Scott; it's because she's tired and sad. Sometimes when people grow old they become tired; so they rest, or they stare."

"Well, Grandma Harris isn't tired. She goes to the store a lot to buy us clothes. When will we see *her* again?"

"Well, she lives far away too, Scott. But maybe we can visit her next summer. I don't know, honey," she says wearily. "Mommy just doesn't know." Scott is a sensitive child; he knows the conversation has ended. He lies back on the cushions and stares at the ceiling through pale blue eyes. If there are other questions, they remain locked in his mind. They may surface in later years, they may not. Norma Jean wonders if she has stifled his curiosity, given the impression that death is too frightening to be discussed.

But before she could turn around, up jumped the little gingerbread man and started running. Out the door he ran; through the garden and out the gate and down the road he ran. "Come back! Come back!" cried the little old woman and the little old man. They tried to catch him, but he was too quick for them. On the road he met a dog. "You can't catch me!" said the gingerbread man. "I ran from the woman and I ran from the man, and I can run from you, I can! You can't catch me, I'm the gingerbread man!"

Once upon a time there was a little old woman and a little old man. They were in their mid-sixties and they lived in a redwood condominium at the edge of the golf course in Leisure City. They were very busy. They were very happy. They played golf, they swam, they joined their little old friends for bridge and barbecues. Every month the little old woman had her hair tinted by Maxine in the little beauty shop at the edge of the swimming pool. Once a year the little old man and the little old woman tell the armed guard at the gate on the edge of Leisure City, "Our grandchildren are coming to visit us! They will be driving a Plymouth Satellite four-door sedan!"

Margaret Mead Studies Her Family

. . . Dr. Mead, who has spent about 50 years studying other people's cultures, describes in great detail in the book her own childhood in a large, close, intellectual family in Pennsylvania and also her later years as a mother.

* * *

She said the book was written out of her passionate belief that what our society lacks today is the mutually beneficial closeness between grandchildren and grandparents.

* * *

"Grandparents give you a sense of how things were, how things are. . . . They've lived through change. Children need three generations to grow up with, and we've done studies that show that older people who are close to their grandchildren are very different than people who are not."

—NEW YORK TIMES SERVICE

The door slams. It startles Norma Jean.

"Ruth Ann is home!" announces Damon. That means cartoons aren't far behind. *The Little Gingerbread Man* slides to the floor.

"Ruth Ann, can I color in your Cinderella color book?"

"No! You can't!"

"I'll let you color in my Dinosaur color book if you let me color in your Cinderella color book."

"No! I said, 'No!'"

"You don't have to scream at him, Ruth Ann. Why are you so cross?"

"I'm tired! I had a hard day!" Look at that! She's picked it up from Martin! Norma Jean has a vision of all the girls in Ruth Ann's generation, coming home in twenty years, throwing their briefcases into the wall, and screaming, "I've had a hard day! I work hard! Why isn't dinner ready!" But to whom would they be addressing their grievances? The robot? The live-in from the sheltered workshop down the street? "What is it, Ruthie? Did something happen at school?"

"Those big guys came up to me on the playground and called me names."

"What did they call you?"

"Oh, you know: 'Motherfucker,' 'Shithead,' 'Fucker Shit'." *That's redundant.* "Well, what did you do?"

"I told them, 'Twinkle twinkle, little star/What you say is what you are.'"

From somewhere in the distance Norma Jean catches the strains of "We Shall Overcome," the second verse, the words, "Black and white together. . . ." It *will* work. It *is* working. They are breaking barriers every day. They will be richer because of it. They are learning to respect one another's cultures; they are cross-fertilizing, re-invigorating, and insulting the shit out of each other. Still, they are also righting grievous wrongs, making history that their children can study without shame. From somewhere in the distance comes a voice. It whispers, "'Twinkle, twinkle, little *star?* What you say is what you *are??*' Sheee-it!"

"I want to color in her color book! She said I could."

"Ruthie, wouldn't it be all right if Scott colored one picture in your book?" Anything to stop this whining. If you're going to pass the buck, pass it to the eldest.

"*Mommy!* You said that book was my very own, that it was special, that it was something I didn't have to share with *them!*" The flush that precedes the knowledge of imminent betrayal is on her cheeks.

"That's true, Ruth Ann. I did say that. Scott, I think you should color in your own book; it's special too, and just for you."

"You just *asked* her if I could! Ask her again!"

"Ruthie, I have a terrible headache; could you stand to let him do it, just this once?" ("*Do not give conflicting advice.*" —Dr. Haim Ginott. "Help me change my life!" —Giulietta Masina.)

"Go and watch cartoons, all of you. I have to feed the plants and start dinner."

"My throat is sore!"

"Well, I'll give you some aspirin now, and I'll take you to the doctor tomorrow."

"Maybe he'll die by tomorrow," offers Ruth Ann.

"Ruth Ann, when I finish with the plants and get dinner in the oven, I want to have a talk with you!"

Norma Jean sighs. Maybe she will get to the jars this afternoon, maybe not. You can't tend the dead when you're surrounded by the dying; it isn't logical. She strokes the leaves on the Boston fern, remembering the article in the paper which claimed that plants respond profusely when they are stroked, spoken to, subjected to string quartets. She remembers *her* grandmother.

Once upon a time, there lived a little old woman in a cottage in the woods. She was very busy. Every day she carried water from the well to water her garden. She had a very big garden. She tended the earth, chopped her own wood, lit her kerosene lamp in the evenings, and read Shakespeare. She had a strength and inner sufficiency that is given to those who respect their place in the order of things, but who also broadcast their seed wider and more vigorously than nature requires.

Her name was Matilda; everyone called her Mattie. Her cottage was on an island in the Canadian wilderness. It was there, in mid-life, that she terminated her marriage to man and embarked on her partnership with nature. And it was there she developed forbearance. It's a hard thing to develop in these conditions. Here, I dream of extending boundaries, shaping new forms. But I can't even stem the tides or control the surfeit of chaos. Here, forbearance turns to impotent rage; I am not sure just how this happens, but I think it has something to do with an excess of stimuli, too many variables. I have not given up. It's just that at this moment the best I can do is forestall disintegration; I cannot manage fertile risks. The plants, as you see, illustrate this point.

Norma Jean reaches into the cupboard for the fish emulsion, stands over the sink mixing it with water. She is breathing hard. She drops the spoon. *My babies need fish oil! All my babies are failing to thrive!* She pours the fish oil, saturates them with it. She puts a little Albinoni on the turntable to aid their digestion.

The cats have smelled the fish oil. They are all lined up in a row on the kitchen floor, jaws parted and fuzzy tongues ready. Norma Jean goes to the cupboard where the cat food is kept. Before she can open the can, Fletcher has jumped on the counter. She swings her arm, sending him spinning to the floor. She empties the contents of the can into the dish and sets it down. Why am I standing here feeding these cats? Once you get yourself whipped up shoveling it into everyone and everything, it's hard to stop. She is distracted by a grotesque sound. The cats are all hunched over the dish: masticating, hissing and growling at each other. Fletcher has attacked Snow White and taken over the food. Norma Jean can't just walk away and let them work it out. She wants to kill them all, for their greed, for their uncontrollable appetites, for their insatiable demands. She hears herself screaming. She screams so loudly her throat feels raw. "You're disgusting! You're *animals, animals!* All three of you!" They blink a few times, then continue hissing, growling, swallowing. She of course realizes that they are, in fact, animals. That is why she is having hysterics now over the sink.

"Mom, when will dinner be ready? We're starving." Norma Jean does not reply. Eat eat eat, in and out, in and out. What good does it do anyone? You can't read it, you can't exhibit it, it does not endure. She considers the thousands of meals she has prepared over the years with unfailing excellence and artistry. Where are they now? Clogging someone's storm drain, gone to feed the fishes, building strong bodies twelve mysterious ways. She begins to prepare a new one, the ingredients spread on the counter as from a cornucopia, flowing through her hands, enduring the knife, undergoing the ancient rite of death and transfiguration: dying, changing shape, in order to sustain new forms. She brings them together in the casserole and places them in the oven where they will perform their obedient alchemy at 350 degrees while she has her talk with Ruth Ann.

She pours herself a glass of wine and takes a long swallow before guiding Ruth Ann into the living room for the discussion; the boys are wrapped around the TV watching "Secret Squirrel."

"It seems that you're angry at me. Do you think you could tell me what makes you angry, instead of saying things like you did about Scott dying?" She talks like that because she's seen how other mothers talk in Dr. Ginott's column. Your task is to communicate to your child that you are displeased with her present behavior, while at the same time being scrupulous not to insult her dignity. At the end of each column it is stated that the anecdotes are meant as examples, and are not to be taken as precise advice. But it's clear they are not general; they are direct quotes from all those other mothers out there who say crisp, firm, gentle, dignity-preserving things to their children.

"Well," Ruth Ann pauses for effect. She is thrown by my sudden understanding, but is not so dull as to be unable to exploit it. We are having a Talk; I am hers. She twists a strand of hair around her finger, the way she's seen the third graders do. She speaks:

"I'm angry at you—first of all—because you won't let us watch 'Hogan's Heroes'; second, you aren't clever, like Jessica's mother: you can't sew. Third"—she enjoys counting: ABC, 123, is just beginning to see its application to everyday matters—"you don't buy us Ding-Dongs." She's hot now; I wait patiently. Dr. Ginott would be proud. "And you're the only mother who doesn't give candy in the lunches."

"And you're the only child in your class without rotten teeth," I shout. I can't help it. I couldn't let her win that one. Oh Dr. Ginott! God damn it. I'm not giving in on the candy in the lunches. "And it sounds as though you want a perfect mother," I add. Fuck them all.

"Well, I do."

"There aren't any," I say, knowing full well there are, millions of them, all over the place; you can feel it when you're surrounded by perfection. Even your children pick it up eventually if they're reasonably bright.

"Oh, there are. Cheryl's mother is perfect." As luck would have it, she has picked a mother I *know*. My ship has come in. I saw her hit her child in front of the store just last week, and not a smack, but blows. With the exquisite confidence that has eluded me all my life, I answer my Budding Beauty (Pre-Teen Products, $3.95 set of three: soap, cologne, nail brush), "Cheryl's mother isn't perfect, darling; I happen to know." It is said with enormous authority. It crushes her, for the moment. She sets the table with respect. Of course it won't last, but you can build on it. Norma Jean knows these talks will go on with each of the children, until they no longer live at home, and will require more of her than Dr. Ginott can provide.

"Just set for four; Daddy has a meeting tonight."

Sitting down, Norma Jean thinks about how the dinner conversation always turns to impossible subjects whenever Martin is away. It is as though the children sense, with unfailing accuracy, that these are the times to go for the jugular. Tonight is no exception.

"Why do plants come back after they die and people don't?" —Scott.

"Do you believe in God, Mom?" —Ruth Ann.

"If you don't believe in God, how do you think the world was made? Who put the moon there?" —Ruth Ann.

"Why does my bottom itch all the time?" —Damon.

"I can answer that for you, Damon." At last, a simple, disgusting question that I am fully capable of answering. "Your bottom itches because we all have pinworms." There is silence for a moment, while they all consider this information, jaws working silently on mouths full of casserole. *Gone to feed the pinworms.*

"Don't you remember, Damon," offers Ruth Ann, "the last time we all had itchy bottoms and we went to Dr. Anderson and got that yucky red medicine that looks just like blood?"

"I don't want the blood medicine! Do I have to have the blood medicine, Mommy?" Damon screams.

"If you want your bottom to stop itching." Norma Jean fights the memory: Dr. Anderson's office, all of them jumping and scratching. "Yes, pinworms are very common. If you have children, and if they play with other children, it's hard to avoid them. Especially in summer."

"Well, we all took the medication last year, and now they're back again. How do you get rid of the eggs?"

"You can't. Unless you want to boil all your bedding and stop biting your nails. Do you bite your nails?"

"Yes I bite my nails."

"And, as you know, the children are always scratching their behinds, then they offer each other cookies with the same hand. You can't fight it. Might as well learn to live with it."

"Live with it?" *Am I going to have pinworms the rest of my life?*

"You see, Mrs. Harris, the larvae are everywhere, even on the chandeliers." *We don't have chandeliers.*

"Isn't there a period of time when they could be expected to . . . dry up? Cease to be viable?"

Anderson: "Well, I can't say for certain that pinworm larvae found in Egyptian tombs would still be viable, but . . ." Why did he say that? Does he know something, or is he just being clever? Do you suppose . . . Hatshepsut with pinworms? Akhenaten? Nefertiti? Impossible. On the other hand, it *is* generally true that nothing of any magnitude is accomplished without some irritant serving as the motivating force. It's something to look into, next time I'm at the library.

"My throat hurts!"

"I have a stomach ache!"

"My bottom itches!"

Norma Jean stares out the window. Well, this is it, she thinks, as she watches the sun setting over Coronado Avenue. This is the little home in suburbia, the little family with two boys for you and one girl for me. There stands Mr. Turner, blowing smoke out of his mouth, standing in the light of the setting sun, watching his dog crap on the neighbor's lawn. Basketball hoops shine like copper, all the way down the block. The dog is straining hard. Mr. Turner blows another mouthful of smoke into the sunset; he has the time. No hurry, he says to the little dog. No hurry at all.

"It's time for bed. Scott, here is some more aspirin. We'll have your throat looked at tomorrow. Ruth Ann, go take a warm bath, you'll be all right. Damon, stop scratching; we'll get some medicine for you when we take Scott for his throat." Damon starts to climb down from his chair, misses the rung, knocks his milk over and falls on his head. Norma Jean wipes the milk out of his hair with a napkin, drops a section of the newspaper on the floor to soak up the puddle which has formed there. She hasn't finished reading it yet, but doesn't care.

After the children are in bed she returns to the kitchen for coffee and leans against the stove, waiting for the water to boil. Everyone is coming down with something; everyone is sick and needing my care. They are dropping like flies. Everything depends on me. She bends down to gather up the soaking newspaper. She glances at it one last time before throwing it away.

Your Horoscope

Leo. There are pressures on you now but you can relieve them if you act positively. Get rid of that problem in your home.

How can you do that to your own son?

Norma Jean turns out the lights. She looks longingly out the window at the garage. Too late. Too tired. The dead can wait. They've had centuries of practice. Slowly she climbs the stairs; her eyes are a little out of focus, her muscles ache. She runs the hottest bath she can stand, soaks in it up to her neck until she feels dizzy and about to pass out. And as she slides exhausted between cool sheets, she sees the full moon as it appears on the eastern horizon. Does that explain why I am feeling crazier and crazier? Whenever the connection is mentioned, she fails to be amused. If it can affect tides, why not human emotions?

A CRIMINAL FAMILY'S PORTRAIT

The "Full Moon" Theory

Two members of a family suspected of killing as many as 22 persons—seven of them in the light of the full moon— were held in Texas and Colorado yesterday.

* * *

The son's wife, Ginger, told her interrogators that she never believed harboring a criminal—her husband—was a crime.

"I love my husband very much and it never occurred to do anything other than to stay with him. . . . I guess that staying with him and doing what my husband told me to do was born and raised into me because I never really thought that there was really anything else for me to do." She has four children. The last one was born in jail.

The elder woman gave police a written statement concerning her involvement in the family's homicidal spree:

"I am guilty of staying with my husban while he cometed roberys because I den't have anywhere else to go. . . . It may sound crazy but I love him very much.

The night moves in her veins like a dark river. She tries to concentrate on tomorrow's demands, before sleep obscures

86

them. Is my appointment with Arndt tomorrow? No, no, that's three days away. Why does the time seem to drag by so slowly, when underneath I know it's passing with the speed of light? My mind is sluggish and doesn't trust itself. It is full of holes where vital fluids seep at night.

She thinks of Anubis, the Egyptian god of the necropolis, the jackal whose role was to protect the dead. His case is an excellent illustration of the manner in which established orders—in this case, religious—can convert a liability into an asset. The jackal, traditional eater of dead flesh, now elevated to the position of one who proudly eats the evil spirits before they help themselves to his former prey. It is not unlike enlisting the services of a master criminal to solve a major crime. It all amounts to the same thing; the basic drives are in no way altered. They are merely channeled by someone who has chosen to assume responsibility and establish order, in the interests of preserving civilization.

> One of the mother's principal roles in the early years is to channel the child's aggressive instincts into acceptable and constructive outlets. To the extent that the child is able to accomplish this, he becomes a willing ally on the side of order and control. His wishes to spoil, devour, and destroy gradually give way to a wish to please and a desire to master his own impulses.
>
> —*Handbook of Infant Care*, p. 144.

It always sounds good on paper; it's when you're actually required to do it that things break down. It isn't possible to list the ways in which the conscience holds itself accountable and renders judgment.

> With the deceased and his wife looking on, the funeral god Anubis weighs the heart of the scribe Ani, in an illustration from a papyrus Book of the Dead found in a New Kingdom tomb. The ceremony took place before the throne of Osiris, in the Hall of Double Justice, while a fierce hybrid monster called the Devourer waited nearby, ready to consume the dead man's heart if it failed to balance with a feather (symbolizing truth) placed on the other scale-pan.
> "Behold me—I have come to you without sin, without guilt, without evil. . . . I have given bread to the hungry, water to the thirsty, clothing to the naked. . . . Rescue me; protect

me. . . ." Pleading for eternal life in the judgment hall of Osiris, the dead stood trembling before the forty-two frightful gods who aided the king of the afterlife in the weighing of souls.

—Leonard Cottrell, *Lost Worlds*, pp. 62–63.

Dear Osiris: Just a note to say I am not without sin, guilt, or evil. But with respect to the feeding and sustenance, I've been giving it all I've got, and they're still not satisfied! Regarding same, I have this to say on my own behalf: tending the living is full of risks; they can eat you alive. Rescue me; protect me. . . .

7

No! Stop! Don't *seal* it! I'M NOT DEAD YET!

"Jeanie? What's the matter? Wake up." Norma Jean sits up in bed, holding her head in her hands. Martin rubs the back of her neck. "You were screaming in your sleep."

She whispers; the dream is still sliding down the bedroom walls and adhering to her skin. Her breathing is rapid, as though trying to avoid suffocation.

"I was in a tomb; and suddenly they started sealing it up. All the cracks of light vanished. I knew if I didn't scream they wouldn't realize I was still alive! The light just kept disappearing." She starts to cry, long hysterical sobs.

"Don't cry. It's all right. It was just a dream." She reaches over to the bedside table and gropes in the dark for a Kleenex.

"Martin, I've just got to change my life. Something's got to give. I can't stand it any longer. I'm losing my mind."

"Kids give you a hard day?" She starts to laugh. The laughter accelerates until she is hysterical again. "It's not that *simple!* What I mean is that I have nothing left for *me* by the end of the day. I have no part of my life that I can claim as my own. Everything is for *others.* I love you. I love the children. I feel torn apart. I am beginning to hate you all, hate this house, hate myself." Martin sighs. It's soft, but sighs like that have a way of permeating the curtains and staying there for weeks. Now that the worst is clearly over, he realizes that he's wide awake at two in the morning and his mind will be shot for the rest of the day. *What does she want from me? She's got everything she's always wanted: a beautiful house, three beautiful children, her garden, me; I don't question her budget, within limits . . . her own car, those fucking jars. I know the children can be wearing, but Jesus, she can make arrangements, get out when she wants.*

"Get a sitter! Go out to lunch! Go out in the garage and pot your fucking head off! Jesus Christ, Norma, I'm not an unreasonable man. No one says you have to be trapped here. All I ask is a little peace. A quiet dinner when I get home, instead of all that screaming and wailing. A man works hard; he wants a little peace in his own home. Do what you have to do. Do what you want . . . within reason. You have my permission."

"*Permission!* What am I, your child? Your slave?"

"All right, all right, my *cooperation* then. You have my cooperation. I want what's best for you, Jeanie. I want what's best for both of us, all of us." He rolls over, stroking her back with his free arm. "Can we get some sleep now? Tomorrow's another day. Everything will be all right if you just stop overreacting to everything, demanding so much of yourself. Why don't you get a sitter tomorrow, go have lunch in the city with Rachel?"

"I don't WANT to have lunch with Rachel! I want to go to the library and not watch the clock! I want to go back to school!" *I want to go away for a year! Forever.* "I can't get a sitter tomorrow. I have to take Scott to the doctor for a strep culture, and Damon for a pinworm smear, and Ruth Ann to Toyland to get a birthday present for her friend Jennifer!"

"Well, do it the next day then! Leave me alone."

"All right, all right. I'll do it the next day. Will you support me, help me out more with the children, give me more breathing space? So I won't have to beg for every crumb? Will you pick up your socks?"

"Yes, yes, dear God, I'll *support* you" *what the hell does she think I've been doing for ten years?* "I'll help out. What do my socks have to do with it? Listen, Norma. I'm all for your liberation. Everyone has a right to his own life. Just don't push me too far."

"Yes, everyone does have a right to *his* own life; what about me?"

"It's two in the morning, and I'm not going to listen to polemics. I'm going to sleep."

Martin goes to sleep. Norma Jean clocks it: twenty seconds. How can anyone who claims to be human fall asleep so quickly, especially in a crisis? Deep, prolonged snores emanate from his quiescent form, swaddled in layers of covers, not unlike a mummy. When did the snoring start? Was it a year ago? Two?

She can't sleep; this time it has nothing to do with the snoring. Leaning on one elbow, she bends over Martin, studying his face by the moon's light. My man, mate, partner. The fact that we have adhered for ten years has to count for something; there is a closeness that runs between us like an underground river. When it surfaces, we acknowledge it, take pleasure in it, sometimes even stand in awe of it. When it resumes its subterranean course, we sometimes doubt its existence. So far, it has always reappeared in time to avert absolute disbelief. She wonders if it will continue this way, if it is one of those things you can count on as a natural constant. It could just dry up. Nature is unpredictable, life is full of surprises. *Will it survive the changes*? How much elasticity do we still retain? His face in sleep: a stone, issuing pharaonic silence. *What planets stir in the far fields of your mind?*

Martin. The years of work to insure a future with security, without want. Vowing, "I will control it; it will never control me." Failing. I think ours was the last generation to have been presented that simple multiple choice: sink or swim. How does it happen that you always see the traps that ensnare others, then fall into them yourself? ("Jesus, her kids are obnoxious; mine will never be like that, because I'm creative, imaginative, resilient." —Norma Jean Harris, 1962. "You don't have to worry, honey; I'm a simple man. We're not extravagant people, we have basic values. Nothing can change that." —Martin Harris, 1963.) And now, in addition to the mortgage and taxes and car payments and food and clothing and furniture and medical bills and nursery schools and corrective shoes and baby-sitters and life insurance and car insurance and fire and theft insurance and home repairs, there is therapy for me, orthodontia for her, hysterectomies for the cats. I have deliberately left out those things whose effects we haven't yet felt, but anticipate. Martin, did you think you were going to get something out of this life for yourself? When did you give up the idea? At which crisis was it clear that it was all over? Or was it the crises at all? More likely it was that undramatic accumulation of small things which, extended over time, has a remarkable ability to promote an attitude of irreversible defeat, especially around the eyes. They say the family is dying. What lousy timing, just when we're right in the middle of it.

IS THE FAMILY REALLY DYING?

Q. What . . . are the biggest threats to family life today?

A. "Our greatest concern springs from the fantastic speed-up in technological changes and the struggle of families to adapt to them.

"The dependence on the family unit for economic security has lessened. The need of industry for high family mobility leads to the breaking of ties with the extended family, creates a conflict of interest between spouses over moving, and increases the demands on the family as a major source of intensive, intimate relationships."

Q. Is the Women's Liberation Movement a source of family change?

A. "No question about it. . . . Certainly women should have the freedom to choose a life-style other than marriage without being termed a failure by society. Certainly men should devote more time to sharing responsibility for rearing children.

* * *

But when you add all of these changes together, the crux of the matter seems to be that such a rapid tempo leads to fear of permanency. . . .   —UNITED PRESS

Martin rolls over, sighs. The move has cost him the section of blanket covering his shoulder and arm. Norma Jean leans over, replaces it; she is slow to withdraw her hand. The phrase "a good catch" passes through her mind. That's how a reasonably attentive, reasonably attractive, and reasonably solvent man was known in the late fifties. You were considered lucky if you got one. She recalls the term with repugnance, all its associations of bait, nets, entrapment, whose ultimate aim is to devour. No wonder so many men ran the other way; it was equally insulting to both sexes—the woman, because it was humiliating to think of yourself as having to employ devices in order to receive love; the man, because it reduced him to an object of prey: his most highly developed sense, suspicion; his most highly developed motor skill, avoidance. Was there still a sense of entrapment? Did it derive from the beginning, or is it something we are all bound to feel with time? She thinks of Rachel's comment about romance, Paul's fear that it was gone, his demanding it back. You don't "get" romance back; it is something which, by definition, belongs at beginnings—where there is the time for possibilities and illusions. Why does it all seem so long ago? And yet, it would be inaccurate to say it is all gone. Maybe for some; not for us. Here is proof. It happened only two years ago.

Damon had croup. We had theater tickets. "I don't think we should leave him with croup." "He'll be all right; turn up the humidifier." The baby-sitter came late. "Why can't she ever get here on time? We'll have to stand the whole first act." The evening began with the usual race against time, disaster, and death. "Look at that son of a bitch! Did you see that, cut right in front of me!" "Martin, the whole world's crazy. Relax, accept it, and drive defensively; it will increase our chances."

And finally we pulled into the underground garage, with ten minutes to spare. Downward we circled, 2nd Level, 3rd Level, 4th Level, into the pits of the earth. Overhead the fluorescent lighting cast its harsh, eye-watering glare over the entire 4th Level, which was almost empty, except for a few randomly scattered cars. Martin became playful: pulling into a slot, hesitating as though to park, then backing out, cruising around, trying out another. I started to laugh; it had seemed so long since he had done anything like this. I choked for the briefest second, recalling how often things had been this way in the beginning, realizing that this feeling of spontaneity seemed slightly foreign now, as though belonging to another time and place, as though when one reaches a certain calendar age it becomes suddenly inappropriate.

Then, standing next to the car, bathed in fluorescent light, while Martin locked up, listening to the Muzak being piped down on us from the ceiling, echoing through the garage, descending in a fine spray from the little speakers next to the vents that suck out the gas fumes, feeling like a figure in Kafka's world, invisible, devoid of human characteristics, about to be swallowed up by miles of concrete corridor, standing there as though in a great grey hall, and Martin coming up softly behind me, taking me in his arms, and starting to dance. I resisted (What are you *doing?* Are you crazy? Everyone will see us.), then yielded, they were playing our song, Martin whispered, "If you could see yourself in this light: you face is chalk white; your lips are purple. You are beautiful, beautiful. I love you," around and around we danced, through stop signs, in and out among stone pillars that supported three floors of automobiles, to the strains of "Fascination," circling slowly toward the Up elevator, completely alone, no witnesses, the whole 4th Level our ballroom; filled with a strange warmth, dissolving, reconnecting, fixed in electronic tableau, fused in an alien configuration of post-industrial love.

Norma Jean lies absolutely still in the blue white of the moon. Why does it always seem that if I stare long enough at the moon I court losing my mind? And how is it that this phenomenon has its counterpart in my everyday life? If I lose myself in pursuit of something *out there*, I run the risk of losing, abdicating, what I have *in here*, those realities which render secure, which comfort and sustain: my home, my family, all my enclosures. Why is it both experiences seem only to apply if you are a woman?

I am the moon; the moon is mine. It doesn't matter that everyone else may have made the same claim at one time or another. The relationship borne to it is always inner and individual, and therefore unique. Women may claim special affinity by right of folklore, mythology, cycles; man, from earliest times, regarded the moon as feminine. (When you can't fathom all that mystery at close range, look to the heavenly body that most resembles it from a distance.) Woman, with her bodily ebb and flow, her cycles, her moods, her dark side, her luminosity, her remoteness, her eclipses. The moon had always symbolized mystery. And now? Norma Jean thinks of the first moon shot: of the peculiar innocence, the energy, the sense of amazement with which Martin had bounded up the steps after work, saying, "Could we eat in

94

the family room tonight? I want to see a little of the moon, if it's on."

And I, defensive, outraged that *my* mystery was being walked on, jumped on, charted, excavated, videotaped, electronically relayed to any idiot capable of flipping a switch and interpreting data. I, saying, "If you're interested in really seeing the moon, go outside and look up." And Martin replying, "What's the matter with you? You crazy or something?"

lu.na.cy (lōō′nə sē), n., *pl.*=**cies.** 1. intermittent insanity, formerly believed to be related to phases of the moon. . . .
> —*Random House Dictionary of the English Language*, p. 853. Copyright © Random House, Inc., 1966, 1967.

And my answering, "The moon is whatever comes in your mind while you're looking at it. That's the only real way to 'see' it. The moon develops the imagination, as chemicals develop photographic images. The only mystery worth exploration lies in its effects on us."

"Will you lay *off*? Can't a man have a little peace in his own home? Your contempt for science is appalling. Your mind is straight out of the Middle Ages." ("Opposites attract." —Anon.)

"Your worship of technology is disgusting; the moon never existed for you, until they landed on it. It's the most grandiose display of chauvinistic, jingoistic narcissism in history."

"And if you start on 'If they took that money and spent it here on earth, we wouldn't be in the mess we're in today' I'm going to hit you in the mouth. This is *history*. Now shut up and let me watch it. Sit down and watch it yourself; you might learn something. Hey, kids! You wanna see the men on the moon? Jesus Christ, this is just amazing. I can't believe it. Ruthie! Come here. Look, *man* is on the *moon!*"

"I know, Dad. I saw it at school."

"Well come here and look again. This has never happened before."

"I just told you, Daddy; it happened once already today. Is that why we're eating in the TV room?" Martin's growing desperation: won't anyone share this momentous event with him? Surrounded by medieval lunatics and blasé ignoramuses, who leave him in cruel isolation, alone with his excitement, he has no one with whom his passion can connect. He stared at that screen with such intensity, it was as though he had been waiting there throughout time for all that space, secrecy, darkness, to be illuminated and finally explained. I couldn't help but think of the parallel with woman's darkness, the things that take place in inner spaces. And man's perpetual amazement and fascination; and his horror and wonder and fear of it. Phallic rocket, speeding toward round moon, it was all one and the same, only this time enacted on the most enormous scale imaginable. MAN ON MOON! AMERICA SCORES ULTIMATE FUCK! The image itself had absolute logic, even beauty, as well as evolutional inevitability. What I don't accept is that it was more like rape than love. But then the entire history of exploration was like that. And in the sense that conquest has been a logical consequence of exploration, this rape lacked neither historical precedent nor logic. We rape our own planet, why not the moon? Littered now with urine bags, Dixie cups, space-ship droppings. What did I have to say about it? Who asked me if I minded?

So you see why it is absolutely necessary to divorce myself from their methods. I don't deny the importance of the discoveries, their impact on the future; but the methods have absolutely nothing to do with inner realities. For this reason, I have developed a method of my own: a method of coping, denying their reality and reinforcing my own. It involves going back in time, and I realize that is un-American, anti-progress, and regressive, but I pass it on anyway. I'm skilled in going back in time; it's the only faculty I've kept up in the past ten years. I don't count things like cooking and fighting for your life; those are conditioned reflexes. Going back in time is a condition of the mind, an emotional state, an act of will, applied to current situations as a defensive maneuver, and can be considered adaptive. It protects the individual from overstimulation, future shock, disintegration, and other such hazards of our age. It is not unique to me, although I have been doing it for some time. Some of our youth engage in it (forming communes in an attempt to reclaim the extended family; going "back to the land"; eating organic; dressing funny). I have refined it to suit my own needs and present obligations. As with all techniques involving the mind and heart, it is most effective if used only when required. Do it too often, apply it to too wide a range of conditions, and you'll cripple yourself altogether for modern life.

Looking at the moon now, I put myself in a trance, not unlike Cabiria's during the magic show. Like her, I reclaim my innocence: I do not know that man has been on the moon. I have erased all traces of that knowledge. I reverse time. It never happened. I do not know that the cost of one discarded piece of equipment from the lunar module equals the entire national budget of the poverty program for one year. I absolutely do not permit myself to pursue this line of association to its inevitable conclusion involving the calculation of: how many kidney machines? how much urban renewal, child care, low-cost housing; how many free clinics, community mental health facilities, educational programs, armed guards in the girls' bathroom at Ruth Ann's school. The moon has not changed in any way, it continues to affect me as before, complementing and reinforcing my moods—not moment by moment—but gradually, in the natural rhythm of things. That which sustained lost civilizations now sustains me.

> The identification of the moon with the power which produces vegetation on the earth is common among many peoples, as Mr. J. G. Frazer* has shown, and we should naturally expect Osiris at some time or other in the period of his cult to be considered a moon-god.

* * *

> . . . at one period Osiris was identified with the moon. . . . Osiris was regarded as the Power of the moon, which produced the Nile-flood and therefore all the fertility in Egypt.
>
> —E. A. Wallis Budge, op. cit., pp. 384–85.

It is my point of focus, my reference, my cosmic model: filling the eastern sky, its light making craters in the folds of the blankets.

Their two forms stand out with a special intensity. Norma Jean begins to think of the varieties of shape and form, and is overwhelmed. I want to go deeper into art, deeper into the stars,

* *Golden Bough*, Vol II. p. 154 ff.

deeper into Egypt. But I am pulled in so many directions by the needs of others. It will take everything I have to reconcile it, but it's a risk that has to be taken; the living dead enjoy no rights in either world. ("Rommel Drives on Deep Into Egypt." —Richard Brautigan.) That was O.K. for Rommel, what did he care if his son wet his bed? She closes her eyes. Shapes begin to swim in her mind with the plasticity of amoebas, then coalesce. Their colors and textures are palpable. *If I had the time, if I had the materials,* her hands lie heavily on the covers, completely disconnected to the ideas that are forming which require their cooperation. She falls asleep with the knowledge that you may be, in the early stages of something new, imprecise; what matters is that you recognize yourself as having fixed your course.

8

Sitting in the pediatrician's waiting room, Norma Jean scans the morning headlines.

A BULLET IN AN UNBORN BABY

KIDS FIND A BODY
IN THE FREEZER

WIFE SHOOTS LOVERS
IN THE TUB

"Mrs. Harris? What are you in for today?" The nurse is standing in the doorway, with her appointment clipboard resting on her hip. She cradles it like a baby.

"To get a strep culture on Scott, and to have Damon wormed." The nurse gives me a look as the children go into the examining room. It's a toss-up where I spend the greater part of my time, at the vet with the cats or here with the children. Procedures, procedures, life requires constant effort to stave off invasions, large and small.

Checking the doctor off her list, Norma Jean loads the children into the car and heads for the nursery. "We're going to pick up some plants and then we'll get Ruth Ann from school and go to the toy store for the birthday present. You can *smell* at the nursery but you can't *pick*; you can *look* at the toy store, but we're just going to get Ruth Ann's present. We are *not* buying cars for you."

At the nursery the boys run up and down the rows of plants, bending and sniffing. Norma Jean stands in the rose section, wistfully examining the bushes, remembering Mattie. Absolutely out. Aphids, bone meal, pruning. Some experiences should be saved for old age; roses will be mine. Their tags flap in the wind. She reaches for one to check the price.

ASEXUAL REPRODUCTION OF THIS PATENTED
PLANT WITHOUT A LICENSE IS PROHIBITED

The rain begins to fall just as they leave the nursery; by the time they pull up in front of the school it is running in the gutters like rivers. Ruth Ann climbs in the car, her hair streaming.

"Have you decided what you're going to get for Jennifer?" The windshield wipers flap from left to right; the windows are beginning to steam up. There is silence, as Scott and Damon busy themselves drawing finger pictures on the steam. Ruth Ann is not thinking; she has already made up her mind. She is attempting to sweat Norma Jean out. She knows that while a mother has the power—and in some cases, the right—to refuse to purchase a Barbie doll for her own child, she is powerless to interfere with her child's choice of a toy for a friend's birthday. She knows this because I have taught it to her: You may choose what you want for your friends' presents, if it falls within the amount allowed; you may select the clothes you wear each day: it's your body; you may wear your hair any way you wish: it's your hair; you may spend your nickel on any kind of candy, gum, peanuts, or other crap of your own choosing: it's your nickel, your stomach. This exercise is known as Developing Responsibility. Dr. Ginott would probably also describe it as enhancing the child's sense of self-worth, body image, and decision making through autonomous choice. It is going to force me to purchase a toy I abhor. There is absolutely no chance that they will be out of stock.

New! Malibu Barbie! Twist N' Turn Waist!
Easy To Pose!
Malibu Ken! Golden Tan! Blonde Hair!

Ruth Ann wastes no time, marches right over to the Barbie section, which takes up a third of the store. She is momentarily thrown by the choices: Barbie or Ken? Francie or Skipper? The skating costume or the prom outfit? Regular Barbie, or Malibu? She takes her time, lifts each little cellophane box up and examines it carefully. Jennifer may get the doll, but Ruth Ann has every intention of appropriating it at the first opportunity.

"Mom! Come and look at this! Couldn't I have a Scream'N Demon motorcycle, *please?*" Scott is holding up two different models, the Lunatic Fringe *vs.* the Dirty Devil.

"Scott, I told you . . ."

"Mommy! Can I have the Batmobile?"

"No, Damon." No. No. No.

DIE-CAST SCALE MODEL WITH
OPERATING ROCKET TUBES.
CHAIN SLASHER BLADE AND TURBINE JET EXHAUST.

Nearby is a water machine gun (the Rodfather). Now Scott begins to slide down the aisle to the male doll section, frantically trying to decide with whom he wants to identify so he can make his demands early, before we have to leave: Action Jackson? G.I. Joe? Big Jim? Big Jack? or Big Josh? All dressed up and ready to kill. Or fell trees. Or score (baskets). Do toy manufacturers produce toys that accurately reflect what we do? Or do they create models that reflect their own dreams of what we should be? Norma Jean thinks of the occupations of the fathers of Scott's friends. Where are the insurance salesman dolls? (Big Tony); the lawyer dolls? (Big Marvin); the teacher dolls? (Big Andrew). These dolls are television models—visible replicas of what the children see men doing in programs. They bear no resemblance to what their own fathers actually do, or what they themselves will be doing years from now. They are electronic images of explorations and conquests, past and present (spacemen; cowboys; lumberjacks; grenade-throwers). There isn't a thinker among them.

"Ruth Ann, have you made a decision yet? We've got to go soon." She is standing there holding Barbie (plain, old, original Barbie; why isn't her hair beginning to grey, her breasts sag, her skin wrinkle?), longing, longing. Can she really want it? Or have I created an artificial desire by my refusal to honor progress?

"Why won't you let *me* have her?"

"It's out of the question, Ruth Ann." Her tragic sigh circulates the toy store; all the clerks are alerted. Finally she speaks: "Why did I have to come out of *your* stomach?"

We have made it to the counter and I am paying the clerk for one plain original Barbie. Why am I experiencing this feeling of pride and relief that she did not choose the Malibu model? Because, by this time, plain old original Barbie has come to represent the past, stand for tradition. We progress that fast.

Driving home in the rain, Damon begins to disintegrate. "I wanted the Batmobile! I wanted it so much! I can't stand it, I can't stand it!" Norma Jean brings the car to a stop at a red light, reciting with patience and firmness all the reasons why the Batmobile was foregone: we cannot buy every toy we see; you cannot have everything you want. Someday, when you grow up, you will thank me for attempting to curb your impulses and your greed. You will thank me because you will have grown into a civilized, self-actualizing adult who can cope with deferred gratification.

YOUTH, 15, ADMITS SLAYING MOTHER

". . . never let me have . . . never understood. . . . When I was 3½ refused to buy me a Batmobile . . ." was quoted by police.

Damon is screaming, wailing, crying, thrashing about in the back. The windshield wipers provide one split second of clear vision, then everything is blurred again by masses of water. If I left my foot on the accelerator we would blast through barriers of time and space, soar for one brief instant, before disappearing altogether in a blinding transformation of matter into nonmatter. She gropes for the radio switch ("Music has charms to soothe a savage breast." —William Congreve.) And precisely because there is no possibility of Albinoni, there is the Adagio in G Minor (". . . the saddest piece of music ever written by mortal man." —Donald Barthelme) filling up the car, mingling with the steam, the screams, the absolute hopelessness. Can you beat your child to the Albinoni Adagio in G Minor? ("Anything is possible." —Anon.)

Turning off Coronado Avenue, Norma Jean weaves down the tree-lined streets, passing the Folletts' house. There is a large moving van backed up against the driveway. Marilyn has moved to New York with her lover. Now Ted will see the children one week at Christmas, and summer vacations. Through the spattered windshield she notes the fallen petals under the tulip tree; they have dropped onto the lawn in a circle slightly wider than the tree itself. She feels shock as she thinks of the quickness with which families dissolve, friends scatter. One minute it is autumn and you're sitting together at a dinner party, trying through conversation to connect, occasionally succeeding; and the next thing you know it is spring and the tulip tree is shedding its skin beside the house where they once lived, and another family is preparing to move in and make the necessary changes in landscape and interiors which will redefine the house as theirs.

Pulling into her own driveway, she alerts the children to the fact that she has had it for the day: "I'm going to work in the garage until dinner, and I want you to play quietly or watch cartoons." She reaches into the mailbox and withdraws the mail. Bills bills bills, and an envelope with a Spirit of Christ return address. Inside, Damon crumples to the floor, grappling with the shimmering image of the Batmobile, which has implanted itself simultaneously in his brain and heart. "I wanted it so badly! I hate you! I'm going to eat you up!" He is thrashing and kicking. When that fails to get results, he begins to throw things—first his jacket and shoes—then, warming to the sense of release, he reaches for the books in the bookcase. Through the air sails *The Dialogues of Plato*, Vol. 1 ("Crito: 'I have often told you, Socrates, that I am in a constant difficulty about my two sons. What am I to do with them?'"). Into the lamp flies *The Tempest* ("Good wombs have borne bad sons." —Miranda). This is it, you little bastard; throwing Mattie's books is going too far. Norma Jean raises her hand and connects with Damon's behind. Shrieks from the old-fashioned rite fill the house.

The Aries Child

. . . As he grows older and stronger . . . your Aries child will begin to show a pattern of temper. You'll notice that he or she can be most unreasonable when thwarted. . . .

* * *

(I'm assuming you don't have more than one Aries offspring. The planets don't do that to parents very often.)

—Linda Goodman's *Sun Signs*, © 1968 by Linda Goodman, Taplinger Publishing Co., Inc., 1968; George G. Harrop & Co. Ltd, London; p. 30-31, Bantam Books edition.

"Damon, I've *had* it with you. I have been *patient* (whack!) and *firm* (whack!) and under*standing* (whack!). I've been listening to your whining (whack!) for a solid hour, and I'm not going to put up with any more." Damon lies on the floor gasping and weeping. BATTERED CHILD SYNDROME ON INCREASE. "Spanking is brutalizing," or words to that effect —Bruno Bettelheim; "Spanking only serves to relieve the parent's anger; it does not encourage trust and cooperation," or words to that effect —Benjamin Spock; "Spanking is uncreative," or words to that effect —Haim Ginott. Norma Jean feels the usual desperation borne of guilt.

Graphoanalyst Finds
CHILDHOOD'S SCARS SHOW UP
IN STROKES OF YOUR HANDWRITING

Frank Budd's use of handwriting analysis to recognize personality traits developed in early childhood has convinced him corporal punishment of children is wrong.

* * *

"If you're going to teach children that a physical reaction, to anticipate threats, is not the way to deal with the problems that arise in adulthood, you have to start by teaching him that his little body is inviolate. Keep your hands off him, at least in anger."

The years before age 6 are the most important, Budd said. He quoted Father Flanagan (of Boys' Town) as saying: "If you'll give me a child at birth, I'll give you back a man at age 5, and after that I don't care what you do to him."

Now why didn't I think of that? Turn him over to Father Flanagan at birth, wait five years, then beat the shit out of him, and not have to *worry* like this.

Norma Jean stands back, breathing hard, glaring at Damon's prostrate, but undefeated, form spread on the living-room floor amidst the Shakespeare and Plato.

"I *hate* you! I *hate* you!" he whispers, with what breath is left. "You're an icky *icky* mommy, you fucker!" ("WHEN IN DOUBT, THROW IT OUT"—Dottie's Helpful Hints.)

She squats down and takes his hands. "Damon. Damon, listen to me. When you are upset you have a wild thing inside you; it gets you into trouble. You must learn to tell it to calm down. Say, 'Wild Thing, calm down, so I won't get into trouble.

Wild Thing, calm down,'" she repeats. His tears have stopped, but his breathing is still rapid. Scott has already switched on the television. Ruth Ann carries Barbie upstairs, cradling her in both hands, hungering after her as though she were something to be eaten in secret. Norma Jean gathers up Damon's clothes and returns the books to the bookcase. As he limps toward the family room she hears him whisper, "Wild Thing! Calm down, or I'll beat your ass!"

> The Lord Jesus Christ
> willing to show his power and mercy,
> and having redeemed the souls of
> Grace Muriel Grovener
> and
> Troy Michael Thompson
> by the gift of his shed blood,
> has now brought them together to be
> husband and wife.
> Mr. and Mrs. Arthur C. Grovener
> hope you will share their happiness
> at the wedding,
> Sunday, the fifteenth of April
> at two-thirty in the afternoon
> Deliverance Hall
> Spirit of Christ Commune
> Auburn, California

("Amazing Grace.") Which reminds me: I've got to call the sitter, or I'll never get out of here tomorrow. Norma Jean has the day planned with exquisite simplicity: she will go to the Egyptian Museum in San Jose, thirty miles south of Pleasant Valley. She has never been there; the experience will be hers alone, a secret. She remembers having read a news article recently which stated that, while the museum couldn't be described as comprehensive, its mummies were exceptionally well-preserved.

The garage is cool and musty. Seated at her work table, Norma Jean pounds the clay. She starts to shape it; and what begins to emerge is nothing like a canopic jar. It is nothing like anything that has ever been before. She feels an indescribable thrill, and some fear. She begins to make impressions on it. Strange designs appear. It grows and grows. An hour passes before she is aware of the rain streaming down the small garage window. From the house the sound of Ruth Ann's voice filters into her consciousness. The creation lies between her hands, moist and solid. Slowly she divides, becoming two distinct women: the one who hears the child, and the one who holds a totally new object in her hands. Ruth Ann comes into the garage.

"Mom, can I read this book to you? I am on page seven already!"

> HI BIG BOY.
> HI PAM.
> I LIKE KITTENS.
> I WANT A KITTEN FOR ME.
> I WANT A SURPRISE FOR MOTHER.
> A KITTEN WILL BE A SURPRISE.
> LOOK, BIG BOY.
> SEE THE KITTENS?

(Yeah, ah sees de kee cats, mu' fu'.) "That's very good, Ruth Ann! That's wonderful. Your reading is beautiful. You're getting to be such a big girl!"

After dinner Norma Jean hazards a request. "Martin, would you mind cleaning up tonight? I have something I'm working on out in the garage and I'd like to get to it early."

"What? Aren't you going to put the kids to bed?"

"Well, I thought you could do that tonight."

"I want some more ice cream!"

"I have to go poopie!" *This place is a madhouse; I've got to get out of here.*

"Hell, honey, I've got a report to get out tonight. What are you doing out there that's so important it can't wait until you've done the dishes and gotten the kids to bed?"

"God damn you, I'm changing my life out there! I'm *making* something. I happen to think it's important . . . at least to me."

"Another jar?"

Norma Jean rinses the dishes in the sink, fondling the handle of the butcher knife. So smooth, so sharp, one thrust under the heart and: no more Martin.

"Martin," she begins, with the same measured tone she assumes with the children. "I am trying to start *doing* some of the things we were talking about last night. You said you'd help out."

"I know I said that. But tonight I've got this report. It's my *work*, Norma. You can do your jars in the morning, after the children are in school."

Jars, jars. What does he know. Strange shapes await me, which themselves await definition. Norma Jean stacks the dishwasher, takes out the garbage, sweeps the floor, wipes the table, makes the lunches, working around Martin with quiet fury while he studies his report. She helps the children dress for bed, presides over the brushing of teeth, the washing, the bedtime eliminations. Martin retires to his study with his coffee. After the last child is tucked in and kissed, she appears in his doorway and reports astringently, "Everything is done. I am going out to the garage." He looks up from his report.

"Could you bring me a hot cup of coffee before you go? I'd appreciate it." She brings him the coffee. "Thanks. God, I'll be glad when this is finished. You understand, don't you? I have no time during the day to do these things." She pauses for a moment in the door before addressing him. " 'Women are the slave class that maintains the species in order to free the other half for the business of the world.' " —Shulamith Firestone.

"What the hell are you talking about?" he says, looking up.

Norma Jean takes the portable radio out to the garage and switches on the overhead bulb that dangles there from the ceiling. It spins for a while, back and forth, casting circular shadows on the stored objects against the walls and over the clay dust on the floor. She readies her work space, lifts the damp towel from her piece, and switches on the local FM station that plays music from the thirties and forties. And there, among the cobwebs, the dim light, the pulsating clay, is Benny Goodman playing "On the Alamo." It is indescribably sweet.

Dear Mr. Goodman,

Do you think the reason we find ourselves returning to your music now is that we are finding our own time unbearable? Or was your time unbearable too, but in different ways? Is this something that is experienced by every generation? Or were you personally able to say you were glad to be alive and in your prime then, in spite of the depression and the war?

Concerning war: once, on a peace march, I was carrying some letters I had written to congressmen, and just as I was about to mail them, the strangest thing happened: I had a vision where I saw them become airborne. They sailed on white wings, pausing once over Kansas. Has anything like that ever happened to you?

The piece is growing. It has expanded, altered its boundaries, assumed energy. Norma Jean withdraws her caked hands and stares at it, and continues to stare: something has been reversed; she has sensed it. The creation has begun to conduct its own mitosis, dictate its own terms. It has agreed to retain its connection to her by a slender, invisible thread. She regards the transformation with awe and respect—and an exquisite chill.

"Jeanie!" The garage door swings open, and Martin stands there, blinking at the unaccustomed light. "You've been out here for three hours! It's time to go to bed." *Time to go to bed?* She resists the urge to say, "If I come right away will you tell me a story?" and instead asks, "Why?"

"Because it's late and I have to get up early tomorrow; if you don't get some sleep you'll be too tired to get my breakfast." Her eyes fall on the Piece. "Go ahead," it whispers; "say it."

"Martin, you *could* get your own breakfast tomorrow."

If love is a product of shared growth . . . and we are to measure success in marriage by the degree to which matched development actually occurs, it becomes possible to make a strong and ominous prediction about the future.

It is possible to demonstrate that, even in a relatively stagnant society, the mathematical odds are heavily stacked against any couple achieving this ideal of parallel growth. The odds for success positively plummet, however, when the rate of change in society accelerates, as it is now doing.

—Alvin Toffler, *Future Shock*, Copyright 1970 by Alvin Toffler, Random House, Inc., p. 222.

"Make my *own* breakfast . . ." Martin stares into space as his words bounce off the walls of the garage and revolve into the air a few times, before hitting the floor. Norma Jean stares at the

Piece. Rapid change is rough on the stomach; she wishes she had some Maalox. *What should I do now?* "You're on your own," it replies, without malice, in a tone that says: Those who would have their progress must incur their own risks.

"Yeah. Get your own breakfast. You managed to do it before you met me. Why do *I* always have to be there doing it? It's such a simple thing."

Martin finds his voice. "It's immaterial that it is simple. What matters is that you are the wife-and-mother in this household, and the wife-and-mother prepares the meals."

"It doesn't always have to be that way."

"Yes it does, because the children and I depend on you to do that. It's what women have always done. I work hard, I go out in the world to earn the money that buys the food. *You* cook it."

"Martin, what if I had work that was just as important to me as your work is to you; and what if, from time to time, it required me to stay with it beyond mealtime. Wouldn't you be willing . . ."

"No. I wouldn't. The point is, your work wouldn't . . . isn't earning the money."

"Everything shouldn't rest on economics; I have a right to my life. I have to begin somewhere!"

"If you're not *there* at mealtime, it's like the children and I are just . . . floating around. There's no center. The wife generates the warmth, prepares the things which sustain the family." Norma Jean sees a large canvas, seventeenth-century Flemish, all muted tones: brown, ochre, mellow oranges, dull whites, faded blacks. In it is a long table where men are holding forth in deep discourse, while around them the women tend the hearth, the ovens, the kettles, the jugs—whirling and spinning, moving with a centripetal force that holds the pieces of the family in place, draws the children from their corners, the dogs from the mat.

Martin returns to the house. Norma Jean lights a cigarette and leans on the table. She thinks how, as children, boys and girls move in and out of a house with a passable degree of equality, move outward from the home toward what they perceive as eventual goals, eventual freedom. Their late childhood and early adolescence is a continual rehearsal for autonomy. Then, by some invisible arrangement, on reaching adulthood—usually at the time of marriage—the woman moves abruptly backwards, assumes the management of a home herself, occupies its center as her mother before her, *becomes* that mother, reverts to and displaces her; revokes whatever goals for achievement and involvement she may have entertained, and whatever freedom she may previously have enjoyed. The man's life, by contrast, continues to move in a direct and logical line—a continuum of the outwardly moving pursuit of freedom and explorations begun in childhood. He embraces the world, to the extent of his ability, and no one questions that this should be. Only the woman renounces it, trading whatever dreams she had for the isolation and certainty of her enclosures.

Norma Jean slowly covers the Piece with a damp cloth. She cannot believe she is responsible for its existence, but she doesn't doubt that it is there. *There is no way you can be undone.* She switches off the light and shuts the door behind her.

She undresses and slips into bed. Martin is still awake. "Martin, I was thinking after you left."

"Mmmmm."

"In recent history boys and girls start out with similar assumptions about their futures—if their education has been fairly equal; but then the girl usually makes so many renunciations. I always dreamed of doing something in the world; I certainly never dreamed of just keeping house for fifteen or twenty years. The boy continues outward and at some crucial point in time the girl draws back. It's not right. It has to change. I don't want that for Ruth Ann. . . ."

"It's true. What you say is probably true. Girls just have to grow up, that's all; boys do not," he says simply and rolls over, signaling the end of the conversation and the beginning of his twenty-second descent into unconsciousness.

"Don't go to sleep on me, you bastard. It's just the opposite, boys *get* to grow up; girls are imprisoned, infantilized, accept no risks."

"Be that as it may, I am too old to change horses in the middle of a stream. And you are not in prison; you've never had it so good. You will succeed in whatever you want to do, if you just budget your time properly. Are we out of eggs? I'm getting sick of granola. I'd like two eggs for breakfast, if we have any." ("The way to a man's heart is through his stomach." —Old saying.) He moves around restlessly in the bed; the moment of sleepiness has come and gone. He reaches for her hand.

"You're making too much out of this, Jeanie. You *know* I have a lot of respect for you. You are a competent woman, you have character." *He knows that the quickest way to a fuck is to say "I respect your character." That will do it every time.* He runs his hand up and down the length of her body. *If he respects me so much, why can't he hear what I'm saying?* Why is she tightening up like that? Why can't we ever get together at the same time any more? Her mind is a million miles away; it's certainly not with *me. Poor Martin; I don't want to refuse him. If I could just loosen up, get into it.* She has become aware of a tiny circle of pain between her eyes. She runs her hand up and down the length of his body, buying time. What the hell is she waiting for? Either she wants it, or she doesn't. Give her another minute and a half; I'm not going to force myself on a corpse. *What will it cost me? People don't have to be in perfect ideological agreement in order to make love.* A man works hard, does what generations before him have done, marries, has children, pays everything on the first of the month; he hits mid-life and what does he have to show for it? Just when things should be easing up, just when all the stability I've been working for all these years should be assured, what have I got? Shrinking dinners, orthodontia bills, and a wife who reads The Book of the Dead and tells me to get my own breakfast. He withdraws his hand.

"I want my wife back!" he demands indignantly in the darkness. Norma Jean stares at the ceiling.

"I want my life back," she finally whispers, just as the snoring begins.

9

Norma Jean stands on the curb next to her car. It is 9 A.M. The day is hers. It is one of those mornings after rain, when the landscape stands out from its foundation. It is a lean, ambiguous spring. She unlocks the car, slides into the low bucket seat, and straps herself in. She starts the motor, letting it warm, thinking back to the time, two years ago, when it first came into her possession. Well, I would see the others driving their Country Squires, their minds fixed on endless grocery lists, the children piled like cargo in the back, all of them locked together in one nuclear mass, riding their cruising machines like ships, sailing, sailing these endless suburban lands. And I knew one thing. It wasn't for me.

So when the transmission gave out in my '53 Chevy in the middle of the freeway in rush-hour traffic, I told Martin that my next car was something over which I wanted a choice. The following Saturday, down at the used-car lot, I pointed to the red MG and said, "I want that."

"You're crazy, Norma. That's for single people. When are you going to be mature and acknowledge your responsibilities? That's a ridiculous car for the kind of life you lead."

"No, it isn't. It's perfect. I can get six children in it for car pools and—when they're not in it—all the groceries for a week. What else could I possibly require?" I had him.

"How the hell can you get six children in an MG?"

"Well, look at it; it has a very roomy jump seat. Four in back, two in the bucket seat in front."

"That's *dangerous*, Norma Jean."

"It's no more dangerous than a station wagon, where they're all crammed in back, with no seat belts, rolling around and hanging out the tailgate window."

"Well, I don't know. It just seems weird, not suited to the kind of life people live here."

"I am people. I live." (*I think.*) "I do it here. I will *not* drive a station wagon." Martin circled the little car, frowning, squinting, patting the hood, kicking the tires, as an animal circles its prey. Aroused, I continued, "It can park anywhere. Have you seen the other women trying to get those lumbering mothers into a parking space? If you want one, you can stay home and car pool children and buy groceries in it. Not me." The station wagon symbolized a capitulation; it represented the final step in the total adoption of this particular way of life. I was not prepared to do that. The MG preserves an illusion of freedom. You can fit the children in when necessary; but you don't have to take all the stepladders, garbage cans, and the family dog, too. If you have to do your living here among the freeways, you should be able to do it in the least painful way possible.

And now she pushes in the choke, releases the brake, and courses through the deserted streets. The same streets that supported all those years of stroller pushing: always deserted, devoid of human life. Where were all the *people?* I used to wonder in desperation. Where are all the children? And the other mothers? Can they all be inside running their disposals at the same time? *Police investigating the murder could find no witnesses during a door-to-door search of the densely populated residential district.* I am Norma Jean Harris, I used to think; I live in Pleasant Valley, where everything is pleasant, diluted, dispassionate. Every street a sterile avenue, winding in circles, coming out where it began. This neighborhood is a necropolis. Witness the highly cultivated, untouchable landscape; the precise planning; the uniformity of style, the thinly disguised efforts at individuality shrinking in the light. See how nothing moves! And all of us sealed in, entombed, dying.

. . . The flight into the home was only a part of a general postwar retreat from the world.

                                    * * *

How could educated women devote their entire lives to a task
so shrunken? How could they make it fill the day, let alone
fill their minds?

                              —Philip Slater, *The Pursuit of Lone-*
                              liness, Copyright 1970 by Philip
                              Slater, Beacon Press, p. 66.

I'll tell you how: first thing in the morning you started with the
diapers. After you changed them, if enough had collected in the
pail, you washed them. If they had ammonia which was causing
diaper rash, you boiled them in a large kettle on top of the stove
for half an hour. While the diapers were boiling, you fed the
children, if you could stand preparing food on the same stove with
urine-soaked diapers. After breakfast, you took the children for a
walk along deserted streets, noting flowers, ladybugs, jet trails.
Sometimes a motorcycle would go by, scaring the shit out of the
children. Sometimes a dog followed you. After the walk, you
went back to the house. There were many choices before nap
time: making grocery lists; doing the wash; making the beds;
crawling around on the floor with the children; weeding the garden; scraping last night's dinner off the pots and pans with steel
wool; refinishing furniture; vacuuming; sewing buttons on; letting down hems; mending tears; hemming curtains. During naps,
assuming you could get the children to sleep simultaneously
(which was an art in itself), you could flip through *Family Circle*
to find out what creative decorating you could do in the home, or
what new meals you could spring on your husband; or peruse
Ladies' Home Journal and read all about "The Operation
Women Fear the Most" and "Secrets of a Perfect Meatloaf." Or,
you could read Simone de Beauvoir and cry. It was all a matter
of choice, and the choices were many. It was quite easy to fill
up a day, even a mind, that way.

Norma Jean pulls onto the on-ramp, shifts into second, and accelerates. The speedometer pushes upward, then hovers between
sixty-five and seventy mph. Mountains of scrapped cars, steel factories, block-long bakeries, auto-assembly plants slip by. Why do I
experience a sense of mastery and release driving the freeway, in

114

spite of my hatred of it? To understand the feeling of exhilaration, you have to take the term literally: free-way; a way that is free. She reaches for the radio dial, runs the indicator up and down the band, searching for some Albinoni, or even some venal rock and roll which—at certain times, particularly on the freeway —is even more edifying, in some inexplicable way, than the classics, possibly because it derives from the same roots as the landscape through which you find yourself hurtling. It corresponds exactly to it, and by turning it up full blast and immersing yourself totally in it while driving at high speeds through wasted surroundings, you can begin to come to some terms with your environment. You do this when you realize you can never hope to reverse things. Sometimes, letting yourself fully embrace and incorporate what you most despise generates excitement. At times it can even lead to understanding.

The landscape is changing: the factories have given way to a stretch of farmland, beyond which there are hills which still remain in a relatively undeveloped state. Two small planes are dipping low over the fields, dusting the crops. As they release the poisons, Norma Jean thinks of Vietnam. DEFOLIANTS LINKED TO BIRTH DEFECTS, SAYS EXPERT. In the distance horses graze in centuries-old postures, beneath the shadows of high-voltage towers. In the air wild birds collide over fields on the outskirts of San Jose.

Entering town, her excitement grows. She passes rows of small frame houses, many with signs in front reading PALMIST or HYPNOSIS. Birds go mad in giant palms. American flags fly everywhere. She remembers having read that San Jose is one of the fastest-growing cities in the west. It seems the archetypal California town that has outgrown its origins in its hurried industrial spread yet continues to exhibit provincial values where it can. Spiritualists cling tenaciously for life next door to Colonel Sanders. Suddenly, it is there in front of her: the Rosicrucian Egyptian Museum. A gigantic yellowing building surrounded by formal lawns and gardens, and terrible replicas of Egyptian columns and statues. Its doors are the color of solid gold. They shine with blinding light in the mid-morning sun.

Director
Egyptian Museum
San Jose, Calif.
Dear Sir:

I visited your museum for the first time last week. As a student of ancient Egyptian history and art, I was shocked to find Muzak being piped into the museum—especially a selection such as Paul McCartney's "Yesterday," rendered by Mantovani. Are you afraid your visitors won't get the point?

In general, your artifacts are good, except in those instances where they are fake and you neglect to state "replica" on the little cards. I raise the point because one tends to look longer, and more lovingly, at the real thing than at a fake. In life, we are left to make this distinction for ourselves—all the time, in fact. That's precisely why we expect it to be provided for us in places like museums.

Another complaint I have concerns those thugs you employ as guards. Why do they walk around carrying walkie-talkies? And why do their jaws hang loose? Are they being rewired? Also, what's the deal with that recorded voice coming out of the tomb ceiling, explaining things? That leaves the guide with nothing to do but shine his flashlight on things at the appropriate moments. (He does keep up with the narrative very well.) Is it because your guide is a mute? If so, congratulations for hiring the handicapped.

One last thing: those Nefertiti fingernail clippers on sale at your gift counter are in the poorest taste. I can't imagine a single Egyptologist who would be caught dead using them.

I'm fighting off a massive depression and tonight six people are coming for dinner. I've taken tranquilizers, but they're clearly inferior to my will power, which dissolved some time back. I can't remember when it was, five years ago? Six? Martin has gone to see the tax man; the children want apples and there are none in the house. I scream at them and their friends, who are circling around the door like a pack of wolves. I hate myself for screaming at them and I hate them for wanting things of me that I haven't got. I hate Martin for deserting me. He's the one who wants me to entertain. "We haven't had anyone over in five months," he says. "That's because all our close friends are far away; I'm not good at establishing new friendships. These

116

people will all be moving away too, sooner or later. It's a waste of time getting involved; we'll never see them again," I answer. "You can't go back in time!" he yells (Oh, I can!); "we're living in the present, and this is the way people do things in the present. They get together and they do the best they can. You complain about your isolation, *do* something about it instead of living like a hermit." "You don't understand." "What's to understand? The close-knit community is a thing of the past; you've got to adapt, or you're dead." When he finally gets home, dollar signs flicker where his pupils once were; it takes two drinks before they disappear.

And now the door, someone has arrived. And the wine glasses haven't been set out! And the candles, where the hell are the candles, it's been so long. And suddenly Norma Jean freezes; *it doesn't matter. None of it matters.* And she feels an immediate lifting of dread, as the past ten years replay themselves in her mind, as she stands in the kitchen, as Martin heads for the door to admit—she doesn't care who it is—all those years, doing all the things that were expected: thin-stemmed wine glasses, no fingerprints; knives facing inward, toward the plate; matching plates (God help the hostess who had unmatched plates); the dinner in layers, rows, stages, perfectly timed; then Martin dropping an ash into the spotless ashtray ("God damn you! Dropping *ashes* in the ashtray! I just *polished* it . . ."). Perfection, perfection. Nothing less was acceptable. *Where was it written?* And in between the dinner parties, the faultless daily performance in front of the stove: bare feet (yes, and pregnant) and loving it, or thinking she loved it; the careful cultivation of flower boxes; the moist seduction of freshly baked bread, the yeast-filled air, breathing it in; the rolling, pounding, kneading, shaping: and the sexual dough, sighing, rising, even while it hung there limp and heavy in her hands; she would bury her face in it, while melodious wind chimes moved outside every window and door.

And now Martin moves toward the door, to admit them, whom we hardly know, with whom we have no connections, with whom we are about to embark on approximately six hours of concerted efforts to find mutual sympathies, common ground.

"Hi, Doris! Mark! Come on in." It's the Morgans. She

listens to the sounds of arrival, the awkward murmurs and nervous laughs that precede the ordeal; the fumbling with coats, the mandatory inspection of anything that happens to be hanging on the walls. Mark. Quickly, which one is he? She fights the amnesia. What does he do? (Remembering all the parties they used to attend, where the first question was always "What do you do?" and it was always addressed to the man. And Norma Jean's mind would race as he began his reply, "I'm Ralph; I'm in investment banking." And wishing she had the courage to break in, just once: "Hi. I'm Norma Jean; I scrub floors.")

You can't stand here in the kitchen. You are the hostess. You must come out now and greet your guests; put the dishtowel down and go out there and say:

"Hi, Doris. Hi, Mark. It's good to see you again."

"Hi, Norma Jean. I was just saying to Mark, we haven't seen you for so long. Where have you been keeping yourself?" Doris, removing her coat, stripping the chiffon scarf from her neck: in five minutes—seven, if she asks for a daiquiri and Martin has to clean out the cupboard looking for the mix—she will be refusing the hors d'oeuvres and wrapping her tongue around the school system instead, how it cripples; her son's latest injury (fell out of a tree; dislocated shoulder; terrible for his body-image, especially at that age). Lightly she will begin wringing her hands, imperceptibly her brow will . . . "Doris. What can I get you to drink?" and if I make the only excuse available (Oh God, excuse me Doris, I smell something burning) under the circumstances, with the exception of committing suicide, which I am keeping in reserve for the time when there are absolutely no margins left, Doris will move, obedient to custom, into the kitchen *with* me on her patented feet. And she will stand there, expectantly, hovering over the stove while I nod, Yes, Oh I sure agree with you Doris; on the other hand, I do not believe private schools are the answer to the bathroom problem. You don't? Well, aside from the psychological damage, think what it is doing to the children, holding it in like that all day. From a purely physical standpoint . . . No, private schools are not the answer. *I think guns are the answer. We should arm the children. An eye for an eye. Mow them down, under the sinks.* Mmmm. Something smells good! Oh, you do it with white wine! I have this fabulous

118

recipe, first you take carrots (chop chop chop) then some dill, then you add . . . "Oh, I'll have a daiquiri; if it's handy . . ." "One daiquiri, coming up." "Thanks so much, Martin." "How about you, Mark?" "Well, ha ha, just give me a scotch and Valium, Marty. That ought to do it!" Well, Mark, you're not that bad, you really aren't. *Make that two scotch and Valiums.*

"So what have you two been doing lately?" Martin is warming to his half-forgotten role as host. Norma Jean can tell by his gestures, his bearing, that he is trying to recapture something. It's the feeling we had when we were first married, getting together with friends, eating on the floor, forming early bonds. Now, with the exception of Paul and Rachel, it would be impossible to gather those we most care about together under the same roof.

"Oh, the usual; been getting in a lot of tennis lately. You two should really join the club. All that exercise! It really puts blood back in your veins. I don't know whether I'm getting healthier or setting myself up for a coronary! Ha ha. Doris, she uses it to trim down, don't you, honey?" Doris blushes. Norma Jean excuses herself and returns to the kitchen; Doris moves ponderously toward the couch, then hesitates, turns, and calls, "Need any help, Norma?"

"Oh, not at all, thanks Doris. Just make yourself comfortable; don't even come out here. It's a surprise." Norma Jean stands before the stove, leaning slightly on its edge. Martin rattles the ice around, swearing under his breath, "Where is that fucking daiquiri mix? Why are these cupboards always such a mess; I can't find anything in them. What are you doing leaning on the stove? Everything is ready, isn't it? You should be out there making them feel comfortable while I'm getting the drinks."

"I can't help it, Martin. I need a minute to clear my head."

"Well, pull yourself together, for Christ's sake. I ask you to entertain once in five months and you fall apart." Clink clink go the ice cubes as they hit the glass. Drip drip goes the faucet which Martin hasn't fixed. Rustle rustle go the Morgans, as they circle the living room alone, squinting at the prints on the walls. God, I hope that psychiatrist can do something; all she does is fade out, right at crucial times. She used to be so competent. I ought to go and have a talk with him myself.

119

I know these things take time, don't want to interfere, but Jesus, I don't know how much more of this I can take. Come home, walk in the door, never know *where* she'll be. He should be told about that; ought to understand it from my point of view.

"When I come home, she's not where she should be. It feels as though there's no center; a home should have a center to it, shouldn't it? She's just not where she should be, doing what she should be doing . . ."

"Where should she be?"

"At the sink! That's where my mo . . . well, in the *kitchen*. I mean, she's off in her studio and I don't know where the kids are, or when she's going to get around to doing what she's supposed to be doing . . ."

"You feel her place is at the sink?"

"Yeah. I mean, she always used to be. Standing there shucking corn or shredding lettuce, when I came home. It used to make me feel . . . well, all I can say about it is that it's like a machine that runs smoothly when all the parts are functioning. She's become a part that refuses to function, so the whole machine breaks down."

"That's a rather mechanistic view of the family, isn't it?"

"Hell no. I mean my mother always was where she should be when my father came home from work. And after dinner, she also was where she should be: at the table, darning his socks, or in his bed when he went to sleep. It united us as a family. It was something you could always depend on. Now, I don't know, Norma is off in museums, or out in the garage, or reading morbid books. She reads everything. They're stacked to the ceiling next to the bed: women's lib, ancient Egypt, sociology, the newspaper. Has she told you about that? How she pores over every morbid item she can find in the paper? It's not that I'm against her reading; Norma's a very intelligent woman. I wouldn't be interested in a woman who didn't keep up, didn't use her mind. What I'm talking about is the way she seems to be moving away from me, from all of us; her mind is taking her places where I have no access. It's as though she is renouncing me, the home, everything we valued. I love my wife! I'll be honest with you, Dr. Arndt; it scares me. I realize times change, and I want Norma to feel fulfilled," *whatever the hell that's supposed to mean now. It used to mean four children, a modern kitchen, and a good fuck three times a week.* "I try to understand, to make accommodations. But it's happening so fast, it feels as though everything is disintegrating. I have needs. I can't adjust this quickly. She's in another world; I play no part in it." *She used to look so good there, standing at the sink in her bare feet, ready for a quick one, before the kids were born; her hair was long, too. She looked so good there, I wanted to keep her there forever. I create images of her in my mind, it's hard to talk about this, but there is a statue of her in my mind, standing at the sink always, thinking of me. She is made of clay and can't ever run away.*

"Jeanie, I'm taking the drinks out now; the others will be here any minute. Are you going to be O.K.? Will you come out and at least try to act like a hostess? Please don't spoil the evening." Poor Martin. Only wants a little peace, a little sociability. Norma Jean reaches over and touches his hand. "I'll be all right; I'll be out in three minutes, I promise." She moves to the cupboard to get out the wine glasses, rattling a few dishes so they will think she's busy with elaborate preparations, not standing there immobilized. The doorbell rings again.

"Come on in: Mark and Doris, this is Stanley and Robin Fleming—Mark and Doris Morgan—and Paul and Rachel Swartz, here Rachel, let me hang that up for you." "Hi!" "Hi!" "Nice to meet you!" "Don't I know you from the PTA?"

Rachel comes into the kitchen, where Norma Jean has just washed down two aspirin with her vermouth. "Thank God you're here, Rachel."

"Listen, what is this? Doris and Robin, together, here, *at the same time?* You could have warned me. I would have passed."

"That's why I didn't tell you."

"Well, just for that, I won't tell you what Robin has found herself . . . you'll drop the casserole, it's so far out; I didn't know whether to laugh or cry."

"The *paper boy?*"

"Norma, what's keeping you out there? Can you give me some idea when we're eating, before I refresh the drinks?"

"Yeah, O.K., twenty minutes, Martin. I'll be right there."

She lowers her voice. "The school *janitor?* Come on, Rachel; I'm on a tight schedule tonight; I'm a Hostess!"

"O.K., ready? The checker, third check stand from the door, at Pay and Save!"

"The one with the mustache?"

"*You've* noticed him too?"

"Who wouldn't, a body like that!" She thinks of Robin, who has no confidence to commit herself to anything, to extend what she perceives as her accepted boundaries, or apply herself to some goal, even conceive of the goal in the first place. She realizes this description fits most of the women in Pleasant Valley: when pressed, almost all admit they are in the process of "deciding what to do with" their lives. For most, the initial recognition that children are maturing and that the kitchen does not necessarily merit full-time occupancy has taken place; and for most this knowledge implies the necessity for some change. Some approach that change actively, with the effort and will which are required after ten or more years of not thinking in terms of goals or growth; and some approach it passively, waiting for something to "happen" which will effect the change for them. Some are immobilized by the choices. All the choices involve risk. All arouse fear. Sometimes, when the fear is experienced as intolerable, new babies are conceived, thus postponing the need for change. Doris Morgan is carrying one; it is her fifth, and is separated by five years from the youngest of her present four.

"Hey! That's terrific, Doris. Congratulations," offers Stanley, proposing a toast. He raises his glass in the air, glancing at Robin. "Honey, isn't that terrific? Goes to show, it's never too late." Robin turns to Doris. "Congratulations," she says quietly. "When are you due?"

"Oh, not for another six months. I hadn't really meant to mention it, so soon," *except that I wanted to have something important to say, something special.* Doris Morgan is glowing. Doris Morgan has a secret inside her, and now everyone has acknowledged it, and she is special; questions are being directed *to her.* And a toast! She suddenly feels very young again.

Dinner is on the table; Norma Jean calls everyone into the dining room, instructing people to sit where they wish—no more boy-girl, boy-girl, which always made her think of kindergarten. Mark is leaning toward Martin.

"You know, Marty, I was serious when I mentioned the club earlier; you and Norma Jean should consider joining. Stanley and I have started playing tennis together over there."

"What about you, Paul? Have you and Rachel thought of joining?"

"No, actually we haven't."

"Well, let me recommend it to you anyway; it's a painless way to get your exercise. And they've got no quotas, they're very liberal."

"Well thanks, Mark. We'll give it some thought." Paul looks over at Norma Jean, who risks a quick roll of her eyes across the ceiling. Paul smiles and asks for more salad. Stanley is feeling out Martin on the Berkeley elections.

"Yeah, yeah, I realize that Marty; but you know, if the radicals get a majority, it's all over."

"If the people who want to maintain the status quo get the majority it will be worse; all the really crucial social changes will get shelved, just as they always have," Norma Jean interjects.

"Hey, I thought you were the one who hated change, Norma! You women! Always changing sides!" He laughs, lifting his wine glass, tipping it straight up, draining it.

"What do you mean when you say 'you women,' Stanley?" ("The polite hostess does not argue with or insult her guests," or words to that effect. —Emily Post; Martin Harris' eyes, casting a laser beam down the center of the table.) Change the subject, something noncontroversial, equalizing . . . "Doris, I heard you were robbed a few weeks ago. Did you recover anything?"

"Oh, you never recover it. What upset me was that it was in the middle of the day; I was gardening out back and Bobby was home with the flu. Can you imagine, just walking into your house like that?"

"Norma, we've got to fix those windows that don't close," Martin says. He's been saying it for two years. She nods, and passes the salad bowl around the table for seconds.

"That must make at least six or eight robberies in this neighborhood this month," Paul says. "I've told Rachel to keep the doors locked, but, at the same time, I agree with her: how the hell can you do that with kids running in and out of the house all day?"

"You know, Mark, sometimes I just wish we could move somewhere else; I have a hard time sleeping at night, since it happened."

"Oh, hell, Doris. It didn't happen at *night*. It happened in broad daylight. And anyway, where would you move? It's not just here, it's everywhere."

"I don't know. With the new baby coming I just feel so, well, stuck here. The dog didn't even bark."

"We'll get another dog. That dog isn't worth what we're spending on him for food."

"The children love him."

"Love doesn't protect you when you're being invaded."

The last guest has departed (Stanley, tripping on the stairs). Norma Jean and Martin sit down, amidst the overflowing ashtrays, with a nightcap. "Don't empty it, Martin; leave it until morning."

"Well," he says, "didn't you enjoy the evening?"

"No. I hated it. How can you say you enjoyed it?"

"Well, I wouldn't say it was ecstatic, but you've got to make an effort. It's better than being isolated."

"No. It isn't. Sometimes being isolated is preferable to sitting around with semi-strangers, saying nothing. Nothing meaningful is ever discussed; I'm sick and tired of small talk and trying to avoid controversy."

"You know, joining the club isn't a bad idea. I could use the exercise." If she got over there, took up tennis, it would clear her head. She wouldn't be so tense if she did something physical, really worked out. She'd be all nice and relaxed. "What do you think? You could play tennis; it might pick you up a bit. You know what they say about the relationship between strain and inactivity and mental depression. What do you say?"

"I'm not the club type, Martin, but if you want to do it, go ahead." He'd probably benefit from the exercise, take all his hostilities out on the courts. His heart, my peace of mind. "I think it's a good idea, Martin. Go ahead and join."

"We could give it a try." Didn't think she'd agree that fast. Fresh air, recreation, she'll be her old self in a month.

"You could take tennis lessons, and we could play together— just the two of us again."

"I don't want the tennis, Martin."

"Why can't you at least *try* it? Why do you have to be so opposed to everything healthy? You know, there *are* ways of taking the edge off things, relieving pressures; what Mark says is true. In fact, the last time I saw Stanley he looked like he was ready to drop dead. Now, since he's been playing tennis, he's got some tone, his attitude seems more optimistic . . ."

"I'm not having that sexist pig in my house again."

"I'm going to bed. I can't talk to you any more, Norma. You've become critical of everyone, everything; you're rejecting your duties; spinning on your own axis. I hardly know you any more." He has the look; he wants the scene. The one where I say, "Oh Darling!" and burst into tears; "I've been so *crazy* lately. I just don't know what's wrong with me." And he says, "It's all right, honey. It's probably just your period. I understand." (That women are crazy; that women never do know just what's wrong with them; that it will pass.) Ancient history, ancient history; I will never go back. She hears herself saying:

"Martin, you *can't* talk to me; you can't even listen to me. I'm trying to make some changes in my life that I feel are necessary, and I can't take the pressure you're putting on me. When you give me that shit about my *place*, neglecting my *duties*, I feel like walking out of here and never coming back. I have *never* neglected what I perceive as my duties."

"Yeah, go ahead; just like Marilyn Follett. Just walk out, do your thing. Never mind *my* feelings; never mind the effect on the *children!*" Now he starts to scream: "You couldn't wait to trap me and have all those babies! And now you're ready to walk out on us. I'll never understand you crazy cunts as long as I live!" It is two o'clock in the morning. I'll admit I'm a crazy cunt and I don't understand myself most of the time. Who can I blame for selling me this bill of goods? Not Martin. *Ladies' Home Journal?* Fixing blame is regressive. You have to concentrate on extending the boundaries outward, at the same time being careful not to lose your grip on the center. It requires both hands.

10

SIXTH DECAPITATED BODY FOUND.
GIANT ADMITS SLAYINGS

. . . in addition to the dismembered bodies of the six young women, the 6'9", 280 lb. Kemper has confessed to slaying his mother. The mother's decapitated, nude body was discovered by police in a bedroom closet of the apartment she occupied with her son.

Kemper told police he killed his mother to keep her from learning of the six other murders. "What's good enough for my victims is good enough for my mother," he said.

RAPIST CAPTURED AFTER
THREE-DAY CHASE

. . . In addition to the fatal knifing of the young expectant mother . . . charged with five counts of rape; one count of attempted murder in the knife attack on the young co-ed, during which he broke off the blades of two knives in her body . . . and two counts of murder . . . who were shot in the head when they . . .

* * *

In discussing Bunyard's extensive juvenile record, one authority was quoted as saying, "His troubles began right after conception, when his mother twice attempted to abort him. . . ."

Making the transition from unconsciousness to reality each morning isn't aided by *No one is forcing you to read the paper* I wonder if anyone has ever pointed out that the really atrocious crimes seem to be committed by white males in their twenties *Yes, the point has been referred to in a number of* And there always seems to be an aborting, absent, negligent or seducing mother somewhere in the background ("Parents should have to have a licence before they are allowed to have a child." —Arthur Bremmer). You know, he's absolutely right. *Well, that's in total opposition to our ideal of individual freedom. You're going to be late for your appointment.*

"Listen, Arndt. I've come to the conclusion that I'm not crazy. I have things to work out, who hasn't. But I keep getting the feeling that I'm in the wrong culture, the wrong time, among the wrong people. I don't want to come here in order to *adjust* to that. But I'm a product of it. You can't just *erase* it. I guess you have to come to some terms with it. That should be an interesting struggle! And I can't just walk away; I love my family, it has meaning for me. Sometimes I think the effort to unite the two goals—family and work—will tear me apart. But since I've been" *shaping the Piece* "working," *he doesn't need to know the details of that, probably wouldn't understand it; I don't understand it myself,* "I don't feel as confused as before, or as angry. I have something of my own, and there are even times when I can direct my full attention and all my energy toward it. It's as though I'm defining *myself* as I'm defining *it*, do you understand?"

"You said 'It should be an interesting struggle.' Does that mean you feel some commitment to remaining here and working on these various things?"

"Well, I do have an urge to quit, because I associate coming here with Martin, the children, with not being able to cope. At the same time, I've come to feel that the therapy, too, relieves pressure, and adds another dimension. It's becoming *mine*, not his or theirs. I've become curious about myself. I'm beginning to see it as another avenue of exploration—one that deals with *inner* boundaries—rather than an indictment."

"What made you see it as an indictment in the first place?"

"What do you mean? You think I just dreamed that up? Every time I feel overwhelmed, it is *understood* that it is due to my inability to cope; it is not that things overwhelm. *It is understood* that I am a rejecting mother; or that I'm getting my period; or that I haven't 'accepted my role.' The message is everywhere, and it says: The problem is all yours."

"By whom are these things 'understood'?"

"By the culture! By the people around me! By the expectations and assumptions of the past. By Martin, when he walks in the door with the look that says: What's the matter with my Housewife? She's not coping any more! I can read his mind, he regards me as defective; he's cursing himself for not having consulted *Consumer Reports* before marrying me!"

"Well, there isn't any doubt that things can overwhelm anyone from time to time, in the course of a life. What we're interested in exploring here are those things which may be making coping more difficult; things which, when understood, can free you to cope better, or to make the necessary changes."

"I'll accept that knowing oneself more fully can be valuable if it results in a greater capacity to effect change." She recalls his words and realizes: Whether to cope or change is up to me. I've heard they tried to get you to *adjust*—usually women—to rotten situations, especially during the fifties. Is that a popular myth, or did they really do it? How tragic to have been betrayed both by your circumstances and by the one to whom you came for help. Maybe it was just the poorly trained, or dogmatic, ones. At least *he* isn't doing it. Yet.

Norma Jean heads for the freeway, but instead of taking the southbound entrance, finds herself steering northbound, toward San Francisco. It wasn't planned, although having the children go to Rachel's after school was. She had intended to spend the rest of the day working on the Piece. But now the need for mobility predominates: the need to *go* somewhere, to move through space, adopting the gestures that are associated with freedom. Even though she knows it's not the real thing, just a rehearsal, there is something about the act of driving away from your home that produces an exhilaration that she hasn't experienced for ten years. It is like reaching back in time and touching an old, original self.

Downtown she squeezes into a tiny parking place on the street; and, locking the car, she gets the scent of ocean fog. She walks toward the cable-car line, a block away. She breathes deeply, moving through the chilled space that bears on its currents a stream of flower stands and street musicians. For the first time in years she is aware of her body, the way it moves, the way it feels moving; there are no small hands gripping her skirt, no restraints. And there, on the right—isn't that the bar . . . where we used to sit . . . looking for men? As she boards the cable car the past throws up its images, overwhelming her.

And at the end of the line she walks slowly in the direction of the beach. Where she sits now, under a low, racing sky, wrapped in her coat, going back in time. She stares across the bay, where the fog lifts its pearls over Alcatraz. The last time she sat here was during the occupation; it had thrilled her to see the flags of the Indian nation flying there on that rock. I spent three hours here that day, thinking about the variety of injustices those who are strong and in the majority find to visit upon those who are weak or small in number. And there is always something about thinking about that, while sitting on the western-most shore of a frontier, that gets you thinking about America. There are two kinds of thinking about America: the kind you do every day after the newspaper, as you make your .ounds—breathing exhaust, tripping over corpses, looking for some-one to talk to, eating Big Macs; and what you do here—staring at Alcatraz, where whitecaps sprout as cool as tusks and gulls tilt their unanimous weight on wind. Sometimes, in late summer, when a hot air inversion settles over Pleasant Valley and not a leaf moves, I lie awake and listen, beyond the freeway hum to the east, and sometimes, far in the night, I can hear the sound of boxcars, slowly parting continental grasses.

Returning to her car, Norma Jean finds a ticket on the windshield. She has overparked two hours; she doesn't care. She doesn't even look in the mirror as she backs up the car, and immediately hears the sound of metal hitting metal. She gets out to see what damage has been done; it is her first accident. She stands there in the street and stares with disbelief at the car she has just dented. It is a Ferrari. *Impossible.* These things do not happen in real life. They happen in Italian movies. Here is Marcello Mastroianni, stepping out of the bar, just in time to see Norma Jean Harris put a dent in his new Ferrari. "Ah!" he exclaims, as he stares. He is *not* looking at the car.

"Please!" I say, "I am entirely at fault, it was unforgivably negligent of me, and I will take full responsibility for all costs and any inconvenience I may have caused you." *Full costs? Do you know what're saying? Martin will evaporate.* I stand in the fog shivering in my pale green *This is Italy! Summer, idiot, summer* silk dress. I have a matching cashmere sweater, but it is in the car. I brush away a strand of hair which the wind has blown across my eyes; I am in great distress, but I do not reach for the Librium. The distress is *suggested* in the 32-frame close-up of my eyes, he is a great director, never overstates; and in the 23-frame wide-angle of my hands, which permits a view of the dent but does not dwell on it. My hands are delicate, the fingers thin and tapered. There is an antique carnelian on my finger; the nails are unobtrusively polished. I have never taken a bite. I am twenty-two.

"Don't speak," Marcello is saying, spreading his arms in the air. "It would be a crime to mention such a trifle." He pauses to brush a cinder *No cinders! Geraniums, in stucco pots, bougainvillaea* from the lapel of his Brioni suit. "But, *si*, we both know the law is petty, requires that certain details, permit me to suggest, my villa, we discuss, over an aperitif, *signorina*, you shiver . . ." There is a vertical scratch approximately two inches long, and a dent where the paint has chipped in one spot, the size of a half dollar. Norma Jean feels around in her purse, finds a note pad and pen, and begins to compose a note. What else can I do? Go down to the Hall of Justice and turn myself in?

After being ushered into the Hall of Double Justice, the deceased stands before Osiris and the forty-two deities who must render final judgment. She makes her declaration:

I have dented a Ferrari.

On the other hand, I have left a note on the windshield. Anubis steadies the scales and notes that the two sides balance each other perfectly. Eternal life is granted.

"You backed into a WHAT?"

"Look, Martin. I have a perfect driving record. I will not stand here and watch you go into the kind of fit that we have been conditioned—from thirty years of cartoons—to expect of every American man whose wife has had an accident."

"Listen, you crazy bitch, don't give me that shit. You don't mind if I *react*, do you? You don't mind if I get *upset* that you wrecked a Ferrari. I only pay the bills around here . . ."

"Will you stop it? It was a *tiny* scratch; it shouldn't cost more than thirty dollars to touch up."

"What the hell are you talking about? You left a note; you could be sued for *anything!* You don't think he's going to give you the lowest estimate, do you? Christ, are you naïve. Didn't you *look* before you backed up? What were you thinking about?" *How it felt to be alone.*

"What's the matter with you, Martin? Can't you reserve judgment until we hear from the owner? Or do you just want an excuse to punish me because I was out, because I wasn't around here mending and baking and scrubbing?"

"Norma, frankly, this doesn't surprise me in the least. As far as I'm concerned, this is simply the latest in a series of insane acts on your part. I think you should consider seeing Arndt more often. I'm not just pissed off; I'm *concerned* about you."

SHOTGUN SLAYING WAS
ACCIDENTAL, POLICE SAY

Redwood City police ruled the death of a Redwood City man— shot while his wife prepared to clean a loaded shotgun—accidental yesterday.

John C. Evandoll, 51, had ordered his wife Edith, 45, to clean his gun Thursday night while the two were watching television. Mrs. Evandoll gave in after some protest and began unloading the weapon.

The gun discharged and struck Evandoll in the back. . . .

"Back off, Martin. You've done nothing but give me a hard time ever since I began trying to work again. You *say* you're for it, but you just can't accept the changes emotionally. So you punish me with incessant complaints and demands! I've got my hands *full*; I don't need this crap!"

"You *want* it? You want a good fight? Come on, baby, I'm ready. I can give it to you!" Martin begins side-stepping around the kitchen; there is a crazy light in his eyes. He really loves cutting loose at 6:30, in the middle of the kitchen, while I'm standing over the stove.

"Come on, come on, come on! I'm ready for you, bitch! Feeding me shit for dinner, making clay baskets like they do in nursery school, running around smashing up Ferraris! You ought to be locked up! Crazy lady!" The children have all lined up in the doorway to watch.

"You're more popular with the kids than cartoons, Martin; did you ever think of going on TV?"

"You *want* it? I'm about to let you have it, you provocative bitch!" he hisses. "It's all right, kids, go on back to your program, Mommy and I are just having a little talk."

"I'd rather stay and watch the talk, Daddy," says Ruth Ann.

"I'm warning you, you've got until five to get back in there and watch TV! If I have to come after you, you'll be sorry! One . . . two . . ." The children slink away. I stay right where I am, whipping and chopping and frying away, thinking. What I think at times like this is: No more. Never again. What a mistake! Next time around, no professor; no one with a mother problem *Well that will be impossible; they all have* No one over twenty-five, only young boys who can adapt to change; no marriage; no children; just a little studio out in the country somewhere, maybe a few orchards, I've always wanted orchards, and chickens. A place in the country, my work, and lots of lovers, all under twenty-five. I really get into it, every time, I never learn. I keep thinking: Next time, it will be different; next time, I won't make the same mistakes. Then I realize there is no next time. These mistakes are irreversible. This is my *last* life!

I know there are women who maintain it can be done, who are trying to do it, having a next time in midstream and taking some of their mistakes (usually the children) with them. But I am not convinced. Not yet. They may be right, I don't know. It's too early to tell. I've decided to wait and see. What holds me back is the possibility that what I often think of as mistakes may turn out not to be, in the end. Of course you have to hang around until the end in order to find that out. Sometimes, especially at night, that gives me trouble.

Martin is making a heroic effort to force his anger underground, as we are about to sit down to dinner and he is afraid that—since I am now officially crazy—I might, if provoked, do something like jumping up from the table and flipping it over, the way they do in the movies. So, while I cook the vittles, he goes carefully into the family room to round up the children for the evening meal. There is a piercing scream; it is coming from the living room. Damon flies into the kitchen, his face white with fear.

"Damon! What's the matter?"

"Aaaagh!" he screams. Martin and I hover over him, asking him to calm down and explain. Finally, he squeaks:

"You said Halloween was over! But I saw a ghost out there on the porch!"

"Come on, Damon, there *are* no ghosts. Halloween *is* over. Now come with Daddy and I will show you there is no . . ." The doorbell rings. Martin glances at me as if to say: The kid was right; the ghost is at the door; what should we do? As for me, I wish they'd all drop dead. The food is sitting there getting cold and I'm standing around in my apron waiting for everyone to get it together so I can go out in the garage and get some work done. The only thing that hasn't happened yet is for the phone to ring, which it usually does, right about this time. I'm also irritated because we haven't finished the fight: before the children came we could get it over with at one time—let the dinner wait. Now, the fights come in four movements, three parts, twenty chapters, with interminable intermissions, often lasting days, even weeks, depending on the number, nature, and duration of the interruptions. It promotes a sense of perpetual irresolution which creates a drain on both the liquor and Librium supplies.

Everything is abnormally quiet; Norma Jean moves out of the kitchen and leans around the family-room door to hear what is happening at the front door.

"Martin? What's going on out there? Who's at the door?"

"Jeanie, it's a . . . it's someone from Hare Krishna; Damon saw the robes in the dark, that's why . . . uh, you know." She peers out the window. Sure enough, there he is with the shaved head and saffron robe, over which he is wearing a Stanford sweatshirt; and there are the dirty tennis shoes—they must buy them from a special dirty tennis shoe store. The Hare Krishnas really provoke me. It isn't just the chanting and jumping around all day and asking people to pay them for it. One night we came out of the theater and they were lined up outside on the sidewalk, holding out lighted incense to people. It smelled good. They were very gracious, in fact, bending slightly from the waist as they offered the sticks; and people were accepting them, touched by the gesture. Everyone smiled and said thank you. Then they stood there and wouldn't let us pass until we gave them money. That finished the Hare Krishnas for me. You expect deception and manipulation from the government, and you defend against it according to the nature of your wish to believe. But people who call themselves holy have a tradition to maintain and its first requirement is to be straightforward.

She studies the strange figure, gesturing earnestly under the porch light. He looks like a high school sophomore from the fifties, in an identity crisis: unable to decide whether to wear his mother's negligee or try out for the team. Norma Jean walks over to the door, where Martin is absorbing all the consciousness and ecstasy, vacillating and equivocating; he has never learned how to answer the door and say NO. That's one of the first things we housewives learn. I resented it at first, but now I'm grateful for the training. It is another one of those little areas where you learn to exercise your autonomy; it is good practice for the future, if you're planning to have one, and it helps maintain the illusion of power. If there is nothing else a woman alone in her home can do, she can close her door in someone's face. I can remember days when doing that sent a thrill through my whole system, waking me from the dead.

"Why are you coming to our door at the dinner hour?"

"Good evening, madam. I was explaining the Krishna consciousness to the man of the house, and I have come to your door in the hope that you will be good enough to make a contribution to our temple." *I read that they don't have any sex, unless it is for the express purpose of conceiving a child. He doesn't look well at all.*

"We have a sign on the door, see it? Can you read?"

"Oh, madam; this is not soliciting. This is . . ."

"You *are* soliciting. It makes no difference in whose name or for what purpose you are doing it; you are asking us for money. That is soliciting." He's clever, starts to pull out a joss stick to offer us, to beat the soliciting rap. "Look, I don't want to offend you; I just want you to go away. I am going to close the door; we don't ask you to subsidize our beliefs, and we don't intend to subsidize yours."

"Mommy! You left the peas on the stove! They're burning. They're all black and yucky!" Running into the kitchen, Norma Jean grabs the pot with a holder and throws it in the sink. I should hit that bastard over the head with it! She's not sure which bastard, Hare or Martin. They're still at it out there, letting all the cold air in.

"Goddamn it, Martin," she screams from the kitchen, "tell him to take his joss sticks and *shove* them! If you don't all get in here for dinner I'm going to burn the fucking house down!" Why is this the only way to get results around here? Now they're all scraping their chairs, shoving, falling all over each other to sit down.

"Why the hell do you have to scream like a madwoman when there is someone at the door?"

"Why the hell didn't you get *rid* of him?"

"I felt sorry for the poor guy . . ."

"Well, feel sorry for *me*, you Motherfucker, Shithead, Fucker Shit!"

"Oh, Jesus, Norma; in *front* of the *children!* You disgust me, you really do."

"What are you talking about? I *learned* it from the children."

"It's true, Daddy; she learned it from me. And I learned it at school." Martin forks the food into his mouth without passion and slowly chews. It's a terrible thing watching a defeated man eat like that. It's terrible because you know he's refueling for Part II of the fight, gaining strength every minute, and there isn't a thing you can do about it.

As I sit in semiparalytic trance watching him, I am thinking that it's a hard thing for a man to reach mid-life and have to revise his expectations and make major changes in the habits and customs of a lifetime. But then I recover. I think: It is no harder than it was for me during those first five years when, if you were a mother alone with your young, you did daily battle with hundreds of crises, in searing isolation. We were cautioned and instructed about the first five years from every source. You can be told what should be avoided, even what should be attempted, but the truth is you can't do it alone. You begin to catch on by the time you're past the first five years, but by then the damage is done.

Sitting here now in the coolness of my garage *Did I say "my?"* —*not "our," or "the," or "his?"*—working the Piece, I am thinking of mid-life. Nowhere is the shock of it more profound than at reunions. The clay is soft, smooth, and it pulsates there in her hands, emitting signals throughout the room. As she shapes it, Norma Jean remembers her tenth reunion, and the feelings that stirred as she entered the lobby of the hotel where it was held; the anticipation and fear which are aroused by the act of going back in time. The lobby was musty; you could pick the dust right out of the air. *Will we be recognizable to each other?* Slowly groups of people began to emerge; they were clustered about the room, and seen as through a gauze lens, antiqued and muted. And coming closer, she is face to face with Roberta, who is almost unrecognizable. Except that, on later reflection, she is a logical extension of what was there before; the basic form, the particular configuration of matter that defines her as Roberta is not obliterated; it has just been altered, deformed, by time. It has assumed all the characteristics: the extra layers of cells, the gray-streaked hair, the shocking changes around the eyes. She remembers staring at Roberta through the cigarette smoke and thinking: She is herself, carried to her most extreme conclusion. Then feeling shame, because the same thing applied to her, to all of them there, although it required an act of will to apply the rules to yourself. And later, amending the thought: we are all still ourselves—carried to our most extreme conclusions . . . to date. Not even the champagne could prevent the sorrow. It had even happened to Wendy, who had always possessed that absolute poise and absence of stress which characterize those who derive from position. ("Alas, that Spring should vanish with the Rose! That Youth's sweet-scented Manuscript should close!" —Omar Khayyám.) ("Mrs. Sterling Sloan [the former Wendy Woodward] writes that 'Sterling has just passed his bar exams. Last summer we visited Sterling's family in Winnetka before going to Europe.'")

The Piece shimmers, sighs, then bursts through its final boundaries with the assurance of a statement that is nearing its completion. She quickly weighs whether to stay through the night and try to realize it. I am so tired, there are no longer the energy or reserves that there once were. How the hours spin, the weeks flash by; before you know it, there are entire years you can't account for.

Part II: We are seated on the bed. I am hurling insults at his back. I am trying to convince him of our fundamental, unalterable incompatibility.

"I gave you the *Rubáiyát* nine years ago!" I scream. "For our first anniversary. You still haven't read it."

"I'm waiting for them to make a movie of it."

"You think what I'm trying to do is a joke, too, don't you?"

"What *are* you trying to do? Besides destroy our family and give me a coronary?" Ignore it. This is what they always resort to whenever the foot they keep on your neck begins to slip.

"I'm trying to regain the part of me that was unique before I renounced it ten years ago to become your slave . . ."

"Slave! You don't even pick up my clothes any more! Or sew my buttons on!" he screams.

"Everyone should be able to sew his or her own buttons."

"You're insane! A raving fanatic! I warn you, I have my limits!"

"To you, a wife is just an extended mother, whom you expect to do all the things your own mother traditionally did: market, cook, wash, sew, inspect every article of clothing for signs of grease or lint, harvest your droppings daily, in whatever field you've happened to plant them—bathroom, bedroom, on the stairs—act as your *interpreter* at the cleaners . . ." Two women stand facing each other, on opposite sides of the counter. The clerk speaks first; she really cares about his pants.

"Now, then, Mrs. Harris; does Dr. Harris want these cleaned, as well as mended?"

"Ah, well, let's see now . . ." *to tell you the truth, the son of a bitch didn't say; we're not speaking this week. Still, after all these years, I should be able to anticipate his desires, read his mind, shouldn't I? Shouldn't I? Tsk! So incompetent! And not coping again! Quick, take a stab at it, before she realizes you don't give a shit about the clothes your man wears when facing the world; before she catches on.* "Oh! Now I remember!" ("Glory je to Besus!" —Marjoe Gortner.) "I think he said he wanted them reinforced in the crotch—yes! Here we are; sure enough! They're coming apart. *What has he been doing? Standing in for the Marlboro man? Exposing himself in class?* And then I think there was a small grease spot on the left pant leg, somewhere around the knee. . . ." The clerk nods with a misplaced passion that brings my breakfast to my throat as the slacks pass from my ruthless, indifferent hands into her welcome, loving ones. It's hard learning not to care about former obligations when more substantial things are vying for your care and attention. It takes a lot of practice. (Why isn't it enough that I love *him?* Why do they always have to attach such significance to your attitude toward their clothes? The first five years: the clothes an extension of the self; Mama spending every week folding, patting, matching; it said: I love *you!*) You have to be sure that your own goals are important enough to warrant withdrawing your attention from things like trousers. You have to convince yourself that your husband will not drop dead from the shock and strain of having to entrust them to a strange woman and describe their symptoms himself.

LOCAL TEACHER SUFFERS
FATAL HEART ATTACK
IN CLEANING ESTABLISHMENT

Wife Held

Norma Jean doesn't wait for his response. The best time to go for the jugular is when the back is turned.

"What men expect is that their wives be like mothers to them, and that marriage be an extension of childhood in every way possible, with some adult surprises thrown in to alleviate boredom." This brings Martin to his feet.

"You bitch! What the hell do you think *you* expect of *me?* I have to *provide,* I have to *protect,* I have to *take all the risks,* and *deliver the goods!* While you sit around and reap all the benefits! You don't have to worry about a thing! *I* do all the worrying! Parasite!" he hisses, hurling his soiled shirt at the hamper, missing.

"You have no exclusive claim on worry! We've just been conditioned to worry about different things. You benefit from all the things I've always provided for you: maid service, cooking, washing, making the home livable, acting as your liaison with the community, taking your car to be serviced. I'm on call twenty-four hours a day to meet your, and the children's, needs!" ("A mother's work is never done." —Anon.) "You come home and sign off; you've had a 'hard day' and hard days merit regular hours. When you do *your* work you grow; when I do mine I *stagnate*. You exercise autonomy, build a reputation, have something to show at the end. *I'm* just working for room and board! Where's my equity?"

"You'll collect it all when I drop dead!" he screams. *What more could any woman want?* Just hang in there, don't complain, play your cards right, bide your time, *keep your mouth shut,* then one lucky day, Kapow! no more worry, no more tears, just what you've always wanted: a dead husband and all the money!

"You see me as just an extension of yourself! When we married, I became Mrs. You! How would you like to be Mr. Me?" *Martin Sommers (the former Martin Harris) writes, "We have moved to New York, where Norma Jean has a one-woman show at the Reese Palley Gallery. I have given up my work as a volunteer with the Little League and Big Brothers, now that Norma's career . . ."* "I don't want to be 'the former'! I don't want to be parenthetical! When you married, you doubled yourself—Mr. Him and Mrs. Him!—I was halved. Can you imagine giving up your original identity, and attempting to assume mine?" Martin stares at the wall. Is he hearing me? Does any of it register? Norma Jean lights another cigarette. There is still no response.

"Look, Martin, just because it hasn't been expected that I take risks and bring in goods doesn't mean I don't want to. That's just what I want to change. If I can create enough pieces to make up a representative sample of my work, I can exhibit; if I can get back into school and work for my master's, I can teach. I want to carry my part of the economic burden; it shouldn't all fall on you. But I want to do the work I originally trained to do.

I can't settle for tending the hearth any more. I've done that, and genuinely loved parts of it, but it's not enough to fill a lifetime. And it's going to take *time* getting back in the field; I've *lost* ten years! Can you imagine how you would feel if it had been expected of you to lose ten years professionally?" Martin is unexpectedly quick to respond.

"You're probably right, I can't even imagine it as a possibility, so it's hard to say how I'd feel. But to the extent that I can imagine it, I would feel tremendous rage and fury." Norma Jean is startled: I expected him to say, "Why are you complaining? *You* wanted the babies, and someone has to take care of the babies." Then I would have said that we both could have taken care of the babies, so I wouldn't have had to carry the load alone and sacrifice my work; and he would have said, "That's impossible; the mother nurses the baby. I can't nurse a baby." And then I would have said, "Why do men always latch onto that? Even if a woman nurses, that period is very short in this culture." And then he would have said, "Women have the wombs, women have the breasts! Men do not! That's why the men go out and work and the women stay home with the babies!" And then I would have stored that away, with all the other remarks of a similar nature, for the next time he decided to give penis envy a whirl.

Martin sits down again. "I didn't think you were looking that far ahead. I didn't know you were that . . . serious," he says, with just a trace of masochism, nothing that would hold up in open court.

"I've never mentioned it because I didn't want your refusal or your permission—whichever it turned out to be. I want to make this decision *myself*. Martin, don't you see? I've got to start somewhere." She looks directly into his eyes; he no longer has his back turned, a concession in itself.

There is a mellowing taking place in this room; you can always sense the subtle shifts, seconds after they have happened. It must be communicated through the skin, by forces invisible to the five basic senses. Still, Norma Jean finds herself suppressing the euphoria which accompanies the knowledge that she's managed to communicate something essential, at a time when the stakes were perceived as high, because such victories are notoriously susceptible to being declared invalid by the loser the following day.

Still, isn't this Martin who is moving closer on the bed, yes, and reaching over, beginning to caress? *And with his other hand dropping his underwear all over the room?* Never mind, you make your inroads slowly and never use more force than is necessary to achieve your ends. *Look how beautiful he is! See how he comes to me, prouder than horses and golden in love.* "Martin . . . there's one thing we have to get straight before: I am not picking up your underwear after; just thought I'd mention it now." His eyes narrow, but only slightly. Is it hate? Love? He speaks:

"Don't kill this moment talking about underwear." He sighs, his lips moving in on me. O.K., let him forget; I've made my statement. That's what will carry the weight when this tape is replayed, the transcript read, and the defense begins its summation. *One last thing, before he immobilizes me: I want to go on record. I have no wish, intention, or need to kill this man! I have sufficient strength to take him on alive, whenever the situation demands.* His tongue is in my mouth, his hand moves between my legs; it is intense. *I can handle anything he dishes out! I don't have to conquer; there's room here for both of us.* Besides, who would want to hurt, to lose, someone so tender? Even a pighead. And why is it often sweeter after conflict? Is it the relief? Down, down we go. Waves of images erupt, mixing with the hot, magnetic sensations. Has there been research on the phenomenon of seeing intense, indescribable designs, textures, and colors during love-making? Is the wrong area of my brain being stimulated?

"Jeanie, I love you, don't you know that?" Martin whispers, overcome, caressing. ("Love is not enough." —Bruno Bettelheim.) Well, how about if you throw in loyalty, constancy, commitment, endurance? *They can make a difference.* He swells and holds outrageous promise there in her hands. How big a difference? Why are those things so susceptible to pressure? *Because life is hard, our resources fragile.* They lie spread out on the bed, exhausted, their fingers entwined. Why is it that once you re-establish contact, anything seems possible? *Beware of illusions!* What do you mean? Some of my best friends are illusions. Been sustaining me for years.

Norma Jean thinks of the ebb and flow of all natural things: life cycles, tides, seasons, sex, love. Martin sighs. There is a sadness there now, he would deny it vigorously, but there are some things which are hard to disguise and one of them is the fact that in the sex act the man loses something and the woman gets it; and every now and then this occasions in him a special sadness whenever he perceives it as being true. ("Well, I've done my part; now there's nothing left to do but go upstream, like the salmon, to die." —Martin Harris, after Ruth Ann's conception.)

As though cued by thought-wave, Ruth Ann begins to stir, then calls out. That often happens when I am thinking about the children after they're asleep, or when they're playing nearby. I mentioned it once to Martin and he said to quit spending so much time in the Rosicrucian Museum; but it was always there.

"Mommy! Daddy! Come here! I'm scared, I'm scared!" Martin is completely out, didn't even get under the covers. Norma Jean pushes the bed away from her and moves toward Ruth Ann's room.

"What's wrong, Ruth Ann? Why are you scared?" Norma Jean settles on the floor beside Ruth Ann's bed. She whimpers halfway under the sheets, seized by some ("nameless terror." —See Albee, op. cit.).

"I had a bad dream. I'm afraid someone is going to come in our house and kill us." *There is no way around it; you've got to address yourself directly to it.*

"Honey, you know no one is going to come in our house . . ." *Did you leave the rest implied because you couldn't say "kill us" out loud, which would have forced you to acknowledge the possibility* No comment.

"How do you *know* they won't, Mom?" *Oh God, what do you want from me, child?* What can I do? Say, "Well I'm not *sure* they won't," and increase her fears? Or keep lying to her, the way I've been doing for years (All the doors are *locked!* Mommy and Daddy wouldn't let anything happen to *you!* No one wants to *hurt* you!).

"Sweetheart, I don't know absolutely for sure whether or not things will happen; no one does. But it's very unlikely that anyone would come into our house to kill us." (There, I *said* it.) They have better things to do with their time. SURGEON'S FAMILY SLAIN IN HILLTOP HOME. Santa Cruz. SEVEN PATRONS DIE IN BEAUTY SALON MASSACRE. Los Angeles. CONFESSED SLAYER OF EIGHT REQUESTS BIBLE IN JAIL. Santa Cruz. . . . KILLED FOURTEEN PERSONS, BEFORE POLICE

FINALLY CUT HIM DOWN. Houston. FAMILY OF FOUR FOUND DEAD IN MASS MURDER; POLICE SAY NO CLUES. Boston. SPECK MAY POSSESS DOUBLE Y CHROMOSOME. Chicago. Mr. Capote was criticized for expressing more sympathy for the killers than for the slain Clutter family. New York/Kansas. "Please let me have my baby!" —Sharon Tate. Hollywood.

This happens every time one of the children has night fears. I am forced to come to terms with the absurdity of a situation where my obligation is to reassure them that their fears are groundless, when in fact I am subject to the same fears, and know beyond doubt that they are not groundless. I always fail. The ritual involves an act of the most terrible deception. You have the choice of protecting them from the knowledge of certain things for a few more years; or letting them have it—in moderate and carefully regulated doses—with the hope that they will be able to bear it when they're older and begin to hear the rumors. The question is not if, but when, they should be told. GOVERNMENT REFUSES TO HALT ALASKA H-BLAST. The cruelest deception of all is the one which requires you to prepare your children for a future which you do not accept, in which you cannot believe, and which you know is inevitable. If there is one thing I envy the ancients, it was their agreement concerning the nature and purpose of such things as the future, and death, and the unquestioned need which all people share to be prepared for them; and their unquestioned right to expect that preparation from their culture.

Now it's all up to each individual family. You can't expect anything of California—to cite the immediate culture—because in California death is one of the most successfully kept secrets there is. If you doubt this, try to find a cemetery. I've lived here fifteen years, and I've found four. While it's true it would be an exaggeration to call me "well-traveled," I should point out that it took me ten years to find the first one. And that was after looking for it. Cemeteries should be places one comes upon naturally, as one moves about. They should definitely not be places concerning which you wake up one day and say, "I just realized: I've been here ten years, and I've never seen a single cemetery. I think the authorities are trying to hide something." They are. They do not want it known that in California people die. And are buried, and change form, and in some vague way nourish the landscape.

My children have yet to see a burial ground, and I sometimes find myself wondering if they run the cemeteries here the way they do the retirement communities: with high membership fees, annual dues, armed guards, swimming pools, dancing girls to accompany the men in their afterlife, and nineteen-year-old swim instructors to take the edge off for the rest of us. What? Oh. Well, what do you mean, "What about it?" Forest Lawn doesn't *count* because it is not a real cemetery. There are no bodies there. The bodies go in the incinerator when no one is looking. They use beach balls underneath, to hold up the ground and give a realistic appearance. The truth is that no *body* ever nourished that landscape; it is kept in shape with the most advanced garden stimulants Dow Chemical is able to produce between bombing raids in Southeast Asia. How do I know all this? Because I'm crazy. You can always trust the information given you by people who are crazy; they have an access to truth not available through regular channels.

This also happens every time the children have night fears: I end up here on the floor with the stuffed animals, touring the necropoli of the world. Ruth Ann has dozed off again; her breathing becomes slow and regular. Norma Jean studies her face in the dim light, because that is what mothers do at night when they are trapped in the rooms of their young and find they have no way of silencing the thoughts that have been aroused by their need for reassurance. And so they look to the child, now lying calm and beyond need. And it is inevitable that there is sometimes experienced an envy that wishes to be beyond need itself. Ruth Ann sleeps with one leg uncovered, dropped like a lead pipe across the back of one of the cats. They are lost in the same undulating, mindless state; together they drift, borne afloat by every illusion in the repertoire of their combined imaginations. Norma Jean reaches out to touch them; and as she soothes the one's fair hair, the other's dark fur, she has a vision which originates deep in the north: pale sentries stroking restless weapons that toss in their sleep. OCEANOGRAPHERS PREDICT SEAS DEAD IN THIRTY YEARS. Scott. Damon. Ruth Ann. Listen. There is something you must know. Your lives are connected to it in mysterious ways. In your veins are swimming all the fish of the sea; under your luminous bones the green underwater moves, precise, cool, forever in love. How shall I give them the news?

She stares out the window. In the east the moon lifts its polar weight out of the hills. *"Who put the moon there?" I don't know; but I hope the forces responsible know what they're doing, haven't abandoned us.* She bends to kiss the child. The cat uncurls. *She has an absolute right to her fears.* Slowly now Norma Jean withdraws, replacing covers, checking the locks, dimming the lights, preparing the house for the night. And slowly falls asleep as the sounds of traffic fade, and snails secrete their ancient pathways toward the choicest blooms. The lines on the moon fill the sky like an engraving, and somewhere a spaceship sighs over pyramids.

11

We recycle. Don't ask me why. I think it has something to do with the children's future. After five years of sorting and crushing all these stinking bottles and cans, I've become less concerned about their future. There are people who learn to do it without cutting themselves to shreds, but I'm not one of them. Then there are the glass shards that pierce through the children's sandals. Sometimes, while sorting through the grease and slime of hundreds of Kitty Queen cans, I start thinking about all the non-recyclers who just throw it in the garbage. "Hey, Harold, take out the garbage, will ya?" "Jesus, Angie; that's the third time today!" "Well, we gotta eat don't we? Don't ask me where all this crap comes from."

Once a month on Sunday we cart it all off to the recycling center. If the children are sick, or if we're having a fight, we go every two months; it's not the kind of activity you want to engage in together if you're not getting along. Once you get the scent of all that blood you can't count on your self-control. The morning sun catches the light from piles of broken glass; the air is filled with the sounds of metal being crushed with sledge hammers and glass being shoveled into tin barrels.

I think I'm falling in love with Gerald. He is in charge of the can section. There are three categories of cans: tin, aluminum, and bi-metal. As you sort through your cans you begin to hallucinate; it's just something you do while trying to separate aluminum Fresca from 7-Up bi-metal and Kitty Queen tin.

"Gerald, would you mind telling me again? I always have trouble with the bi-metals." Gerald is sweet; he has one tooth missing in front, but he takes the environment seriously.

"Sure. The bi-metals are an alloy. If you put them in the aluminum bin, we're all screwed up and our contractor won't deal with us any more."

Gerald is very patient. When I offered him the sardine can, which is a combination of tin, bi-metal, *and* aluminum (counting the key, which is always twisted inside the aluminum top, and can't be separated), he just looked into my eyes and said, "Hey, babe; why don't you just stop eating sardines?" It had never occurred to me before.

Every few months Martin decides to put his foot down. "I'm putting my foot down," he says, stomping on the cans. "I work hard all week and I'm fed up with all this bi-metal, tri-metal shit. Why the hell are we doing this?" That's when I remind him about the children's future. Once you start being concerned about things like that, it's hard to stop.

After we're finished recycling, we come home and drink a lot of coffee and sit around with the Sunday paper.

WARNING ON THE END
OF CIVILIZATION

Sydney, Australia

Famed flyer Charles Lindbergh warned yesterday that over-civilization could bring a breakdown of the environment, returning man to the primitive.

"Nothing that has been accomplished is going to be effective if we allow the human environment to break down," he said. "It is possible that we are in the latter stages of a civilization."

—REUTERS

IF ICE DOESN'T GET YOU
WATER WILL

New York

The current 12,000-year-old era of comfortable climates around the world may be coming to an end, closing another chapter of what a University of Miami scientist believes has been a history of relatively short-lived ice ages and warm ages.

147

Cesare Emiliani, a leading authority on the use of sediment cores in studying past climates, called his findings a "warning from the deep sea that the present episode of amiable climate is coming to an end."

Earlier this year, at a conference of global climatologists, Emiliani and others agreed that a new Ice Age could come within 2,000 or 3,000 years. It could be even sooner, they agreed, if man's effect on the environment tips the balance too far.

* * *

"Man's interference with climate through deforestation, urban development and pollution must be viewed with alarm," Emiliani wrote. "If the present climate balance is not maintained, we may soon be confronted with either a runaway glaciation or a runaway deglaciation, both of which would generate unacceptable environmental stresses. . . ."

A deglaciation would melt the water now locked into ice at the poles. It has been calculated that there is enough ice above present sea level that if it were to melt, the oceans would rise enough to drown every coastal city to a depth of many yards.

Measured in human lifetimes, a new Ice Age would, of course, come quite gradually with seasons becoming steadily colder over the long run until the summer high temperatures no longer rose above freezing. From then on snow would simply accumulate, burying cities.

—NEW YORK TIMES SERVICE

I hate Sundays, because Martin always gets the good sections first and I can't argue with him because I get them the rest of the week. So I sit around, pouring coffee and flipping through the dregs and fillers, biding my time. The children are all afflicted with the aimlessness that pervades everything on Sundays; sometimes they can find a friend to play with, and sometimes not. Good parents usually take their children for a drive somewhere on Sundays, leaving the neighborhood more deserted than ever. When the weather is good, we take ours somewhere too; sometimes we take them hiking through the environment so they will appreciate it when they're grown, just on the chance that there will be some left.

Today Jennifer has wandered over to play with Ruth Ann.

They are upstairs in Ruth Ann's room with the boys, and they are unusually quiet.

"That kid is on the doorstep every Sunday morning; what do her parents do, stay in the sack all day?"

"You're just envious, Martin."

"Damn right I am. It's been seven years since we've made it on a Sunday morning."

"You're forgetting the weekends when we've gone away . . ."

"I mean in our own home. It's a form of deprivation to have to always schedule it at night, when they're asleep." ("The birth of children is the death of parents." —Hegel.)

"It's awfully quiet up there, Jeanie. What the hell do you suppose they're doing?"

"Playing doctor probably."

"I'm going up."

"That's an invasion of their privacy, Martin." Together they tiptoe up the stairs LOVE NEST RAIDED and pause at the closed door, listening. Complete silence. Martin opens the door. The boys continue pushing their cars around the room without looking up. Jennifer and Ruth Ann are staring at us; they've both got the same look on their faces. There, in the doll house, are Ken and Barbie; without their clothes; in the missionary position.

"O.K., pick up the toys, kids; I'm going to make lunch." As they back out of the room and start downstairs, Norma Jeans turns to Martin.

"You know, Martin, it's not fair."

"What's not fair?"

"Ken doesn't have a penis."

"I never thought of that."

"Well, you have to think of those things before you buy. Think of Jennifer, mating Barbie and Ken for years on end, then imagine her surprise the first time she tries it herself. ("Yi! What's that you've got down there?" "Christ almighty, that's what all my girl friends ask me! It's a *penis*." "Well, I can't understand it . . . Ken didn't have one.")

"You're right; I know they'd probably imagine it anyway, without the doll, but I don't want Damon and Scott thinking it falls off when you grow up. Get Ken out of the house."

"What about Barbie?"

149

"What's the matter with Barbie?" *She looks all right to me!*

"She has no nipples and no vagina."

"O.K., O.K., get Barbie out too. Let them do their perverted fucking in their own house!"

Martin pulls a beer out of the refrigerator as Norma Jean makes the children's lunch. This is where Sundays usually begin to go downhill. He'll sit around getting sleepy, avoiding all the little domestic tasks that require things like screw drivers, debating whether to sit around awhile, waiting for me to nag ("You said you'd repair those windows that don't close after Doris was robbed. You said you'd fix the gate the year Ruth Ann was born."). I am not going to nag. No sirree; you've got to save your steam for the real crises. Then I'll go out and water the garden, feed the plants, mess around, wishing I could go in the garage and work on the Piece, but not dumb enough to try it; because the minute I get my hands covered with clay is when Damon will knock out a tooth. We both know better than to try to work on Sundays. That's why, unless we're careful to plan something as a family, structure the day, we always end up snarling at each other and feeling uncared for. Sundays are terrible because it is clear that there is no one in charge of the world. And this knowledge leaves you drifting around, grappling with unfulfilled expectations and vague yearnings. Sundays reactivate all the memories of your childhood, when things were planned for you and done with you. If you're not careful, if you just sit around, you find yourself waiting for them to happen again; and things begin to disintegrate when you realize it isn't possible. All your own needs for sustenance and nurturing come crawling out like worms on Sunday; it's the day when you're the most aware of the relentlessness of the parenting task, and of your own irreversible adulthood. ("You can't go home again." —Thomas Wolfe.) But of course no one ever quite believes that, not entirely; that's why you've got to be on your toes on Sunday. It can be a real killer.

So after lunch, I've got plans. "There's a fair going on over at the shopping-center parking lot," I say to Martin. "I thought I'd take the kids. Do you want to come?"

"Naw. You go ahead. I want to stay here and rest." The front

section lies there, discarded and tempting, at his feet. Norma
Jean steals a glance.

CANNIBALS EAT SOCIAL WORKER
IN YELLOWSTONE NAT'L. PARK

I ask you: who needs it? Especially on Sunday.

"All right, kids; are you ready? Let's go." Norma Jean grabs her
purse and starts out the door, then abruptly returns to the house
for something to read. It is a conditioned reflex, acquired from
years spent on park benches, at children's swimming lessons, in
pediatricians' waiting rooms, veterinarians' waiting rooms. She
spots the paperback lying on the shelf beside the kitchen table:
The Pursuit of Loneliness by Philip Slater. I keep it with the
cookbooks; it's what I read every time I get the urge to try a new
recipe. It's my hot line. Every time I start reaching for the food
books I tell myself: *No more recipes. No more in and out and
down the drain, but something which speaks of conditions.* She
stuffs the book into her purse, herds the children into the car,
and heads for the freeway.

Where they join the swirling mass of autos, trucks, motorcycles,
vans, and campers. She is forced to slow, then brake, almost immediately. After a few minutes it becomes clear that they will have
to sit there until the inevitable accident has been cleared. The
shopping center is five miles away. She can already feel the heat
of the midday sun beginning to penetrate the small car. *Why
the hell didn't I take the top down?* The children begin to os-
cillate in the back with little queries concerning the nature of the
delay: ("Why did we stop?" —Scott. "Are we going to sit here all
day?" —Ruth Ann. "Do they have toilets on the freeway?" —Damon). She wonders how long they will be able to hold out. Then
she remembers the little bag of lollipops tucked under the seat for
times of unbearable stress and dire emergencies. She distributes
them and settles back to wait. You can't see anything up ahead,
but there is the sound of sirens in the distance. Norma Jean
closes her eyes. She tries to imagine the accident, in order to prepare herself; speculates on the degree of carnage. And the memory surfaces, she *does not want it!* But it is precisely because you
resist a memory that it thrusts itself into your consciousness with

the force of a pneumatic drill. Two years ago, driving past the burning remains of a late-model Ford which was hanging over the edge of an overpass by its rear wheels, dangling there, suspended in midair, wrapped in a mass of flames. The doors were all shut, she noted that; so there *had* to be someone inside. The police were waving everyone past; they were agitated because there was nothing they could do. The driver couldn't be reached either from the top of the overpass, or from the ground. There was nothing to do but wait for the car to burn itself out. The following morning the paper carried the details. The only ones Norma Jean remembers were that her name was Pearl and that she had screamed for a long time. "Help me! Help me! Help me!" she screamed, as people stood by. She remembers having thought the image the ultimate metaphor of the times: to be betrayed by our technology and consumed by our passion for speed and isolation. Can you do that to someone, make her a metaphor without her consent? Is it fair?

Norma Jean flips on the radio and reaches for her book in an effort to wipe out the memory and fill up the time. Philip Slater is calm and does not provoke the feelings of rage the feminist writers do. You read the feminists at night, in bed, when chances are good that you are too tired to act immediately on the feelings that are aroused, and trust that your mind will digest the material during sleep in a way that will lead to purposeful action later. You do not read feminists while in the pediatrician's office or on the freeway. (CHILDREN ABANDONED IN DOCTOR'S OFFICE. Police are seeking information concerning the identity of the three children pictured Was last seen on Interstate 580, passing commuter traffic in the on-coming lane, just south of the Seminary interchange, after a chase climaxed by speeds up to 90 miles an hour. Officer Charles ("Chuck") Romack, a 12-year veteran of the force, was quoted as saying, "Every time I'd get close, she'd give me the finger. She was driving the ——— out of that car. Then suddenly she pulls out, crosses the divider, and just keeps going, on the wrong side of the road. The reason we lost her was we were stuck there in rush hour traffic; we couldn't move." In response to a reporter's question, Officer Romack stated, "There was no way I could have done that; it's against the law to drive on the wrong side of the road. . . .") As a stage in the process, agitated rage is as essential to growth as death is to rebirth. But it's not something you can live with day and night; you have to take breaks, back off, and give yourself the margins that are required for rapid change to be mastered with a minimum of collapse.

The main factor facilitating the ultradomestication of the middle-class American female was the magnification of the child-rearing role.

—Philip Slater, op. cit., p. 66.

"Mommy, I'm thirsty!"

"Yeah, me too. And we're hot. It's too hot in here." Norma Jean reaches under the seat. "Here, have another lollipop and shut up; there's nothing I can do about it." It's amazing what you can accomplish reading Philip Slater, whipping yourself up and not giving a damn.

The emotional and intellectual poverty of the housewife's role is nicely expressed in the almost universal complaint: "I get to talking baby talk with no one around all day but the children." There are societies in which the domestic role works, but in those societies the housewife is not isolated. She is either part of a large extended family household in which domestic activities are a communal effort, or participates in a tightly knit village community, or both. The idea of imprisoning each woman alone in a small, self-contained, and architecturally isolating dwelling is a modern invention, dependent upon an advanced technology. . . .

This is in striking contrast to her pre-marital life, if she is a college graduate. In college she is typically embedded in an active group life with constant emotional and intellectual stimulation. College life is in this sense an urban life. Marriage typically eliminates much of this way of life for her, and children deliver the *coup de grace*. Her only significant relationship tends to be to her husband, who, however, is absent most of the day. Most of her social and emotional needs must be satisfied by her children, who are hardly adequate to the task. . . .

This is, in fact, the most vulnerable point in the whole system. Even if the American housewife were not a rather deprived person, it would be the essence of vanity for anyone to assume that an unformed child could tolerate such massive inputs of one person's personality. In most societies the impact of neuroses and defects in the mother's character is diluted by the presence of many other nurturing agents. . . .

—Ibid., pp. 67–69.

"Hey, lady, traffic's moving again. Move it or milk it!"

"They're honking at you, Mommy."

Norma Jean quickly throws the book aside and reaches to start the car. It goes oya oya oya. God *damn* it! Not *here!* She switches off the radio so she can concentrate (when these things happen, it is required that you not be distracted; it is essential that you experience the full force of your agony, humiliation, and panic without props of any kind. Don't ask me why; that's just the way it is. Everyone whose car stalls on the freeway knows it). She turns the key again and this time the car starts. By the time they pass the site of the accident nothing remains but a few twisted fenders and the ubiquitous fragments of glass.

Eventually they pull into the parking lot of the shopping center where the fair is being held. Here we are, and there's not a single place to park. Sweat streams down Norma Jean's forehead; the children are screaming for water. I promise, I swear: Never again. *I don't want it never, never again. I'm callin my mother and I don't care if she don't speak to me; I'm goin home.* ("You can't go home again." —Thomas Wolfe.) "Shut up, you nagging son of a bitch!"

"I didn't do it!" squeaks Damon, in surprise.

"She didn't mean you, Damon. She's talking to *herself.*" Don't lose your mind. Not now, not here. Just keep circling around and around and keep your mind focused on the fact that you're looking for the three most important things in the world: a parking space; a bathroom; and water. (Norma Jean Harris [the former Norma Jean Sommers] sends us her new address. You can write her, all of you out there from the class of '58! c/o California State Hospital for the Insane. . . .)

"Mommy! Mommy! There's one! Right there!" screams Ruth Ann. It really helps to have a child who can scout, who's skilled in the art of scanning the terrain for things that maintain life functions. Norma Jean hits the brakes, which sends Damon's face into the back of her seat. He starts to scream.

"His lip is bleeding, Mommy!"

"Aaaa! My *lip* is bleeding!"

You've got to move fast, or some bastard will slip into it front-first while you're backing up. She reverses the car and hits the brakes again, sending Damon's head into the rim of the jump seat. "Just suck on it a few minutes and the bleeding will stop," she shouts over the roar of the motor and the sound of his wailing, and pulls the car to a stop inside the two white lines of a genuine, undeniable parking space. She turns off the motor and wipes her forehead with the back of her hand. She experiences the sense of peace that always follows hard-won achievements. Moments later she begins to cry.

Sinking onto a vacant bench as the children race toward the bathrooms, Norma Jean closes her eyes. The form of Martin Harris takes shape behind her lids. He is stretching. The Sunday paper lies at his feet. God, it's great to just sit here, everyone gone, no noise. Never get to do this—just sit quietly in my own home —looking around, drinking it in, *nothing required.* Images of articles put aside for weekend study come into focus, but he doesn't act on them. He continues to sit, his body deflated, concave, marveling at the lighting, the structure, the arrangement of his home.

She gets to do this, to absorb and enjoy the house. Well, I suppose if you have to be here every day, and it's filled with noisy children making demands, you could come to hate it. She should have her own work, I can't argue with that; it's uncivilized to ask a person to waste her education, her talent. But she should be able to wait; the children need a mother, need someone. I can't turn the clock back, can't give up what I've achieved. It took too long. If we were younger, and starting over, would I be able to split things half and half? Could I delay my own progress so as not to retard hers? She doesn't want to take my work away; just wants some meaningful work of her own. She has a right to that, any human being does. Hell, would I be satisfied living her life? *It's not required of men, so you've never had to consider the question as though it were a serious possibility; and therefore the integrity of any answer you give is compromised before the fact.* Still, nature gave women the womb, the breasts, there must be Well, this is the twentieth century and requirements change. Actually, I might have liked it, in a society where the division was expected; I would have known the kids more intimately, been more of an influence on them.

"Mom! We peed and got a drink of water. Can we go and buy things now?" Slowly Norma Jean comes back; she leans over and zips Damon's pants.

"Listen, children: I have a headache, so I'm going to stay here on this bench—right by the bathrooms, you can't miss it. Here's a quarter for each of you, but you must come back here when you're finished looking around. Understand?" She deposits a quarter in each sweaty palm and watches as they scatter—Ruth Ann toward cotton candy, Scott, the midget race track. Damon stands around for a while, looking confused. There is a Batting Practice booth right next to the bathrooms; she encourages him to give it a try (THREE TIMES AT BAT—10¢). He's shy, but starts inching over slowly; it's his favorite game. The smell of hot dogs is overpowering. Norma Jean lights a cigarette and leans back, pinching the bridge of her nose. *I should have stayed home* while *he* took the kids. Well, it wouldn't have been fair; he works hard all week, deserves some time to himself, to just sit around and think. Thinking is one of the most restorative things there is. She fans herself with *The Pursuit of Loneliness*; the heat is searing. She pictures Martin, alone in the cool house. She hopes he appreciates the quiet, for which she now suffers. She grinds out the cigarette with her foot and closes her eyes again.

Martin eases himself out of the chair and walks slowly toward his study. He is going to get the articles, finish reading them while it's still quiet. As he sinks into the chair at his desk, he does not reach for the articles; instead he leans back with his feet on the desk, dreaming of his wife. Norma Jean Sommers. *When I first met you I used to tell my friends: I'm going out with an artist.* Yes, it's true. I was moved by that; it set you apart. *Then why are you opposing her now?* I didn't think it would require so much of me! All my supports, the things I rely on, are being withdrawn: her focus on me, her *availability.* It isn't just the little things like the buttons, and refusing to take my clothes to the cleaners (bitch!); there are deeper assumptions being challenged, issues that have to do with the very way I see her in relation to me and my needs. It was enough that the entire balance of needs had to be redistributed as each of the children came along. It was a delicate balance to begin with, it's always a delicate balance; you can't ask a man to do that twice. It's a major adjustment. *Life is change; change is growth; growth requires continual readjustment.* I have never denied that. *Just regarded it as a theory in books, huh? To be applied to the species as a whole, not as something that would be required of you personally.* Maybe. Maybe. I always thought: you do your changing and adjusting when you're young. After that, you apply yourself, settle down, work hard . . . for me, and my generation in general, there were no margins for fooling around.

The very worst thing was the unyieldingness of the choice: you could either sign on for a lifetime commitment, and hang by your teeth trying to fulfill it; or you could blow it all in one moment of indecision or rebellion—and there would go your chances for self-respect, security, achievement, love; a wife (who would want to marry a bum?), children, home, the approval of parents, society, the respect of peers. Kiss it all good-bye. No address, no money—to invest, manipulate, as a visible index of your power. No *power!* That's what it all comes down to in the end. Power. Without it, you might just as well call yourself a woman. . . . And if certain vital parts of yourself began to atrophy in the struggle to maintain it, it was understood that every goal had its price. Anything might be possible, but you didn't get it for nothing.

Martin gets up and walks through the silent house, running his hands lightly along the walls as though to confirm that it is indeed due to his sense of honor, his integrity, his responsibility, that they are standing, and can be called his own. I have honored my obligations; where is the praise? I have met the requirements; what is the reward? This house? The family? No. No. They . . . came with the deal. *They* are not what you get in return, are they? Where is that one thing, that burning core, profound pleasure, inner light, ultimate treasure, the dream of which was implanted under your skin at an early age? Where is the proof that you have fulfilled a crucial expectation? I paid the price they asked and the laurels didn't arrive. It didn't even buy their love. And now, as though to ensure absolutely that the lesson has been learned; as though to make certain I do not escape the full impact of the betrayal, the loss; and in the event I am tempted to sustain the least illusion against despair, here is Norma Jean, right on cue, obliterating my few remaining assumptions, withdrawing all my small privileges, *one by one*.

Norma Jean sits up with a start; you shouldn't just sit here dozing The children could get What time is it? She scans the crowds, the booths; she sees Damon's hair stirring like a meadow above home plate. Give them another fifteen minutes; it took us so long to get here. She lights another cigarette. He can't complain; we've been away over two hours. It would please him to see Damon there. . . .

Martin stands by the window, staring into the yard. He is thinking of his sons. Scott, the quiet intellectual; strange how he keeps most of it in, his stoicism. Ponders everything in complete isolation and silence, weighs all the information before making a statement, before committing himself. He'll be O.K. if he develops that; it will be a strength, the system can't crush him. Crazy Damon, he'll be the athlete: hyped-up, springing, ready to throw himself into the absolute center of all things. He sees Damon in twenty years, has a vision of Damon. His hair is still the color of dry grass, it ripples on the spring wind as he removes his cap and drops the ball inside. Martin smiles as he stares across the yard where the sunlight lies in patches. A cat crouches there, coiled for the bird it will never catch. And suddenly the crowd becomes excited. It is Damon, blowing a wad of spit onto the pitcher's mound; snapping his gum; rubbing his hands together while casting glances to the right and left; he touches the rim of his cap; now turns, And it's Damon Harris in the wind-up! Every muscle was born to preside over this moment. And now the stretch. The pitch. *Strike three!* Listen to that crowd! Sports fans, Damon Harris has done it again!

Martin runs his fingers through his hair. He clears his throat. Turning away now from the window, he feels an intense desire for a beer. He walks slowly into the kitchen, withdraws the can from the refrigerator, and inserts his finger into the ring; a quick hiss escapes as the tab is pulled back. The sound conveys a sense of promise that takes him by surprise. He puts the can to his mouth and, throwing back his head, stares at the ceiling as he draws in swallow after swallow, without pause. Something on the ceiling moves. It is Damon, in center field; and he's going back,

back, his form there on the sweet turf, the blinding white of him, floating backwards on that green sea; the fibers in his up-stretched arms where lightning flows like rivers, back, back . . . and he's *got* it! Has drawn it out of the sky like a wounded bird whose fall he breaks, and holds a moment in the curve of his body, before he sends it spinning on its homeward course. For those of you who just tuned in, what you're hearing there in the background is a crowd that has gone *wild*. They just won't let him go! A stu*pen*dous catch by Damon Harris!

Norma Jean opens the front door and the children stagger in; they are weighted down with sweat, grime, fatigue, and the as-sorted trinkets which are always acquired at fairs and thrown out the next day. Coming out of the kitchen, Martin almost collides with Damon, who is running to show him the one purchase he hasn't eaten: a little hat, made of pink feathers, with silver-spangled letters in front which read HAPPY NEW YEAR.

"Jesus Christ, what is *that* he's got on his head?" Martin de-mands, stepping back.

"What does it look like? It's a Happy New Year hat. He got it at a white elephant booth for two cents."

"What are you trying to do, make a goddamned *fag* out of the kid? Damon, take that thing off your head."

"Will you cut it out? He thought it was pretty. Leave him alone! You're the one who's going to confuse him, with all your damned sex-role stereotyping!"

"Bunch of man-hating lesbian misfits, trying to lay your neurotic shit on a little kid. You just wait; there'll be a whole generation of crippled fucked-up kids who will have to pay the price for this so-called liberation!"

"There already are! And they got that way because of overpro-tective mothers and absentee jock fathers like you!" Damon is crying now. "I want my hat! I want my hat!"

"Come here, kid. Wanna bat the ball around with Dad?" Bat the ball, knock over the Empire State Building, stand on your heads. I'm going out in the garage, before I lose my mind.

In the silence of the garage Norma Jean unwraps the Piece. I'm going to stay with it this time, until it's finished. She begins to work and it surprises her that new ideas for other pieces begin to suggest themselves, even as she is applying *these* ideas to *this* piece. She hadn't thought it possible: that two, or more, entirely separate systems of creative thought could evolve and develop there in the mind simultaneously. You would think one would cancel the other out. Maybe the mind knows that the Piece is now conducting its own birth, can make it on its own; and has decided it can take leave of it now in order to preside over the genesis of new forms.

Two hours pass with such speed that Norma Jean jumps when Martin stands in the doorway of the garage to announce, "O.K., Jeanie, I've kept the kids out of your hair for *two hours* now. They're tired and hungry. Are you about ready to get dinner?"

Dear Piece,
   With your graduation so close at hand, I want you to know what you've come to mean to me.
   Although it seems that I've been creating you, the opposite also obtains. ("Who *is* the Potter, pray, and who the Pot?" —Omar Khayyám.) Your existence has redefined growth for me. By declaring new boundaries for yourself, you have extended mine. You, your example, have convinced me of something I had always disbelieved: that boundaries are movable; there is always more space beyond. That people are not fixed; our possibilities are fluid and infinite. When I look at you it tells me things about myself I never knew.

"Did you hear what I said, Norma? Will you bring your mind back from outer space and answer my question?"

   Before I close, I thought you might be interested to know how I met this particular challenge. What I said to him was:

"I can't leave my work right now; fix yourselves some soup and sandwiches. The stuff's all there."

I would be lying if I said I felt no doubts, no guilt; but, amazing as it might seem, people are sometimes helped in their struggles by simple reason; and reason said: *They won't die! The food is there; all they have to do is put it in their mouths.*
   Soon you will be "finished." Don't envy the new ideas; you were the first. You set the tone, established the frontier to which the others now migrate with ease. You were there at the beginning.

"I've had it, Norma Jean. I can't take it any more. I want a divorce."

"Wait 'til I turn the water off; I can't hear you." Norma Jean replaces the cap on the toothpaste and switches off the light.

"What did you say?"

"I said: This is *it*. I want a divorce." Norma Jean is walking toward the bed; now she stops and stands motionless in the middle of the room.

"Why did you tell me while I was brushing my teeth? Did you feel it needed a rehearsal?"

"Don't get sarcastic with me. You've pushed me as far as I can go. I want a divorce."

"Well, I don't." *Not now! I'm not ready. . . . The son of a bitch! I was saving that to use myself, and he beat me out. . . . Let's see; think fast, don't look stricken! Act nonchalant, bide your time. I've got it: agree with him. He'll panic.*

"You're probably right, Martin. I feel you're pushing *me* as far as I can go. It's sad, but we're probably too old to change."

"My main concern," he continues, "and I'm sure yours too, is for the children." Norma Jean slowly lights a cigarette, a gesture which has always signified a willingness to negotiate and to postpone hysteria. *Those fucking men, they've had centuries of practice detecting bluffs, stepping over land mines, taking the offensive, calling the shots. The reflexes are all there, written in the history of their cells, and I—I need to sit down, I'm about to cry, the dirty bastard has me right where he wants me: I can not go backwards, will not give up these small but significant gains; but I do not want to lose him. Because then I'd have to manage those blood-sucking kids all alone! Because I haven't been alone for ten years, and I've gotten used to having someone there in bed every night; come to value the special feeling that someone cares, and would take note, if you were to disappear. Because I'm still his chattel, any way you slice it. I'd have to ask him for every cent! There must be other reasons for not wanting to lose him; it goes deeper than that. Nothing I can think of now!*

"Why can't you see me through this struggle? I saw you through yours; I am not asking that much! Why can't you cope? You're so rigid; you're not the person I married. You used to have flexibility. Where is it now?" She flicks an ash and waits for his answer: *My* flexibility? Oh. That. Well, it's gone. They took it away on my thirty-eighth birthday, don't you remember? The age varies, but they always come for it sometime in mid-life. They exchange it for rigidity. One never suffers total loss; everything that's taken away is replaced with something else: energy with fatigue; dark hair with grey; spontaneity with caution; optimism with despair. For everything that's lost, something takes its place. You have to replace what goes out; it follows some law. You'd cave in otherwise.

After studying his thumb, Martin answers. "You are no longer meeting my needs."

"Well, you don't meet all mine either; I've learned to live with that."

"Well, I'm not sure I can."

"Listen. I want some of *my* needs met for a change! Not my needs as perceived by *you*, or Madison Avenue, but ones which *I* perceive as authentic: autonomy, mastery, self-respect. I love you and I care about you, but I am not going back. I want nothing more than what you have always demanded for yourself. How can you claim I have no right to that?"

"You probably do have the right. I just can't accept it in practice." *Things are way off center, out of balance. You work and work, you think you have a home, a haven, with something at the center, something warm, always there when you need it, which gives you the will to keep going . . . and then you wake up one morning and find that everything has shifted: and what have you got? An equal! Fuck it, fuck it . . .*

"What can't you accept? My attempt to create a body of work that represents what I can do? To participate in a life *outside these four walls?*"

"You have a right to explore your ideas. What I can't tolerate is that you're" *not there when I need you any more* "in outer space half the time, off somewhere—God knows where—in your own world; your mind is not *here!*"

"What do you mean, 'here'? Where is 'here'? Where should my mind be the other half of the time?" She feels a growing sense of desperation, *trying to make me give it up! take it away!*

"On me! You are not *here*, with *me*; your mind is not with me!"

162

"God damn you, Martin; what do you *want* from me? I can't be hovering around you every minute! If I did, you couldn't stand it; you'd say, 'Don't you have something to do?' (A few floors that need . . . A few buttons . . . maybe a cake!) You want me to be *subtle* about my availability. Just float around unobtrusively, waiting in the wings, out of sight but not out of calling. Well fuck that, fuck you, I don't want it never, never again. . . ."

"Look at you—you're getting so hysterical you can't even speak correct English."

"Listen, you pigheaded bastard, you demanding prick: You spent years establishing yourself, working nights, discovering your potential, growing; and I waited, I gave support, understood, stuck around. Your work didn't preclude your having the gratification of a family. Why are you asking *me* to make that choice?"

"A lot of women realize their full potential when their families don't need them so much, and they have time" *He's thinking of those women with the beady eyes, who sit on the rocks painting the sea!* "to develop themselves without jeopardizing the needs of others! Why can't you do your sculpting" *when no one needs you* "when there are . . . pauses in the day, in between your chores, in a more . . . leisurely way?"

" 'Pauses!' 'Leisurely!' I'm not on *vacation!* I didn't study art to be a dilettante! It's my contribution, my statement; and it's important when you make statements that they represent your best effort. And that requires time."

"Well, you wanted *children! You* chose marriage and a family! And people have to stick by their choices! Why did you have a family if you wanted to be an artist?"

"People change! Their times change, and their own needs change. You can't condemn them for having changed; you can only ask if they've acted with integrity, if they've dealt with that change as conscientiously as they could." *You always walk a tightrope between your needs and the needs of others. I don't subscribe to the idea that complete selfishness is a legitimate requisite for attaining goals. It doesn't suit the human condition. Still, people have the ultimate right to act according to their own interpretation of their needs. And this sometimes causes pain to others.*

"Well, being conscientious doesn't cut it when you're asking someone else to give *up* something so you can *get* something. That's what this all boils down to: you're asking me to give up things so you can achieve your goals!" Martin spits out, his voice rising.

"Why *not*? What's wrong with give and take—we've been compromising for each other throughout the marriage; that's fundamental in close relationships. It proves you don't consider me equal to you, you don't really believe I have the same human rights as you do. I gave up 'things'! I sacrificed so you could attain *your* goals! It's all right for *me* to do the giving up, but unacceptable, *unthinkable*, for you. And you consider yourself a progressive and civilized man. You're still living in the nineteenth century!" she screams.

"You sound like a fishwife! Lower your voice! You'll wake the children."

When a man wishes to regain the advantage in an argument with his wife, he first employs a maneuver designed to provoke her vigorous protest; the basic aspect of this maneuver—in addition to the *content* of his statement, which contains the emotional ammunition—requires that he raise his voice higher than the prevailing conversation; but not so high that it could be defined as screaming. And after she has risen to the bait and shouted her objections, his second tactic (effective only if executed *immediately* after she speaks her last word) is to veer toward her with index finger cocked and make a statement such as the preceding.

In simple terms, what this maneuver seeks to accomplish is to convince the wife that she has overstepped the boundaries governing the argument, which were defined earlier, and in secret, by the husband; and to arouse her inherent guilt and shame for having behaved with less control than he. This device usually results in the husband's regaining the balance of power. Occasionally, however, it fails. When this occurs, there are still two auxiliary maneuvers he can employ.

In the first of these, he must begin to make statements—always addressed *to* or *about* his wife—which gradually increase in their degree of incoherence and the intensity of abusiveness. It is helpful to include references to: her weight; the fact that her facial expression is hard, ugly, unfeminine (do not be diverted by the logic of the situation, i.e., that this is so because she is angry and fighting; your objective is to *exploit* this fact in a way that will distract her and prevent her from using it as a legitimate defense. Remember that the point of all the maneuvers cited in this exercise is to assist the husband in recapturing the edge). The reference to the face is often successful because she still thinks, in her profoundest depths, that it is "unfeminine" (i.e., unnatural, *wrong*) to have a facial expression that is anything but serene, nurturing, expectant, soft, passionate, compassionate, accepting, forgiving, and extremely beautiful by whatever standards prevail. Other references which have proven consistently provocative and which are equally acceptable are: her frequency and attitude regarding sexual relations (frequency, being tangible, is often harder to attack than is attitude, whose universal ambiguity makes it an excellent target); her origins (national, religious, economic, and, of course, sexual); her parents; her siblings, if any; and finally, her general adequacy as a mother. The latter in particular has been found to have a high index of guilt-arousal.

The ultimate aim of this second maneuver is in many ways similar to the aim of the first, in that it employs tactics whose goal is to arouse guilt and self-doubt; and its similarity extends also to the fact that—when effective—it results in loss of emotional control on the part of the wife; and that, further, the form that this loss of control takes is, in both cases, screaming. Here, however, the similarity ends. For while the first maneuver calls for the husband to attack the wife simply for *screaming* (on the basis of its unfemininity; its potential to arouse the children, or the neighbors, or the dog—you see the possible variations suggested here; if one fails to arouse the guilt required to produce remorse and submission, others can be tried), the second maneuver requires him to cite the screaming as evidence of *insanity*. The simplest method is for him to point the index finger directly at the wife, while she is screaming, and comment, "Listen to your screaming! You must be crazy to scream like that!" When she responds to this with increased fury and noise, he has simply to mutter "Crazy lady, crazy lady" a few times to drive the point home.

This maneuver has rarely been known to fail when instructions were carried out as given. What happens, quite simply, is that the husband himself uses extreme irrationality as a device to arouse a corresponding response from the wife; and after this has been obtained, he then focuses complete attention on the *wife's* irrational screaming, and makes the link between screaming and insanity by means of the following logic: there is documented evidence that crazy people sometimes scream; therefore, screaming is an indication of insanity. The task is facilitated immeasurably by the enormous weight of historical precedent establishing extensive and intricate networks of links between loss of control, mental imbalance, and women. And since, throughout most of history (and continuing to the present) the consequences of craziness were so extreme, a woman can be expected to respond with near-flawless conditioning, expressing a fear quite sufficient to indicate that she feels the accusation might be true. When this occurs, you may consider the battle won. Incidentally, the effects of this tactic often last much longer than actually required for the initial purpose. This is only one of the reasons why we consider this the Rolls-Royce of maneuvers: smooth, dependable, with a performance you can always rely on. A thoroughly elegant tactic. Highly recommended!

The third maneuver is one which should be considered only after previous battles have established that the wife is sufficiently capable of defensive actions which render the first two plans ineffective. This is because the final maneuver is one which accomplishes the least, in terms of reinforcing the husband's self-esteem and in terms of his long-range ability to hold and maintain the edge once he has acquired it. In spite of its acknowledged tactical inferiority, it is included here in accordance with our philosophy that, in combat, men must be accorded the widest possible range of alternatives in order to maintain the superior position. Greater choice results in greater morale. And morale, as we know, is of the utmost importance. A man without morale is a defeated man. And a defeated man has no power. And a man without power is not a man.

To conclude: the instructions for the third maneuver are quite specific. Unlike the first and second maneuvers, individual latitude in the areas of interpretation and execution is inappropriate and not suggested. The third maneuver, for all its deficiencies, has one basic appeal and that is its simplicity. When the husband senses he is losing, or about to lose, his edge (remember to think ahead; it is always preferable to employ maneuvers against a suspected loss of sovereignty than to require the maneuver in order to regain positions already lost), he simply interrupts the dialogue—regardless of whether it happens to be his wife's or his own—and excuses himself to urinate. While maneuver number three, as we have stated, has its limitations, it has one feature—besides stopping the conversation and permitting memory lapses which favor the husband—which renders it foolproof, and therefore unique among maneuvers: the wife cannot contest it. There is no way for a woman to challenge a call of nature and win, provided there are locks on the bathroom doors which cannot be tampered with from the outside. In extreme cases, where the wife suspects a ruse and attempts to authenticate your claim by means of listening at the door, a child's rubber duck—filled with water, and held over the bowl—has been proven to produce an excellent facsimile of the appropriate auditory effect.

Maneuver number one has had a short-term effect; Norma Jean lowers her voice. "I don't want a divorce; I'm tired of fighting. I just want a reasonable amount of time to do my work, and a reasonable adjustment on your part toward a more equitable sharing of responsibilities so I can make use of the time I have."

Martin scratches his head. "One minute you're cooking great meals and having babies; the next thing I know you're in outer space! What's your *hurry*? You have all the necessities of life, and many of the luxuries—things that would" *make any normal woman* "make any woman happy. Can you give me one good reason why you can't wait a few years, until the children are grown and you will have unlimited time to develop your interests?"

Well, aside from the fact that no one ever asked that of *you*; and aside from the fact that most people don't begin their careers at fifty, and aside from the fact that *you have no right to control my life by offering me choices that benefit you and cripple me,*

"Yes! I can give you one good reason why I can't wait fifteen years to do my work: *Because my ideas are coming now!* If I can't connect the idea to the work when it's fresh, it dies. And killing ideas is just like killing babies. They are my products, they come from me, and they have a right to live."

"This whole business is clearly symbolic; when you can't have any more babies in *there*," he points to her stomach, "you manufacture them out *there*," gesturing toward the garage.

167

When attempting to prevent a wife from engaging in an activity which the husband cannot tolerate, it is usually sufficient to suggest that the activity is merely a symbolic representation of some other function—usually having to do with her reproductive system—the duties of which she is attempting to avoid. That this may or may not be so in a given case has no bearing on the wife's reaction. She invariably responds *as though* the symbolic action were not only inferior to the actual one, but wrong. In most cases you can count on her cultural conditioning to produce this reaction immediately, and nothing further needs to be done. In stubborn cases, the principle of Mother Earth can be invoked to advantage. Remind the wife that since she is designed in a way that permits conception, gestation, growth and harvesting, it is her obligation to honor the purpose for which she was designed, and that deviations from this purpose are unnatural. Cite as many examples from nature as necessary; they are abundant.

"I do not give a shit what *you* think it means. ('You can't scare me!' —Three Little Pigs, p. 6.) I care what it means to *me!* It means I can shape *matter*. I can organize *chaos*. I can achieve *mastery*. It *requires* something of me. You can be totally paralyzed and brain damaged, and still have a baby. It's something that happens *to* you. When I work I *make* things happen. You want to know my theory?"

Norma Jean's Theory

In the beginning, before primitive man made the connection between intercourse and conception, he would stand around in the afternoons, after the hunt, making observations. One of the first things he noticed was that all the women were getting bigger and bigger bellies. "Umph. Gee. She's getting fat," he would think. Then later, he would stand around in the evenings by the fire and he would see all the women giving birth to babies. "Fantastic!" he would say; "Whooo-ee! Looka that, come right out of nowhere!" He was ignorant of cause and effect, what with coming home tired from work, and the effort required to stay alive, etc.

After a while, his mind began to wander during work. He'd think: "Here I am every day, out here whuppin and clubbin these animals; she git to stay inna cave, nice and warm, givin suck to those things what come outa her. How come nothin ever come outa me 'cept shit? Still, I got this pleasant thing on me that rises when I needs it and goes down when I don't, and she don't have that. But a baby's bigger, and it can grow and do things by itself, and brings in extra food when it grows up. And she can have lots of them! I only got one of this. And it don't *do* nothin, 'cept go up and down, and in and out, and pee. Well, shit. I don't know." (This was the first recorded depression.)

Later on he made the connection between intercourse and conception. "Hey!" he said. "I made a discovery! If you fuck, you get babies!" It was as important a discovery, in its way, as the discovery of fire. After some years, however, he developed extreme melancholy. He confided to a friend, "I am *so* blue. I fuck and fuck, but *she* still gets all the babies!" His friend replied, "Yeah, I noticed that too. It's damned unfair that we don't get to have people growing inside us. Just imagine it— having another person *inside* you! It give me chills. I'd sure like to try it to see what it's like, but I don't know any way to do it." (This was the original sex discrimination.)

The first recorded case of the defense mechanism known as overcompensation occurred shortly after this, as primitive man stormed out of the cave one morning, just after his woman gave birth to their fifteenth child, and said, "I just can't stand her no more! She lie there alla time havin babies, got no use for me. I am *so envious* I fit to die! Ungh ungh *ungh!*" "Well, cheer up," the voice of overcompensation whispered to him. "You still got your thing there." "Sure enough I do. I'll show her. I can do more things with this thing than she can do with her non-thing! I'm gonna have me some rape and pillage! And I'm gonna build me a great big weapon, shaped just like my thing, and I'm gonna kill a lot of dirty bastards with it! And then I'm gonna build me a monument in the shape of my thing, big as a mountain! And everyone gonna get down onna knees before it and they gonna say 'Whoo-ee! You are the *greatest*'." So he went right out and laid waste to the land. And it felt so good he never stopped. And when he came home at night he kicked his woman in the head and said, "Nyaa, nyaa, nyaa! You can't come out with me and rape and pillage and smash things and lay waste to the land, cause you justa dumb broad; you gotta stay inna cave, havin babies cause you got gypped; you got no terrific fantastic thing on you like I do! And don't you go trying to steal it inna night, either. It don't come off . . .

169

(I don't think). I *knows* you envious; but you just gonna hafta make do. They's that got, got; they's that don't, don't." And as he lay there that night, he found himself in deep reflection about his woman. He thought: "She do mysterious things I can't do. She got mysterious things inside her I can't see. She *bleed* alla time but she never die! Weird. She scare me. I gonna keep her down so she can't do nothin funny, like eat me up."

Martin gets up. "Interesting theory," he says. "I've got to go to the bathroom."

"Don't pull that on me! You started this argument; you can stay until it's resolved."

"There *is* no resolution. I've put up with all I'm going to. I no longer have a *wife*. You're more excited by your work than you are by *me!*"

"I learned to share you with *your* work years ago; you'll just have to learn to share me with mine." *Had me to himself all those years, then the children came along and staked their claims on me, and now my work has a piece of the action; what's left for him? One third? You've got to be precise about these things; they want to know.*

"I'm sleeping in my study tonight," he calls out over his shoulder. "You want to work, do your work. We'll both give the children what we can. There's no reason they should be made victims of this, if it can be avoided. I have nothing more to say." He exits.

In the event that the edge has been lost completely, and the combatant finds that, due either to lack of ammunition or fatigue, he is unable to employ any of the previously mentioned maneuvers in a way that will maintain his advantage, there remains one final device which he may use. Known as Withdrawal with Honor, this maneuver calls for the husband to *remove his pillow from the bed*, while simultaneously stating, "There's nothing more to say," or words to that effect. All human beings, women in particular, hate to hear that there is nothing more to say. This derives in part from their conviction—thought by some to be an illusion—that from communication proceeds understanding, reduction of tension, mutual respect, emotional closeness, and a more tolerable life in general. So it is helpful to keep in mind that it is all these needs which are being threatened when you say "There's nothing more to say." It cuts them cold—which of course is its purpose. Removing the pillow is a back-up gesture, designed to reinforce the terror you hope was engendered by the verbal statement. It is a power play whose purpose is to hint at desertion and abandonment; its strength obtains from the basics of its symbolism, e.g., the associations with sexual gratification and security.

If added insurance is desired, it does not compromise the effectiveness of this maneuver to throw in a comment concerning the vulnerability of children to parental discord; it is guaranteed that the implication this comment always carries is that the *wife* must stop being discordant if she wishes to protect her children against victimization. It is, for this reason, a smooth and dependable device, as it places the wife in a double bind, the classic dimensions of which are not easily comprehended or resolved. This buys you time.

There are no stars tonight. Storm clouds have gathered since the searing heat of the afternoon. Humid and dense, they lie impacted in the night sky, dropping their rain like marbles over the bedroom roof, where Norma Jean lies alone, and listens. She stares into the semidarkness, watching the loquat tree fill up with rain. "I want a divorce." Did Martin say that? *Yes; he said it twice.* MID-LIFE DIVORCE: INCREASING PHENOMENON. How can this be happening to us? We were different. *Were we? How much pressure, how much change, do you think people can take? What makes you different?* Our inner resources! Our . . . stability. Our love for each other. *Forget it. Inner resources are like natural resources; they both dry up eventually when the demands on them are heavy. Stability? That belonged to another time. It's meaningless now. Love? You know love is not enough. . . .*

I used to cry all the time; now I hardly cry at all. Right now I feel I should. Because I think—whether we divorce, or separate, or live like strangers under the same roof—Martin is not going to change. I keep hoping I'm wrong, but there is a quality of alienation this time, a degree of differences, that makes me wonder: how far can you go before it is impossible to recover ground, heal wounds? Only a year ago I was mourning the divorces of friends and feeling certain of our own stability. I don't want to

be a casualty in a revolution; I don't feel heroic. But to go backwards would be to die the kind of death that has no resurrection.

Am I expecting too much? But it's expectation that differenti-
ates you from the dead. The dead, so low in their stone rows,
making no demands, without desire. He would like me that way.
He would like me better dead. *Don't start that again; you've been
clean for a year and a half.* True love can overcome anything! All
the books said! I'm sorry I disappointed you. I'm sorry I couldn't
meet your needs. I'm sorry we had to be the generation in the
middle. Sorry the years went by so fast, and took us by surprise.

It *has* been a year and a half, but I am losing Martin and the
knowledge makes me want to die. I am staring at the loquat tree.
For seven years it has borne witness to our acts of love. Now it has
nothing to say; it is not a symbol, just a tree, with leaves like
troughs where the rain runs like silver. It seems only natural to
think about dying. I have considered it before; I have rehearsed
it in dreams; I have rehearsed it in G minor in the stillest of nights.
I have chosen the place: it is on the coast, in dry grass, directly
beneath the route of migratory birds from Canada.

12

Norma Jean wakes to an empty bed. There is a unique feeling which accompanies waking after loss; its first manifestation, and most disquieting feature, is the knowledge that something has happened, but the inability to recall it. And while you lie there fielding the vague dread, groping for it, it's hard to know which is worse: the not knowing, or the fact that at any moment you might remember, and find the fact worse than the dread itself.

It is coming back to her. My work. Asking too much. Killing my family. Killing babies. Better to kill the ideas, before you lose everything. She curls up and tries to go back to sleep. The children's voices intrude, mixed with the sound of the TV dial being switched from channel to channel. Monday morning. Must get them off. Did I finish the Piece? or was I going to do it this morning? Would have remembered if I had finished last night; you don't forget a thing like

"Mom! I don't have any clean socks left! Mom! Did you hear me? I said, 'I don't have any clean socks!'" You've got to get up. They need you. "You aren't meeting my needs." Need you. Need you. Need you. There are so many of them, and only one of me. The thought of it makes you want to sleep forever. "Father! I trusted you! I believed you when you said the purpose of our mission was to bring peace to the world!" "Please stay out of this, Loretta; there are things you cannot understand!" "I can't go with you, Father! These men took you at your word! I am staying!" "Don't be foolish, Loretta! Get out of the way! I don't want to hurt you!" "Father! Father! Put down the gun!" "Loretta! Do what I say! Don't force me to do something I will regret! I have dreamed too long, I have worked too hard, to lose everything now!" Norma Jean's eyes slowly part their lids and stare, unfocused, at the wall. God damn them; they *know* Only allowed to watch Captain Kangaroo in the morning Fuck it So tired So sad Can't even scream at them.

"I can't tie my shoes! Mom! Come and tie my shoes!" "The car is waiting, Loretta! I beg you: Move out of the way! Don't force me to choose!" Just lift the covers and then swing your legs over the You've got to try. You've got to keep going, even when it seems impossible. ("Although shot once in the right temple, and once in the mouth, Mrs. Oakes still managed to . . .")

I have made it to the breakfast table, where the children are dribbling granola all over the floor; I have set out the orange juice in three little plastic cups. I am not hungry. I am trying to decide whether to finish the Piece or go out to the ocean and take an overdose. The last time I thought of doing that was when the children were babies. It strikes me as ironic that at one time I felt them to be the cause of my wanting to die; and that now they have acquired some mysterious power to draw me back whenever the thought comes up.

"Mom, what are those things we saw on cartoons, those 'mommies'?"

"I don't know what you're talking about, Ruth Ann."

"You know. Those 'mommies' that are all wrapped up."

"Oh. You mean 'mummies.'"

"Yeah, 'mummies.' What are they? Are they real?"

"Yes, they are real. They are dead people who lived long ago. The ancient Egyptians used to wrap people like that after they died. They put special oils and powders on them and wrapped them to preserve them."

"Do they come alive?"

"No."

"Why did they wrap them that way? What would have happened if they just left them the way they were?"

"Well, then they would have decayed. They would have crumbled, turned to dust."

"Oh! Then you mean . . . *people* are . . . bio-degradable?" *Absolutely. As sure as you're sitting there. We're just about the most bio-degradable thing there is.*

"Where did you learn that word?"

"At school. The teacher told us."

"You better eat quickly; it's almost time for school."

Norma Jean finishes packing the lunches, writing the names on each little bio-degradable bag. Well, you've got two choices: you can use plastic to wrap them, which is not bio-degradable, and fouls the environment; or you can use paper bags, which are bio-degradable, but which cause deforestation. Those are the choices. Unless you want to tie a salami around their necks.

As the last child slams the door, she runs her eyes over the paper before going to the garage.

Leo: Avoid one who is drawback to your progress.

As she begins shaping the final stages of the Piece, all the flashing ideas, all the connections of the day before seem to have vanished. In their place, image after image surfaces: Martin filing for divorce; Martin standing by the stove with his mouth open; Martin at work, with two buttons missing; Norma Jean cooking *paella* for Martin; Norma Jean throwing the Piece under a truck; Norma Jean throwing Martin under a truck. She smoothes down the rough edges on the Piece, stroking it with her wet hands. The Piece recoils. Something is wrong; it isn't coming together at all. She stares at it awhile, but nothing happens. It's either there or it isn't. Today it definitely isn't. My hands don't know what they're doing; there's no connection to the brain. How is it possible to feel so fluid and in control one day, and then stand here paralyzed the next? Well, how the hell can anyone work when there is no support? Nothing but hassles and guilt. If I feel I have a right to do this, then why can't I do it? *Because the guilt was there longer than the recognition of the right, and has prior claim.* With practice, it may be possible to reverse that. Everything takes time: time to know yourself, what you want; time to set it in motion; time to fight for your right to do it; time to recover from the fight for your right to do it; time to do it; and time to establish your credentials in the world. Who has that kind of time? The young do. They also have the added advantage of not having to fight so hard. It is understood: they are free to choose from a range of options. As for me, I think about the past and wonder what became of all that time. There are such terrible gaps, and long, unaccounted-for years. In my sleep Time is the god to whom I pray for more.

Norma Jean covers the Piece and slams the garage door behind her. A fury whose intensity she hasn't felt for months is rising in her, positioning itself to attack the vocal cords and the eyes. She tries to suppress it; everyone is away, there is no one to take it out on. In desperation, she looks around for Fletcher, but everything is still as a tomb on a windless day. Of course it's hard for him, he never expected He's an adult! He should be able to I never walked out on him when Well you were conditioned to be It was expected of And besides, where would you have gone with small children and no money? So what if you finish the Piece? So what if you finish twenty pieces, and have a show? Even sell? They'll say: you threw away a good man for that? To not make the effort amounts to throwing *yourself* away. You can't do that to keep any man, however good. Do that, what good would you be to anyone? One of these days And you're all alone You'll regret, you'll see. You can't go to bed with art. The men of this generation have become the casualties of The *women* were the original casualties! ("You can't ask *me* to pay the price." —Martin Harris.) Never wanted you to pay a price. Don't want to lose . . . Bastard, bastard!

Shifting into second, Norma Jean maneuvers the car onto the freeway. In third she keeps her foot on the accelerator. Go south; just keep going and never come back. She leaves her foot on the pedal, as the tachometer jumps wildly, and tightens her hands on the wheel. You should slow down You're a wife and mother, you have an obligation The speedometer climbs to eighty. There is a special significance to the act of pushing limits further than you normally would; it introduces an element of risk that requires constant alertness to the split-second nuances of such variables as road conditions; your reflexes and degree of control; and your mental state. When you have to concentrate this hard to avoid sudden death, it leaves no room to dwell on conflicts. It is a way of controlling pain.

Norma Jean has left the industrial area behind. The road now bears west, where it winds and slices through entire hillsides. The landscape appears uncontaminated, pure—at least to the naked eye traveling at eighty miles an hour. She imagines it as having looked this way to the first settlers. Did it correspond to their visions of it? Did it thrill? How does it feel to have pushed beyond established limits and to look upon the unexpected for the first time? And this longing that stirs now like a prisoner in my throat: it is the wish to relinquish the act of hurtling through space, to leave the freeway far behind, where it curves like a silver river on the land, and throw myself on the green of the hills, to bury myself in the silence, and be reborn. ("You can't go home again.") You can't go back in time. You can't reverse progress. Every inch of land, on either side of the road, is ringed with barbed-wire fencing. If they won't let you into their hills, you can still blast down their roads, that much remains; that option is still open. She accelerates again and the land blurs; and is renounced, with the kind of vengeance that first refuses and then despoils that to which it has been denied access.

("Ah Love! could thou and I with Fate conspire/ To grasp this sorry Scheme of Things entire/ Would not we shatter it to bits—and then/ Re-mould it nearer to the Heart's Desire!") But I have no love. He is about to separate, disconnect, withdraw, dissolve. And all because too much is being asked? Too much has been required, of all of us, under conditions which are impossible? Because we can't adjust? Because times change? (". . . what boots it to repeat/ How Time is slipping underneath our Feet . . .") It's always hard to manage; but overwhelming as you age, and expectations rise and possibilities shrink.

Norma Jean brakes abruptly; a car up ahead has spun out, and the air is suddenly filled with smoke and the possibility of multiple collisions. Everyone manages to negotiate it with quick braking and skidding and some rocking from side to side. And a second later she sees that the driver has spun in order to avoid hitting Beautiful dog! Irish setter But the car in the next lane hit it instead It floats there on my right, rolling over and over The ears rise and fall like velvet flags, its body bending and twisting, caught in slow motion She sees it frame by frame Assuming grotesque positions of indescribable beauty. And no one stops because no one can stop; it would interrupt the rhythm. There is no way to stop once you are on the freeway; provisions have not been made. Dog, person, it's all the same. *You can't go back.* Your life depends on keeping up with the flow.

The freeway is the last frontier. It is unsurpassed as a training ground for the sharpening of survival skills. You can use it to revive feeling or to blunt feeling if you wish; those are individual variations which have nothing to do with its basic effect on your life. Once this is acknowledged, you have a certain freedom to experiment in whatever ways will maintain the number of illusions required to endure the fact. When you do the freeway you find that, after a certain length of time, the mind slips into another gear, whose requirements are minimal; and thus stabilized, it cruises at will, exploring its own geography. Passing now into this state, Norma Jean notes another phenomenon characteristic of the transition: the sense of having fused with the car, of no longer having to exercise any conscious control over it. This is the ultimate freeway state. Unlike risk driving, which seeks to avoid the inner life by focusing on external hazards, this state enlarges unconscious territory, and facilitates the creative process. It is the more difficult state to attain, as its realization depends on a greater number of variables: the time of day or night; the type of road (two lanes, four lanes, eight lanes, straight or curved); the amount of traffic; and, of course, mental set. The mental set itself is dependent on another group of variables, which includes time (do you have the time to pursue this state, and let it develop? Or are you expected home to get dinner by 5:30?), and freedom (will your husband ask: "Where have you been for the last two hours? Who's been running up all the mileage on the car? Where have you been *going?* What have you been *doing?* Who have you been *seeing?*"). It would be impossible, for example, to achieve this state of the Bayshore Freeway at any hour and regardless of mental set; it is not designed for the release of creative energy. On the other hand, both the section of Interstate 5 between Tracy and Bakersfield and the section that connects northern California with southern Oregon are ideal, especially at night.

Interstate 5 is very good for realizing unconscious states, *if* you can keep your fear under control. In this, 5 poses a double challenge: it incorporates the essential feature of risk driving, and elevates it to an art. For example: you are on 5, at night; you are going ninety miles an hour and have been on the road for an hour. You are fused with the car and the ideas, images, and their interconnections are starting to appear in your mind. At this point: are you able to stay with it and ride it out? Or do you begin to take note of such things as (1) the indicator on your gas gauge and its relationship to the complete absence of service stations; (2) if you had a flat, you couldn't see to fix it, as you are in total darkness; (3) if the car ran out of gas or broke down, you would sit here all night, because no one would stop; *or,* someone would stop, but would rape (kill; mutilate; terrorize) you; (4) you have become so accustomed to the props of civilization (fluorescent light, gas stations, telephones, Denny's twenty-four-hour restaurants), that your natural sense of relatedness to the land, night, sky, space, isolation, has atrophied and you risk disintegration and collapse every minute you stay out here? The choice is crucial, and it is what gives doing Interstate 5 its challenge, its special flavor. How you respond to the choice is another way of defining and determining the limits of the self. Isn't that one of the functions of frontiers?

Now the hills and trees are passing by on either side with a speed that fuses them into a single image. There has been a gradual blurring around the edges, a subtle erasing of distinctions. And they are seen as through a filter, and they form a tunnel through which Norma Jean becomes a river that always moves, but at the same time always is. And the substance of her mind now is opaque; nothing stirs but the single thought: *You could make time stand still if you traveled west at high speed forever.*

Here we are about to enter the health food store; I have just thrown my cigarette in the gutter. They go crazy if you smoke in there. Ruth Ann still has a school note pinned to her sweater; she looks like a refugee. My little trip made me late for Damon, left them all standing around sucking their thumbs, wetting their pants, wondering if their mother had died. It touched off the usual round of questions on the subject.

"We thought you died."

"No, no; I didn't die." (See, here I am!) *I did my best, but it seems they wanted a dog this time.*

"I don't want to die," said Scott, after a pause I had hoped meant the end of the discussion. Now it's my turn again.

"Why?"

"Because I haven't died before and I don't know how it feels." Well, I understand your reluctance, Scott; we all worry about the unknown, but you can't let that hold you back. There's a first time for everything, know what I mean? *Where is this bitterness coming from? What kind of mother are you?*

They're throwing sesame cookies in the basket while I pick through these apples, trying to find some without worms. I am buying the groceries. I will put them in the house. But I do not plan to be home tonight when he gets back from work. ("I can run from you, I can!" —Little Gingerbread Man, p. 5.) Just take the kids to McDonald's and sit around with all the other just-divorced or about-to-be-divorced, getting the feel of what separation is going to be like. All parents succumb eventually to McDonald's, but it is a special haven for the divorced and separated. It eases the transition you have to make from comfortable family meals—however chaotic they may have been—to sitting home alone with the children, trying to ignore the empty place and staring into your coffee, holding back tears.

Someone is standing next to me, humming a song I heard on the radio recently. There are some people whose presence next to you in stores you scarcely notice, and some whose presence you can't shake. I take a peek out of the corner of my eye, taking care not to move my head. I have very good peripheral vision, all paranoids do. She's standing there watching me pick out apples, tapping her foot as she hums. About fifty, but small as a bird, and dressed as an Indian. Her grey, uncombed hair hangs down straight beneath her headband. Why does it bother me that she's forgotten the feather?

She swings away from the apples now and does a dance, a little shuffle, lousy rhythm, with the moccasins, toward the refrigerator where the yoghurt and fertile eggs are kept. And there she breaks into full song, just as Ruth Ann comes over and stares rudely, with her mouth hanging open.

"Mommy, is that a real Indian?" she asks, loudly.

"No, honey; it's a lunatic impersonating an Indian," I whisper.

"'I'm the train they call the City of New Orleans . . .'" she sings, reaching for the yoghurt. "'Good night, America, how are ya? Say, don't ya know me? I'm your native son . . .'"

"Mom, I have to pee." The clerk is popping a Vitamin E and washing it down with a half pint of kefir. Looking at his complexion makes you think of something that just crawled out from under a rock.

"Excuse me. Could my son use your bathroom?"

"Sorry, we're not allowed to do that. There's a gas station down the block." I think he's the owner's son. There's a quality about both of them that reminds you of overcooked cabbage.

There's a sweet clerk who works here part-time, on Tuesdays

and Thursdays. He'd let Damon use the bathroom, because he's in love with me. His name is Tomaso Ruggiero. He's dark and young and the veins in his arms are alive with nervous fish. He's Italian, and he doesn't give a shit about things like who uses the bathroom. His eyes are so beautiful they make you want to rip off his green apron and jump in some river with him at midday, if you could find one. When it's not crowded, we lean on the counter and shoot the breeze. He knows I'm a "housewife," but it doesn't bother him at all. He says things like: "See that counter full of pills? They should throw them in the street! It's *food, pure* food, that makes you feel alive! You know, it makes me glad that *you* don't waste your money on pills. Your body is strong and slim— has grace!—because you get your energy from the *source!*" And I think: Well, actually, it's more from pushing the vacuum around and from nervous tension than from those things; and actually, I buy an awful lot of the poisoned crap down at Pay and Save, I just come here for the produce. But of course I don't say these things to Tomaso. If he's got an image of me as slim and graceful, it's all right with me; I've often said illusions are crucial to the maintenance of life functions, and I wouldn't want to do anything to jeopardize his. He said to me once, "You know, Norma," —he rolls it: Norrrma, like an aria—"you shouldn't smoke. It *robs* you of vitality! Our bodies are meant to *breathe*, to *move*, to . . ." That was it, because some woman was drumming her fingers on the counter. I'll never know if he was about to say "celebrate life," in which case I would have vomited, or "come together," which would have been O.K.; but either way, there was a look in his eyes that left no doubt as to the sexual implication. He gives off a sexual energy that has to be experienced first-hand to be believed. And I thought it significant from the beginning that he has the same first name as Albinoni; I can't explain why I've never mentioned that to him. *Because more than likely he'd throw his head back and laugh. He'd fail to see the significance.* ("Albi-*noni?* Who's-a he? I know him? You gotta *nother* Tomaso? *Non è possibile!* I die! I go drink Coca-Cola!")

Damon is jumping up and down, clutching himself. As for me, I've had it with stores that want your business but won't let your children use their bathrooms.

"You don't have to cry, Damon. Go in the street." He stands on the curb, arching his stream like a bridge over Coronado Avenue *His first try for a gold medal, and it looks like he wins it! By seven inches!* His hair is a field where crickets hum, his rare beauty, Damon, my son. "I'm afraid I'll have to take him in." "Can't you just give him a ticket? He's only three years old." "No, ma'am, it's a violation of Section 434 to urinate on a public thoroughfare having more than two lanes." "Well there are no provisions! What are people supposed to do?" "That's not my problem, ma'am. My job is to enforce the law." "It's a crime against nature! A crime against humanity!" "That's what they all say, ma'am. Come along son, and zip your pants, or I'll have to cite you for violation of Section 433, too."

Putting the groceries away, I keep looking around the house, focusing on details that were never noteworthy before. It's as though I am asking myself: is it worth preserving—it, and all it stands for? Were we really happy here? *What's happy?* Don't ask me. Why is it that my name seems to be stamped on everything here? I want to see all our names, on an equal number of things. Where was it written that the world was his and the house mine? It's very nice, beautiful in fact; I've done my best to create an environment that pleases and warms. But what more can you do after that is done? Norma Jean thinks of Doris Morgan: after you have spent years furnishing and decorating your house, there comes a time, you detect it like a scent, when everything is nearing completion. It sends a thrill of panic through you to know that it's *done,* in the same way that having the last baby does. Because it raises the question: what will you do with yourself now? What Doris Morgan does is begin all over again: when the last room is redecorated, she goes back to the first, which, she convinces herself, is in need of a refresher. No new ground is broken, no boundaries extended; just the same old boundaries endlessly rearranged in infinite variations within the same space.

Have you noticed the way single fathers look in McDonald's? It makes no difference if they've got one child or six; if they behave well, or like animals. The expression on the father's face is always the same. There is a haunted look about the eyes; and in this particular ambience of efficiency and immediate gratification of need it is intensified to the point of despair. The contrast with the way life really is becomes unbearable; they lean over the tables and bite into the hamburgers, and slowly chew.

There is something about restaurants which are always open that says: you don't ever need to be alone. And this unfailing availability of food, light, and warmth eventually corrupts the feeling of security it was meant to arouse, intensifying the sense of loneliness and want. Because the only other time when things were that way was in infancy. Can McDonald's hold you? Is it tender, can it love? So right away you understand the look about the eyes; someone else is probably observing the same thing in you. Single fathers have no claim on it, they just seem more vulnerable because they've remained naïve longer, haven't spent large amounts of undiluted time with ravenous children. Mothers have always known. You can see them the minute they enter, casting their eyes around, checking out who looks promising among the single fathers. The single fathers do not do this; who needs another desperate woman? In the end, no contact is ever made on either side. We're all prisoners in the same cell; we are repelled by the sight of our mutual condition, and keep our distance.

As we approached the counter, six immaculate voices asked in unison, "May I help you?" *Oh, I'd be so grateful. My husband wants to leave me because I am not meeting his needs. Do you make house calls? Have any live-ins who could whip up a batch of fries whenever Can you tell me what I should do?* "Four cheese, three shakes—two chocolate, one vanilla—two fries and one coffee."

The children are sitting three in a row in the booth; I am alone on the other side. I want to be as far away from them as possible while they're swinging the catsup-drenched fries into their mouths. I know it doesn't fit to be reading Breasted here, but I don't give a shit for appearances tonight. Let the others stare into space; I need all the help I can get.

If already in the Pyramid Age there had been some relaxation in the conviction that by sheer material force man might make conquest of immortality, the spectacle of these colossal ruins now quickened such doubts into open scepticism, a scepticism which ere long found effective literary expression.

* * *

Behold the places thereof;
Their walls are dismantled,
Their places are no more,
As if they had never been.

* * *

None cometh from thence
That he may tell (us) how they fare. . . .

* * *

. . . Scepticism means a long experience with inherited beliefs, much rumination on what has heretofore received unthinking acquiescence, a conscious recognition of personal power to believe or disbelieve, and thus a distinct step forward in the development of self-consciousness and personal initiative.
—Breasted, op. cit., p. 181.

"Mom, I have to go to the bathroom." Norma Jean looks up from her book; her eyes feel strained. She comes back to the knowledge that things are off-center. She stares at the unending stream of people swirling in and out of McDonald's with undreamed-of speed.

"Well, go ahead, Ruth Ann; you can find it. You can read. Just look for the door that says WOMEN, W-O-M-E-N . . . no, wait a minute; it might say LADIES: that's L-A-D-I-E-S."

"It's O.K., Mom. I'll *find* it." They say this is the age when they get sarcastic, think they know everything; because they've developed to the point where they can see that you're over the hill, and having nothing new to offer them that they can't discover for themselves. Norma Jean looks at her watch. Is it possible to sit in McDonald's for another hour? We can't go home until we've been out long enough to make a significant statement. She rips some pages out of the notebook in her purse, instructing the boys that if they're good they can stay here a little longer and draw. They fall for it because anything is better than going to bed. She buys another cup of coffee and lights up, staring across the room through the smoke. The same tables are all there, just a completely different set of faces suspended above them with open mouths.

> To whom do I speak to-day?
> I am laden with wretchedness,
> Without a faithful one.

. . . The story of the Misanthrope was one which owed its origins to individual experiences through which the men of this time were really passing, and they found profit in perusing it. It is a distinct mark in the long development of self-consciousness, the slow process which culminated in the emergence of the individual as a moral force, an individual appealing to conscience as an ultimate authority at whose mandate he may confront and arraign society.

—Ibid., pp. 194, 198.

Ruth Ann returns, announcing in a loud voice, "They have a *dumb* bathroom. When you sit on the toilet
    "Lower your voice, Ruth Ann!"
cold air comes out of this place in the wall and goes right in your *bagina!*"

Damon climbs out of the booth. "I have to go pee; I want the cold air to go in my bagina too!"

"You don't have one, Damon; only *girls* do."

"Aaaa! Ruth Ann said I don't have a *bagina!* That's not fair! I want a bagina! I want a bagina, like Ruth Ann!" People are staring, especially the family with the two little girls in party dresses and ribbons, Dad in his bow tie, and Mom in her pearls; they've gotten all dressed up for their big night out. They've never seen a crazy family before.

It was after dark when we got home. The children fell asleep exhausted, and Martin's only comment was, "Where have you been?" Two possible responses went through my mind, one having to do with McDonald's bathroom, the other with what did he care? I rejected them both in favor of silence, which, being ambiguous, carries more impact. Keep him guessing.

An hour passes and he's still sitting in his study working; he isn't guessing. He doesn't care. He hasn't moved out yet, but he's not here. Norma Jean is filled with a sudden and overwhelming isolation: of course it doesn't happen all at once. It goes by pieces, and this is the beginning. And the process? Is it irreversible? She imagines a time when much that was perceived as unbearable was borne, because one was surrounded by a fundamental stability. Certain expectations were held by everyone close—family, neighbors, community—and they were rarely questioned; few conflicts arose. There were interconnections between people, whole networks of links and roots; she can see how it could hold a couple together. Now, what's there to hold you? Everyone's an island, everyone's free, drifting; there are no requirements any more. Why not divorce? It will disrupt no network. It's no tragedy any more; it's a way of life. And the more frequently it occurs, the easier it becomes for you to consider the possibility, and to minimize the consequences. Are there no longer sufficient reasons to bind you together? Times change, but what of inner requirements?

They say a highly mobile culture predisposes to shallow relationships. By the time they're grown, the children should be well prepared; most of their close friends have already moved away, in just the past three years. They're catching on; I have seen the gradual hardening of expectations, their increasing acceptance of loss. They're becoming smooth and thin, adapting to their reality. Still, there are times when they will speak of missing someone with such depth of feeling that it shakes me if I'm not careful. That too shall pass, in time. They will make the necessary adjustments. They will be ready for their time, when it comes. But what about us?

If there is to be a resolution, it isn't going to come tonight. You can see the way I still adhere to old assumptions: that conflicts can be resolved within traditional contexts; that patience is a virtue of which we are still capable and which allows for shifts to occur over time, rendering slow change, the kind that gives you half a chance. And aside from the instinct to preserve something you assumed had value, there are always the children to consider. They make the old assumptions too, the most significant being that it is our sole purpose to acquaint them with life, and that we are qualified for the job. Shouldn't we both be on hand when they make the discovery that we haven't finished acquainting ourselves, and never will?

The Piece sleeps in the silence of the garage, not breathing, inert; it represents not a stillbirth, but a labor in remission. Norma Jean leaves the house. As she shuts the door behind her she looks up, checking out the stars. They burn there, older than stones, casting their dim light down the rows of empty streets. She takes down the top on the car and folds it into the trunk. And just before starting the motor, she thought she heard Orion sigh in his western height.

I can't explain the reasons, but I know, even before I reach the on-ramp, that I'm going to drive until I find the moon. It was here this time the other night; it should be on its way right now, only further to the east. Norma Jean heads north on the Bayshore. Driving top down, letting the stars fall right into your car, is one of the solaces of living in California. She switches on the radio just in time to hear the announcement that the Verdi Requiem is being broadcast live, from the Opera House, where the San Francisco Symphony is now in session. There is a silence, followed by some crackling sounds, then the music begins. When you're out tracking down the moon, it's a bonus to be able to do it to the Verdi Requiem, she thinks, at the same time hoping the Requiem has no further significance. Events which carry deep significance, and which are timed to coincide precisely with other deeply significant, but otherwise unrelated, events in order to form symbolic meanings whose weight is made more profound by the coupling, are a device of directors with tight schedules and low budgets, whose goal is to bring the film in on schedule, but with no loss of impact. They have to cram everything into a limited space in a limited time; that's why it happens only in movies. In life, we have what seems, until later on, all the time in the world. We can afford to forego the drama, stretch things out very thin. Sometimes events which should—for maximum artistic and emotional impact—have coincided, happen light years apart. This dilution is necessary to keep our focus on all the small, killing details which ensure our survival.

As she steers the car toward the approach to the San Francisco-Oakland Bay Bridge, the city rises before her; its windows simmer in the night. On the bridge the salt air is sharp and fills the lungs with possibilities, and she thinks: if you travel east at high speed, you can be the first to see the moon rise every night. Coming off the bridge, she takes the ramp to the freeway that leads through the Berkeley-Oakland hills. And there, where lines of traffic cross and counter-cross, she accelerates and joins the flow: hypnotic chains of light—one white, one red—speeding in opposite directions, winding, spilling their beads, as the *Sanctus* blesses. Sometimes, late at night, beneath deserted overpasses, it is even possible to recover a sense of worship, where concrete pillars, bathed in fluorescent light, lift their arches to the stars.

The car enters the tunnel that runs through the hills. Norma Jean can hardly breathe with the top down; carbon monoxide fills the air and lies impacted in the tiles. Under white lights, the walls of the tunnel shine like a morgue. Marcello Mastroianni escaped from just this kind of situation in *8½*, when he was trapped inside a tunnel in a car during a traffic jam. When he could no longer bear the sense of confinement, his spirit simply squeezed through the car window, and floated up, out, over, and away from everything. It took your breath away to watch. Emerging from the tunnel now, the road rushes eastward, bearing her along its surface as though, seen from above, on a conveyor belt moving between black hills. Here she races through the corridors of night, giving birth to herself mile after mile.

I came upon the moon just after the *Libera me*; I was hoping the two events might coincide, but you know how it is in life. It was a good moon, one night short of full, but it wasn't possible to fix on it; you have to watch the road every minute out here. Therefore, there are no images or insights to report, at least nothing that is directly moon-related. Still, I have no cause to complain, because if there is one final discovery you make driving the freeway, eventually, it is the confirmation of your essential loneliness. And, as with all knowledge, it is better to have it than to not have it, even in cases where you didn't want it. I am not sure why that is so, or what ends it serves. But driving home there are no doubts that I have gotten what I came for. I wonder if others are aware that it takes eighty miles to do the Verdi Requiem, start to finish. It isn't often you get a run as good as that.

13

So low, here I am back at the kitchen table, shooting up:

MAN'S HEAD FOUND   SHOOT-OUT
IN TRASH   AT WEDDING

The Piece isn't speaking, just lies there, wrapped in its shroud, moist and aloof, refusing to confirm my existence. Martin doesn't speak, either; it has been three days, nothing is resolved. We circle around each other like poisonous fish in a partitioned tank; no way has been found to communicate through the glass.

Ralph Bosco, 51, of Rand Associates on the first floor of the building, said he dialed the telephone operator when he heard the shots and asked for police.

"I said, 'Give me the police, some nut is shooting away here,'" Bosco recalled. "The operator said, 'I'm sorry sir, you'll have to call 411 (information).'"

As she leaves the house, Norma Jean reaches into the mailbox and withdraws the mail. As she slides into the car she notices one letter, bearing an unfamiliar return address. Sitting behind the wheel, letting the motor warm, she reads.

Dear Ms. Harris,

I was touched by your note. I didn't think it was possible that anyone could be so conscientious, especially these days. The damage to the car is very slight, as the estimates confirm.

I can't decide if your note was prompted by feelings of guilt for having cracked a Ferrari, or by admirable integrity. Assuming the latter, please be assured that I consider the note itself as payment enough—you have restored my faith in humanity. If you still feel guilty, call me the next time you are in the city and I will be honored to let you take me to lunch.

Sincerely yours,
Rex Porter, III

Stapled to the letter is a business card, bearing the name of his company; the phone number has been underlined in red ink. Well, fancy that. Norma Jean feels a flush come over her. *He's probably living off his father's fortune; he can afford to pass it off.* Aw, jump in the lake. He used *Ms.*, didn't he? *Sometimes people do that when they're in the dark. Doesn't mean a thing.* Well, he was *touched*, wasn't he? If you're touched, it means you can feel. That makes up for a lot of things. How can I answer it? Was it guilt, or do I have integrity? He thinks integrity. It would be nice to believe that, *in which case you'll have to send him a check. Say guilt and you can have lunch with him.* As she backs out of the driveway, choices revolve in her mind as wheels on a road; and as she turns onto the freeway, feelings stir which have slept over a decade. *I restored his faith. It's not every day you get a chance to do something that important.*

By the time she reaches Dr. Arndt's waiting room, the mood has dissolved. What can I say to him today? *My husband, who pays your fee, feels I am not meeting his needs?*

Norma Jean focuses on the split-leaf philodendron. *It's trying to speak! Yes, yes, I'm sure of it.* It is struggling there next to her chair; she leans a little closer. It whispers, *"He doesn't feed me! I need water!"* She pulls back. What do you want from me? I've got enough mouths to feed. She reaches for a magazine. They have all been stamped with invisible ink; the message is activated whenever one of them is taken from the office. "Stolen from Dr. Rudolph Arndt," it says. The door swings open.

"Hi."

"Mmm." Norma Jean shuffles over to the chair and sits down. It is positioned in a way that requires an effort to turn and look directly at Dr. Arndt; she stares ahead at the opposite wall. He settles back in his chair, jingling the change in his pocket. *He's got the time, can sit there like that, enduring me. Every now and then he will stir himself to make a sincere comment on my condition.*

"Martin has declared war on my piece. He said he wanted a divorce three days ago, and hasn't spoken since. He's drawn a line which says: Art or me. He's waiting for me to declare him the winner. I haven't been able to work since it happened." *He listens and listens; his ears are avenues where the loveless walk in their speech.* "My feelings are: fury at Martin for creating a choice I consider artificial; despair over not being able to work; guilt for not meeting Martin's needs; certainty that I can never go back to where I was before; uncertainty over whether I can handle the consequences of going forward. I don't want to lose Martin and I don't want to give up my work. Is this inner conflict, or outer?"

Arndt remains silent. *He's holding himself back. He is filled with love for me; every day is a struggle between his longing and his professional standards.*

"I got a letter today, from the man whose Ferrari I dented last week," she continues, shifting her position. *If I hadn't worn Levi's today, he could see my legs.* ("Where there's a will, there's a way." —Anon.) "He said he thought I had 'admirable integrity.'"

"What do *you* think?"

"Me? How should I know? I think I left the note because I would have hated myself if I hadn't. Who can say whether that's guilt or integrity?"

"It might have something to do with self-respect."

"I don't think I should come here any more; it's not right to ask Martin to pay for it, feeling as he does."

"It's *his* money?"

"Of course it is!"

"You feel you haven't earned your treatment?"

Well, I've paid for it emotionally, every fucking minute. "You probably think that half of everything a husband earns belongs to the wife. That's the standard you've accepted all your life. I don't subscribe . . ."

"Haven't your services been worth something?"

How can you put a figure on *that*? But now that he mentions it, I have always felt I was . . . just working for room and board. *That he was being kind to keep you on.* That if I slipped up anywhere, the arrangement could be terminated without notice—no benefits, no equity, no *acknowledgment*, because there was no real contract. Still, I remember having read in the paper, not long ago, that Underwriters of America had done a study and, on the basis of their findings, estimated the annual net worth of the American housewife at . . . I think it was somewhere between $9,000 and $10,000. The figure $9,000 sticks in my mind. Then I must be worth at least

"Underwriters of America estimates that my 'services,' as you call them, are worth at least $9,000 a year. I read it in the paper."

"Do you need Underwriters of America to tell you what you're worth?"

"Yes! I do! How else can you measure intangibles?" *Self-respect, self-respect, it's out there somewhere, the only problem is how to* There are probably thousands of people who should never have married, wouldn't be married now if *"I'm sure that in your"* don't say "time"; *he'll think you think he's over the hill, and it will ruin any chance* "experience it was typical for marriages to break up, when they did, because of such things as sexual incompatibility, or infidelity. What do you have to say about this shift that's taken place overnight, where the wives have begun to want a change in the balance of things?" *His wife: weeding, mending, standing at the sink, tending his needs. Poor woman; he leans on her so I can lean on him What am I doing here?* "I'm sure you think fixed role-division makes for smoother marriages. Well, you're right! It does! My friend Rachel says, 'Any marriage can survive, if the wife is willing to be a masochist.' How do you feel, knowing that you got where you are today at the expense of your wife's personal growth? *What are you talking about, you don't even know his wife.* Doesn't matter, the odds are high she's standing at the sink this very minute. "Philip Slater says,

Having created a technological and social-structural juggernaut by which they are daily buffeted, men tend to use their wives as opiates to soften the impact of the forces they have set in motion against themselves. Consider, for example, the suburban living pattern: husbands go to the city and participate in the twentieth century, while their wives are assigned the hopeless task of trying to act out a rather pathetic bucolic fantasy oriented toward the nineteenth. Men in their jobs must accept change—even welcome it and foster it—however threatening and disruptive it may seem. They do not know how to abstain from colluding daily in their own obsolescence, and they are frightened. Such men tend to make of their wives an island of stability in a sea of change. The wife becomes a kind of memento, like the bit of earth the immigrant brings from the old country and puts under his bed. . . .

And *I* say: The balance of needs has been highly skewed in *his* favor for ten years!" *So why do I feel this guilt for putting my finger on my side of the scales? Isn't it Justice who carries the scales? And isn't Justice a woman?* All those years of refinishing furniture, ironing shirts, *hand* washing socks that clearly said "Machine Washable" on the toe. ("It strains the *elastic!*" —Martin Harris; heated discussion, 1963.) (What about the *woman?* —Norma Jean Harris, ten years too late.) Preparing the meals— made with fresh ingredients, never canned or frozen, feeding the babies, changing their diapers, shaking the shit out of the diapers in the toilet ("Why is it every time I have to go, there's a diaper in here?" —Martin Harris), putting them to bed, clearing the dishes off the table, washing the dishes; then sitting down with coffee, listening to the account of Martin's day:

"Boy, am I wiped out. Wiped out. Sometimes, I swear, I'm not sure teaching is There are days, though, when it all comes together, and you get fired up with the promise of it. Got this kid in class, you should see the way his mind It's as though you and the student were creating something totally new, something that never existed before, just by the exchange of thoughts; it's completely intangible—you can't *preserve* it—but you know it's there. The act of exploration, the process of two minds—or, some days, three minds, or six minds—coalescing like that creates something that is greater than the sum of any one mind. Now when *that* happens, it's thrilling! But it doesn't happen that way often. Today was typical. I'm pouring my guts into it, trying to *make* it happen, and those kids are sitting around chewing gum, staring at the ceiling, scratching their asses—I swear half of them are on dope. And I think: I'm not God. What am I pushing myself for? That's when I get depressed."

So I'd listen and then, when he got to saying things like that, I'd get right in there, murmuring encouragement, feeling his forehead (why do all women have that reflex? Where did it originate?), trying to get my man back in shape, so he could face that terrible world out there. ("A man needs that feminine sustenance when he comes home from the front lines." —Paul Swartz, argument at dinner party—at the Morgans'? Our house? —1971.) What do they mean when they make that analogy between work and the front lines? Are they nostalgic for a war they can call their own? Have they seen too many combat movies with Deborah Kerr playing the nurse? Does the dream of the all-nurturing mother ever die? *You couldn't call it a death. It simply attaches to someone else, usually the wife. And once embodied there, it undergoes the kind of change that occurs in theater, for instance, when an actress assumes another identity. And however excellent her performance, it is understood she remains herself, behind the portrayal. These things are understood in art; in life, we succumb to the most outrageous confusions regarding who we are, and whom we expect others to be. Roles must be shed, eventually. It would amount to a crime to require people to become the characters they're asked to play—a homicide against their first and original self.* In that case, a lot of husbands are guilty of attempted murder.

It happens occasionally in art that a few choose to merge so fully with the character they're asked to portray that it is no longer possible to detect the original self in them; it disappears, usually for good. And when this happens, it is regarded as a tragedy— except by the one who has undergone the transformation: who, being someone else, has no means to remember what he was, and so perceives no loss, and fails to mourn. In life, when this happens to wives, it is not regarded as tragic, but natural.

Whenever they spoke of what they did in the world, their attitude always suggested vast legions clawing their way to victory, toward some intangible goal. They maintained from the start, and still do, that they do it for the wife and children; but we're just a screen. After years of close-range observation, you can see they do it for themselves, would do it whether we were here or not. And so I would listen and I would always feel, in some vague way, that it was up to me to see that he got it, whatever it was. I can't say I listened only from a sense of duty; part of it was because I couldn't very well give *him* an account of *my* "day"—without feeling like a fool, that is; because where was the promise in it?

Arndt has been silent all this time. A news bulletin is flashing through Norma Jean's mind: YOU'VE RUN 15 MINUTES OVERTIME AND ANALYST IS DEAD . . . YOU'VE RUN 15 MINUTES OVERTIME AND ANALYST IS DEAD . . . YOU'VE RUN *Quickly she checks the pulse and raises the lids. Stone cold dead. No need to panic; you've got to remain philosophical about these things. It's just like praying—what difference does it make if no one's there? It's the BELIEF that someone is listening that matters, isn't it? It's what gives you the opportunity to listen to yourself.* We all *think* we do that—hear ourselves—but studies have shown that we don't. I know. I read it in the paper.

It's my turn to drive the car pool today. Norma Jean drives to Scott's nursery school and pulls up in front.

"O.K. Everyone remember the rule? No poking, tickling, shoving, hitting, biting, spitting, or standing up while you're in this car. Keep your hands to yourselves. Don't sit on your legs; keep your feet on the floor. *You should have been a WAC.* And remember to hold onto your drawings; if you don't, they'll blow away." The children are telling riddles.

"What is black and white and red, and black and white and red, and black and white and red?"

"I don't know, Joshua. What *is* black and white and red, and black and white and red, and black and white and red?" You go insane repeating it, but they expect it; it shows them you're paying attention, instead of the usual Yeah, yeah, that's nice, unh huh. It spoils the effect if they feel you're not interested.

"You give up?"

"I sure do. I just can't figure out what could be black and white and red, and black and white and red, and black and white and red." Do you know how it feels to have squandered your whole week's supply of interest in three minutes?

"It's a penguin with a diaper rash rolling down a hill." Ha ha ha ha ha! *Is that you laughing?* It must be; *they* aren't, they've heard it a thousand times.

Norma Jean negotiates the car from lane to lane, through Coronado traffic. The children are comparing infinitesimal details from the cartoons they watch in the afternoons. (Why is

Atom Ant's belly button missing? Why doesn't Popeye ever cut his mouth on the spinach can?) It would never occur to them to ask why Olive Oyl is so helpless, always screaming, "Popeye! Help! Save me, save me! Oh, Popeye!" They just accept it as natural. Their voices become louder; I think the fumes are getting to them, inhaling all these ozones. The air is like brown paper; the city simmers in its thick juices. *Is this the best we can do for them?* Where did this pain in the back of my head come from? Norma Jean switches on the radio. She runs the dial back and forth across the band. "You've just heard the number one song on KFSX this week: 'Brain Damage.' . . ."

After the children have been delivered and Ruth Ann arrives home from school, Norma Jean decides to give the Piece another try while they watch TV. She opens the door to the garage and cautiously steps inside. *So long since I've been in here! Why do I feel afraid? I am afraid of the Piece. Afraid it has died because of my neglect. Even if it has managed to sustain itself in my absence, I am afraid of finding it changed. It will no longer remember me; or, remembering, will shrink in disgust.*

She unwraps the damp cloths, unwinding them slowly. Howard Carter must have felt just this way: entering the tomb and unwrapping the mummy shroud; the sense of trespass, the uncertainty of what will be discovered. As the last cloth is lifted away, she stares at her creation and tears fill her eyes; it is unrecognizable.

Don't fall apart. You've been away from it, lost the connection. It's bound to seem Not my work! Has nothing to do with me! *strange after an absence. Pull yourself together, you'll get it back.* As if it had never been! Can't think, can't face it now; come back later tonight, after dinner, children in bed, see what happens then. Norma Jean replaces the cloth on the Piece as though changing a dressing on the mortally wounded. She fastens the latch on the garage door and goes back to the kitchen. And there she puts her head on the table and cries. The children are all in the family room with the TV blaring, can't hear, can't see, won't know I've killed another baby. *If all artists collapsed at every setback, there would be no art. You have to be tough to succeed, force yourself if you want to create something of value.* The newspaper lies under her left elbow where she leans; something is trying to make its way into her line of vision.

YOUR BRAIN: USE IT OR LOSE IT

United Press International

The brain, like the body, can become dull and inactive through neglect.

But like muscles that develop by physical conditioning, exercising the mind with exciting and lively environments may keep the brain active and growing.

Well, it's finally out; now you know. Just what you've always suspected. Would you like a sedative? My LIFE is a sedative! No, I mean something that will take away the pain altogether; you still feel your life. That's one of the drawbacks.

A 14-year interdisciplinary study with laboratory animals at the University of California has shown that anatomical and chemical changes occur in rats placed in an enriched environment, compared to their litter-mates living a more secluded, impoverished life.

Implications from the research are that the brain—including the human brain—can be expanded by experience regardless of age.

See? "Regardless of age!" I know that should really excite me, give me the green light, so why do I keep thinking of the litter-mates? Because you both have the secluded, impoverished life, dummy. But I've got choice, I can change my condition ("Accentuate the positive." —Bing Crosby.) They are stuck in their cages because the researchers still aren't convinced that a woman alone in a little box, on a deserted street, with few social contacts and little mental stimulation, will end up with a shrunken brain. They have to see if it works on rats first—fewer variables that way —then apply their findings to us.

"Daddy! Daddy's home!" The door slams. He's here, whose funeral I conduct once a day in my mind. Norma Jean reaches for the vermouth and pours it in a red, white, and blue tumbler. She lights a cigarette. If I had a joint handy I'd smoke that too. *Try. You've got to keep trying.* She takes a long swallow of her drink and, wiping her mouth on the back of her hand, sweetly turns and addresses Martin as he reaches inside the freezer for ice:

"I made dessert," she says. There is a pause.

"As far as I'm concerned, you've already deserted."

"I *said*, 'I—Made—Dee-zert.'" What's the use? I *may* desert. More and more women are doing it. Private detectives claim business has never been better. I read it in the paper.

"Listen, you bastard! Stop punishing me! I have a right to call at least *half* my life my own! This has got to stop. I can't work, I can't do anything. I feel like running a knife right through your heart!"

"Go ahead, crazy lady! You've got no use for me anyway! Rotten blood-sucking bitch! Take all the things I've worked to give you, then say it's not enough! I could cut your heart out!" Animals go for the jugular; humans, the heart. It's unbelievable the primitive feelings that are aroused by rapid change. Crazy. He called me crazy again! If there's one thing I can't stand *Because it's true?* Yes! It's true! True true true! Now I know why I have always felt a profound sympathy for all crazy people everywhere ("Birds of a feather . . .") Well, *my* crazy is better than *his* sanity—his warped, rigid, screwed-up . . . CRAZY IS BEAUTIFUL! CRAZY POWER!

"Aaaaaaaaaaaaaaaaaaaaaaaaaaaaaaaaaah!"

"What the hell are you doing?"

"Aaaaaaaaaaaaaaaaaaaaaaaaaaaaaaaaaah!"

"Norma! What's the *matter* with you? *Stop* it."

"Aaaaaaaaaaaaaaaaaaaaaaaaaaaah! Aaaaaaaaaaaaaaaaaaaaaah!" He wants crazy, I'll give him crazy. "Aaaaaaaaaaaaaaaaaaaaaah!"

"NORMA! STOP SCREAMING THIS MINUTE!"

"Aaaaaaaaaaaaaaaaaaaaaah!"

"Norma, please! I beg you, stop."

"Aaaaaaaaaaaaaaaaaaaaaaaaaaaaaaaaaah!" If I'd known it felt this good I'd have done it long ago. "Aaaaaaaaaaaaaaaah!"

"Norma . . ." I know what he's going to say: The Neighbors and The Children. "Aaaaaaaah!" (Fuck the neighbors). "Aaa-aaaaah!" (Fuck the children) "Aaaaaaaaaaaah!" (Fuck you).

"Mommy, what's the matter?"

"Dad, why is Mom screaming? Did you hit her?"

"Shit. No, Ruthie, I didn't hit your mother."

"Then why is she screaming?"

"BECAUSE I'M CRAZY!" It's lots of fun, Ruth Ann; when you grow up you'll be crazy too, just like me!

"Norma Jean! We'll talk about it later. Please just stop *scream-*

ing." Got to get to her before she starts throwing the pots and pans; once they get going with the pots and pans, you've lost the whole ball game.

"Aaaaaaaaaaaaaaaaaaaaaaaaaaah!"

"Make her stop. She's hurting my *ears*."

"Shut up, Damon. If you don't like it, go back to Popeye." You like Olive Oyl's screaming better than your own mother's?

"No one can stop me! Do you all hear? I can scream all night if I want! I am my own person! Aaaaaaaaaaaaah!"

"Now you've made Damon cry, Mom; and I'm about to cry too." No, no, Ruth Ann; the Woman of Tomorrow doesn't cry. She screams!

Norma Jean's throat is tightening; it's becoming harder to get an effective sound out. She pauses, getting a second wind. Martin leans his head against the freezer door; Ruth Ann is standing there crying, Damon is lying on the floor crying and kicking his legs. *All because of me!* ("Concentric circles spread outward from the point of disturbance." —Law of nature.) Where is Scott? The tableau isn't complete without Scott here, rolling around, showing some sign of collapse.

Martin throws his ice cubes in the sink, storms out of the kitchen and into his study, slamming the door behind him. He feels it's safe to do that because he thinks I've stopped screaming. *You have stopped, haven't you?* I don't know . . . I had thought of it as more of a pause. Damon is throwing his cars all over the floor; Ruth Ann is "Why did I have to come out of *your* stomach?" again; and *there* is Scott! Still quietly watching TV. Why is Scott so stable? Where did I go wrong?

"Get up, Damon. Everything's all right now. Mommy was just upset about . . . something. Come on, go wash your hands and we'll eat in a few minutes." She bends down and holds Ruth Ann, burying her face in her hair. "I'm sorry Ruthie; you know Mommy loves you all. She . . . I just get upset sometimes." The trouble with going crazy is that you have to go around making it up to everyone afterwards. It seems they should be making something up to you.

Norma Jean slips into Martin's study. "Dinner's ready." He looks up briefly from his desk. "Feeling better?" It is the kind of question whose ultimate aim is to foster penitence; it is definitely not concerned with acquiring information. Norma Jean remains silent. I don't answer penitence questions any more.

"Norma, I can't take it. You're asking me to absorb ten years of accumulated fury. It's too much."

"You liked it better when it was repressed, didn't you?" *Hidden, buried, eating me alive.*

Things were much better then; she used to take it out on the dishes, or scrubbing floors, woodwork, tiles. Now everything around here is filthy. "And not only that. We haven't fucked in two weeks; what kind of life is that for a man?"

"You've been hassling me for months! You haven't spoken to me in three days! What kind of a life is that for a woman?"

"Two weeks . . . That works out to two fucks a month! You call that a marriage?" *It's true what he says; I don't know how to explain it, but I'll try: It's as though you were in prison, and the warden sent you a message that said: Fuck me 3.2 times a week and we'll see about getting you out! Now what would you do in a situation like that? Me, I just keep chipping away at the mortar with my nail file.*

"The Folletts went a year and a half without fucking."

"How do you know a thing like that?"

"Rachel told me."

"Should have known. Christ. No wonder they split." Hell, that's insane. Why do they go around broadcasting things like that? Christ. Everyone knows all the intimate details of everyone else's life in this neighborhood. And yet, at the same time, no one really knows anyone.

"Do you go around spreading *our* business all over this neighborhood?" Crazy women, their mouths would be going twenty-four hours a day if they didn't have to sleep.

"I don't gossip!" *Any more.* "I've got all I can do just staying alive! And you're no help. No help at all."

God, it's been so miserable around here I've forgotten what normal feels like. "Look. Finish your goddamned sculpture, or whatever you're doing out there." Give her the green light, get the damned thing finished, maybe things will ease up, get back to where they were before. "I don't know how much more I can take, but I'll do what I can. All this screaming is bad for the kids. Do what you feel you have to do. We'll see what happens, see where things stand when you're through." Don't want to have to move out of my own home. Don't want to be pushed into that Worked too hard That girl in class, what's her name? Jeanette. She's attracted to me; it wouldn't take Funny thinking of her like that, the way things just pop into your mind. Hot. She's hot. No doubt about it.

Martin pushes his chair away from the desk. "Let's eat. O.K. Norma? We'll see what happens." He puts his arm awkwardly across her shoulder as they walk toward the kitchen. Why don't I feel relieved and grateful, the way I always used to whenever a fight was concluded? Where are the warm, secure feelings that used to accompany the resolutions? *Because this isn't a resolution. This is a skillful maneuver to get you to stop screaming and to buy time.* ("Don't look a gift horse in the mouth.")

The reason I'm taking so long with the dishes is because I'm afraid of going back to the garage; it's so much easier to scrub away at these bits of chicken adhering to the bottom of the skillet than it is to confront something you think you've killed and may have to resurrect. Still, you've got to try. There is only one road away from the sink.

This is the hardest thing I've ever done in my life. ("Nothing ventured, nothing gained.") *Lift the cloth and look it right in the eye. Say: Do you forgive me?* Norma Jean begins to knead, shape, add. And slowly, the sense of mastery returns; gradually the rhythms that flow between the idea and the act re-establish themselves, and she and the Piece are moving together, flowing back and forth along delicate networks, forming a cooperative bond. Technically, nothing is ever "finished." Possibilities are always infinite; and life, being fluid, requires continual forward motion. So why should it seem unexpected that, while the Piece was a statement I hadn't known I would make, now there should be this absolute certainty that a declaration has been made? So, Piece, I guess you are "finished." Everything about it feels right, so it must be true.

Norma Jean wipes her hands and switches on the portable radio, tipping her stool back and leaning against the wall. She reaches for a cigarette and stares at the "finished product." *How do you feel? Elated or disappointed?* Everything came together—but not in the way I had expected. Everything feels "right"—

but then I have no yardstick of what's "wrong." I have nothing to measure it against, no standard. Only that I presided over a birth, and that it exceeded my expectations—both the process and the result. What else can be said? *You could say: What next?* That's indecent; I've just this minute finished *this! What about all those other ideas you had? Killed off, to preserve peace in the home?* They'll be back. I'm beginning to believe that ideas don't die; that they're different from babies; that in art, you get a second chance.

Frances Langford is singing "I'm in the Mood for Love." Norma Jean stretches; the light bulb casts the shadows of her arms across the room. And then she leans back against the wall—the clay dust speechless as snow on the floor, the smoke curling upward, reaching through light and shadow—overcome by the mellowness of the song, the pure simplicity of it, the warmth. *How did we move from this to "Brain Damage" so fast?* Watching the smoke curl and rise under the hanging light, you can't come to any other conclusion but that anything is possible: see how it moves on the currents of air in the room; the way it twists and changes, its shape could only be held by a photograph—and even that would represent only one fragment of all its possibilities. Norma Jean's eyes become a lens through which one shape is now caught, and realized; the new ideas are instantaneous. Her hands move toward the clay. When I do this I am merely the developer; I process the image in a way that renders it intelligible. And even while that is happening, it has already moved on, is light years away: mutating, regrouping, changing, its energy untapped, its course unaltered. She glances at the Piece. It whispers, *Go ahead; you are free.*

She works on the new piece until her body refuses to obey orders. When she looks at her watch it is four in the morning. She leans her head against the wall; the garage is a tomb where nothing moves: under the light, these objects which live, yet are so still! She stares and stares. Why can't I leave? *I am Anubis, guarding my treasures against decay.* Al Bowlly is singing "Close Your Eyes": Ray Noble, 1933. Norma Jean closes her eyes. Indescribably sweet. Someone is holding her. They are dancing. The setting is unfamiliar, but that causes no confusion. This is what everyone wants, deep down, sooner or later, this going back: always the mystery of what was wished for but failed to happen. Does this longing for new beginnings flourish most in conditions where endings are perceived as imminent? Why do I keep thinking that the future was not supposed to shrink? *Because we all think we have forever; it's built in.* Why does it take me by surprise, the feeling that this is the end of possibilities? *Because the knowledge is new. It takes many years for it to sink in and stop surprising. That's why they introduce it at mid-life—to give you enough time to absorb it so you'll be able to withstand your old age.* Old age cannot be withstood; that's why people die. Fools speak of growing old gracefully; but the heart knows what it knows in the thin afternoons, the long silences, unspeakable nights. *I'd swear you were having a post-partum depression.*

The music fills the small garage. Norma Jean wraps her arms around herself in the early-morning chill, wills herself back to exactly that point in time that matches this mood: tender, tender, everything strange, long ago, and happening for the first time. . . .

14

Ding Ding Ding. "Children, may I have your attention?"

"Gimme the eraser, you fucker! Gimme, I kick your ass."

"Teacher! He call me a fucker . . . I beat your butt!" *What am I doing here, on three hours' sleep?*

. . . Los Angeles officials confiscated guns from no fewer than 40 students during one recent month, and the homecoming parade at the city's Jefferson High School ended with a shoot-out in which five students—including the homecoming princess—were wounded.

"QUIET DOWN THIS MINUTE! Your assignment for today is to write a story of something you saw on the way home from school. Do you understand? I want you to write a *de-scrip-tion* of something you saw after school."

"Mrs. Harris, while they're doing their stories, would you mind returning these books to the Media Center?" God in heaven, what would it take to get them to rename it the Library?

Norma Jean walks down the hall toward the library, the books in her arms. What am I doing here? *You ask that question everywhere you are.* I've never asked it in the garage. The door is locked, but there is a note:

The Media Center will be closed between 9:30 A.M. and Noon today. Signed, (Mrs.) Helen Farnham, Media Specialist.

What am I doing standing here, with my arms full of media? I could be in San Francisco, sipping a Campari with Rex Porter, III. "Mr. Porter? You probably don't remember me . . . Rex? This is Norma Jean? I smashed your Ferrari?" Norma Jean deposits the books on the floor in front of the Media Center door. I'll go back and put in—she looks at her watch—another twenty minutes; then I'll say I have an appointment. They can't fire me, because I'm a volunteer.

She spends the next twenty minutes helping the children with their spelling and making sure the eraser is shared without bloodshed.

"That's a very good story, Mason. Is it true?"

"Sure it true! Teacher said tell whatcha saw comin home from school. I saw it!"

AFTER SCHOOL A COP CAR COME AND SHOT A BAD GUY IN THE STOMACH AFTER HE ROB A STORE.

MASON

Norma Jean moves on, checking the rest of the stories at the next two tables.

AFTER SCHOOL WHEN I WAS LOOKING OUT THE WINDOW I SAW A MOTHER TAKING HER LITTLE GIRL FOR A WALK AND A CAR HIT THE GIRL.

JESSICA

ON THE WAY HOME MY FRIEND TOLD ME THAT A BOY BUST HIS HEAD AND HAD TO GO TO THE HOSPITAL IN A EMERGENCY.

HENRY

ONE DAY AFTER SCHOOL MY FATHER CAME HOME AND TOLD MY MOTHER THERE'S GOING TO BE BLOOD IN THIS HOUSE. BUT I NEVER SAW NO BLOOD.

RUTH ANN

As most school administrators see it, their agonizing safety problem springs from forces outside their terrain. "Our whole society is based on violence, even within the family," says one San Francisco principal.

"Ruth Ann!"

"What? What's the matter? What did I do?"

"Uh . . . how many times have I told you it's bad grammar to say 'never saw no'? Erase it. Erase the whole thing!" she hisses.

"The whole thing? *Why?*" Well, there must be something else you can write about! Some other disaster that you've witnessed after school, something that isn't so personal. *Pull yourself together.*

"Look, honey, I think the teacher wanted you to tell about something you saw *walking home* from school; something that happened out on the *street.* Here, I'll get you another piece of paper, you can start over. Now: What have you seen *on the way home from school* lately that's interesting?"

Ruth Ann is sullen; she doesn't like the way I threw her story in the wastebasket, shredding it so that even the janitor wouldn't be able to put two and two together.

"I don't know. I don't know what you mean." Sure you do. Automobile accidents, shoot-outs, mass murders. Norma Jean is sweating; it's almost time for the recess bell.

"Listen, honey; I'm going to have to leave now. I have an appointment. I won't be back by the time you get home from school, so I want you to go over to Rachel's. I'm going to call her now and she'll take care of you and the boys until I get back." Yes, I'm sure this is her day off work, out of school, at home.

"You can't! I have to get my *braces* on today! Right after school. Did you forget?"

"You're right, Ruthie; I did forget. What a responsible girl you are for remembering!" *Good-bye, Rex. It was swell while it lasted. No regrets Smile through your tears Don't look back Here's looking at YOU, kid, etc.*

"Damon, will you *please* sit still? This is an office, not a football field. I know you're tired, Ruth Ann should be out soon."

"Mrs. Harris? Could you come into my office for a minute, please?"

Ruth Ann is sitting opposite his desk, her mouth all hooked up, banded, and wired. It seems that all that's left is to plug her in somewhere.

"She'll have to brush now every time she eats. She will not be able to eat candy, ice cubes, french bread, raw carrots, apples— things that might cause damage to the wires." *But she loves raw carrots and apples. That's practically all she ever eats.* "And as soon as she gets home from school, she will have to wear the headgear apparatus for at least sixteen hours, through the night. The wires are too small for her to be able to insert them into the tubes herself. You will have to do it. It can be removed while she eats dinner, and then reinserted immediately after dinner. You will have to be available to insert the headgear twice a day for the next eighteen months." *But I had planned on running off to Mexico with Rex Porter, III. Or was it Tomaso? Arndt?*

"Aw, Mom! Not the health-food store again! We were just there!"

"That was quite a few days ago, Scott." *The wrong day, to be exact.* "Besides, we need eggs." *Nice, big, fertile eggs, full of possibilities.*

"We're tired! We want to go home and watch cartoons."

"Why don't you kids just stay in the car, then; sit here and relax. I'll only be a minute. Don't get out, and don't . . ." You can't very well say ". . . open the door for anyone," when the whole top of the car is open.

Mrs. Peterson told police she left the baby unattended in the car because he was asleep. "I was only gone for a minute," the distraught young mother said. "I just needed milk; I would have been back sooner, but the lines in there were so long. . . . When I got back, he was gone."

Police are attempting to locate witnesses who may have been in the parking lot at the time.

"Hi, Tomaso. I need some eggs; are they fresh?"

"*Ciao*, Norrrma! *Si*, just came in today. Stay there! I get them for you." He reaches under the refrigerator and withdraws a carton. "How are you?" He asks as though he really wants to know. Why should I lie to him? There's no one else in the store. He places the eggs on the counter but does not ring up the sale, just folds his arms and leans there looking at her.

"I'm O.K., Tomaso. How are you? How's school?"

"You don't sound so O.K. What's the matter? You seem sad." What could the age difference be? Ten years? Fifteen? Older men with young girls are regarded as exhibiting their power to attract, declaring their vigor; any woman over thirty with a young boy is seen as desperate. Is this feeling desperation? Is it really

Tomaso, or merely a wish to stay in the game, prove I'm still in the running? *What difference does it make? You analyze everything to death.* It makes a difference when people have some idea what they're doing; it makes your life more your *own*. When you have understanding, there are more alternatives. *You can also go crazy with alternatives.* I'm already crazy. *How do you feel, right now? Who do you think you are? Arndt?* I *feel!* Isn't that enough? It's one of the first signs of rebirth. Does a newborn have to account for its sensations? Does it know what it's going to do?

"Norrrma. I know: you're *smoking* too much!"

"Yeah, that's probably it, Tomaso."

"Listen. I know *just* the place; I eat lunch there all the time after class, fantastic place, all natural foods. You are *not allowed* to smoke there! Light up, they THROW YOU OUT!" He laughs. His hand moves across the counter and touches hers. "You let me take you there sometime? I would like that very much." It was just the lightest touch, but he continues to wait for the answer with his eyes. He is not laughing. And I am not speaking, only feeling, not a new feeling, but one that is newly re-created—a feeling central to one's youth: that you matter, that something unexpected could happen.

"I just went in to buy some eggs!" the distraught middle-aged mother told police. *But then I got turned on by the clerk, what could I do?* ("Falling in love again/ Never wanted to/ What am I to do?/ I can't help it." —Marlene Dietrich.)

"You're a good man, Tomaso," I say as he rings up the eggs, still refusing to look away from me. "You're the only reason I shop at this crappy store." And then I walk quickly out, without looking back, cradling the eggs in my arm like—you want me to say it, don't you? It's what you're thinking; and thinking is the only absolute freedom there is, so be my guest—a baby.

And driving home, I consider the questions. I am a contestant on "Queen for a Day"—yes, I know that goes way back, but doesn't everything?—and if I come up with the right answers, I get to be Queen. I also get a new refrigerator. I have refused to answer the first question. I insist on my right to remain silent, on the grounds that it has at least two possible answers, maybe more; and that either one could be correct; either one could be incorrect; or both could be right. Contrary to what you might expect, open-ended multiple-choice questions become harder to answer with age. However, for the benefit of the court, let the record show that the first question was: Why do you want Tomaso Ruggiero? The M.C. is pissed. *Women like you, who refuse to play the game by the rules, give this show a bad name, lower our ratings.* I stand firm. The risks, after all, are mine, not his. He moves quickly on to the second question; he's given up on me, I can tell; has no interest any more. But that does not affect me as I thought it might; my major concern is not with pleasing him. ("To thine own self be true . . ." —William Shakespeare.)

The second question: What makes you feel that, as a wife and "mummy," you have a *right* to Tomaso Ruggiero? Where does this feeling come from? From what source does it derive its conviction? (Keep in mind that, in the early stages of resurrection, the labor is long; there is no reason to expect the birth to be any different.)

> . . . The dead man would rise like the sun at the dawning of the world, emerging from a blue lotus-flower . . . dominating the waters of primeval chaos. Thus the final phase of the mummification ritual would be his passport to eternity: "You live again, you live again forever, here you are young once more forever."
>
> —Christiane Desroches-Noblecourt,
> *Tutankhamen*, George Rainbird
> Limited, London, p. 221.

Therefore, to answer as directly as I can, I call your attention to the early years, when I was giving birth to *others*. (You might not have thought it possible to give birth to others before one has given birth to oneself, but I assure you it is quite possible, it has been done; I offer myself in evidence as Exhibit A.)

"Would counsel please approach the bench." What does he want? *He's inquiring about the body.* Well, tell him I was just getting to that.

"Witness may continue."

With respect to the body: they crawled all over it, day and night; they considered it their home. Long after they had been borne of it, they continued to inhabit its folds, its recesses, all available aspects and apertures. There were all those years when babies would be sucking on breasts and rambunctious sons ramming their heads into your pelvis; and there was absolutely no way to view the body other than a giant receptacle, an endless repository, for tears, snot, blood, shit, dirt-caked hands—pawing, pinching, kneading, clinging. To spare you the trouble of further questioning along these lines, let me say I have already forgiven myself that, when Martin would come home at six o'clock and whisper, "Mmm, baby, wanna fuck tonight?" I used to scream, "What did you *say*? Don't come *near* me! I'm not a *fountain!* You can all drop *dead!*" (If it please the court, this was never meant to be taken literally . . . to the best of my recollection.) (". . . And it must follow, as the night the day, thou canst not then be false to any man.")

It is central to the argument that you understand that for many years it was not possible for the defendant . . . that is, the contestant . . . *Well, which are you? The difference is crucial* . . . to regard the body as other than a mother ship—for the simple reason that there were always so many people lined up on the gangplank waiting to climb aboard. And I would lie awake nights, posing the question over and over: When will the body be my own again? To do with what I choose? Does that answer the question? The M.C. isn't giving any clues. I think I may have blown the whole thing by refusing to respond to the first question, but you never find that out until the end of the show.

Norma Jean puts the dinner in the oven and, while the children watch cartoons, returns to the garage to work on the new piece. As she sits there stroking the clay, she sees Tomaso Ruggiero standing in a field of grain.

> To assist the deceased to reconstitute himself and be reborn, the great silhouette of Osiris, laid flat in a coffer at the bottom of the tomb, was covered with grain which was watered. The corn soon germinated, its tender young shoots giving promise of a harvest.
>
> —Christiane Desroches-Noblecourt, op. cit., p. 253.

She is shocked when she realizes two hours have passed. The dinner is probably burned. But the new piece is nearly finished! Second births are quicker and easier, as a rule. ("It's always hardest getting that first olive out of the bottle." —Michael Ward, M.D., natural childbirth class, 1964.)

"Well, what's she doing out *there?*" Martin's voice filters into the garage. "What's *burning?*" She throws a cloth over the clay and runs toward the house. *Are you going to tell him you finished the Piece?* What? And spend the rest of my life at the sink? You must be crazy, too. No. This is definitely not the time to say I've "finished." I've just begun! I need more room; entire armies have perished because they claimed victory too soon. You have to push on, claim more ground than is absolutely required, because you never know much you may lose later on, in the course of a surprise attack. It is always more difficult to reclaim a loss than to foster a gain. The goal is to extend the boundaries far enough to assure unobstructed breathing; then hold the line. ("Power concedes nothing it isn't forced to." —Popular truism.) I bide my time, largely out of fear.

"Hi, dear. Welcome home. Have a hard day? Want a drink? Did you see Ruthie's new braces?"

"What's going on around here? Something's burning in the kitchen, Damon's running around without a stitch of clothes on, and *you're* out there in the *garage.*" There is a pause whose obvious purpose is to give me enough time to dislodge the cyanide capsule from the hollow tooth, and bite it open with as much discretion, and as little *fuss*, as possible.

"Damon, why are you bare?"

"Because my skin needed air. It wanted to come out of its clothes and dance around."

"That's not true, Mom," explains Ruth Ann. "There was this real scary man with a ray gun on 'Speed Racer,' and it made Damon pee in his pants."

"Well, get your pajamas on; we're going to eat soon" *if there's anything left.*

Norma Jean pulls the casserole out of the oven and lifts the lid. Martin is standing nearby, pretending to inspect the mail, so that when he is called as a witness he can claim to have been on the scene. "Would you describe the defendant as a bad mother?" "No, your honor; not bad. Crazy. She doesn't willfully seek to hurt others and create chaos; those are simply by-products of her condition." "Well, now, can you tell us if the dinner in question was, in fact, *dead* when you arrived on the scene?"

"Ah, there." She breathes a sigh of relief. "What you were smelling was just some drippings that overflowed in the oven. This is O.K., just a little hot, is all."

"You didn't even *know* Damon had wet his pants." ("When I can't get at 'em—when they's got they left pretty well-protected—I lets 'em have it on the right." —Floyd ("Flingin' Floyd") Faluchi, U.S. Middleweight Champion; interview, Madison Square Garden, 1942.) As I stand over the salad bowl, breaking the lettuce into perfectly sized pieces, my mind is made up: if Rudolph and I marry, we will *not* have children. We will sit at small tables in the most intimate cafés, feeding each other bits of cool melon for the rest of our lives. *Rudolph? You mean Arndt?* What the hell are you talking about? Didn't you hear me? I said, if Tomaso and I marry, we will definitely *not* have children. We will . . . *No, you said "Rudolph."* You're out of your mind. Well, I suppose it's inevitable when you're in such close proximity for a long period of time, you're bound to pick it up. *Pick what up?* My craziness. They call it symbiosis. *Don't worry about that; it's all yours. I'm the SANE part of you. I'm immune.* You're an arrogant little . . . if I weren't so lonely, I'd ask you to leave.

"Dinner's ready, everyone. Turn off the TV and wash your hands." Martin walks away from the table.

"You and the kids go ahead; I don't feel like eating," he mumbles, as he heads for his study. When direct frontal attack is not feasible, assault via the midline is the recommended tactic. All that is required to incapacitate the woman, for periods of time ranging from twenty-four hours to infinity, is to refuse to eat her food.

"Are you going to pull that just because I failed to catch the casserole the minute it spilled over? Because I failed to catch Damon's pee the minute the ray gun went off?"

"Go ahead and make it sound trivial. The plain fact is I've had enough of this crap. Enough! Go find yourself someone who will put up with it. Not me, baby. Not me." He exits.

Arndt puts up. Of course he's paid to; still, in spite of what the philodendron says, it's begun to seem like an oasis in there lately. Especially since all this crap with Martin began. Rudolph

Arndt sets his umbrella carefully in the front hall. He removes his raincoat slowly, in a manner that suggests he has come here in order to relieve himself of a heavy burden. "No, thank you; I'll just hold it here over my arm," he replies, in answer to Martin's offer to hang it for him. He refuses a drink; a man with a sense of purpose doesn't prevaricate, he gets right to the point. "I never thought it would come to this, but I am deeply in love with your wife," he says, as I pour the children's milk.

"You said we could have ginger ale for dinner because we had milk while we were watching cartoons!"

"Well, it's already poured. Drink that first, and then you can have the ginger ale." Martin doesn't seem surprised; it's as though he had been expecting it. "She's yours," he answers immediately, "assuming you can put up." Arndt is slow to understand. "Well, I didn't bring much cash with me; will Master Charge do?" Martin is patient: "No. I meant you can have her if you're strong enough to put up with all her shit." Arndt chuckles. "Oh, *that!* Leave it to me," he replies, winking. "You sure you won't have that drink? Not even a small toast?" "Well," says Arndt, "maybe I will after all! You know," he adds, "you've been very decent about this, I didn't expect . . ." Martin replaces the lid on the ice bucket and looks up in surprise. "Didn't expect to find me a civilized man? Has she been making me out to be some kind of animal?" "No, no, of course not . . . that is, not entirely. She's a balanced woman, understands the basic duality which underlies much of . . . mmmm. This is just right. Dry." He smacks his lips. Martin smiles. "Good! I'm glad you like it." He doesn't mention that it's imported, French to be exact, and cost $2.99 over the price of the local brand. No need. When gentlemen confer it is understood that one refrains from speaking of certain things. He feels a flush of pleasure to have been able to help. Still, sipping his drink, the thought occurs with sufficient force that he feels he should inquire: "Ah, I don't want to seem intrusive; but as her husband, I feel a certain duty to ask. Are you certain, that is, do you feel sure you *know* her well enough to take this step? I'd like to avoid any hard feelings later—you understand my intentions, I hope. I would feel responsible if there were misunderstandings and I had failed to inquire." Arndt is quick to reassure. "My dear man, I understand. Please, be assured: I *know* your wife—I have *studied* her these past months; it's my work, after all. I make it my *business* to ascertain certain facts before I enter into any transaction." ("Examination of the teeth and hoofs is advised before purchase." —*Horse Trader's Handbook*, p. 2.)

"I don't think it's fair to make us drink the milk after you promised us ginger ale." Norma Jean clenches her teeth. Well, you can't expect a fantasy to go the way you want in the face of these constant demands on your libidinal energies.

"It's probably not one hundred percent fair, Ruth Ann. But people are not one hundred percent perfect. You may have the ginger ale when you've all finished your dinner, not before." That's where I stand. That's my position on the ginger ale. Arndt suddenly appears before me in the kitchen. "What you saw in there just now is a figment of your imagination, my dear; it is not as it seems. How many times must I remind you? I am on your side. And as your (paid) representative, I think I should take this opportunity to ask: Why did you have me 'acquire' you by making a deal with your husband? Does that ring a bell?" The bells are all kept in a back room, way in the past. You have to go there in order to ring them. I hate it because it's dark and full of cobwebs; you're always tripping over debris and hurting yourself. Thomas Wolfe was wrong: you can go home again, if you don't mind getting torn to shreds. The place is in such a state of decay, you require the services of a guide before you can go in. After that, you're pretty much on your own. He just sits there on the porch and has a beer while you're feeling your way through the rooms. (The upstairs is especially bad; you wouldn't believe the things that were left lying around up there.) Sometimes I holler to him, "Get me out of here, I can't see where I'm going," and he usually answers, "It's *your* place; you're the only one allowed in there, them's the rules. I'm only paid to *get* you there. You can describe it to me, though; that's part of my job, to interpret what you find there. Got real good ears; they cleared all the wax out during training with a special purifying agent, supposed to keep the passages clear of obstruction permanently."

"It was *your* fantasy, you know. And it should tell us something about *you. Does* it ring a bell?" Yeah, O.K., I found it; they left it under the couch in the . . . parlor? We never had a parlor. "Never mind, go on." There are two men and a woman there;

the two men are talking to each other, the woman is off somewhere in the background. She's either clasping her breast or
wringing her hands, I can't tell because of the light. Anyway, it
doesn't matter—she's not part of the action, the men are. One is
her father, the other is her suitor; he's asking for her hand. The
father is stringing it out, making the poor guy sweat, because you
can't just give a daughter away (snap!) like that; you've got to
make a man work a little first, to show she has some value. The
father's enjoying it; it takes the edge off his knowledge that he's
losing things to see someone that young, with everything ahead of
him, have to wait on his decision. It's a rare privilege to be able
to take your time, to exercise discretion, when disposing of valuable
property; it restores a sense of power and well-being, the way a
fine cigar does. That's why he's stringing it out. Has nothing to
do with the girl. He wants to make this moment last as long
as possible. If this isn't my house, what am I doing here? No one
asked my father for my hand. I've never seen these people before; what do they have to do with me?

"History, customs, traditions, all have their effect on the individual, whether or not they happened to be experienced first-
hand. Your fantasy seems to say that you see your husband and
me in collusion, and having some ultimate power to control what
happens in your life. If you see yourself as that helpless, then we
must analyze *why*. *Not* knowing is an impediment to your having
real control over your life." Wait. You're missing something: are
we analyzing why I *see* you both as having all the power, or why
you *have* all the power? I've got a headache. Look: you have the
power, have always had the power; and that is why I see you as
having the power. A woman can *try* to equalize things, but even if
she succeeds, the change is so radical, and so rapid, her attitudes
can't always keep pace. Even after changes have occurred, we're
still victims of attitudes.

"I'll drink to that." You *will?* ("You could knock me over
with a feather!") I have some very special imported stuff here that
I keep just for men who understand. Been in the cupboard since
1938. "Oh, no thank you—I was speaking metaphorically; I don't
drink on the job." Aw, come on; don't be so stuffy. Just a little
one, for me. "It wouldn't *be* for you. That's the point; it wouldn't
be fair to *you*." Well, if you say so. Then how about lunch Satur-

215

day? Someone I know ("I grow as 'Grain' . . . I am barley") told me about a terrific little restaurant . . . O.K., O.K., I can take a hint. If you're not interested, who needs you? Not me. Tomaso! What a surprise! What are you doing here? "My Ferrari ran out of gas" HIS Ferrari? Aren't you getting things mixed . . . Get out of here! You are never, *never* allowed in here! It's a total violation, it is never permitted! "on the way home, I was just passing your house" (funny; it's on a *court*, how could he . . .) God damn it! You get out of here too! All of you! Tomaso. Tomaso?

"Norma? What are you doing sitting alone at the table, staring into space? Haven't you done the dishes *yet*? Where are the children? It's nearly dark." What is that disgusting mess on that plate? Where did it come from? Who put it there? Where am I? What day is this?

"Norma! I asked you a question. Where the hell are the kids? It's after nine." Oh, it's the *kitchen*! How did it get dark so fast?

"Martin, where are the children?" I could have her committed; don't know why it didn't occur to me before. She'd be taken care of, get a good rest, a chance to pull herself together, and *I wouldn't have to be a witness to this sideshow any longer!* It would cost, but it would be worth it, every cent.

"God damn it, Norma! Wake up! I've been working in my study for the past hour; how the hell should *I* know where the kids are? *You're* their mother, you tell *me*!"

"Don't scream at *me*! They're probably next door. *You* go out and find them! I've got to get this garbage cleaned up."

Standing at the sink, the steaming water spilling over her hands like a caress, Norma Jean dials again: Tomaso? Are you there? Tomaso—ratify my existence! Martin stalks back into the kitchen.

"The kids are upstairs getting ready for bed. They were *not* next door, they were running wild in the street. It's one thing for you to be in outer space as far as *I'm* concerned, but when you start fading out on the *children*, you'd better know I think you're in serious trouble, lady!" Drop dead, drop dead. *Try to understand that it's hard for him—hard for anyone—to absorb so many changes so quickly. It throws people; they become confused and lash out. If you can forbear, it will pass.* Listen, stop being so goddamned coy; I've been onto you for months now. You hear me? I know who you are! *Well, I try not to blow my cover; sometimes when people know, it tends to scare them off—especially these days. But go ahead. Say it. Who do you think I am?* You're the Voice of Reason! And haven't you heard? They've cut back funds, deleted your job, phased you *out!* Go back to the nineteenth century and find yourself a nice fresh field to gambol in. *It's my duty to tell you I think you're trying to avoid thinking about Martin and making sure you've left no stone unturned in the struggle to find a reasonable solution to the problem.* I'll bet you always turned your homework in on time and washed behind your ears. I always hated your type. *It's true; I've never been wildly popular, but we all have our place, and I've noticed that people like you are always glad I'm around when the chips are down.*

Norma Jean draws a bath and lies back in the steaming water with the newspaper before her eyes.

RAPE IN AMBULANCE   GAS CRISIS IMMINENT

Good God! If that's true, it's good-bye to Interstate 5, Interstate 580, the Bayshore, the Eastshore, 101. . . . How will I survive?

Count Marco

HOW TO FIND YOUR
HUSBAND'S TRUE VALUE

While dining out the other evening I found myself seated next to a table occupied by an acquaintance of mine and three of her female companions. I had heard via rumor that my acquaintance was having marital difficulties. I soon overheard that the rumor was true.

Her friends were so sympathetic. . . .

"I wouldn't put up with him for one more minute," was the advice that each of them gave. Each soon found an excuse to leave my acquaintance sitting alone with her thoughts.

I invited myself to her table and gave her some advice for which she has not yet stopped thanking me. I will give you the same advice. It is perhaps cruel, even morbid, but I guarantee it will help save an unhappy marriage: Think of your husband as dead!

When he leaves in the morning, go through the whole terrible routine. Imagine that he will never come home again and what you must do when that occurs. Go to his closet and remove his clothes, fold them and put them in boxes to be given away.

What will you wear to the funeral? Who will come to the funeral? And, when it is over, who will remain behind with you in the weeks that follow?

"Take my arm, Norrrma; the Ferrari's parked just down the road." The little group of mourners breaks apart, as people walk off slowly toward their cars. I am wearing a light green *peau de soie* afternoon dress with long sleeves, and the antique earrings Mattie brought back from Perugia in 1910, because I am secure in my conviction that life is sad; I do not need to wear black to prove it. I have decided against the hat and veil, for the same reason. The grave is banked with fresh flowers; they stand out with a special intensity under the low, overcast sky. Rachel is approaching me. She whispers, "I'll take the children, Norma. You go on ahead with Tomaso. We'll keep them fifteen years—that will see Damon through to college and give you a chance to get your bearings." ("A friend in need is a friend indeed.")

Tomaso grips my left hand with his, while embracing me with his right. As he guides me *You're a feminist; you should be able to navigate that place yourself. They've got markers all over . . .* If you violate the rule one more time, I am going to stop recognizing you! It is a law of nature that *reason* cannot intrude on a fantasy. Now fuck off and stay on your own turf, do you understand? *You're right. I have been out of place. It's just that I take my job so seriously, I get carried away sometimes.* Well, take a vacation. *Oh, gosh, thank you! We're not supposed to ask, you know, but* GO, GO, GO!!! Get away from me! Oh, God! Give me strength! "Norrrma, please. Hold on a little longer. I *know* you're upset. It's been terrible, terrible, and you've been so brave. Just a little further, I hold you. *Coraggio, coraggio.*" As he guides me down the gravel path, I see Doris Morgan out of the corner of my eye; she's whispering something to Mark. As it passes through his ear and out the other side of his head, the wind carries it gently down the slope and I can just make it out: "Still warm in his grave, and she's running off with the grocery boy! Oh, oh! Ungh! Tsk! Mmm!" The fifth Morgan child beats its fists against the walls of her belly: "Let me out of here, I'm suffocating!" it screams.

"You all right? Stay. I unlock the car." As Tomaso bends down to insert the key, the wind stirs the leaves overhead; they move heavily, as though on water, *lentamente, adagio,* casting a delicate network of light and shadow across the top of the Ferrari. "Get in," Tomaso whispers; his lips just brush the side of my face. Eat your heart out, Doris Morgan! And that goes double for all you horny sixteen-year-olds. With flawless coordination I glide into the bucket seat; with a composure unequaled anywhere outside foreign films, I lean my head against the headrest and allow one tear to form in the eye nearest the driver's seat, as Tomaso slides in and shuts the door. As we pull away, I notice Fellini sitting on the mausoleum roof, peeling a banana. When we finally come to a stop in front of his penthouse, Tomaso turns off the motor and holds me, as the tape deck plays the Albinoni Adagio in G Minor—both speakers, front and rear. He strokes my hair and whispers, "Believe me, Norrrma; this will pass." I believe him. As our mouths come together, the Ferrari fills with exquisite sensations until it seems about to burst. It is the finest *Liebestod* of its kind in the western world.

Suddenly the bathroom light goes out, throwing the room into total darkness. Norma Jean lies there blinking. The water laps gently against her skin. She closes her eyes, then opens them again; everything looks the same, open or shut: black. Lying there in her watery darkness, she feels the house contract; it sighs as it bears down, and she thinks: *It has finally agreed to let me out!*

Stepping from the bathroom, she feels her way along the wall with her hands, and it strikes her: It wasn't just the bathroom bulb; all the lights in the house are out. She looks out the window. The entire neighborhood is dark. The whole house sleeps. She makes her way to the kitchen and feels around in a drawer for a candle stub. Lighting it, she places it on the table and considers calling the electric company. I wonder if it's local, or worldwide. Why do I feel I can't go to sleep until I know? She turns on the radio and moves the switch up and down the band, but there's no news, just "Good night, America, how are ya? Say, don't ya know me? . . ." and talk shows. What difference does it make why it happened? It's dark, that's all that matters. *No, that's not all that matters; all your frozen foods are melting. Can't you hear them? Drip, drip.* Well, there's nothing I can do about it. Still, if I called . . . *Why do I have this need to know what's happening? Because you were taught to look for explanations. You still believe there are answers—that it's just a matter of inquiring of the right source.*

"Hello? Uh, my name is Mrs. Harris, on Palm Court? The lights are out all over the neighborhood, and I thought you might be able to . . ."

"Sbeenafailure. Wha? Ya, ya, hold it willya? I'm on line two."

"What?"

"S'been a failure, ma'am. They're checking it now."

"Oh. O.K. Thanks. Uh, say, you have any idea what caused it?"

"Lady, don't ask me. These things are getting more and more frequent, that's all I know. One of these days there'll be no power left."

Replacing the receiver, she casts her eyes around the room, squinting in the candlelight. *Well, now you know. Or don't know. In any case, you can go to bed; you've done what you had to do.* Can't go to bed. Don't know why. What is it about unexpected crises, disasters, that produces the need to be near someone, to make contact, to talk? Rachel. I'll call . . . wait, it must be . . . probably too late . . . asleep. Well, maybe it isn't; she often stays up to work. Damn, my watch is in the bathroom. Time! I'll call Time. Ah, that's it, see, there's still something that continues to function. As long as the phone isn't dead, you're O.K. Norma Jean dials Time and waits. "The time is . . ." (she always pauses like that before she gives it out; it makes you think there's really someone there, looking at her watch) ". . . eleven forty-two." Too late. She replaces the receiver slowly and sits back down at the table and stares into the tiny flame burning in the center. It flickers there beside the radio, so fragile; it illuminates most of the room, though, except for the corners. That's a lot of light, coming from such a small source. *Go to bed.* Can't. Have to

. . . absorb? Is that the right word? Ponder? this sudden absence of light. When things are cut off suddenly, you can't just go to sleep; you've got to give yourself time to reflect on it, to adjust. *Yes, speaking of Martin, have you considered* I wasn't speaking of *him!* I was talking about the blackout! *Come, come. No!* You go, go!

Power failures, gas shortages—it doesn't seem fair to be running out of time and resources all at once. What is there left to look forward to? Tomaso. Better get together soon, before I'm too old; what can I lose? I've lost it already. *You could do Interstate 5 with him, go out in a burst of glory, kill two birds with one stone.* I thought you were the Voice of Reason! *Well, I'll be honest with you. Sometimes, in (stubborn? difficult? impossible?) certain cases, we do what's called "entering in": that is, we share the (patient's delusion? fanatic's vision?) other person's point of view; we adopt her voice for a while; assume her way of thinking. It helps to encourage trust, and at the same time gives us a deeper understanding. It amounts to standing in another person's shoes; that's always being recommended by the moralists, but you'll notice damn few ever really do it. As I was saying, it's a sure way to achieve empathy, take my word.* Are you sure you're not working for Arndt? *Why, whatever gave you . . .* Interstate 5 with Tomaso . . . wait, I'd need the Ferrari; couldn't do it properly in the old MG. And that would involve Rex. . . . Did you ever stop to think of all the things that never take place because of the sheer weight of the mechanics involved? *You could do it in your mind; the funeral went off all right, didn't it?* No thanks to you. Besides, it's a perversion to do everything in your mind; I'm getting sick of it. *That may be so, but it has one big advantage, which is that you never have to account to anyone for it.* The day is coming when people won't have to account for anything; times are changing fast in that respect. *I don't think so; as long as there are people, there will be things they're held accountable for. You have to have standards, values; otherwise, what's the point of existence?* Feeling good. *Always pain, always pain, no matter what you do; Lord, haven't I been around enough to know.*

The candle sputters; what's left is just a stub, no more than an inch, but it refuses to go out altogether. When you get down that close to the last of anything, you might as well hang around for the end. Norma Jean switches on the radio and stares into the flame. Can that burn an image on your retina? Or is it just the sun that does that?

"Hello? Hello? We have another caller here. Can you hear me? Hello, this is Al here, on the KGX Hot Line Talkathon, midnight to six. Anybody there?"

"Mr. Speed?"

"Right, sweetheart; speak a little louder, will you? We can't hear you too well."

"Oh, yes, of course. Mr. Speed, I just wanted to call and say I listen to your program every night. I . . ."

"Hey, now! That's terrific. Say, you sound like a real old-timer. How old are you, sweetheart? If you don't mind me asking."

"No, of course I don't. Well, Mr. Speed, I was seventy-eight last February. I live alone here in the city; I've been a widow for twelve years." She speaks slowly, as the air waves crackle. Al is saying "Uh huh. Uh huh."

"Mr. Speed, there is something that is troubling me; would it be all right for me to tell you about it?" Al sighs, but it's off-mike, no one picks it up. "Sure, sweetheart, sure, you go right ahead, that's what I'm *here* for!" It's a slow night, no callers on the other lines. When you host a talk show you depend on callers to carry it. You can't sit there talking to yourself midnight to six; people would tune out.

"Well, Mr. Speed, a week ago my dog ran in the street and was killed. I had had her seven years." There is a pause; Al closes his eyes. Last week, the one whose husband beat her; week before that, guy up in Humboldt county, they never send his social security check on time, upsets him so much he wets his pants—Whoo-boy, what a way to make a living.

"Aw, gee; that's a shame. Guess you were kind of torn up about it for a while."

"Yes, I was. I still am. That's why I'm calling you. She used to sleep on the bed with me—I'm calling you from bed; I put the radio beside the bed and listen to your program before I go to sleep. It helps me."

"Aw, that's *sweet*. Really is."

"Mr. Speed, I've tried, but I . . . just can't seem . . ." She chokes; the radio bristles with her silence there in the dark room. It's hard to believe that a seventy-eight-year-old woman, with an intact mind and a well-modulated voice, would be calling Al Speed, but here she is. Al is quick to fill in the pause; the worst thing that can happen on the radio is unintentional silence.

"Well, I can understand, I really can—I mean even if it was just a dog, you know? Because after all, anything's better than nothing, even if it's an animal. Matter of fact, some animals make better companions than people, ha ha! No, I really mean it—they're loyal, don't talk back . . ."

"Yes," she sniffles. She's trying to pull herself together, regain her control. "You see, I miss her so much. It may sound silly to you, but she was all I had in the world. . . ." She's crying now, groping for something to hold back the tears—Kleenex, bedsheet. *Got to get this one OFF THE AIR.*

"Listen, I know it must be rough, being alone like that, but try to think of it this way: the dog had a good life. You know what they say: ('Into each life some rain must fall.')"

"Yes."

"When you come right down to it, everyone's alone. We're born alone and we die alone, know what I mean? Listen, I understand, I really do. But you have to realize: each and every *one* of us is alone, when it gets right down to it."

"Yes, dear, I *know* that . . ." she says quietly. She has regained her control. Al sighs, off-mike. ". . . it's just that I had no one else to call." *I think I'm going to die. Right here in my General Electric kitchen.* Al lights up; the crisis is over. When he exhales, his teeth shine whiter than the panels on the studio ceiling. There is the sound of the connection breaking, then silence. Norma Jean switches off the radio and sits alone in the dimly lit kitchen. The candle has a quarter inch to go. She rests her head on the table. *I can't imagine a loneliness so unbearable that I would have to call a young snot like Al Speed in the middle of the night. Well, you should start imagining it; I've found that, in general, those do better later in life who begin to make the realization early on. I've imagined it—late at night on the freeway. A beginning, but not nearly enough; it in no way duplicates the actual situation: family*

223

gone, no mobility, poverty. I've realized it often, reading the paper.

FOSTERS WEST IS SWINGING TO THE YOUNG SIDE

The venerable chain of Fosters restaurants soon will . . . become budget-priced, fast-food outlets this summer.

"Face it, we're living in a hamburger world," said Larry Browning, the intense 33-year-old executive director of Fosters West. . . .

"The time, I regret to say, is past for the raisin toast and prune crowd—and please don't think me callous," he added.

Browning was referring, of course, to the gentle stereotype of Fosters—lunchrooms peopled with old folks, often one to a table. . . . "We couldn't make it with just the old people sitting over their chicken a la king and tea all afternoon," Browning said. "We had a hell of an image problem."

Yes, of course, you realized it; but did you apply it to yourself? Did you "enter in?" Yes, I applied it to myself. I apply everything to myself; that's why I'm crazy. Before I began to work on the pieces, I did what we all did once or twice a month—got a sitter and went to the city to shop. But I always ate lunch at Fosters: as though to remind myself of something; as though I were getting the feel of it, trying it out early, to see if it could be borne.

I would order the Friday Special, baked macaroni and roll, $.59, and sit among the elderly, watching. I used to pretend I was one of them; I would think: Martin, gone these many years, the house sold, the children grown and far away. They write four times a year, but do not visit. They spend their holidays traveling, sailing, skiing—things an old woman can't do. And then I would think: strange, that they should all three have decided not to have children! As I sat there, lingering over my tea, I wondered if it was due to the times, or to their having had me for a mother; and then I began longing, in spite of myself, in spite of everything, for the plump, seductive, never-to-be grandchildren. The ones with the special shine to the skin, which comes from being rubbed lightly with the hand over time, and, like a stone, grows smoother each day. And the smell: each child has its own special smell. You get so used to drinking it in; it's a special protective device they all have, to ensure that they're not abandoned. And then I would think, I've got all that! Right now! They're all three at home, wetting their pants and driving the sitter nuts. What am I doing here in Fosters, on my day off, thinking of *them?*

But just before I gathered up my packages to go, I'd give it one more whirl: I'd imagine the tiny hotel room, no kitchen, toilet down the hall, medicines on the night table, the children's photographs, maybe a fern or two, where I would now return and, after hanging my coat in the closet, rest, and wait for mail. *No getting mugged on the way to the mailbox?* No, no, I didn't think of muggers then. *No panic, no incontinence, when your social security check failed to arrive on time?* No . . . I didn't think that far. It wasn't an *elaborate* fantasy; just the basics: eating alone, loss of family, things like that. *Well, if you're going to do it at all, you must be thorough. It's the details, after all, that do it.* Do what? *Give old age its special poignancy. When you fail to consider the variety of possibilities, you leave yourself wide open. What about living in fear? You do that?* No. *Falling, breaking your hip? Lying in some hospital ward, full of tubes? A nursing home?* ("They're animal farms. I know. I worked in one." —Unidentified woman in drugstore, to clerk, 1971.)

Norma Jean stares as the wick struggles, then drowns in the pool of melted wax. When there is no light from any source, the sense of sound predominates by default. And what she hears is the slow, regular, trickling sound that things give off as they melt; it seems to be coming from far away. Is it the polar ice cap? Or just the frozen foods? One thing is clear: what once was fixed now burns, loosens, and redefines itself. She leaves the kitchen and makes her way to the bedroom by touch. There is no moon.

When I close my eyes I see ideas for a half-dozen works, and can't sleep for the stimulation. I wonder if I'm the only one who sees things after closing the eyes, or if others have the same problem. She glances at Martin, who sleeps like a stone. Martin, I just don't know about us; I really don't. Zzzzz. Zzzzz. I know it's been hard for you; but it's been hard for me, too. Strange, I never expected you to retreat when things got hard. Well, I can't tell you what to do; you've got to square things with yourself. I stay right here, and see what develops. *If I can stand it.* The moves are all yours now. It's up to you. You son of a bitch.

"Norrrma. How much longer you gonna hang around there,

225

waiting for him to make up his mind? You think I can wait for-ever?"

"Shhh, Tomaso; he wants to be sure he can adjust. Every person deserves a chance—as long as he's trying. He does puzzles with the children after work and puts them to bed; he hasn't said 'I've had a hard day' since late March; he's taken the garbage out eleven times. . . . We're creatures of habit; everything takes time. You have to respect individual differences in the ability to master change; I read that somewhere."

"But Norrrma! With me, you don't have to *wait* for change! I love feminists! I *am* a feminist (Mmmm!) I love art! Sculpt! Mess around all you like! I even eat your shitty dinners—sprouts, seeds, soybeans, grain! I no *complain!*"

"You don't *understand*: I don't want to lose him." (*I don't understand it either.*) Still, everyone has limits, even me. And when I think of Tomaso, I, too, burn, loosen, change form, just like the polar ice cap—or was it the frozen foods?—like anything that's subjected to overwhelming stress, change, or has lost its connection.

15

MOTHER, THREE CHILDREN

FOUND WITH THROATS SLASHED

. . . Police discovered the bodies of Mrs. Jane Coates, 35, and
her three children, sprawled in the bedrooms of their neat suburban home.

They could have been *us*. . . .

"Mom, would you like me to get you another cup of coffee?
I can reach the stove now!"

"Oh, that's sweet of you to offer, Ruth Ann. But I don't want
you lifting anything that hot until you're older. You and Scott are
doing just fine with the jobs you already do."

"But Mom, I've *grown*. I'm bigger now, look." She raises herself to her full height, and sure enough, my Budding Beauty is just
about ready for the prom—just a few more years—*What generation
are you in?* No, Wait. The pill; that's it. In any case, just a few
more years.

"Come here and give me a kiss; you're such a fine girl." Ruth
Ann gets on Norma Jean's lap. Can't lift her very well any more,
getting so big. ("Time flies.")

"Mom, I been thinking . . ."

"I *have* been thinking, Ruth Ann." Screw it; school's out, she'll
talk the way *we* talk this summer. "What were you thinking?"

"Well, I was thinking of calling you 'Norma Jean' instead of
'Mom,' cause that's your real name. You don't call me 'Kid,' so
why do I have to call you 'Mom'?" Fantastic thinking, Ruth Ann.

Of course Martin will "You're their *mother*, you trying to *deny* that? Finding it hard to accept your *role*, your *function?*" but then again he might not.

"Ruthie, that's a very nice idea; it's fine with me. You can call me either one, whichever you feel like. What are Scott and Damon up to? Why is it so quiet upstairs?"

"They're doing puzzles. When you finish reading the paper, will you take us to the park?"

"Sure I will; you deserve a trip to the park. Would you like a picnic?"

"Goodie! Yes! You're such a good mommie, you make me so happy!" *I do?*

Norma Jean lights a cigarette, tosses the match toward the ashtray, misses. That friend of Marilyn Follett's—what's her name? —with the gallery. Got to give her a call. Can't let the Piece—any of the pieces—just sit there in the garage any longer. Got to put them up for sale, come out of the closet. Two more will be enough for a show. It shouldn't take me much longer, if I work every night. *You'll get tired, strung out, then you won't function well.* Listen, what happens during work, the *ideas,* are what permit me to function. Don't you understand? I've been sleeping all my life. Norma Jean's mind begins to drift. She gets up and pours herself another cup of coffee. How did school let out so soon? Wasn't it Halloween just the other day? The thought of the seasons, and the absolute conviction that they are changing faster every year, makes her catch her breath. It makes no difference whether you think of time as linear or cyclic; any fool can see it's accelerating.

Well, there have been compensations; look how quickly you made it through Scott's and Damon's birthdays. The parties were over before you knew it. Reason sighs. *I can STILL hear those* ——*horns. . . .* You have a point. And how could you forget Mother's Day and Father's Day? *Come, come; that wasn't so bad. There'll come a time when you'll treasure those drawings the children gave you, mark my . . .* Ah, their drawings: Damon's chaotic, unintelligible masses—O.K., I know he's only four, but it was all in black. *That's perfectly logical; it's his favorite color, you know that.* "I want a *black* ice cream cone!" "They don't have black ice cream, Damon. Look, they have thirty-three other colors;

how about . . ." "I want *black!* Black! Black!" "Damon, get up off the floor this minute, or I'm taking you out of here without *any* ice cream." "Aaaa! They have colors for everybody else! Why don't they have black?" "Sir? What are the chances of your . . . *creating* another flavor one of these days?" "What flavor did you have in mind, ma'am?" "Uh, well, the color has to be black . . . ah, you see, my son . . ." "Well, as you can see up there on the board, we have to have special *names* to go with all our colors; and we already have one that's called Licorice Stick, only it's not black; it's vanilla with little bits of rubber, I mean licorice, embedded throughout. . . . Uh, ma'am, we can't let him throw the chairs around like that; the manager's kind of touchy about those things." "DAMON! Get your hands off those chairs!" "So, like I say, you see our problem: even if we *could* invent a black ice cream, what could we call it?" "Well, I don't know; what about Death?" The clerk stares. I can't blame him, with a fruity four-year-old throwing chairs around and the mother requesting Death ice cream. So I tell him, "Listen, wait; don't back away like that; don't call the police. You think I don't understand the bind you're in, but I *do!* An ice cream like that—all black and yucky, with a name like Death—it would never sell. So forget it, O.K.? Sorry I brought it up." *You're going to have to decide which period of history you're operating in. You know what Christiane Desroches-Noble-court says about black, don't you? No, what? She says, ". . . black —in Ancient Egypt the colour of re-birth and not of mourning . . .' (op. cit., p. 250.)* I'll be damned. That changes everything.

Scott's picture: the entire page filled with rocket-nosed phallic shapes; and everything had *wheels,* even the race-car *driver.* Why do you suppose he's putting wheels on *humans?* What do you think it means? *My, you do worry, don't you? Look, the driver probably wanted to get from the pit to his Mark V with as little wasted time as possible. So. He roller-skates.* And Ruth Ann's: I have to admit, the content really got to me. The cross-section of a castle, showing a King; a Queen; their daughter, the Princess; and their two sons, the Princes. Would you think it was reaching if I said that the Princess was in bed with the King? While the Queen busied herself downstairs with breakfast, and the two Princes watched cartoons? Well, it's true, every word of it. You don't forget a Mother's Day gift like that in a minute.

Well, Martin's little gift to you—that was very sweet, consider-ing. Considering we weren't speaking? *Yes. He still made an effort to show his affection on Mother's Day.* You mean that box of Whitman's "Tender Moments" chocolates? He knows I hate chocolates. He knows that *anything* which would have "Tender Moments" printed on it would make me want to vomit. Those things make *him* want to vomit. And it was *heart*-shaped! Left over from Valentine's Day! No, there's simply no other way to view it: the box of chocolates was an act of pure hostility.

U.C. ASTRONOMERS FIND
MOST DISTANT QUASAR

Astronomers at Lick Observatory have discovered an immensely powerful star-like object believed to be lying farther out in the universe than man has ever seen before.

Their calculations show that the object is more than ten billion light-years away, and that it is speeding outward as part of the expanding universe at a velocity more than 90 per cent of the speed of light.

Light waves from the object that reached Lick Observatory's big telescope last night actually started on their journey through space more than ten billion years ago—at a time when, accord-ing to current cosmological thinking, the universe was new-born.

There have been a lot of quasar articles lately; this is the second one in the past month. Where did I put the other? Didn't even have time to finish it that day, but wanted . . . Wait. I clipped it and put She checks the cookbooks, turning them upside down and flipping the pages rapidly. No quasar article. Bedside table? Garage? That's it—under the glaze jars.

"Mommy! You're taking a long time! Ruth Ann said you would take us to the park. We done all the puzzles."

"*Did* all the puzzles, Scott."

"Yeah! We done 'em all! Are you proud of us?" Hopeless. When they reach college—*if* they do—literacy will come as such a shock to them *No dear; where have you been this past decade? Literacy is no longer required; hasn't been for some time. Everyone talks in the way that suits him or her best. There are no longer any rules. My, you have been cut off, haven't you? To have not heard about that.* Of course I've been cut off. Except for helping out at Ruth Ann's school, I've spent the past eight years right here in my hermetically sealed, split-level inner chamber. How would I know about a thing like that? You don't see bad grammar in the paper.

"Yes, Scott. I am proud of you. You are all playing so nicely" *I thought I was in the wrong house.* What has happened to them lately? They seem so much more reasonable, more . . . accessible —even Damon. Could it be just that they're maturing? Or could it be that since I started working I've begun to really see them for the first time?

"If you'll play for five more minutes, while I finish this article, I'll pack a special treat in our picnic."

Thus the astronomers have used their ground-based optical and electronic equipment to make an incredible voyage into the past, peering at a part of the universe that already existed billions of years before earth and our solar system even began to form.

The object detected by the Lick telescope is called a quasar, one of a mysterious class of bodies that is now exciting astrophysical researchers all over the world.

Glimpses of quasar and other bizarrely energetic objects in the night sky may yet help reveal how the universe was formed, how it evolves, and whether its ultimate future will be decay and death or infinite existence.

"Mom!"

"What?"

"I hate to tell you this."

"Ruth Ann, I've told you before, I don't like those dramatic suspense-filled openings; just *tell* me, straight out." Next to candy, the thing that gives them the greatest pleasure is watching each other get in trouble.

"O.K. Here goes: Damon karated your geraniums, and all the tops are off." Would you accept it as a significant sign of change that it bothers me more to hear karate used as a verb than it does that the geraniums were violated? A year ago, TODDLER STRANGLED: MOTHER HELD. Now I figure, they'll grow back. If rebirth involves anything, it is just these kinds of distinctions—the paring down to fundamentals; the purification; recognizing the difference between that which perishes and that which regenerates.

Norma Jean gets the scissors and clips the quasar article. This isn't something you can concentrate on when children want to go to the park. You work on it at night, when they are in bed, and the quasars are sending their signals. She takes it out to the garage, to file with the other one, passing the fallen geraniums on the way. Didn't I read in one of Mattie's journals that plants do better when you cut them back? Pick off the dead and dying blooms?

It's chilly for June, but the children don't seem to mind; as long as they can run around and climb, they're happy. I sit here on the bench and watch the wind corrugate the surface of the lake. I brought no books this time, figuring my mind would do. Damon waves from the top of a pine; the gesture almost costs him his balance. How does he do it? *Wings. A mutation often found in Aries sons. They're hidden in back, under the skin, only come out when mothers turn their backs.* And where else would Scott be but down there with the ants—squatting, burrowing. And Ruth Ann, leaning there against that tree, her hair flowing, is . . . *non è possibile!* Oh God, not yet, not so soon! *Looked like it to me, too.* She's only seven and a half! *They mature early these days.* My baby, my baby! *Relax. She's not looking FOR them yet; just AT them.*

How do they come to be what they are? How much of it has to do with me? They're changing so fast they bear no resemblance to the babies they were before. Nothing is so strange as that which is most familiar; if you don't believe it, look at the children. One day you are busy having babies, and the next thing you know you're surrounded by these mysterious creatures who grow and change form right before your eyes. You quickly catch your breath and take stock. You squint your eyes, and regard them closely, from many different angles. And you begin to weigh: Well, they're noisy as hell, and that little one under the table still bites sometimes. Still, notice how thoughtful they can be, and loving— amazing in anyone so small. Wonder where they picked it up? On the other hand, defiant, primitive, drinking your blood.

As the years pass, you bear witness to their changes, shaping where you can. Everything shifts so fast, conclusions are impossible; you bide your time, withholding judgment. It's hard living with all that ambivalence, but you adjust to it after a while. Everything on earth is highly adaptable; why do you think it's still there? Different things tip the scales for each person, eventually. For me, it happens on a park bench, when I realize for the first time that they have changed me absolutely and forever; have reshaped the substance of what I am. My little Pieces, that I should also be your product alters everything. It may be premature to say this, but I think I am grateful.

Is that Scott I see running this way?

"Mommy!" It is Scott. He throws himself onto the bench, breathless and hysterical. I take back what I just said, every word.

"What's the matter, Scott?"

"Ruth Ann keeps bossing me around! She been being so bossy I can't stand it! Make her stop!"

"Tell her to come here, Scott; I'll talk to her." There should be one adult for every child; that way everyone would have equal representation. No one person would be required to spread herself thin. Why should I have to drag these scales around everywhere I go? My name isn't Justice.

"Scott says you've been bossing him. Is that true?" Ruth Ann folds her arms and slouches in silence on the bench.

"You know, Ruth Ann, a lot of little girls, when they're seven and eight, become very bossy for a while. Did you know that?"

"No."

"Did you think you were the only one?"

"Yes! I don't know what makes me be that way! I can't help it!"

"If you thought you were the only one, it must have made you feel pretty bad. Did you think you were turning into a terrible bossy girl? Did you think you would be that way forever?"

"Yes! Yes!" She holds back tears.

"You won't. You're still your old self underneath; you're a fine girl, you always have been, and we love you. You'll be that way again soon."

"Really?" Yes, really. There are some ways in which people don't change. I think. The important thing is to let them know you'll stick around, stand by them, until they re-emerge. *Is that what you're doing with Martin?* Is that what he's doing with me?

It's a funny thing about parks; they're supposed to be happy places—at least I think that's what they're for. But notice how they're always filled with lonely people—like that old man over there, casting his vote for the ducks. They're unbearable on weekends: their paths become avenues where people pass without touching, and their benches rock the newly divorced to sleep as their children roll in the grass. Why does the sight of an empty bandstand and rows of unfilled benches make you want to turn and run forever?

It's time for lunch; I should round up the children, but I can't take my eyes off the old man. He roams the park like a blown-out tube, his overcoat dead and brown, the color of old baggage; it rides on the wind, thin as a kite. *Don't get started on the elderly again. The children are hungry, it's getting late.* What is it about old men's overcoats that's always so sad? *Take it up with Arndt.* Get lost. See how it floats around his frail form, like a spirit struggling to depart; notice its refusal to adhere, its negligence. *He's not complaining; eat your lunch.* His future has abandoned him; there is nothing left. *You don't even know him.* Anyone can see. How does he bear it? Why doesn't he throw himself in the lake? *Maybe he has his illusions.* You mean people never give them up? I don't believe it. *You spoke once yourself of their importance in sustaining life. He's alive, isn't he?* I always thought that at a certain age they had to go; that the one thing common to old people everywhere was the loss of illusions. *Well, I couldn't say; you'll have to ask one of them.* I don't know any. *Ask him. He's right there. Probably welcome the company.* You must be crazy. I can't just go up to him and ask something like that! "Excuse me, sir." "Eh? Oh! Heh heh." "I'm sorry to bother you . . ." "No bother, no bother, mmmm." "Sir, do you have any illusions?" "Eh?" "ILLUSIONS. Do you have any?" "Na, na, I *gave* already; they take it out of your social security. Go away, leave me alone. I gave 'em everything I got. Here, ducky, ducky."

I think he knows we're talking about him; see, he's moving away. The ducks move off too, gliding above their reflections, faithless, obedient to need. As she watches him stumble down the path, Norma Jean tries to imagine what his features had been like before. He stares ahead, through revised dreams. *What secrets stir in the brown bag under your arm?*

The wind ripples the grass and brings water to her eyes. The children are nowhere in sight. Norma Jean burrows into the curve of the bench and folds her arms tightly around herself. As usual, I be thinking. About how it all passes so quickly. And I be thinking of you, Tomaso; oh, I do be thinking of you all the time. I'm not going to correct Ruth Ann's black English any more; it is intense and immediate, gets to the very heart of things. It rolls like a rich river through your feelings, rendering a special poignancy to everything it describes. Who am I to cling to what was once considered "proper" language? Mattie wouldn't understand; but Mattie's dead.

And I will/won't/will say to Arndt, I can scarcely sleep cause I be thinking so of Tomaso. And Arndt will say/think to himself, Mmmmm. Could be any one of (1) patient so desperate for love and gratification, one man is not enough. Tsk, tsk. (2) patient restless, dissatisfied, voracious, *unfaithful* woman All you women In which case, Tsk, tsk, *tsk*. (What *do* they———?) (3.) patient in conflict over transference Wants to act out Let's see, there is a procedure here somewhere for that Just had it a minute Mmmm. Is that what Arndt thinks? Or is that what I think Arndt thinks? Only Arndt knows for sure, and he don't be telling. And I will/ won't say, I be thinking of history, and the concept of community, and the early foundations of the family. And I be going back to feudal times and I be thinking of hard work, few pleasures, struggle for survival, the importance of property, the begetting of children and the handing down of names, the continuity of identity (passing through the male line, the females being swallowed up by history, generation after generation). And then I be thinking of courtly love. And then Arndt be thinking something like: Romantic fantasy O.K. but romantic dobedobe*do* bad for society. Structure of family collapse. And then I be saying to Arndt: that be true once but not true now. And I be shouting, Times change! Requirements and environments change! And our needs, they be the same or greater in the face of all this change. And I be weeping, Do we be weaker? or do we be needing greater now than they been needing then? And after a while I be dryin my tears, and I don't be sighin no more. I be sayin: Society don't be meetin my needs, so I be takin care of my own.

If someone had come up to me and said, "Guess what? It's the Fourth of July already!" I wouldn't have believed it. But there it is, in black and white, on the front page. Norma Jean tosses the paper on the table and starts the breakfast. She has been up all night working on the last of the pieces. Images have been spilling forth like fruit dropping from trees. Martin is up early, too. He's out jogging. He's doing it because he's scared. All the men in this neighborhood are out jogging, for the same reason. The outfits they're wearing were created just for jogging, and cost between fifteen and twenty-five dollars. They come in four colors—dark blue, green, maroon, and grey; and four sizes—S, M, L, and X-L. The sight always moves me; but if the feelings aroused were in a race, it would be a dead heat between laughing and crying every time, so I've trained myself not to think about it. Once, during a heavy smog, I said I thought he might do more damage to himself running around out there than just sitting quietly in a smoke-filled room as usual. He didn't comment, but the look in his eyes described a conflict so painful that I keep my mouth shut now.

Sometimes, from the kitchen window, I'll catch a glimpse of him as he bounces down Flamingo Avenue; and I suddenly receive a flood of images that makes my heart contract: I see him among fields—he's not just standing there with an erection, like that useless Tomaso; he is bending, straining, lifting, and the roots of his heart spring straight from the earth. He is hard and proud as a tree; his body shines. As the sink slowly fills with water, I convince myself of the futility of projecting nineteenth-century proletarian images on twentieth-century man. I say: unfair, unfair; see him as he is. I've tried to stop, but every so often, when I least expect it, he appears before me, drenched in sea foam, his teeth white as breakers. He is casting rough nets over muscular seas, luring the pale fish from their sleep. I tell no one how beautiful he looks drawing the luminous harvest in; how, in some long forgotten way, it becomes him to chart those sinuous tides, whose memory sleeps in his nerves like a coiled spring. *You're shooting this through a gauze filter; you've left out grief and blood, pain, hardship, things like that. It's not a balanced presentation.* Feature-length realism isn't required of dreams. They're meant to *focus*—usually on something that is unattainable, or something that's been lost. These center on the connections men once had with the natural world. Women have always had their inner rhythm, which regulates and serves as a natural connection. There was a time when man's life depended on his alignment with tidal rhythms, seasonal cycles; the strength of his connection to those things determined his survival. Why shouldn't that relationship have given him profound pleasure, as well as beauty, in spite of the hardship? It provided him with a rhythm of his own, a cycle as fundamental as women's. I don't know if it's fair to call it compensation, but it must have compensated all the same, brought him into harmony; equalized. What is left to regulate him now? Is the 8:10 traffic flow on the Bayshore a natural rhythm? When a man connects himself to it, how does it affect him? *There's* your pain and grief.

Well, all that romanticizing won't accomplish anything for Martin; just makes it more difficult to reconcile yourself to his reality. I've already acknowledged its futility. Still, ("Somewhere, over the rainbow . . ." —Judy Garland.) *And it's rather arrogant applying those bucolic images just to Martin. What would you say if he were to see YOU rising out of some traffic jam, cradling a bushel of apricots, fresh from the orchard? What if he were to think: How beautiful YOU would be, putting up preserves, knitting sweaters, having babies? What would you say to that?* I'd tell him to drop dead.

Martin staggers into the kitchen, breathing heavily; he slumps into his chair and lifts the front section from the table, bringing it up to his eyes as he tips his chair against the wall.

"Breakfast is ready," Norma Jean says, carrying the plates to the table. "Could you round up the children?"

"Shit. Are you asking me to *move*? I just sat down!" Norma Jean doesn't speak; silence is far more devastating than words at times like these. What does jogging around the block a few times compare with staying up all night and laboring over a set of masterpieces that will alter forever the way *a few people who frequent the Pleasant Valley Arts & Crafts Assn.* mankind perceives the world and its relationship to *how it would look on the table next to the sofa . . . or maybe on the mantel?*

"Where are the kids? What are they doing?" he asks. It's the kind of question that buys time; anyone could see through it. But Norma Jean finds herself softening anyway.

"They're turning on . . ."

"What?"

"You know; injecting; siphoning it in. Reading the comics in front of the TV. The comics are taken visually, while the cartoons go in the ears. Doing the two together produces the best high possible before the third grade."

"Come here." He extends one arm in her direction; it gestures a moment in the air as he keeps his eyes on the newspaper. "Sit down and look at this." So what if the food gets cold? Wasn't that my husband who just asked me to join him at the table? And aren't we the only ones in this room? ("Strike while the iron is hot.") Setting the plates down, she sits beside him and reads.

SLAYING IN GAS RATION WAR

An Oakland service station attendant was shotgunned to death yesterday after he refused to sell a motorist a second tank of gasoline.

"My God!" he says, before she can finish the article. "It's just unbelievable. Shouldn't be, I guess; after a while people adapt to just about anything." He shakes his head. "It's turning into an armed camp. . . ."

If I'm not mistaken, I just saw Martin "enter in." I'll have to check my records, but I think this is the first time (not counting the sports section, World War II movies on TV, and his work). *Wait a minute; didn't he get up in the night with Damon a week or so ago—whenever it was he had the cough, couldn't sleep? Gave him the medicine too, if I remember right, and sat up rocking him until it took effect.* You know, you're right. I vaguely remember. . . . *If I hadn't been lying down at the time, I would have fainted. And in addition to the "entering in," there've been other indications of a shift: have you noticed those models he's been building with Scott? With both boys: planes, racing cars, dinosaurs?* No, I haven't seen them; I avoid their room as much as possible, except to go in for the kisses at bedtime—and it's dark in there by then. *Well, that's what I'm talking about. All this time you've been working on the pieces nights, HE'S been putting them to bed.* I know that. I just haven't *acknowledged it? Afraid it might stop?* You're damned right. In a situation like that, you ("Don't rock the boat."). I know he said Go ahead, finish; we'll see what happens. But I figured it was just a matter of time before he came out to the garage, discovered the Piece, grown to maturity, nursing all her little baby pieces, and screamed: Well that *does* it! All this time And I thought Well, I kept my end of the bargain I've done *my* time, baby, You won't have me to kick around any Enough's enough Here's the house key Good-bye slavery, hello divorce *Arrivederci Sayonara Auf Wiedersehen Au Revoir Ciao . . . Well, now aren't you ashamed? He never questioned, never came into the garage to check, never violated . . .* That's true, he didn't. But was it because of a belief in what I was doing, a respect for my work? Or was it disinterest? ("Only time will tell.")

Norma Jean picks at her eggs. "I suppose it's some comfort that there are still things that are unbelievable, unacceptable; when you're no longer outraged, that's a form of acceptance." Martin tosses the paper aside. "Yeah," he whispers, stirring his coffee.

"Remember when I took around the anti-gun petition after Kennedy was shot?" Martin nods, chewing silently. "And almost no one would sign it?"

"Well, that was futile. Never happen, not in this country. You don't take away a man's gun. Next to his car—maybe even *before* his car; they're both primary extensions of himself."

His prick, his rod; where was I reading about the association between the phallus and a gun? For some men, fucking is the same as shooting. It was some sex study, and a woman was quoted as saying, "Shoot me! Shoot me!" and her partner came in a minute.

"I'd better get the kids; their breakfast is getting cold." Martin pushes his chair away. He *going* to get them, he's not *calling* them. I'd call that "entering in," especially on a holiday morning, after jogging. What's going on here? What does all this mean? Is it possible . . . Do you suppose . . . Can it be . . . *Well, go on; say it!* Norma Jean sets the children's plates in the oven to warm. Well, it just crossed my mind suddenly and I found myself wondering: Is it possible that Martin is being reborn too?

Breakfast is over, but I'm still here in the kitchen, putting the finishing touches on my contribution to the block-party supper later this afternoon. They just started having the Fourth of July block party here last year; we were on vacation then and missed the first one. So I have mixed feelings, don't know what to expect. After this is done, I'll go back in the garage and work until party time. *You should get a nap in somewhere.* It's strange, but I'm not that tired. In fact, I feel regenerated. *By the way, did you thank Martin for offering to take the children swimming while you work?* No, I did not thank him. If I thanked him every time he did something with the children, emptied the garbage, picked up after himself, it would just strengthen his illusion that he's just doing it all as a *favor* to me; and we all know about favors: they're intermittent, sporadic, and unreliable.

Norma Jean shuts the garage door behind her and switches on the overhead light. No sooner has she removed the cloth and immersed herself halfway to the elbows in clay, than she hears Martin's voice. She can make out her name, but the rest is unintelligible. Better go out there, meet him halfway; can't risk his coming in here and blowing everything so close to the end.

"Norma! Will you come out of there for a minute? There's a problem here." Norma Jean walks quickly to the house, holding her caked arms in front of her as though in casts. Martin is standing in the kitchen with his arms full of towels; Ruth Ann and Scott languish nearby. Damon is not in the group; so I cleverly conclude that the "problem" concerns Damon. Mothers get so they can tell these things, even with their eyes closed.

"What's the problem, Martin?" I ask, trying to affect nonchalance; there is something about the situation that has my name written on it already, even at this stage. It won't be easy erasing my name and writing in his without the use of my hands, but I suddenly think of a man I once saw in a sideshow, who did these amazing charcoal portraits with his toes, and it gives me strength.

"Listen, that kid" *he must mean Damon* "has a HOLE in his bathing trunks!"

"He does?" I ask, in my most carefully modulated conversational tone.

"How could you not see a thing like that? It's right in the seat of his pants."

"I don't know, Martin. I don't worry about those things very much any more. If it's in back, it will only show when he bends over. Don't worry about it."

"Don't *worry?* Sometimes I don't understand you at all. You can't let that poor kid go swimming EXPOSING HIS ASS!"

"Oh for Christ's sake, he's just a child! What difference does it make? As long as it doesn't bother *him*, no one else is going to get worked up about a thing like that!"

"I won't *have* it. I absolutely won't have it. No son of mine . . ." Damon enters, stage left. He is grinning in the manner of evil spirits and fanatics everywhere. The reason he is grinning is because he has reversed his bathing trunks, so that the hole under discussion is now in the front. What a coincidence that it should be located at precisely the latitude and precisely the longitude of his penis. It smiles at us, and waves. Damon begins to dance. I start laughing. So do Scott and Ruth Ann. I figure it's either the theater, night clubs, or the nut house for him.

"This is NOT funny," Martin says. Ruth Ann and Scott stop laughing. Not me. It has just occurred to me that the Pleasant Valley Country Club might have been liberated by Damon Harris, if his father weren't such a stuffed-shirt. On the other hand, a second glance tells you right away that the father isn't fooling around with this business of the hole in the son's bathing trunks. No siree, he's doing a slow, but hot, burn. So we can no longer afford, funny as it is, to take the matter lightly. We can't afford it because already the lines are being drawn, and the issue over which this war is about to be declared is: WHO WILL SEW THE HOLE? I suppose some would see it as a good sign that the father is burning; he would have no need to burn if he were secure in his conviction that it is the mother, and only the mother, who can, should, or will sew the hole. I concede that it's a good sign; but I also know that this is my last stand. Needles and thread is about as far as you can push it. Of course, I intend to give it all I've got; I always do.

"Are you going to sew that poor kid's trunks, or does he have to stay home?" A weak opening, using a pawn; it surprises me. Still, it's well known that things can and do throw the best of players, and there are big stakes riding on this one. Now the question is, do I counter with a weak move myself, ("Gee, my hands are covered with clay!") or do I reduce him to jelly at the very start, with a show of my power? I decide to restate the rules, which could be considered a move in some circles.

"There *are* other alternatives, Martin." He reads me right away; he doesn't even bother to say, "Well, then, where is his other suit?" There's no doubt, this is going to be a short game.

"Oh *no*; unh unh," he says, or something like that, backing off. This is where you have to move fast; it's the whole game, right here. Lose them when they first back off and you lose it all.

So I scream. I haven't done that for a while, it startles him. "*You* know how to sew, just as well as I do!" I yell. "When you couldn't even afford the Chinese laundry, you sewed yourself! Before I met you you sewed your own buttons! You were a Boy Scout!" I pause briefly for breath and, when I resume, I am in full control. I speak with a cold-hearted authority from which there is no appeal; it frightens even me. "The needle and thread are in the left-hand drawer of the sewing machine. You can choose your own style: machine or hand. He is *your* son, as well as mine. I'm busy working right now, and you're not; my hands are dirty, yours are clean; you *do* know how to sew; and since it is *you* who is concerned about the hole, it is *you* who will repair the hole. And since it is I who is *unconcerned* about the hole, it is I who will do nothing about the hole." He is silent. And sullen. He is also stunned that I have pulled it off. I am not convinced that I have pulled it off, so just for good measure, as a form of insurance, I say lightly, as I make my way back to the garage, "Nowhere is it written that I must do all the sewing. And at no time did I verbally promise to do all the sewing. Therefore, I shall *not* do all the sewing. And Damon's suit is the very *first* of all the sewing that I shall not do!"

I would be lying if I said I went right back to kneading and shaping. I went back to the garage and had a cigarette and thought to myself: You blew it. Blew it. You went through months of hell, it was in the palm of your hand this morning, and you blew it over a little one-inch hole. Reason tries her best (*I think your argument is basically sound . . . although my Jack never would have stood for it*) but I am unconsolable. Twenty minutes pass this way; and although it crossed my mind in the first five seconds to run upstairs and mend the damned hole, I stayed right there on the stool. I figured, blowing *two* things definitely does *not* add up to a recovery, any way you cut it. Having become familiar with biding my time, I decided to master it now, if it killed me.

There is a strange scraping at the door. Suddenly it swings open and the garage is flooded with light. And standing there smiling are the father and the son—the little one, with the hole. I am thrown off-guard by their sudden appearance, and all that light hitting me in the eyes, but it doesn't take me long to recover. I read the situation in a flash. They're smiling because they are proud of themselves—the father in particular. And they're here because they want my approval. Well, in spite of what you might have thought, I'm not as cold-hearted as I sometimes appear. I'm not all business—not me. I can spot a victory when I see one; and the truly exceptional thing about this victory is that it is shared equally, three ways. There are no losers.

So I slide off the stool and hug them both. Martin, (can I do this without using war analogies or baseball emotions?) *Keep those man-and-nature images out of it, too.* Well, that just leaves sex. There are any number of things he *likes.* But as for that flush of ecstasy, I don't know; even a triumph at work doesn't fit. There aren't many triumphs at work, and none that produce the flush of ecstasy, that I know of. Sex isn't accurate either, because eventually you roll over and relax. He doesn't relax; he isn't going to come down for a long time. This one is going to go on and on, this sudden mastery and unexpected pride.

"Well. I can't believe it. You *did* it!" I say.

"I did it," he says, feigning modesty.

"See? Dad sewed my hole!" Damon demonstrates, bending over. Sure enough. *Good Lord! Look at that! He did a better job than you do!* Anyone can do a better job than . . . You know, you're right. He really did. You can't even see the stitches. How did he do it? *You sound envious!* Well, there was just a trace, but you couldn't see it without a microscope. I have repressed it already. Just the tiniest trace, very manageable. Needle-and-thread envy. How times change.

Damon runs back to the house to join Scott and Ruth Ann. Martin continues to stand there, beaming.

"You did a fantastic job," I say, then suddenly become embarrassed; I'm not used to this. *Keep trying.* "I really mean it. I didn't expect you would do it, and I was sure if you did attempt it you'd do a clumsy job, on purpose. Just to ensure that you'd never be expected to do it again. I'm proud of you, Martin!"

"I didn't do it for you. I did it for my *son*."

I decide to kid around a little; after you've passed Needle and Thread, you can relax; that's as high as you can go. So I say:

"See, Martin; it just goes to show what a man can do when he has to. I promise I'll never tell."

"Ha-ha-ha," he says sarcastically, but the bloom is still on the rose. "Can I come in?" he queries, craning his neck around the doorframe, peering into the darkness beyond. There is something so disarming about his manner, I am touched; I don't hesitate for a minute. In fact, I laugh nervously, like a girl on her first date. *Ah, ahm. Excuse me . . . Norma? Ah, shouldn't you throw a cloth over the PIECES first? Relax! He's my husband.*

"Sure, come on in. You really want to see it? It's kind of a mess." He steps cautiously over the threshold and stands there a minute getting accustomed to the light. I stand here getting accustomed. He's here. In my tomb. With me. At first, the feeling is one of novelty and autonomy: *I* have invited *him* into *my* room. Because he *asked*—didn't just come barging in as though he owned the place. For a second I consider the possibility that *I* own it; that what would have been my accumulated wages—based on Underwriters of America figures over the years—plus the work I do here, inside these four walls, have somehow made it mine; and that his asking to come in was a kind of transfer of ownership. But then I get scared; I think, nah, who do you think you're fooling? He owns it—we both know it—and he's come to take it back. It has also just dawned on me about the pieces. I light a cigarette and lean against the workbench. This is it.

"You've done all *those* since . . ." Neither of us can remember just how long it has been; it seems like twenty years.

"I did them," I respond, cautiously. I take a long drag as he moves to get a closer look. He lightly touches one with the tips of his fingers.

"Those are really stunning, Jeanie," he finally says. Not believing my ears, I say:

"What?"

"They're *very* unique. I had no idea . . ." *that I could do something like that?* ". . . that you were doing things like *this*."

"What did you think I was doing?"

"I really don't know; I don't think I thought about it specifically—except for those jars. They bothered me, really did. Gave me the creeps."

"Well, I'm not doing those any more."

"I can see that; I can see. These are really something. I like them very much." It's a strange feeling, after all these months, to see him look at the pieces for the first time, and to witness his reaction. It throws me back in time: seven and a half years, to be exact, and I am sitting propped in the hospital bed and the nurse has just handed him a tightly wrapped cocoon with YOUR DAUGHTER stenciled on it. He sits in the plastic rocker next to my bed, holding it in front of him, with both hands, the way men in goggles and asbestos suits hold incendiary bombs which they are about to dismantle. There is the same look in his eyes now as there was then: the pupils set at the widest opening in order to admit the maximum amount of light, so that what he sees before him can be fully comprehended. "I can't believe she is ours," he is whispering. And now that I've been thrown back here, it's hard to leave; the whole nursery has begun to stir. I hear Scott; he's yelling and screaming before he's completely left my body. And Martin is holding onto my hand and peering down between my legs at the same time, looking for the balls. Surely it will be balls this time. And surely it is. And I am staring through a steamy haze at the white ceiling. I have done it. A daughter and a son: we're both represented now, we can relax; any further achievements will be frosting on the cake.

And that final night in April: peering at tiny Damon through the glass. "He looks like a grapefruit," I am saying and Martin isn't even looking at him, he is looking at me. I am wearing a thin robe with tiny flowers on it. "You've never looked so beautiful to me," Martin says. Who, me? I look quickly around, but there is no one else there, we're the only ones in the nursery; it's after hours, but the nurses were kind because Damon was premature, let us come in here anyway. There must be some mistake, surely you mean someone else: I am barefoot, my hair's a mess . . . "I love you so much." Then I think back to the flowers in my room, the lilacs he brought to celebrate the birth of the little April son. They must have been for me.

As I watch him acquaint himself with the pieces I become aware of a tremendous feeling of relief—he knows what's been going on. That he finds them pleasing, even exciting, is a bonus. A terrible pressure has lifted; I will never have to fight this particular battle again. The fact that all this time I was working on many, instead of the one, never comes up. It's hard to know what to do with this unfamiliar mixture of feelings. Martin's approval pleases me, and adds to what's already there. But it matters more that it was not required to authenticate either the work or the works themselves; they were authentic to me from the start. But now that he's here, and the works have the power to move him, there is a sense of working with, rather than struggling against; what was rich to begin with is enriched. Everything shifts once more. It would be naïve to think that there will be no more conflict; but if the past six months could be endured, anything can. That the pieces have affected him is another way of making a difference to someone, of being understood.

After Martin has subjected them to as much scrutiny as they can bear, he comes over to where I'm sitting on the stool. I can't remember when I ever saw him so serious. I know it sounds crazy (why stop now?) but I think this is the first time he has really respected me. I don't mean respect for what one inherently is; we have always had that for each other—give or take the usual intolerable defects. This is a respect for having achieved something that never was before, and for having somehow rendered it intelligible.

"Dad! Are you going to take us swimming or not?" The children are running toward the garage.

"You guys go get in the car, I'll be right there. I have something I want to say to your mother."

"Aw, Dad. You said that half an hour ago! We been sitting out in the car, then we been waiting around the kitchen. We're tired *already!*" I know just how you feel, Scott; when you been sittin and you been waitin, you get tired fast. There's no logical explanation for it, but it's true all the same.

"Come on, kids; do as I say. I promise I'll be there in five minutes."

Now that they're gone, we sit here among the embryonic mounds of clay, strangely silent. Martin has made himself at home on top of the work table, where he sits opposite me. The pieces shine in their mute rows, watching us. I'll admit, there have been more impartial juries.

"Jeanie, I want you to know I have a lot of respect for you." See? Delicious. He pauses. That's bad; you have to look out for pauses. They're usually followed by the word "But." "And I love you. You're a very creative woman and you have the right to do whatever you have to, or want to, in your work. I'm not saying this now because of . . . them," he gestures toward the pieces. He doesn't exactly say "Forgive me," but I do anyway. "Although they're startling. I'm impressed, really impressed, with them." For a minute there, I thought they would smile. But they're so far above that sort of thing, I should have known. Besides, they know the hell he put me through; they're on intimate terms with that. As far as they're concerned, he has to sweat this one out alone. "Actually," he continues, "I've wanted to say something for some time but it's been very difficult. You've been inaccessible and I've been hard to reach—I admit that. I've done a lot of thinking, and I'm sure you have too; we've both gone through a lot of changes in a very short time. You've pretty much moved with yours—it was what you wanted to do, and you were ready for it. I've resisted, I'm aware of that. Lately, though, some things have shifted. There are some areas where things seem better than before—the children, for instance."

"I've noticed it with the children, Martin. You're much closer than before. You were always a good father, but now you seem like a *real* father to them as well. Regardless of what happens with us, I will never regret having pushed for that. It's as though they're really *yours* now, too: you've gone through some of the fire."

"Well, I don't know what else to say at this point. I'm very happy for you, Norma Jean. And I want you to understand one thing: I do *not* expect you to 'come back home' as it were; to get back to your 'place' after you've finished these pieces. I know you *think* that's what I expect, what I've been waiting around for, what I had in mind when I referred to things getting back to normal." That sure is what I think; it's what I fear the most. "But it's not true," he continues. "You have this part of your life now, and you deserve to live it." I light up another cigarette at this point.

"I realize the last few months have been hard on you, Martin; I know the changes I've asked you to make require a lot of time to get used to, and probably a lot of flexibility. I don't know that if I were you I could have done it. I don't want to lose you; but I can never go back. You probably don't agree, but hard as it's been, and even in this short time, the balance of things feels much fairer, much more equitable now. I'm starting to feel better, and that can't help but have a lasting effect on the whole family."

"I'm sure that's true; but it's still unbalanced for me in some areas. It's too early to say, at this point. I've seen the good effects on the children, and certainly on you. You say I'll reap my reward later; well, I don't know. For me, at this stage, that's just a theory. I'm not sure I believe it, and I'm still not sure I can live with it."

"What do you mean? You've *been* living with it; you're still in one piece. Some things have changed for the better, while others have dragged. Why are you being so melodramatic?"

"I'm not being melodramatic; I'm just saying it's asking a lot, and I'm not sure if I can do it. I am *not* quarreling with your right to do what you're doing."

"Listen, Martin, the kids are waiting. We've come this far. We haven't lost everything. There may be a lot of changes going on around us, but *people* don't change overnight."

"No, no; I think things have leveled somewhat. I'm not trying to be difficult, Jeanie; you've got to understand that. It's just that a man can take what a man can take—no more, no less. That's it."

"What about a woman?"

"You know what I mean; don't split hairs. We both have our limits; maybe some of them can give, maybe they can't. We'll do our best—the children deserve that . . . and so do we. And we'll see what happens." If you want a portrait of a man in the eye of a hurricane, in the dead center of rapid change, here he is.

I've found there's a fine line between sympathizing with Martin and doing what I feel I must do; I walk that tightrope every day. I'm becoming quite skilled. He loves me, he loves the children; he's worked hard for the little nuclear mass we've got here, and he doesn't want to give any of it up. Not just because it cost and not just because he worked hard. He values it. In addition, he now sees some genuine merit in what I'm doing, it even excites him a little; but, since it's also a direct threat to some of his security and a lot of his privileges, he can't go out on a limb. Not yet. Furthermore, he's lonely as hell in his post-industrial purgatory, and horny besides. He looks around at friends who are separated or divorced, and he figures he'd be just as horny, and twenty times as lonely that way. So now he's positioned himself dead center; he waits there, slowly dividing. Has he begun to lean? Is he moving slowly in my direction? He's a cagey bastard, always has been; he'd only say if his very life depended on it, and it hasn't come down to actual life yet.

For my part, I'm still closer to the center than he realizes, or than I want to admit. It's just my *foot* I've got out there on the left—at least for now. But that's the way I want it, for the time being; I resist speed in every way I can, except on the freeway, which was designed for it. People were meant to move at a much slower rate than is currently expected; that's why I continue to hold the line, wherever possible, without sacrificing what has to be done. That's another tightrope. They're all over the place. It's the biggest circus I've ever been to. You might think it contradictory for a person to be extending boundaries and holding the line at the same time. You'll just have to accept it as another one of those things which sound crazy, but which can be done. It's all a matter of where you choose to extend the boundaries and where you choose to hold the line. There are some boundaries beyond which I haven't been able to look yet. One of them involves the children. I still feel that since we have them, we owe them something. One of the things we owe them is each other. Together. Martin feels the same way. You'd think that would make for complete accord, wouldn't you? Funny, the little tricks life plays. I still can't decide whether the family is decaying from within or whether there are just too many outside pressures; all this puts me at dead center too. If anyone had told me ten years ago that my position in the future would be dead center, I would have died laughing.

"Jeanie, I have to take the kids swimming. We'll talk again, we'll re-evaluate things as they come up. Let's not wait this long to do it next time, O.K.?"

"*You* were the one . . ."

"I know, I know I was; it was the only way I felt I could manage all the things that were happening while you were" *running around half out of your mind* "trying to get your work started. I had to protect myself. I never really wanted to interfere with your work, never. I respect it. I've always respected the fact that you've wanted to do it. But with your being involved to that *extent*, especially in the beginning, mentally and emotionally divided every which way, what was there for me?"

"I figured you were the biggest one around here, you're an adult, you could hold out. So I gave to you last. I tried to explain all that before; you wouldn't listen."

"I heard what you were saying; that doesn't always change things."

"I appreciate what you said about the pieces. That means a lot. And what's happening between you and the children—they aren't just *my* responsibility; they don't deplete me any more. I can see them for what they are, and enjoy them, because they're *half yours* now, too; I can't tell you what a difference that has made. I wish it had happened earlier . . . God, when I look back . . . the comparison . . ."

"Don't get started on that again; I've got to go."

"O.K. Well, I'll see you at the block party then. What time does it start?"

"Five? I don't know. Six? Call up someone and ask." Martin eases himself off the work table and brushes the clay dust off his pants. I'm getting jumpy again; I hate loose ends. So I light another cigarette, in order to string things out a little longer, and say:

"I feel things are more ambiguous than ever now." Why can't I stay cool, be sophisticated, keep my mouth shut, the way they do in the foreign films? *There*, everything is understated. Everything is implied. *There*, they float through situations like this with such restraint; it gives everything intense meaning. *Here*, I flick ashes all over the floor, and say things like

"Well, what are we going to *do*? Just sit around and see what *happens*?" And that gives him the opportunity to repeat, with infinite poise:

"We'll see what happens." It is so open-ended it makes me want to scream. I can't say that I could think of an alternative, on the spur of the moment, that would make more sense. But still, it's so ambiguous that I finally do scream:

"Things don't just *happen!* People *make* things happen!" And of course he responds:

"We're trying, aren't we? What more can you ask of people?" If Marcello Mastroianni had said that he would have shrugged his shoulders ever so slightly, while extending his hands, palms up. The gesture would have carried tremendous emotional weight. Actually, even with Martin saying it, it comes across well. I'd give anything to be able to rewrite the script and give that line to myself. Why should *he* get to say all the mature things? He's the one who's been the fly in the ointment from the beginning.

But he does a very nice thing just before he leaves; he kisses me, and holds it for a long time. I've never been kissed in my studio before. And because I have my eyes closed, and because he's never been in here before, it strikes me that he could be anybody; I don't think of him as my husband. He's just some stranger who walked by on his way for a swim, and happened to notice my stunning pieces. Or was it stunning me? *Make up your mind; you have to cut the cord sooner or later.* And then we sat around having a deep conversation, and he kissed me on the way out. Whether we'll get together again or not isn't clear. One thing is clear: he's *not* that crazy bastard who calls me a blood-sucking bitch over at the house. This one has a lot of reserve; he speaks softly, and thinks before he opens his mouth. He kisses with finesse. Very subtle, and therefore doubly sensuous. Could this be a "Tender Moment"? It's been so long, I don't think I'd recognize one if I saw it. When he leaves, everything is ambiguous. It's exciting, in a way, if you can tolerate ambiguity. I can't, but I'm taking a course where it's taught, in the hope of acquiring the skill. It's called Modern Living, and you get no credit.

It's late now; the block party leaves me only a few hours to work; they'll be setting off firecrackers all night. Norma Jean starts to work, spreading the materials quickly over the table. Because of the time pressure, she attempts to clear her mind and focus directly on what is before her; but the harder she tries to concentrate, the more her mind wanders. That's just one more example of the unpredictable nature of the human psyche. Looking at the clay, I begin to see houses there, in neat little rows, with fences and yards and so forth. So I look away from the clay, shake my head and blink my eyes a few times, and wait for the shapes and designs to come out; the curtain went up ten minutes ago. What the hell do you suppose they're doing back there? I stare into space and wait; it's all I can do. You're not allowed backstage. It's a private world. But the designs don't appear. Just a single word, in giant letters, and illuminated by a single spotlight, for dramatic effect. The word is F A M I L Y. That's it. That's the whole show. I hate these avant-garde productions, where they leave all the work to you, where you just have to sit there, finding your own meanings. It's true you can compare notes with people later, but for the moment you're stuck with the damned thing—no cues, no action, nothing. You're working in the dark; and the dark, for some people, still produces anxiety, confusion, and loneliness.

I sit and stare at F A M I L Y. I know there's the option of walking out, but I never do that once I've paid for the ticket. I believe in getting my money's worth, even in cases where I have to do the work myself. In this case, I feel some irritation because I'm sure I've seen the show before. They must have revived it and changed the title. There should be a law against that; people have some right to know what they're getting into before they commit themselves. Then I remember: what *should be* and what *is* have always been worlds apart. You can never be sure, in any situation, what it's like in there until *after* you've gotten into it. (*And then it's often too late.* You think I don't know that?) So I tell myself, there might even be some advantages to having seen it before. Sometimes you suddenly get the meaning the second time around. *And then again, you sometimes never get the meaning, no matter how many times the show comes to town. You can go to all the lectures, read all the reviews, and STILL not understand the meaning. Sometimes the controversy over meaning can go on for years, and the explanations still fail to clarify. Sometimes EVERYONE is in the dark. There's something in human nature that keeps most people pursuing it, though, even in cases where reason would clearly indicate the futility. . . . And then there are those who go out in the lobby for a smoke, who realize there are some things they're never going to understand; some of them develop perpetual despair over it, others make their peace with the ambiguity.*

What the hell. You've paid for this one over and over; it's certainly been the most expensive. It's had the longest run too, with the possible exceptions of L I F E, and D E A T H, and B I R T H, and perhaps W A R. It's been a smash hit, you have to admit; there's something about F A M I L Y that keeps them coming back, time and time again. There are the factors of overexposure and saturation to consider, which take their toll on you, and compromise your ability to find meaning. But still, when you've invested that much, you owe it to yourself to search as thoroughly as possible before concluding it's not there. So I be thinking hard about F A M I L Y again. I be thinking and thinking.

I think about communes, and the divorce rate, and the way all these streets around here are laid out in a way that throws each little family back in upon itself; they've made it so awkward and unnatural to just wander around freely anywhere else, among others. You usually have to call first. Or have an appointment. It discourages spontaneity and all but prohibits intimacy. I be thinking of the wheel, and transportation, and factors which facilitate mobility and encourage separations across great distances. I see all my friends, as though borne along on swiftly moving rivers, flowing away from me. We've survived all the moving around, but what did we have to throw out to keep from sinking en route? Was the cargo valuable? I think it was. Can we live without it? *Depends on what you call living.* Rivers make me think about something Leonard Cottrell said, regarding the Nile:

> Why did the earliest civilization on earth grow up beside this great river? Because civilization can only flourish where communities can live together in one spot over long periods of time.
>
> —Leonard Cottrell, *Lost Pharaohs*,
> p. 16.

The way these communities are designed requires each family to feed upon itself. And everyone knows what happens when you feed on yourself; individual resources and appetites may vary, but you can't keep up a thing like that forever. The government doesn't even give the family a depletion allowance. Speaking just for Martin and myself, we could certainly use it.

It is up to just the two of us to make this family run. We must bring unimagined efforts to bear on the task. It requires everything we have. We've given birth to a new generation, but there's no one around from the old one to take note. We have become our children's only past; it has aged us prematurely.

Thinking about communities, and the way they're designed, brings on images of the children as babies. I can't figure out why I'm seeing babies; I'm not able to make the connection. I light a cigarette, and suddenly it all comes back. It comes back with such intensity, in fact, I could really get worked up if I let myself dwell on it. You don't forget the major crisis of your life overnight. I be thinking of mothers and children, about how it begins innocently and slowly enough: you're all shut in there together, there's a lot of close contact. It's prolonged and intense. And then gradually, over time, your egos blend; it begins to scare you a little—in those cases where it's recognized—but what can you do? With all that isolation, you're on top of each other all the time. Under such conditions, it's only natural to absorb one another; what else have you got to eat?

So I be thinking that gets the family off to a bad start right there; it takes years to reverse that process, years to undo it. Some mothers never get their selves back. Which cheats their children out of theirs; why should you develop your own, if you can borrow your mother's? That partially explains why so many fathers come home, take a look around, and think: Who are all these people? What the hell am I doing here? They're running the whole show; I just pay the bills. What are they to me except a noose around the neck?

FATHER KILLS WIFE, KIDS

Boston

A security guard, who reportedly complained once to a neighbor that his family was a "noose around my neck," apparently killed his wife and five of his children in their rented home and then took his own life, police said yesterday.

One neighbor quoted him as saying once that "The family is a noose around my neck and someday I am going to kill them all."

—UNITED PRESS

And I try to recall that point in time when I shifted from being given to, to being the giver; because in this culture it's when you become the giver that they kick most of the supports out from under you, and things start to get rough. How can you ask a question, for instance, of someone who isn't there? *What was it you wanted to ask?* Oh, things like: What was it like for you? What are the things that helped you manage? How do we differ? How are we the same? For me, the feeling is like the one expressed in the Egyptian inscription that describes the period where the old values are breaking down; the one which speaks of the neglect, and subsequent loss, of the links with the past:

> Their places are no more,
> As if they had never been.
> None cometh from thence
> To tell us how he fares . . .

You have to ask the questions and attempt to find answers because you're right in the middle of it; they've put you in charge—and during a hurricane, too. Leaks are springing up everywhere, most of the crew has abandoned ship, and the navigator is dead. That leaves just you and your mate, and three little ones who stowed away somewhere along the route. It's a big responsibility, especially with all the maps and charts missing. And questions always become more pressing when there's no one around to ask. So there's just the five of you, who huddle together for warmth when you're not bailing and steering and searching for food, or scanning the horizon and calling for help; each other is all you've got. You wouldn't be human if you didn't ask yourself: is it worth it? Didn't think of jumping ship from time to time.

16

They've blocked off Palm Court by running picnic tables across the end of the street. I set the chicken down on the table reserved for the main dishes, and look around for the wine. It wouldn't take much to knock me out, not having slept last night, so I plan to have just a little. I spot it under a table on the other side of the street, and as I begin to pour, Doris and Mark Morgan come over.

"Hi, Norma! We left Martin and the children at the pool; they'll be along later."

"I was wondering where they were."

"We had to get back early; Doris hates to be late for a party! Ha ha." The Morgan children have turned on their hose and are firing it at the house across the street. People are beginning to mill around in the street. It's supposed to be just for this block, but it looks as though a number of people have invited friends who live somewhere else; that would account for all the strange faces. Norma Jean squints her eyes. At least I *think* these people don't live here. On the other hand, they could just as easily live next door. You can't always tell.

By eight o'clock some of the fathers are considering doing the fireworks, even though it's still light. We've been standing around eating and drinking for an hour and a half, and there are some people who would just as soon throw in the towel now. They're the ones you see sitting on the curb, slowly spitting out watermelon seeds and drinking beer. They don't talk to anyone, just sit there watching the whole thing as though it were a show.

I started out doing that too, because that's the way I tend to approach everything, initially; but after a while we got to talking to a few people, and it might have been the wine, but it began to feel as though we had known them for a long time. It must have looked that way too, because we were all standing around, leaning on the tables, laughing. I can't remember anything we said, or what it was that was so funny; I only remember feeling warm. It was just as though we were among friends.

While they're arguing over when to light the firecrackers, someone puts some records on, turning up the volume as high as it will go, dragging the speaker partway out of the house. Some people start to dance. The children love it. All but a few drop their hoses and join the adults, in the middle of the street. Things really start to pick up. Everyone's dancing; neighbors, strangers, adults and children, even the dogs are circling around. The most amazing thing is the transformation that takes place in the children; they are ecstatic.

I'm sitting on the curb watching Martin dance with the children. I don't think I've ever seen that particular expression on his face—or theirs, either, for that matter. It is a mixture of mirth and amazement; people just don't do things like this in Pleasant Valley—or didn't, until now. What thrills the children is that they're doing something exciting with adults. There are no age barriers, no distinctions or prohibitions. The people who aren't dancing begin to clap their hands in time to the music. This ignites everyone; some even stamp their feet. A few fanatics start to set up the fireworks, drawing the children away from the dancing; within ten minutes all the children have been siphoned off, and only a small circle of dancers remains in the street. The music has changed now; everything is slower, more mellow. I join Martin and we begin to dance as the first flares start to go off. I think we stayed that way for half an hour, while the children screamed with excitement half a block away, and the flaming colors filled the sky.

The loss of sleep finally hit me, and I was finding it hard to stay on my feet; but I realized, even before the fireworks subsided, that the whole thing had been a show, after all. This was not a real community; just a block full of strangers who shared a common yearning. We had consented to stage an illusion in honor of this yearning; it wasn't that difficult to do, because the calendar said it was O.K. As we gather up the children and walk slowly toward the house, I think of how happy they had been, and wonder if I could be wrong. Had there been something authentic there? And I think, whatever it was, it has produced a *sense* of community. It was a near-perfect imitation; even I was fooled for a while. The whole celebration was an enormous flashback to the way things were before. We are not in *our* time, I kept thinking—knowing you had to be, in order to call the event authentic—at the same time wishing it weren't true. You can re-create the past, but there is no way to resurrect it. An event like this, in order to be considered real, must proceed organically out of the life of a community; it must be a natural extension of that life. All I could say about this Fourth of July on Palm Court was that it was an unnatural event, created in an attempt to deny the isolation of our lives. I must be very tired, because I keep asking myself: are we doing the best we can under the circumstances? Or are we making fools of ourselves? I can draw no conclusions, not a single one.

The children fall exhausted into bed. I give them all kisses, and as I turn to leave Ruth Ann whispers, "Could you stay a few minutes and talk?"

"Oh, honey, can't it wait until morning? Mommy is so tired."

"You been working out there every night. I never get to talk to you at bedtime anymore."

"I know, Ruth Ann; I have been working hard. But I'll be finished very soon, and then I'll be able to talk to you more often before bed. Night time is the only time I have to do my work now that school's out; I explained that to you."

"Well," *she's getting ready to go for the jugular; I sense it coming, tired as I am,* "you think your old work is more important than your own *children . . .*"

"That's not true, Ruth Ann. You are very important and my work is important too.' ("Who do you love the most?" —Ruth Ann, 1967; Scott, 1969; Damon, 1971.)

"A child is the most important thing in the world," she states, with absolute authority.

"Where did you hear that?" Who's been indoctrinating her? Her teacher? Martin! He's been slipping it in while my back is turned, feeding her small doses every night, patiently waiting for nature to take its course, right to the mother's heart.

"*You* told me once," she says, touching my nose with a delicacy that makes me want to die. *I did? Have you forgotten? It was back in the old days.*

I don't know what to say, so I just kiss her and leave. She is tired and doesn't stir.

Martin and I collide in the hall; what else is there to do but embrace? We make our way into the bedroom, sinking slowly onto the bed. And it is understood that we will undress each other here in the dark, the way we did in 1962. My arm brushes the bedside table; *Patriarchal Attitudes* falls softly to the floor. I can afford it.

Rachel and I have an arrangement for the summer; I take her children for two days each week while she goes to her part-time job, and she takes mine while I go to Arndt and try to finish the pieces. It has taken the pressure off with respect to working nights, but I still find it hard to give them up; the middle of the night is the only time you are completely free from interruption. That's the way it is once you start extending yourself. There's no reasonable way to keep it in check. Martin ("Give you an inch and you take a mile,") but once you've taken that first mile, you never go back to inches. Rachel and I have it perfectly planned; it will get us through to August, when the children will all be in day camp.

I'm running late today, so I just yell, "Hi. I'm running late," as I drop the children off. Rachel doesn't speak, just waves her arm. She looks depressed, I think, as I head for the freeway. This is the hottest July I can remember; Arndt's air-conditioning really hits the spot. Sometimes I think it's one of the major things that keeps me coming back.

"I was unfaithful to you," I tell him, as I sit down; "I slept with my husband last night." If he prefers that woman who spends all her time at the sink there's no reason I have to take it sitting up. His silence infiltrates the room, rising to the ceiling, slowly filling every corner. Breathing becomes difficult. So I open my mouth and start reporting; it's what you do in the silences to give yourself more air.

259

"Martin's finally seen the pieces; he likes them. We have some kind of . . . understanding; we're seeing what happens. It's a way of buying time, giving ourselves the margins to see what changes we can master. I should finish the pieces in the next month or so, then I'll start trying to exhibit and sell them. I've also sent in the application for graduate school. Well, that's about it."

"Is it?"

Just about. Except for a few loose ends. You, for instance. I know you're not real, I've begun to suspect it, but I'll have to stick around a while in order to be absolutely certain. Tomaso too. Not real, either of you. Aside from Martin, and Rachel, I don't know anyone real; that's how it is on Palm Court. With Martin there are times when everything seems to fit together, everything falls into place. And I think: This is just as I always imagined it would be. This is sufficient; I require nothing more. In the end, it all boils down to the questions of how much do you require? How much can you expect—from people, from life, from yourself? How much do you have to give, and where do you want to put it? When things are going reasonably well, you don't have to ask the questions. On the other hand, I sometimes get to reading things like *Patriarchal Attitudes*, and instead of saying, well, that's interesting but it has nothing to do with me, I discover a lot of things that confirm exactly how I feel. It's always disturbing. So when that happens, I hit the freeway for a while.

And out there on 101, I start thinking about M A R R I A G E and T H E   N U C L E A R   F A M I L Y : they're playing everywhere. As I drive along, I get out my scales—which is rather tricky at eighty miles an hour—and I weigh the idea that marriage and the family are inimical to personal freedom, against the idea that there are enrichments that come from responsibility to others which are impossible to obtain any other way. I don't know just why Ruth Ann should come to mind, except that she's the oldest, and was therefore the first unexpected enrichment. Martin, it's been hard to tell lately if he's an enrichment or a noose around the neck. But one thing is certain: we've changed each other in unforeseen ways; our imprints are there. Of Ruth Ann

I think: She is life itself. I know that sounds banal, but it's true. I wouldn't have missed her for the world.

And Scott, down there under his rocks, respecting the smallest things—which will of course ensure his ultimate respect for larger things; Damon, who flies—aren't they life itself? Damon, memorizing the rhyme at nursery school, then reciting it for me in the bath:

> Engine, engine, number nine
> Going down Chicago line
> If the train should leave the track
> Would you want your money back?

And my praising him, "That's wonderful, Damon! You have a clever mind." And Damon, pensive, thoughtful for once, pushing his boat slowly through the bath water: "Mom, if your train left the track, would you want your money back?" In books, when they would speak of the thrill that comes from witnessing a new mind at work, I always yawned. Now I get chills, and can't open my mouth at all, not even to speak.

Once they all stop drinking your blood, and start functioning on their own systems, they become galaxies, spinning away from you, covering greater distances with every passing year. They're moving fast, but they leave their imprint. You know they've been there. You know it forever. *You mean like the lines on Mrs. Hatch's face?* Mrs. Hatch? *The neighbor who once said, "They take years off your life."* I thought you were . . . *Reason doesn't always take the sentimental view; my goodness, no.* See? This is the kind of thing that happens when you weigh: so many voices enter in, so much to consider. I think of Anubis often, and the delicate job he has to perform, the strain of it. Few realize . . . Listen, do you think I don't know that as every mother holds her child, as she drinks in the sweet weight of it, she doesn't also know she has to fight the thought of being eclipsed by time, by her own young? Fathers have to do it too; it's part of the human condition, if you're a parent.

Well, I tell Arndt, a year from now I'll be back in school, where others come and go just as naturally as I sit and wait. Perhaps I'll find the meaning there, perhaps not. It's possible that the only way to approach the problem of meaning is to change perspective from time to time, enter into other alternatives and view the matter from different angles. In the meantime, I continue to weigh. You never know when you might strike something—a balance, for instance. As long as there's reason to think something's there, what else can you do? I keep seeing signs that say SLOW, so I conclude that these are probably questions which can't be properly weighed while traveling at high speeds, watching the road and keeping track of all the traffic at the same time. So I pull over to the side where it says REST STOP, figuring it must have been put there for a reason.

"Well, there are times when the wisest thing to do is to suspend judgment," he says. Yes, that's what I'm doing, that's what I mean: biding your time, giving yourself margins, suspending judgment—they're the same in the end.

Pulling up in front of Rachel's, the first thing I see is Damon, standing stark naked on the lawn with the hose between his legs, refreshing everything in sight like an ancient rain god with an endocrine problem: small, but qualified for the job. The image is imprinted and filed; I will remember him this way forever.

Rachel is still in her robe. Unusual for her, I think; it's almost noon.

"Do you have to run off," she asks. "I've fed the kids; can you stay and have some lunch?"

"Sure," I say, sitting down and lighting a cigarette. Rachel puts the sandwiches together and heats up the coffee. Something's wrong; you can feel it in the air.

"Well," she finally says, *She and Paul are getting divorced. That's it. She's pregnant? That wouldn't account* "I might as well tell you the news." She pauses. I look up from my coffee. "Paul's been transferred. We're moving." *Transferred—as though you were freight, cargo, baggage . . .* Why didn't I think of that? *You're so far back in time you're bound to miss the obvious.* That's the first thing you're supposed to think of. It's the most likely, the most expected. Why am I so stunned? Why can I only say:

"When?" As though it made any difference.

"End of summer, early fall. It came up so suddenly, we haven't had time to set a date."

"Where?" I light another cigarette. *When are you going to learn to anticipate? When you anticipate, you can bear.* I'm learning; what do you want from me? See, I'm not crying, for instance. You don't do that when friends move away; it's not modern.

"New York." Far. Very far. Suddenly I have an image of jets streaming through the skies, bearing all the California people away from their friends to New York, passing the jets that carry all the New York people away from their friends to California.

"How do you feel about it?" I say. What else is there to say?

"Terrible, what do you think? Paul's ambivalent, of course, but he's not losing sleep. Same old reasons: better position, better pay. You know what it means for me, I don't have to tell you." But she tells me anyway; sometimes repeating what you already know is an effective antidote to despair.

"I was just beginning to feel settled here. So were the kids. The job I won't miss that much, always find another somewhere else. But there's no way to replace the people I knew here, the friends I made, the friends I have, you and Martin . . ." She's not going to cry either; it's never done at high noon with the children running and splashing nearby, not even with friends. It's done at night, usually behind locked bathroom doors.

"I feel terrible, Rachel. There's nothing more to say." We spend the rest of the time on those little details—the ones which help you focus and ensure survival: selling the house; what to take and what to leave behind; when to hold the garage sale that signifies the end; and whether or not she could bear a going-away party. Thank God she says no.

"Absolutely not. Thanks for asking, Norma, but I couldn't bear it." Neither could I.

As I herd the children into the car and drive away Rachel stands there on the porch, holding her coffee cup in both hands, as though it might take off. There goes one more support, one more link, I think, as we approach Palm Court. Ruth Ann is sucking her thumb, something she hasn't done in years. She was in love with their son. Cheer up, Ruthie; there's more than one apple on the tree. The world is full of sweet little boys; you'll see, you'll see. Before they leave, we'll take a picture of you and Scott and Damon with Peter and Dan; we'll put it in your baby book, under Friends. And in a few years you will look at it and ask: "Mommy, who were they?"

We wouldn't have planned it this way, but their schedule was tight so we said our good-byes to Rachel and Paul over a nightcap, directly after Family Night at camp. It didn't bother us that the children were running around the house, two hours past their bedtime; there wasn't much any of us could think of to say. We talked in quiet tones, mostly about the strange ambivalence that always afflicts us on Family Night at camp. There is something about eating communally on the ground, and gathering around the fire as night comes on, that is capable of evoking the deepest longings. This year it was especially hard to reconcile all the warmth and communality with the fact that so many families there had recently divided, leaving just the mother to share Family Night with the children. In a few cases the father showed up too, standing just off to the side of the fire, as everyone sang songs. You couldn't help but see it as another one of those events which imitate institutions that no longer exist; it left us with a double sense of loss. You think of all the campfires of your past and you want to cry, but usually don't. What would be the use?

We talk for another hour or so, debating the issue of whether, by exposing the children to these experiences, we aren't fostering something they won't be able to use, because it won't be around when they're adults, and have the most need for it. Martin takes the position that every bit of contact helps, and Rachel and Paul agree. As usual, I'm not sure, but this is not the time to get out the scales. We all realize we aren't just talking about day camp. We embrace at the door and say the usual things about writing. Then, after we've tucked the children in, Martin and I embrace in bed, and I lie there thinking it's a universal trait people have of clinging to what is left. It's another one of those thoughts that both comforts and disturbs. It comforts Martin for twenty seconds, and disturbs me for two hours. I finally put on my robe and go out in the garage. And I sit there on the stool, under the single bulb, among the nearly completed pieces, smoking away and driving myself nuts. The riddle of the Sphinx was easy compared to the kinds of things they're throwing at us now. As I put my cigarette out, I notice the quasar clippings lying there under the glaze jars. I take them out and read.

MAN AT THE EDGE OF TIME
The Expanding Universe

LOS ANGELES TIMES SERVICE

Pasadena

It wasn't all that long ago that the universe seemed to astronomers to be a compact and orderly place, a sort of cosmic English garden of stars, dust and cloudy nebulas.

But in the space of ten years, from 1924 to 1934, a young astronomer at the Hale Observatories—Dr. Edwin P. Hubble—overturned that concept of the universe and revolutionized the field of astronomy almost as much as Copernicus had nearly 400 years earlier.

* * *

In 1924, Hubble presented the first concrete evidence that the universe and our galaxy were not one and the same thing.

In 1929, Hubble also proved that these other galaxies were moving away from us, and from each other, at very high speed. . . .

* * *

Far from being a staid English garden, the universe was suddenly revealed to be a wild jungle, extending out in all directions to distances that numbed the mind.

* * *

These findings, taken together with work done by astronomers at other observatories around the world, give rise to the so-called big bang theory of the universe. According to this theory, the universe began as a superdense ball of energy. The ball exploded—astronomers refer to this as the "creation event"—and the energy was scattered, gradually becoming matter as the universe constantly expanded.

Today, using the 200-inch diameter telescope atop Palomar Mountain . . . and some very sophisticated electronic equipment, a new generation of Hale astronomers believe they will soon be able to see the "edge" of the expanding universe. They may already be looking at it.

* * *

"The 'edge' of the universe is not really an 'edge' in the sense of a spatial surface," said Allen R. Sandage, a senior Hale Staff astronomer.

"What it really is," Sandage said, "is a time horizon. It is a threshold in time, prior to which galaxies had not yet been born in the already-evolving universe.

"As you look far out into the universe, you are looking back in time. You are, in effect, looking back at the birth pangs of galaxies at this time horizon.

"Can we see this far?" Sandage asked, and then answered himself: "Yes. Have astronomers already done so? Perhaps."

Sandage and other Hale astronomers . . . hope to find answers to these questions during the next five years or so in the light shed by quasars and far-distant galaxies.

* * *

Quasars—for "quasi-stellar radio sources"—are mysterious objects that emit disproportionately large amounts of energy for their comparatively small sizes.

* * *

About 350 quasars have been observed in the sky since the first was found little more than ten years ago. They share this one common characteristic: the light emanating from them is strongly red-shifted.

The movement of a star affects its light, as perceived by an observer. . . . If the star is moving toward the observer, its light will be shifted toward the blue end of the spectrum. But if the star is moving away from the observer, its light will appear to be reddened.

The biggest mystery, however, is what and where quasars actually are. Because of their large red shifts, most astronomers believe they are located far out in space, beyond the most distant observable galaxies. A few astronomers, however, think they are much closer.

The problem is that if quasars are far away it is almost impossible to imagine how they can generate such tremendous amounts of energy that their light still reaches earth with enough strength to be detected.

What could create such an unimaginable light from such a distance? There are no answers, only mysteries.

There are no answers, only mysteries. Norma Jean's eyes rest on the line until, eventually, they lose their focus. All these years, looking at stars and not thinking of it as looking back in time. We limit ourselves in the strangest ways—as though the only way to go back in time were right here on earth, as though the Egyptians were the absolute outer limit; or, occasionally, when reading to Damon, dinosaurs . . .

Quasars may be hugely massive stars collapsing under the weight of their own gravity and spewing out all their energy as they die.

All these years, thinking of *myself* as collapsing under the weight of my own gravity, right here in Pleasant Valley, California. At night the days' events would settle like a fine, but lethal, dust; and when I considered the weight of them, their endlessness, I used to think: This is my destiny; for these tasks I spew out all my energy as I die. This is all there is. This is it. Forever. If I were to join one of those communes where the members give themselves new names to signify their rebirth, mine would surely be Quasar. Because now, whenever I think of expansion, I have the conviction that if the universe can expand, so can I.

One quasar, in fact, appears to be moving at the incredible speed of 90 per cent the velocity of light, or some 165,000 miles per second. If this figure is correct, it would place the quasar quite close to the time horizon described by Sandage and date it back almost to the creation event.

17

Things are moving fast now. Time is accelerating, you can't fool me. I read all the signs; this year they have appeared in my face and in the leaves at the same time. Scott and Ruth Ann have been back in school for a month, and I sit here shaping the very last portion of the very last piece. Damon will be home from nursery school within the hour, but I think I will finish it tonight. Then, after the firing and glazing and refiring, I will photograph them. And then I will take the prints, with one sample piece, to the galleries in the city to request that they be placed in an environment conducive to life.

I've developed new habits too; I use the morning hours for work; I read the paper later, when there's time. It's still a window to the world, but not the only one. I have my lunch with Damon when he returns, and sometimes we go to the park or to the museum, and sometimes he goes around the block on Ranch Road to play. The family living in Rachel's house is a little strange, but they have a nice kid Damon's age. When he's down there, I make myself a cup of tea and read. I still do the whole paper, front to back, the way I always have, but skip the dregs. The fillers, though, are as instructive as they've always been; you never know what you'll find hidden there on the back page, just before the obituaries. I treat them with the same respect I do the main news.

Imagine my surprise this afternoon at finding, in the same paper, both a filler and a main news item which, together, form a link.

GRAPPLING WITH DEATH OF UNIVERSE

Scientists are on the verge of discovering the ultimate fate of the universe, one of the world's leading astronomers said here yesterday.

"We are in a golden age of discovery," said Allen R. Sandage. "In the past 30 years we have learned how stars are born, live, and die. Within another ten years, I believe we will know exactly how the universe itself will die."

Specifically, he said, most scientists have narrowed the future of the universe to just two possibilities:

* It will continue expanding, as it is now—forever. Young stars will get old, old stars will die and cool. Eventually all energy and matter will settle into an eternally quiet, cold sea of dark, burned-out galaxies. There will be no life and little change.

* The expansion will gradually slow and, over billions of years, the universe will fall back on itself until it becomes a "singular point" of enormous energy. Conceivably, this point could explode, and create a new, young universe.

* * *

Astronomers already know how the sun will die . . . and the process should begin about six billion years from now. (The sun is now about 5.5 billion years old.)

At that time, he said, the sun will expand 30 times larger than now, becoming a "red giant" that will engulf the planet Mercury and boil the seas of the earth away.

That process will take about 100 million years, undoubtedly destroying all life on earth. With its fuel exhausted, the sun will then cool for another 50 million years until it finally is nothing but a tiny lump of rapidly spinning matter.

* * *

"It's just a guess, because we need more information, but I think there is no turning around. Our universe will just get bigger, colder, and darker, forever," he said.

And over here on page forty-nine, the filler, which, in some strange way, breaks my heart.

STATIC ABOUT MICROWAVE OVENS AND HAIRNETS

Alarming blips on radar screens used by the West German Army have turned out to be static electricity from hairnets worn by their own soldiers.

The Germans have had to throw away 200,000 hairnets previously required to keep long hair from fouling up machinery.

Britain's radio astronomers are having similar problems. They complain that radiation from microwave ovens used in homes and restaurants near the Jodrell Bank Observatory are scrambling up messages from deep space.

This leads columnist Patrick Ryan of the British publication New Scientist to ask a provocative question: Could it be that all the mysterious quasar and pulsar signals U.S. and British scientists keep discovering are but emanations from microwave cookers at the Hamburger Palace or static electricity from housewives adjusting their hairnets?

Tonight, after dinner, everyone clears as I pour the coffee. We have devoted the meal to the discussion of killing bugs *vs.* not killing bugs; killing some bugs sometimes, under certain conditions; and how to decide what rules to apply to the issue of life *vs.* death in the insect world. The problem arose this afternoon when Damon crushed a bug which Scott had wanted to preserve for the purpose of examination. Quickly grabbing the scales, I applied the rule that nothing is to be crushed indiscriminately; that unless it's coming at you with a stinger, it has as much right to exist as the rest of us. Later, however, in the course of attempting to extend the concept that we all share responsibility for the various household and garden jobs that surround us, I made a fatal existential error by seeking the children's cooperation in picking geranium caterpillars off the blooms they were consuming, and suggesting that they help me crush them underfoot. I figured it would be a perfect job in which they could all participate, thereby saving me the trouble. Clever Ruth Ann. Who not only saw through the inconsistency, but also spied a mother caterpillar curled on one of the leaves, with her eggs. This child may be only seven and a half, but she recognizes an emotionally charged situation when she sees it.

"Oh, no!" she cried. "You won't get *me* to kill that mother! Look! She's waiting for her eggs to hatch! *Babies* are about to come out of them!" Boo hoo, boo hoo.

"Well," I tried to explain, "I know what I said before, about not killing unless something was hurting you." *However, I've decided to reverse myself in order to have some geraniums left.* "I know it's inconsistent, children, but ('Nature is cruel.') If you want to have flowers, you've got to be willing to crush these caterpillars when I say 'crush.'"

("Never! Never! Over my dead body," or words to that effect), cried Ruth Ann, picking the mother from the leaf, along with a handful of tiny black eggs. The family nestled there in her hot little palm as she declared:

"I won't kill them! You can't make me!"

"I'm not going to make you, Ruth Ann. I know how you feel." I really do. *Oh God, not the scales again; I absolutely refuse. I draw the line at caterpillars.* Ruth Ann searches desperately for a solution.

"I know! I'll take her to the other side of the yard! Her babies can hatch there and they'll all be safe!"

"No, Ruth Ann; that won't work. She'll be right back on the geraniums in the morning; it's what they eat."

"Well, I'll take them far away then! Where you can't kill them!" So she takes them half a block away and places them gently on a leaf in the gutter, which happens to be a variety they don't eat. They'll all be dead by tomorrow, I think, but say nothing. Either starve, or get hit by a car. But then a strange thing happened. One of the eggs hatched, right before our eyes. A tiny baby caterpillar, the size of the head on a pin.

"Mommy! Look! It's a *miracle!*" cried Ruth Ann. And indeed it is. That I should have raised such a child.

Over coffee, I let Martin in on the news; so near the end, what can I possibly lose? So I say:

"Well, you may not believe it, but I think I will finish for good tonight." He's heard that song before, knows the tune by heart. He fiddles with the dial on his transistor, trying to find another station, preferably the one broadcasting the ball game.

"No, Martin; listen. I mean it this time. Except for the glazing, this is *it.*" Don't let me down now, after all this. He sets the radio down and strokes my arm; the thin smile that breaks across his lips is charged with exquisite ambivalence. He hasn't taken the course but he's still doing better than I am, on his own. There was a fleeting second there when I could have sworn we understood each other. And were proud—not only for having borne the change, but for having expanded into roughly the same space at roughly the same rate of speed.

"I always knew you could do it," he says. "It's a real achievement. Of course they'll sell; there's never been any doubt in my mind since the first day I saw them." *It's wonderful what she's done; I admire her tenacity. Even though I never bargained for all this. Why should she have all the babies? Where do I come in? What's my part in all this? To go upstream to die? Again?*

Tonight I stop work early; it's exactly midnight when I pull the garage door shut behind me and step outside, beneath the flock of stars that fills the October sky. I stand and stare, trying to form a link between myself and the things I see, and things I do not see but know are there: at this moment, and through all time, breaking their boundaries and expanding as the space around them expands.

The house is still; everyone sleeps. I stand before the bathroom mirror and look for signs of change. What's reflected there is never what you want to see; I have found no way to reconcile it with the changes within, although they correspond. I remove my watch and prepare to sleep. It ticks there on the sink, trying to get my attention. *One o'clock already*, whispers the big hand. Concerning the big hand: when I was seven my mother told me, "It moves so slowly around the clock you can't see it with your eyes, but it's moving all the same." Now, I tell Ruth Ann, "The big hand spins around the clock so fast you cannot see it with your eye. It makes one complete revolution every second." *Who steals the time and my years?*

Lying in bed, thinking about beginnings and endings, Norma Jean closes her eyes and sees the pieces shimmering there behind her lids. They are waving good-bye. And she envisions her own end. It is inescapable. The only real question is: how will it happen? What are the possibilities?

PLEASANT VALLEY FAMILY
SLAIN IN SLEEP

Police are investigating the deaths of Martin J. Harris, 39; his wife, Norma Jean, 35; and their three children, Ruth Ann, 7½, Scott, 6, and Damon, 4. The family of 29 Palm Court was found shot to death early yesterday morning. Their bodies were discovered by a neighbor who became suspicious when the younger child failed to show up for his nursery school car pool. Police

Chief "One of the most senseless" Were not able to determine a motive There are as yet no clues.

No; that's not how it happened at all. I could explain but ("None cometh from thence/To tell us how he fares.") They were nice kids, actually; meant no harm, at first. But they were desperate, all strung out. They were looking for money to support their habit—but the tragedy was, we carry nothing but credit cards. If it hadn't been for the children, I could have understood, I really could; life is so hard, I forgive everyone his or her weaknesses. And it wasn't the neighbor driving the car pool; she just drove off without him, figuring he had an ear infection. No, actually, if you were to rise above the house, you would see how small it is, how unobtrusive, nestled down there among the pines, the loquats, the palms; that's how you would see it if you were to rise above it as a helicopter might, or bird, or a spirit leaving a body. It was weeks before they were discovered, weeks before they were missed.

Wait. That's *not* how it happened. I just remembered something. I've got it here, somewhere. . . . It was not by inundation, as you might have expected. It was, in fact, the reverse. There had been warnings, but who pays attention to them? You know how it is with warnings; if you acted on everything you read in the paper, you would go crazy. No, it simply happened much sooner than expected. And it was exactly as they had described it: "snow would simply accumulate, burying cities." It happened just like that. Down it fell, deaf as silk, settling over us, over everything—even Ken and Barbie, frozen in their plastic fuck forever. Our places are no more, As if they had never been. All that remains are cold winds that blow through the spaces between stars.

No, *dear; in spite of the fact that* ("Imagination is a wonderful thing." —Walt Disney), *be realistic. You know, as well as I* Yes, I do, and I was just coming to it. I was saving it for last for just that reason. You see, all that snow made me think of a documentary I once saw on TV about the Eskimos. And the most impressive custom, the one which really stands out in my mind, concerned the aged. Among the Eskimos, it is understood (or *was* understood, times change so fast) that when a member of the community becomes too old to be able to contribute to

273

the welfare of the whole, he or she simply goes for a ride. It is understood that it is the individual's *own* responsibility to recognize that he or she had ceased to become of use, and could only be a burden to the others. The documentary concerned a very old woman. No one had to tell her; that just isn't done. To tell her of her own condition would have violated some rule—more than likely the one concerning an individual's right to recognize and respond to her own condition and take action on her own behalf.

At a given time—unplanned, unspoken, and mysterious—she simply got on the back of a sled. And then someone took the reins and, urging the dogs on, moved across vast fields of snow. The ride continued until the old woman had made her decision and chosen her time. At which point, she simply fell—with indescribable simplicity, so softly it made no sound—then lay there waiting to die. I thought it cruel at the time, but now I see the beauty in it. The gesture, being autonomous, preserves dignity. *What about you, though? Where do you come in? No sleds around here that I know of.* You know where I come in. *Of course I do, but you're the one who has to say it; that preserves your dignity.*

Last year, two weeks before Christmas,

(KIDS MOB SANTA AND BEAT HIM UP

ASSOCIATED PRESS
Fort Lauderdale Fla.

Santa Claus swooped down in a helicopter at a local shopping center Saturday and was greeted immediately by a crowd of about 600 youngsters who knocked him down and emptied his goodie-bag.

"I thought I was going to be killed," said Lee Garen after he was rescued by police. . . .)

I was stalled in traffic in front of a rest home for the aged. There was a large plate-glass window in the . . . lobby? . . . living room? which faced onto the street, and in the center of it stood a giant, flocked Christmas tree. It was all white; even the ornaments were white. Through winter light I could see the faces pressed against the glass, staring through the branches with their bleak, Sumerian eyes. And I had a vision of my own future. Tucked away, wrapped in white, sedated, and no trouble at all.

Preserved there behind glass, like the mummies in the Egyptian museum. And I thought of the children, and the thought of them made my heart jump with love, and fear. Where are you now, my golden creatures? Where is my F A M I L Y? Scattered and useless, like the petals of a flower whose season is over. And I wondered what it had all been for. I was sure that, in the end, memories were not enough. And then I became aware of activity behind me, so I turned from the window—moving wasn't easy, but I've learned to do it slowly, preserving energy—and there, of all things, was Santa Claus! He was at the sanitarium to make the presentations. Slowly I remembered the season; they had briefed us about this, but memory fades quickly here.

Vision fades too; what? Oh, he's beckoning me! He's getting ready to pass out the presents. That must be why everyone has gathered around the tree, waiting quietly in wheelchairs. But why have they formed a circle? And where are they taking me? Why am I being wheeled into the center? *Isn't that where you said you were, dead center?* That was forty years ago! You never think of yourself as staying in a place like that forever! And he is bending down, whispering something to me And the nurse is putting something on my It's a I reach up slowly and feel it; I've always had good tactile perception, I know what it is immediately. I begin to shake; i don't know if it's because I am thrilled, or appalled. But it is a crown, there is no doubt about it. I am the Christmas Queen. Everyone begins to clap and sing; I've always hated groups, especially noise like that. Santa says ho ho ho. I think he's Dr. Ward, underneath the disguise. But no, it's the *others* who are all dressed in white: the nurses in their uniforms, the patients in their sheets; the rows and rows of dentures, the white walls, the flocked tree If I close my eyes I see fields of snow that stretch to distances vast as my longing. You never lose it, longing; no matter how old Never do. And just before I make my decision I see Martin and I reach for his hand; we've been through so much together, so much, it's only right that he be here now. And the touch of him after all these years, across great distances, the warmth of it startles so, there is a stone in my throat. And Ruth Ann whispers, "Look! It's a miracle!" Scott and Damon stand beside her, holding geraniums. My blossoms, my miracles, I think, as I fall.

18

Norma Jean Harris stands before the throne of Osiris. Anubis waits beside the scales where her soul is about to be weighed. It must balance with a feather, which symbolizes truth. Osiris addresses her:

"Are you ready to declare?"

"I am prepared," she replies. "I stand by the actions of my life. I am not ashamed. I have done my best and that is all that can be required of anyone." If it doesn't balance with the feather, tough shit.

She steps forward. The monster god known as the Devourer waits nearby, ready to consume her if her soul fails to balance. Doesn't scare me; not after what I've been through. *But Look. The others are there too: the Breaker-of-Bones, and the one known as the Eater-of-Blood.* What are you doing here? You come to rebirths, too? *I stay with you to the end; I do not abandon.* Well, I have nothing to fear; the Breaker-of-Bones doesn't look so fierce to me. Don't forget, I raised two sons. And as for the Eater-of-Blood, he's out of luck; it's all gone. They got it all. My babies . . .

Osiris repeats, "How do you declare?" Norma Jean stands before the great scale; it's the most exquisite one I've ever seen, its precious metal gleams, even in this dim light. "In my life

I honored my obligations to my family as I perceived them, and according to my heart, in a time of ambiguous rules. I created new codes as change required, and passed these on to my children.

I honored my obligations to myself. I discovered my voice and produced works according to that voice. I gave them life and they live after me.

I never faked an orgasm. Not even to keep the peace. I was true to myself, and therefore never false to any man. Every one real, my very own.

The jury stirs; murmurs ripple through the cast of assembled monster deities. ". . . unique among women," ". . . perjuring herself . . ." ". . . strains credibility . . ." ". . . thoughtless bitch!" were some of the comments.

I recycled all waste products that threatened my environment, except for Kitty Queen cans when I was depressed.

I supported all movements for liberation, including animals." (Anubis will like this.)

She looks at him out of the corner of her eye; he is suppressing a smile and tipping the scale ever so slightly with his paw.

"I boycotted zoos!" *Don't overdo it.*

Anubis interrupts: "We have a memo here which states that you kept *Anatole the Mouse* out of the library for two years. Can you account for this?"

"Oh. I certainly can. The memo is inaccurate. *Anatole* was only out for three months, February to April, if I remember right. I was so busy working on my pieces at the time. . . . Actually, it was *The Easter Bunny that Overslept* which was out for two years. But I can explain."

"Please do."

"I hated that book. The children picked it out, but I hid it so I wouldn't have to read it to them." *You blew it. Right there. Blew it. Blew it.* Calm down, I can handle this.

"My beautiful, sleek Anubis, (*"Flattery will get you nowhere."*) would you believe me ("I throw myself on the mercy of the court.") if I said I did it as much for the children as I did for myself? What I did instead of reading *The Easter Bunny that Overslept* was to have the children write their own stories. In that way they created something unique, something which had never existed before."

Anubis glances at Osiris. Osiris nods.
At the end of the voyage, the battle won, all obstacles overcome
and annihilated, solar birth could take place. The following address could then be made to the deceased:

> Awaken, O sick one, thou who has slept,
> They have lifted thine head toward the horizon.
> Appear! Thou art justified against him who sought
>   to harm thee;
> Ptah has overthrown thine enemies and has ordered
> Him who stood against thee to be pursued.
> Thou art Horus, son of Hathor,
> He whose head was restored to him
> After it had been cut off;
> Never again shall thine head be taken from thee;
> In the future never again for all eternity
>   shall thine head be taken from thee.
>
> —Christiane Desroches-Noblecourt,
>   op. cit., p. 274.